*Never
Say Never*

## Bethany House Books by Lisa Wingate

# Never
# Say Never

# Lisa Wingate

## BETHANYHOUSE

a division of Baker Publishing Group
Minneapolis, Minnesota

© 2010 by Wingate Media, LLC

Published by Bethany House Publishers
11400 Hampshire Avenue South
Bloomington, Minnesota 55438
www.bethanyhouse.com

Bethany House Publishers is a division of
Baker Publishing Group, Grand Rapids, Michigan

Printed in the United States of America

New paperback edition published 2019

ISBN 978-0-7642-3303-6

The Library of Congress has cataloged the original edition as follows:
Wingate, Lisa.
   Never say never / Lisa Wingate.
      p. cm.
  ISBN 978-0-7642-0492-0 (pbk.)
  1. Drifters—Fiction. 2. City and town life—Fiction. 3. Texas—Fiction.
  4. Love stories—Fiction. I. Title.
  PS3573.I53165N48 2010
  813'.54—dc22                        2009040684

Unless otherwise indicated, Scripture quotations are from the King James Version
of the Bible.

Scripture quotations labeled NIV are from the Holy Bible, New International Version®.
NIV®. Copyright © 1973, 1978, 1984, 2011 by Biblica, Inc.™ Used by permission
of Zondervan. All rights reserved worldwide. www.zondervan.com. The "NIV" and
"New International Version" are trademarks registered in the United States Patent and
Trademark Office by Biblica, Inc.™

Cover design by Paul Higdon
Cover illustration by Paul Higdon and William Graf

19  20  21  22  23  24  25       7  6  5  4  3  2  1

To the homefolks of Burrel-Wingate Road
and points beyond—
the Tullys, Hidalgos, Joostens, and Kikers . . .
Thank you for wonderful memories of
hours spent along the coast.
And to
The determined, resilient folks of the Texas Gulf Coast,
Still rebuilding after Rita, Dolly, and Ike . . .
I wish you fair skies and gentle winds.

# Acknowledgments

When I'm out and about at book events, it never fails that someone with a particular favorite among my stories will ask me what inspired the book and how much of it is true. After that, the discussion is a little like one of those chats at a family reunion, in which a gaggle of aunts sits near the vittles, eyeballing passing children and trying to decide whom each one favors. "Why, he's the spittin' image of Uncle Clee," one will say, and another will argue, "Not either. Clee had them big ol' ears, remember? That child's cute as a bedbug. Looks just like his mama. Takes after the Lumleys, for sure." The arguments go on from there, and usually there are as many opinions as aunts at the table.

Stories are a little like children. None of them drop out of thin air. The DNA of *Never Say Never* was pieced together from shreds of family history, bits of personal experience, a few colorful real-life characters, and a hurricane tale or two shared by readers and relatives along the way. As always, I'd be remiss if I didn't thank the folks who so kindly contributed.

7

Thanks to our friends and family in southeast Texas for always hosting us on trips to the coast, for chatting and talking during the numerous "hurrications" of the past few years, and for being willing to share hurricane experiences, even when it was painful to recall them. To Uncle Buck McAdams, thanks for sharing the long-ago hurricane story of floating mattresses and flooded farmland that inspired Mamee's history. You never know when a chat over coffee will inspire a book. Thanks also to reader friends for sharing evacuation stories and tales of God's little miracles along the way.

On the print and paper side of things, enormous gratitude goes out to the amazing folks at Bethany House Publishers. To Julie Klassen and Dave Long, you are simply the best editors a writer could dream of. Thank you for your astute suggestions, guidance, and encouragement along the way. Julie, thanks for the notes in the margin—you're as good an editor as you are a writer, and that's saying a lot. To the awesome folks in publicity, marketing, and art—what can I say? Even when you're making snow at forty below there in Minneapolis, you're coming up with hot new ideas. To my agent, Claudia Cross, at Sterling Lord Literistic, once again, thanks.

Lastly (but not leastly), my thanks once again goes out to my family for being . . . well . . . awesome, and always willing to eat "deadline dinners," otherwise known as frozen pizzas and peanut butter and jelly sandwiches. Thank you to my friend Theresa Loman for creating wonderful digital scrapbook pages for my website and to top tech guru and friend Ed Stevens for online help, video production, website assistance, and especially for your encouragement. How lucky I am to have such friends. Thank you also to reader friends far and near for sending notes, sharing stories, recommending the books to friends and book clubs, and delivering encouragement on days when I needed a pick-me-up. Little angels must whisper in your ears, because every time a mullygrub day comes along, a sweet note arrives. God does His best work through the people we meet on our journeys. Thank you, all of you, for being my peeps and for your little acts of kindness. What a blessing!

*When thou passest through the waters,*
*I will be with thee; and through the rivers,*
*they shall not overflow thee.*

Isaiah 43:2

# Chapter 1

## *Donetta Bradford*

You'd imagine, livin' high and dry in the middle of Texas, with the jackrabbits and the prickly pears, you wouldn't close your eyes at night and feel the water. In this country, people think of water like the narrow string that runs over the rocks in Caney Creek, or drifts long, and slow, and lazy down the Brazos or the Guadalupe. But when I close my eyes, I feel the kind of water that surrounds you and seeps into your mind and soul, until you breathe in and out with the tides.

Where, in heaven's name, would a person get a dream like that in Daily, Texas, where the caliche-rock ground's so hard the county's got no need to pave roads—they just clear a trail and let folks drive on it. It'll harden up quick enough and stay that way three quarters of the year while the farmers and the ranchers watch the sky and hope for rain. Life here hasn't got much to do with water, except in the waiting for it. But every night when I close my eyes, I feel a tide, rockin' back and forth under my body. I been feeling it for sixty-nine and a half years now, long as I can remember. I never did anything about it, nor

11

told anybody. They'd think I was nutty as a bullbat, and when you're a businesswoman in a small town, well, you got to protect your reputation. That goes double if you're the hairdresser, and a redhead. We all know what kind of reputation hairdressers and redheads got.

All that's even more important for someone whose people, historically speaking, ain't from Daily. In a little town, even if you been there all your life, you're not native unless you can trace your roots back generations. There's still folks that'll point out (in a backhanded way mostly, because they're all gonna need a haircut sooner or later) that I'm only a Daily girl by half, on my father's side. On the other side, there's a bit of scandal the biddies still cluck about.

My daddy was what you'd call a prodigal. After leaving behind his fine, upstandin' family and a half-dozen brokenhearted girls of marriageable age in Daily, he wandered the world for so long everyone thought he'd either landed in jail or got hisself killed in a barroom fight. Then one day, he showed up at my grandparents' hotel building on Main Street, as mysterious as he left. He wasn't alone, either. He was driving a 1937 Chevy folks thought he musta got in a bank robbery, and he had a girl in the passenger seat. When she stepped out, my grandma Eldridge fainted right there on the spot. The girl was pregnant, *and* she was Cajun, *and* a Catholic. She was thumbin' a rosary ninety-to-nothin'.

It's hard to say which one of them three things Grandma Eldridge fainted over, but it took her two full weeks to get over the shock and humiliation, and welcome my mama into the family. By then, I guess there wasn't much choice. My daddy was married to the girl, and I was on the way. Grandma Eldridge was happy as a boardin' house pup when I come out with the Eldridge bluish-gray eyes and light-colored skin.

When she'd tell me that story, years after my mama'd passed

on, I never understood it. My mama, with her hair the deep auburn of fall leaves, and her olive skin, and her eyes so dark you couldn't see the centers, was beautiful, exotic like a movie star. When she talked, the words fell from her mouth with a lilt that made her voice ebb and flow like the currents in the bayou. Mama's people knew the water. They lived on it, and farmed rice alongside it, and felt it in their very souls.

Every summer, Mama gathered me and my little brother, Frank, and carried us on the train to southeast Texas to see her people. I'd come back afterward and tell everyone in Daily that Mama's family lived on a plain old farm, just like folks in Daily. That was as far from true as the east is from the west. Those trips to see the Chiassons were like going to a whole other world.

After my mama passed on, there weren't any more lies to tell. Daddy never sent us back to her people, and I didn't hear from them, and the secrets from that final summer, when I turned fifteen on the bayou—the biggest secrets of all—never got told.

I thought I'd take the secrets to my grave. And maybe I would've if Imagene Doll, my best friend since we started school together at Daily Primary, hadn't got a wild hair to celebrate her seventieth birthday by catching a cruise ship out of the harbor near Perdida, Texas.

It's funny how from seventeen to seventy can be the blink of an eye, all of a sudden. Every time we talked about that cruise, I had a little shiver up my spine. I tried not to think too hard about it, but I had a strange feeling this trip was gonna change everything. That feeling hung on me like a polyester shirt straight out of the clothes dryer, all clingy and itchy.

The day we sat looking at the map, using a highlighter to draw the path we'd take to the coast, static crackled on my skin, popping up gooseflesh. I imagined them east-Texas roads, the piney woods growin' high and thick, towering over the lumber trucks as they crawled with their heavy loads. I followed the line down to the bayou country, where the rice farmers worked their flooded fields and the gators came up on the levies to gather the noonday sun. Where the secret I'd kept all these years lay buried, even yet.

"Are we really gonna do this?" Imagene asked, tracing the road with her finger. A little shimmy ran across her shoulders. Imagene'd never got out in a boat on anything bigger than a farm pond in her life. Even though we'd already booked the trip and paid our money, she was trying to wriggle off like a worm on a hook. Sometimes what looks like a wild hair at first looks harebrained later on.

Across the table, Lucy, who came from Japan originally (so she ain't afraid of water), had her eyebrows up, like two big question marks in her forehead. Her mind was set on taking the cruise. After all these years away from the island country where she was born, she wanted to see the ocean again.

They were both looking at me, waiting to see what I'd say, since right now the vote was one *for* and one *against*. I knew they'd probably go for it if I told them, *Oh hang, let's just go to Six Flags instead. It'd be lots easier. We can ride the loop-de-loop and say we done somethin' adventuresome before we turned seventy.*

I sat there, staring out the window of my beauty shop, where the wavy old glass still read *DAILY HOTEL*—from back in the day when wool, cotton, and mohair kept the town hoppin'— and it come to my mind that I'd been staring at that same window almost every day of my whole, entire life. How many times over the years had Imagene and me hatched an idea to do something different, then sat there and talked ourselves right back into the same old chairs?

Imagene swished a fly away from her cup. Early September like this, the flies hung thick as molasses under the awnings on Main Street.

"You know, it's maybe not the smartest thing to be headin' down to the coast when there's a hurricane coming in," Imagene pointed out.

Lucy frowned, her eyebrows falling flat. "I hear it on TV the storm is head to Mec-i-co." That was Lucy's way of saying she thought we ought to go ahead with the cruise, but she wasn't gonna be pushy. If Lucy had a disagreeable bone in her body, it hadn't poked through the skin in the forty years she'd been in the beauty shop with me.

Imagene's lips moved like she had something stuck in her teeth and couldn't get it out. She did that when she was nervous. If I let her cogitate long enough, she'd spit out our adventure like a bone in the sausage. She'd decide it was safer for us to stay home, because that's Imagene—careful as the day is long. She was already in a fret about packing all the right things, and asking my brother, Frank, to water her flowers and feed her cat. She was even worried about whether the cat (which was a stray she didn't want to begin with) might get lonely and run off.

Last night, she'd sat down and wrote letters to all of her kids and grandkids. She left them on the kitchen table—just in case we, and the whole cruise boat, got shipwrecked on a desert island and never come back.

"We're goin' on this trip," I told her, and Imagene sunk in her chair a little. She was hoping for Six Flags. "I checked on the intra-net this mornin', and it said the boat was leavin' at four p.m. tomorrow out of Perdida, right on schedule. I even called the toll-free number, and they told me once we get on the boat, it'll sail right around the storm, and there's not a thing to worry about."

"That's just what people say when there *is* somethin' to worry about." Imagene took a sip of her coffee, her lips working again. "Hurricane Glorietta's somethin' to worry about. She's a whopper. A person hadn't ought to be goin' out on the ocean when there's a storm like that around, Donetta. It's . . . silly . . . reckless, even."

*Reckless*. The word felt good in my mind. "We're near seventy years old, Imagene. If we're ever gonna get reckless, we better start now."

"I hadn't got any desire to turn reckless." Imagene tipped her nose up and squinted through her bifocals. She looked a hundred years old when she did that.

"The lady from the cruise line said boats sail around storms all the time. They got to durin' hurricane season."

Imagene's eyes went wide, and I knew right away *hurricane season* was the wrong thing to say. I got that All-timer's disease, I think, on account of I'm all the time saying things I didn't even know were in my brain yet. I don't lie much because mostly these days, there ain't time for it.

"We ought not to of *booked* a cruise durin' *hurricane season*." Imagene's voice was shaky, and she had worry lines big as corn furrows around her mouth. "Someone shoulda thought of that." By *someone*, she meant me. It was me that finally (after weeks of idle yappin' about how we were gonna do this big thing) got on the intra-net, looked at prices, and found us a cruise.

"They're cheaper right now. We saved almost half." I didn't mention it, but without the savings, Lucy never coulda come up with the money to go in the first place.

"Well, that right there oughta tell you somethin'." Imagene was headed into a nervous rigor now, for sure.

"What oughta?"

"That it's cheaper by half. Of course it's cheap when you might get sucked up in a hurricane and never come back."

"Like Gilligan I-lans," Lucy popped off, and grinned. It was hard to say whether the joke was helpful or not.

"Those ships hit things sometimes." Imagene stared hard

at the pecan pie she'd barely touched. "They hit a rock, or a iceberg, and next thing you know, you're in the drink."

I leveled a finger at her. "You turned on *Titanic* last night, didn't you?" The minute I saw that movie was on, I'd called Imagene's house and told her not to go to channel 136. She musta clicked it right away.

She tipped her chin up, like a kid turning away a spoonful of green peas. "I just saw a minute's worth."

"I watch it all," Lucy chimed in.

"For heaven's sake, you two! There's no icebergs in the Gulf a' Mexico." I stood up and started gathering coffee cups, because if we sat there any longer, our trip would be ruined. "If we don't go like we planned, every last soul in town's gonna know about it, and we'll be the laughingstock. Just think what Betty Prine and her snooty bunch'll say." I pictured the next meeting of the Daily Literary Society. They'd be happy as cows on clover, havin' us for lunch right along with the finger sandwiches. Betty'd been thumbing her nose at me and whispering for weeks about how three ladies *our age* didn't have any business driving all the way to the coast alone. "Come wild horses or high water, we're going on this cruise. We're getting up in the mornin' and we're headin' for the water, and that's it. I'll be over to your house at seven a.m. to help load the cooler, Imagene, then we go after Lucy and we're off."

"We're off, all right." Imagene looked like her dog'd just died, instead of like a gal headed on vacation. "Frank said he'd take my van tonight and gas it up, then check all the belts and hoses one more time, just to be sure. He thinks we hadn't ought to be driving to the coast by ourselves, though. And especially with a hurricane comin' in."

"Oh, for heaven's sake, Imagene, you and my brother act like we're about to get the roll call up yonder. We're grown women. It's six hours' drive—if that. And Kemp's got me fixed up with a special page on my new little laptop computer. It tells everything about the cruise. I've had the computer going all day long, and nothin's changed with the weather or the boardin' time. I tried to tell Frank that, but you know how he feels about computers."

"Frank's only looking after us." Imagene was defending Frank, of course.

Lately, when Frank and I had the kind of disagreements brothers and sisters have, Imagene took Frank's side. My brother'd been over at Imagene's even more than usual—mowing the lawn, helping her with her garden, stopping by to get a sample when she was baking pies for the Daily Café. Once or twice, I'd looked at the two of them and wondered . . . well . . . him being a widower, and her a widow, and all . . .

I slapped a hand on the table to knock Imagene out of her funk. "Come on, y'all. Take off them long faces. We're gonna have an adventure bigger than our wildest dreams. I can feel it in my bones!"

That night, what I felt in my bones was the water. Ronald was down the hall snoring in his easy chair, the sound rushing in and out like the tide. I closed my eyes and let the waves seep under my bed, lifting the mattress, floating me away to that secret place I'd never told anyone about. Imagene and Lucy didn't know it, but this trip to Perdida was gonna take us within a whisper of the mystery I'd been wondering about since my last summer on the bayou.

# Chapter 2

# *Kai Miller*

I've often walked the shore and wondered if all things drift according to a larger plan. For each message in a bottle, each straw hat blown from the hand of a strolling lover, each sailor far from home, all the lost coins from all the ancient ships, is there a designated landing place? I've marveled at the seeming randomness of the treasures pushed up on the tides, corroded by salt, encrusted with barnacles, at home in the ocean, now tossed back to the land.

A street preacher on the pier told me once that God stirs the currents with His fingertip, the winds with His breath, and that even in the vastness of the sea He knows each ship at sail, each tiny creature beneath the water, each shifting patch of sand. Nothing lost, said the preacher, is ever lost to God. A homeless man, begging for change from tourists, took a free sack lunch from the preacher and held it in his blackened hands and agreed that nothing adrift is meant to stay adrift forever.

The homeless man had eyes as dark as coal, as deep as the waves on moonless nights. I gave him a dollar that had been washed and dried in my pocket. He smiled as he unfolded it and straightened the crisp paper.

His hands reminded me of Grandmother Miller's hands, but I knew Grandmother Miller would have said I was a fool for giving the man anything. She would have talked about *shiftlessness*, the results of it, and the fact that those who find themselves destitute have caused their own misery. *Teach a man to fish*, she'd say, and then, if my father were in the room, she'd give him a narrow-eyed look. My father would put up with what he called *the sermon* for whatever amount of time was necessary. He'd play Grandmother Miller's game—pretend he wanted to get a real job and keep it, promise to start going to church again, agree that a family needed stability. He'd vow that if Grandmother Miller would just help us out one more time, he'd give up his dream of making it in the music business. He'd promise to become normal, conventional, faithful, devoted. To comply with her wishes. Then, once we had what we needed—usually money—we'd leave. We wouldn't come back to Grandmother Miller's big house in McGregor, Texas, for another year, or two, or five, depending on how soon we were destitute again.

Maybe I gave the dollar to the homeless man *because* I knew that Grandmother Miller—wherever she was by now—wouldn't like it, and even at twenty-seven years old, I was still trying to prove she wasn't right about everything. She wasn't right about me. I was nothing like my mother or my father, and I never would be. Or maybe handing over the dollar seemed like a good thing to do, because, when a storm the size of Texas is just over the horizon, it's probably smart to get some good karma going. Even though weather forecasters had predicted she'd stay south and make landfall somewhere below Brownsville, I could feel Glorietta swirling across the Gulf of Mexico, closing in. The sky was as blue as a baby's eye today, but Glorietta was coming. Three nights in a row, I'd dreamed she hooked north and headed our way.

My landlord, Don, was sure there was nothing to worry about, but then that was Don. A few quick looks at the weather reports and he was chillin' like a tall glass of iced tea with a little paper umbrella on top. In his mind, Glorietta was already a non-event, an uninvited tourist wobbling across the Gulf. In the meantime, the surf shop was doing a brisk business in boogie boards, water bikes, and jet skis, with the waves up and tourists rushing to have a little fun, in case they had to cut their vacations short and run from the storm. Even though half of Perdida had already boarded up, Don didn't want to mess with putting the storm shutters on the shop, or on our apartments upstairs, so I'd started doing the job myself.

Don finally gave in, after watching me single-handedly drag hunks of plywood from the storeroom. He grumbled about the unnecessary preparations as we covered apartment windows upstairs. The big apartment with the ocean view was his, and the little one around back was mine.

Don jokingly called my apartment the *mother-in-law suite* because he said I acted like someone's mother. That was funny coming from Don, a surfer dude deluxe, who was forty-eight going on eighteen, with a long salt-and-pepper ponytail, skin like leather, and the weird idea that women found him sexy. He grew on you over time, and as a landlord, he was easygoing, which was why I'd kept the apartment for two years now. Living at the end of the strand, I'd become part of an odd little family of people like Don, who were happy enough to have someone to hang out with but didn't require any strings. It was nice having a place to come home to when I wasn't working entertainment and social staff contracts onboard one of Festivale's cruise ships, teaching everything from ballroom dancing to crafts and jewelry making.

Don gave me a dirty look as he carted the last of the shutters upstairs. "What'n the world you worried about, anyway? In the morning, you'll be headed out." He motioned vaguely in the direction of the port, where the *Liberation* would be finished with one group of passengers and getting ready for departure with a new group at four p.m. tomorrow.

"I want my apartment to still be here when I get back." For some reason, I could never resist arguing with Don. His laid-back, no-worries attitude reminded me of my father in some psychologically twisted way I didn't really want to contemplate. The last time I saw my dad, we were living in a camp trailer and working the roller coaster at a carnival. I finished my final high-school correspondence lesson—an essay on the Cold War—dropped it on the table with the mail, then grabbed my stuff, walked out the door, and just kept going. Not the smartest decision for a seventeen-year-old, but at that point, I had to do something.

Right now, Don was looking at me like my father had those last few years—like he wished I'd buzz off and leave him alone so he could do what he wanted. "Glorietta'll go south. Everyone says she'll go south."

"Everyone, who?" Even with the day bright and clear, I could feel the air growing heavy and the sea changing. Couldn't Don sense it? "Maggie and Meredith boarded up this morning." Across the street, Maggie and Meredith were operating their coffee shop with the shutters up, the stereo playing seventies music, and incense burning to attract benign weather spirits. "They're heading for the airport this evening to fly to Maggie's son's place in Kansas. Maggie said the traffic's already getting bad and she almost couldn't find a flight."

"People are stupid." Spitting a stray hair out of his mouth, Don slipped a shutter into the brackets.

"No one wants to get stuck here if it comes." Before sunrise, something instinctive had prompted me to pack all the things I'd normally take on ship. But while gathering the usual items, I'd slipped a hand under the mattress, the place I didn't tell anyone about, and grabbed the mementos of my childhood—a family photo of my mother, my father, my brother Gil, and me; a ticket from a racetrack in Ruidoso, New Mexico; a birth certificate with a sticky note still attached; a heart-shaped drink coaster made from flowers pressed between two sheets of sticky plastic; and a smashed penny from the Tulsa State Fair. They were tucked inside a Bible Gil took from a motel nightstand in some town that was nameless in my memory. Gil had a thing for Bibles, though none of us could figure out why. Maybe he knew he'd be heading for heaven pretty early on.

Don's mutt-slash-black Labradors came to the inside of my screen door and whimpered as Don revved up the drill to secure the shutters.

"What're they doin' in there?" Don pointed the drill like a pistol and gave the dogs an irritated look.

"Getting hair in my bed, probably," I muttered, holding out a box of self-tapping screws so Don could reach them. The dogs had chewed their way through my screen door and ended up in my bed sometime in the middle of the night.

"Well, kick 'em out," Don ordered, like it was that easy. A hundred and forty pounds of combined Labrador went pretty much where it wanted to.

"If you'd fix the gate, I wouldn't have to." Technically, according to city codes and probably my lease agreement, Radar and Hawkeye were supposed to be locked in the little yard behind the shop. "Anyway, they can tell something's wrong. That's why they're acting weird."

"Pffff!" Don's lip curled. "Don't let 'em in and they'll quit."

"They *ate* a hole in my *screen* door."

Holding the plywood with one hand, Don leaned back and

checked out the mangled nylon netting that had been the only barrier between me and the host of Texas-sized mosquitoes that frequented Perdida at night. "Shut the door and turn on the air-condition, there, blondie."

"I like to hear the water, and besides, the air-conditioner's broken, remember?"

Don didn't want to talk about the broken air-conditioner. "Just tell 'em to get out." He shook the drill at Radar and Hawkeye again. "Get outta there!"

The dogs whined and retreated into my apartment.

"They're all right," I said. "They won't stay outside. I'm telling you, they know something." Radar and Hawkeye had been pacing the floor between the bed and the door for hours. "Maggie told me that when she was growing up, the animals always knew days ahead if a hurricane was coming. The cattle went to the hills, the horses were skittish in their stalls, and the barn cats moved their kittens to the loft. Animals can sense things."

Don let the drill rip, then cussed a blue streak when the screw sheered off and the drill bit went skittering sideways. His arms strained as he struggled to hold the plywood in place, sweat dripping from beneath his Willie-Nelson-style bandanna headband. "This is ignorant."

Leaning over the veranda railing, I gazed around the corner toward the beach. Today, it was full of sunbathers and swimmers ignoring the riptide warnings. "No it's not. I have a feeling about this one."

A chill ran over me, chasing away the sticky heat on my skin. Over the past two years, Perdida had become the closest thing to a home I'd ever known. After a lifetime of drifting, I was finding out what it felt like to spend time in one place, to put down roots. With Maggie and Meredith's help, my jewelry-making business, Gifts From the Sea, was growing, and in a few months, I'd be able to quit the cruise ship contracts and spend my days combing the beaches in the early mornings after the tide and creating art jewelry from beach glass and other treasures the water had surrendered overnight. With more shops around Perdida showing and selling my pieces, I was slowly becoming an artisan working in a medium of found items. A soul at peace with the sea.

If Glorietta came this way, all of that could change.

Don raised the drill and drove another screw with one quick swipe. "Hand me the box," he barked. "You worry too much."

"You don't worry enough."

"Ffff," Don scoffed, but his mouth was twitching upward at the corners. "I don't know what you're complaining about. You'll be down in Mexico someplace, soaking up the sun."

"Yeah, right." Nobody here had any idea that working on a cruise ship wasn't like an episode of *The Love Boat*. The hours were long, and the work was usually far from glamorous. Even the jewelry-making classes, where I helped passengers create lasting keepsakes from treasures discovered in distant ports, were usually less than inspiring.

Don tucked several screws into his pocket, and I moved around the porch turning over the plastic tables, bracing the tops against the wall of the building. Standing at the railing, I watched a flock of seagulls fly inland while Don finished the last of the shutters, then walked down the deck. "Guess I'll do the door tomorrow morning after you leave . . . if it's even headed this way. Which it won't be." He set the drill against the wall. It would stay there until tomorrow morning, or the next time he needed it.

"If it turns north, promise me you'll evacuate, okay?" I pleaded, even though I knew what his answer would be. "Just go, all right?"

He pulled off the headband, wiped his neck with it, then put it on his head again. *Gross.* Don had the couth of a baboon.

"Go where? Where am I gonna go? Every motel from here to Oklahoma's full of idiots runnin' from a storm that's not even coming here. Half of Houston's gone on the run already. I'm not sleeping in some high-school gym with a bunch of screaming brats."

Tears prickled in my throat—the desperate kind that wouldn't be denied. "Just do this for me, okay? If they order an evac here, leave, okay? Take a . . . a little vacation."

"A vacation?" His head fell to one side and his mouth hung open. "Darlin', I live on vacation. Besides, how in the world am I gonna evacuate? No room for the boys on my bike." He gazed lovingly at his Harley, lounging in the shade of a palm tree below.

"You can have my van. I'm taking the shuttle to the port. I'll leave the keys tomorrow morning, and the van'll be here in case you need it. If they call an evacuation, you can take Radar and Hawkeye, and go."

"In that junker? We probably wouldn't get ten miles." From day one, Don had been vehemently opposed to the antique VW Microbus I'd been lovingly restoring as my official business vehicle since I'd started Gifts From the Sea, moved to Don's building, and finally had a place to keep a car.

"Come on, Don. Just promise me you'll leave if you need to."

He threw his hands up, sighing. "Sheesh. All right. If I see it's coming in, I'll go."

"When?"

"When I see it's coming."

Which meant never, of course. "You won't be able to get out by then. Every road north will be stacked bumper to bumper. By tomorrow morning, if the storm turns, it'll be stop and go. If I wasn't headed out on the ship, I'd be hitting the road today, like Maggie and Meredith."

Don shot a dirty look toward the coffee shop. No doubt Maggie and Meredith had already harassed him about his lack of evacuation plans. "I gotta get back to work. I'm a big boy, Kiwi." At some point after I'd rented the apartment, Don had taken to calling me Kiwi, because he couldn't remember my name, Kai.

"You don't act like one."

"Go make some jewelry. Your counter downstairs is getting low," he grumbled, then headed for the steps, his gaze scanning the sky. "Glorietta'll hit south. You can bet your big blue eyes on it. And that'll just mean more people'll come here for the end of the season. Big bucks, baby."

"I'll leave the van keys on my table. If you need them, take them," I called after him.

He stopped momentarily at the top of the steps, his posture softening. "Take care 'a you."

"I will. You too."

Giving the thumbs-up, he started his descent. "Bonfire at Blowfish Billy's tonight," he called, motioning down the beach toward one of his favorite haunts. "Gonna boil some crawfish, pop open a keg, rock out to a little Cajun music."

"I think I'll pass."

He waved me off. "Suit yourself. Peace out."

"Yeah," I muttered, rubbing my hands over my arms as the lonely, hollow feeling I'd known all my life came creeping in like an unwelcome relative. *You gotta look out for yourself, Kai-bird,* my father used to say. *When it comes right down to it, you're all you got.*

I felt the loneliness closing in hard and fast. Before it could grab me, I opened the apartment door, took Radar down to the yard, then let Hawkeye follow me toward the street. Radar wasn't allowed anywhere near Maggie and Meredith's coffee shop, but Hawkeye heeled with the discipline of a professionally trained guide dog, which he may have been, for all anyone knew. Hawkeye's past was a mystery. He'd been discovered hiding among the piers under the coffee shop, with a chain so tight around his neck the skin had grown over it. Don took him home, because, as he told the story, Maggie and Meredith would have *made a sissy dog out of him.*

Hawkeye stayed closer than usual as we headed across the street and climbed the stairs to the coffee shop.

Maggie and Meredith were in rare form when we walked in. "I see you convinced the bubblehead to board up," Maggie observed, tucking her hair, glazed an unnatural red this week, behind her ear.

"He's convinced it won't hit here."

"Meridee's got a bad feeling about this one, and so do I." Maggie leaned over to greet Hawkeye and scratch his ears. "This old fellow looks worried, too."

"I tried to tell Don that."

"Don-schmon." Cupping Hawkeye's head in her hands, Maggie gazed into his eyes. "I wish I could take you on the plane with me, big boy. Yes, I do."

"Do the two of you need a ride to the airport tonight?" Anything would be better than sitting alone in my apartment, or going to the crawfish boil at Blowfish Billy's, watching old hippies beat their chests and shake fists at the storm.

"Nope." Standing up, Maggie flipped a towel over her shoulder. "We're just leaving the car at the shuttle stop. If Glorietta sweeps it off to Timbuktu, then so be it."

"Maggie!" Meredith protested from the back room.

"Well, you never know. This could be the big one." Maggie grew serious. Bracing her hands on the waistline of her long cotton skirt, she peered out the door. I couldn't help looking myself, thinking that far out on the horizon, the water was darker and choppier now.

Maggie chewed her lip. "If Don weren't such an idiot, he'd pack up and go."

"I tried to tell him that, but he won't listen. He's headed down to Blowfish Billy's tonight. If the storm does turn before morning, he'll probably be passed out somewhere."

Tossing the towel onto the counter, Maggie snorted and rolled her eyes. "If he ends up being right, we'll never hear the last of it."

"I hope he *is* right." But no matter how much I tried to tell myself that everything would be fine, the words were like a magician's illusion—foggy, muted, ready to vanish at any moment. The image in my dream, the one in which the storm was coming and I couldn't run fast enough, seemed real.

## Chapter 3

# *Donetta Bradford*

In the mornin', I was awake before the first glow of sunup pinked the horizon. It was too early to call Imagene, so I went to my sewin' room and checked my new portable computer I'd got off QVC. The page about the Festivale Cruises was still there on the screen, same as the night before, and the *Liberation* was settin' sail at four. Not a thing'd changed.

I jumped up and down and cheered all by myself, right there in the sewin' room. "We're goin' on a cruise!" I, Donetta Bradford, was gonna sail the high seas of adventure, starting today. Who'da thought it, plain old Donetta from Daily, Texas, leaving behind the beauty shop for exotic ports a' call. It just goes to show, you should never say never. Amazin' things can happen in a regular life, if you let 'em.

I couldn't hardly keep from dancing and singing Broadway songs in the halls while I dragged my suitcases to the porch. If it wouldn'ta been for Ronald there, sawin' logs in his recliner, and that persnickety old Miss Peach probably watching our house from outside, I mighta just waltzed down the hall and into the yard to sing to the sunup. "California Here We Come" was runnin' through my head, only in my mind, I'd rewrote the song, and I was singing "Liberation Here We Come." I did a little dance right past Ronald's chair, and he didn't know anything about it. *Liberation here we come. Gonna go and get some sun. Got to run to catch that boat. Then we'll be . . . la la . . . somethin' . . . afloat. . . .*

By the time the last suitcase was on the porch, I was trying to think of what would rhyme with *Thumb your nose at Betty Prine*. Ever since word got around town that we gals were planning this trip, Betty'd started bragging how her and Harold were gonna take a cruise to Alaska. "Harold's giving me the cruise for an anniversary present. Ten whole days in a luxury suite, just like on that movie *Titanic*. Isn't that romantic?" Betty was in for a wash-and-curl when she said that. I wanted to hold her under in the hair sink, which ain't a very Christian thought, but Betty could bring out the ugly in anybody.

"Sounds nice, Betty." I couldn't think of anything romantic about bein' locked in a cruise ship cabin with Betty Prine for ten days. If I was on the *Titanic* with Betty, I'da jumped off 'n paddled for shore, icebergs or no. You didn't have to be bright as a washed window to know what was behind that satisfied smirk of hers. Her cruise was *twice* as long as mine, and besides that, *Harold* had bought it for her. We both knew there wasn't any way my Ronald was gonna get on some ship and sail off into the sunset—not unless they loaded him, the TV, the recliner, and all.

Just thinking about it got me a little sad. Here it was, the mornin' of my big adventure, and Ronald didn't even bother to wake up and help me load the suitcases, or tell me *bon voyage*. Instead, it was my darlin' nephew Kemp who rolled up in the driveway to make sure I got off all right. Even *he* knew Ronald wouldn't be up. Sweet as it was for Kemp to come, having other people see the way things were between Ronald and me just made an old ache hurt again, like a bum knee that shoots out a twinge after a wrong step.

Kemp didn't have any idea about that, of course. He was just doing for me like he'd always done. Even now that he was all grown up, had gone out in the world to play pro baseball, and was back coaching at Daily High, he was still my precious boy and the closest thing to a son I'd ever have, since Ronald and me'd never been blessed with children of our own.

"How about a bite before you head off to work?" I asked when Kemp finished loading everything. "It'll only take me a minute to whip somethin' up." Lots of mornings, Kemp stopped by for breakfast on his way to open the field house for the football and baseball boys. Since he was the newest coach at Daily High, and he wasn't married, Kemp got all the early morning and late night jobs nobody else wanted. He didn't seem to mind. Kemp was restless, living back here in Daily instead of up in Dallas playing for the Frisco Rough Riders or the Texas Rangers. Last year with the Rangers looked like it would be his big year, but after two surgeries on his pitching arm in four years, I figured that door was probably closing for good, even though Kemp hadn't quite faced it yet.

"I'll grab something at the Dairy Queen." He already had one foot on the trail, like usual. That boy never stood still for long. "Need to get to the field house early. Got kids coming in to make up workout time so they can play in the game."

"Seems like since Mr. Groves is the football coach, and it's *football* season, that oughta be his job," I pointed out.

Kemp just smiled again and shook his head. "If the boys don't get in their workout time, they don't play. That's the rule." Which was Kemp's way of saying, without saying, that if it was up to Coach Groves, the kids that'd missed workout sometime during the week would be out of luck.

I touched Kemp's cheek and felt mother-love bloom in my heart. "Kempner Rollins Eldridge, you're too good. I've got half a mind to call the superintendent's office and give them a piece of my mind."

He rolled his eyes, embarrassed like the little boy he used to be, and then he pointed a finger at me, his brown eyes goin' serious. "Aunt Netta . . ." he warned.

"I've got half a mind to. You hadn't oughta let them treat you that way." Sometimes I was afraid that, if Kemp couldn't pitch in the big leagues, he didn't care what happened to him.

He closed the tailgate on my pickup with the arm that hadn't had all them surgeries. "*No* calling the school."

"Well, they deserve to hear about it."

"No *calling* the *school*."

"All the kids oughta have a equal chance to play. Them kids out on Caney Creek can't always get to workout if they don't have a ride. It ain't their fault—just because their folks don't have the money to buy cars for their kids. If it was the banker's son or the doctor's son who didn't get to play, well, then you'd hear about it, I'll tell you."

"I'm working on it."

"I know, but . . ."

"*No* calling the school."

Kemp stood up straight, all six foot three of him. He put his hands on my shoulders and looked me in the eye. "Don't worry about the boys out on Caney Creek. Just go on your vacation and have a great time. It's fine. We're fine. Everything here'll be fine."

I sighed. "I just worry."

"Don't. You've been waiting all summer for this trip. Have fun. I know it's hard to believe, but the homeplace won't fall apart while you're gone. Y'all get some sun and live the wild life." He kissed me on the top of the head, then started off, but

33

stopped halfway to his truck. "Make sure you keep track of the weather reports, all right? I forgot to look this morning."

"Oh, hon, I been checkin' it on my new computer since yesterday." I was pretty proud that, at almost seventy years old, I could still learn to use the latest technological wonders. "The boat's gonna leave at four and sail right around that storm, so there's not a thing to worry about."

"Just keep track," Kemp warned, then headed on to his truck. I had a little twinge of being sad that Ronald hadn't said one word to me about that storm. He was too mad over the cruise to hardly even talk about it. He thought it was silly, us gals goin' off by ourselves, spendin' all that money. He'd never break down and say he was worried about me, or he'd be lonesome here and didn't want me to go.

Kemp waved good-bye, and I put on a smile and waved back. "Love ya, sweetie," I called, and my voice cracked a little. I guess I understood why Imagene'd wrote the letters to her kids and left them on the table.

"Love you, too, Aunt Netta."

I watched him drive away, then I went in, closed up the computer, and got my purse. On the way through the living room, I stopped and stood over Ronald's chair.

"I'm leavin'," I whispered. "I'm headed over to Imagene's now."

Ronald pushed his mouth into a big ol' frown, and his eyes squeezed shut tighter, like he was in pain.

"I've got to head out now," I said a little louder. "There's plenty of food cooked ahead in the fridge."

His head rolled and one eye blinked partway open. For a second, I thought he might say he was gonna miss me while I was gone. Every once in a while, when I looked in Ronald's face, I thought I saw the handsome boy I married all those years ago. "All right," he grumbled, and that very moment all I saw in the chair was an old fart too stubborn to say something nice.

All of a sudden, I didn't feel a bit bad about leaving. "I'll be back next Thursdey." I didn't wait for an answer. I just headed out to my truck with heaviness in my chest. But the farther I drove down the street, the more it floated away. Not Ronald nor anybody else was gonna ruin this trip.

By the time I got to Imagene's house, I felt free as a bird. Imagene was scramblin' around trying to get ready, and there was my brother in her kitchen cleaning up the dirty dishes. That was something, considering he didn't hardly clean the dishes at his own house.

"Mornin', Frank," I said, and he jumped like he'd been caught robbin' a bank.

"Mornin'." Frank dried his hands, then leaned up against the counter and took a sip of his coffee, trying to act like there was nothing strange about him bein' in Imagene's kitchen first thing in the morning. "I was just thinkin', I could drive y'all down there, then come back and git y'all when the boat docks again."

I felt a twinge of tenderness for my little brother, but then I pictured Frank cooped up in the van for six hours with three women. He'd be grunchy as a spring bear. "That's real sweet, but this trip's gals only. We got movies and I got my computer. I can check the weather anytime I want with my wireless intranet, and Imagene borrowed Timmy's cell phone, so if we run into any trouble, we can call."

Frank didn't want to talk about the computer. It bothered him that I'd learned to work one, and he still didn't know a keyboard from a keyhole. "Just make sure y'all remember to check the weather."

"We will."

"Every little while."

"Every thirty minutes, maybe more." The kitchen door swung open, and Imagene walked in. She had big bags under her eyes, like she'd been pacin' the floors all night.

"What's every thirty minutes?" she asked, like she was searching for somethin' new to worry about. When Imagene latches on to a fret, she's like a gator on a warthog's leg. She don't let go until she can drag it down in the mud and chew on it.

"Nothin'." Hooking my arm into hers, I tried to drag her toward the door, but she ain't the lightweight she used to be.

"I think I forgot to lock up in front," she fussed.

"Frank'll get it." I pulled her toward the back steps—the fastest way out to the car. "Let's go. Lucy'll think we forgot her."

Imagene rubbed a fingertip against her temple, pushing her glasses up and down. "Did anybody turn off the coffeepot?"

"Frank'll check it." I got her through the door and dragged her down the steps and to the driveway, then wondered how hard it'd be for me to shove her into the car single-handed. Frank was following along, but not helping any. Imagene kept lookin' back at him, like she was waiting on him to save her.

"Y'all two go on and git in," he said finally, and I could've kissed him. "I'll load your stuff for ya."

I hugged Frank, then started toward the driver's seat, because I didn't figure Imagene was fit to drive right now. "All aboard," I said. "I'll take the first shift behind the wheel." When I turned back, him and Imagene were just standin' there. They had a look that was lovestruck, if I ever saw it.

"Say good-bye, y'all," I hollered, and Imagene turned pink as a pig's ear and hurried into the car. She didn't look back . . . except in the mirror, while Frank finished loading everything, then waved us off.

"Here we go!" I said, and we headed on over to Lucy's house, with Imagene just sitting there in the seat chewing her fingernails. While we were waiting on Lucy's son to load stuff, I got out my computer and set it on the console, because it was clear that Imagene needed somethin' else to think about.

She frowned at the computer. "What's that for?"

"So we can check the weather."

"Here?" she asked, looking around, because there wasn't a thing nearby except Lucy's little house.

I opened up the computer, and the page about the cruise ship come up on the screen right away. "It works anyplace. See? And it plays movies."

Imagene's eyes got wider and wider, and I figured out she was looking at the hurricane update box in the bottom of the screen. Good thing Lucy got in right then and we could head off before Imagene took it in her head to jump out and run for her life.

"I brought a surprise for us," I said, and while we rolled down the driveway, I fished movies out of my computer bag. "I got *The King and I*, *The Sound of Music*, and *Steel Magnolias*. Had to rent them from the Prines' video store, which is against my principles, strictly speakin', but I figured we needed a little onboard entertainment. Which one do y'all want first?"

Imagene picked up *The King and I*. "Lands! I haven't seen this in years!" she said, and for the first time, she looked excited about our trip.

"Alrighty, then. Just slide it in the little hole there on the front of the computer and mash the Enter button. It'll play all on its own," I told her.

"Do tell." Imagene opened up the DVD, then sat there looking at the computer.

"My grandson have one," Lucy put in, and she took over getting our movie going. It started up with an ad for a sing-along tape, and we rolled off down the road singing "I Whistle a Happy Tune" the way only three best friends alone in a car can do.

## Chapter 4

# *Kai Miller*

In the morning, I opened my eyes to a close-up of Radar's tongue vibrating on the pillow as he snored softly. Hawkeye had squeezed in behind me, so that I was wrapped in my covers like the filling in a dog burrito. The boys smelled salty and smoky, a little like crawfish, probably from a wild evening at Blowfish Billy's last night. I'd finally gotten tired of Don and the bonfire crowd calling to entice me into joining them, and around midnight, I'd turned off the ringer on my phone. This morning, Don's window AC wasn't running outside, which probably meant the dogs had come home alone and Don was crashed under a beach umbrella at Billy's.

Hawkeye's eyes drew together with concern as I sat up. His graying muzzle twitched as he raised his head and sniffed a shaft of sunlight.

It took a minute for the light from the screen door, the angle of it, the fact it had already risen over the palms outside, to register in my thoughts. I twisted and checked the clock, and a rush of adrenaline zinged through my body. *Eight thirty!* I was supposed to report to the *Liberation* in less than an hour.

Squirming from under the covers, I hurled complaints at the alarm clock, then hit the floor and moved around the room like a one-woman tornado. Within a half hour, I'd showered, pulled my hair into a snaggly blond knot and popped a clip into it, thrown on shorts and a T-shirt, grabbed a granola bar and a lone banana off the counter, and tossed the last of my things into a duffle bag.

Opening the mangled screen door with my hands full of luggage, banana, purse, and car keys, I hollered at the dogs, "Come on, you two. Out."

Hawkeye inched forth a few steps, then tucked his tail and backed away, embarrassed by his own disobedience, while Radar yawned and belly-crawled to the edge of the bed, then laid his head on his paws, his tail thumping the mattress with a complete lack of chagrin.

"Nobody's listening to me!" The door flapped open in the breeze, then came back and smacked me hard on the rear end. "Out! Now!"

Radar whined, and Hawkeye turned his face away with a look that was disquieting. It wasn't like him to act this way. He never disobeyed an order.

Piling everything on the porch, I headed back into the apartment, grabbed both dogs, and dragged them across the floor, thirty-two toenails (not including mine) plowing furrows in Don's ugly green linoleum, until we made it across the threshold and I deposited the dogs on the deck outside. Radar tried to crawl back in through the screen door, and Hawkeye checked the boarded-up windows for another point of entry.

"What's the matter with you two?" I muttered, but the question quickly became rhetorical. I could feel the answer as I kneed Radar out of the way, pulled the door shut, and locked it. Something was wrong with this day. On the horizon, clouds were closing in. The surf was rough, the tide higher than normal, the water brown and churning with sediment and depositing tangled mounds of seaweed on the beach. Along the walkway, the palms bowed to the west, their fronds waving like the streamers on a giant wind sock.

Glorietta was closer than she was supposed to be.

As I started across the deck, the dogs whined, their eyes framed by worried furrows of fur. They followed a few steps, then retreated and continued pacing the deck near my front door. Their toenails clicked on the hollow wood as I left Don a note downstairs, telling him I was too late to catch the shuttle and he could pick up my vehicle at port parking. Tossing everything into the Microbus, I gave the dogs one last apologetic look as they watched from the top of the stairs.

Before I was halfway to the port, I knew why Radar and Hawkeye hadn't descended to the yard. They were looking for higher ground, and the dogs weren't the only ones. Perdida, normally just waking and dragging out the beach gear at nine in the morning, was in a state of pandemonium, people everywhere loading cars, securing shutters, and tying up patio furniture. The highway leading down the coast was already clogged with traffic, and at the gas stations, the lines stretched down the curb. For the past few days, cautious residents had been filling vehicles and gas cans, just in case. Those who hadn't were now stuck in a frustrating tangle, sweltering in the heat.

While I was sleeping, then oversleeping, everything had changed.

Absently counting the cars in a gas line, I pulled out my cell phone, flipped past the list of missed calls from Don and the bonfire crowd, and dialed the cruise terminal. The call failed. All circuits busy. As the drive to the port slowly ticked by, I scrolled down my phone list, tried members of the *Liberation* staff. Every attempt ended in a *circuits busy* message or a roll to voicemail. A check of the missed calls showed that no one from the ship had phoned me during the night, but along with the wild bunch from Blowfish, Maggie and Meredith had been trying to contact me since the early hours of the morning. The M&Ms wouldn't have been calling unless something was very wrong.

By the time I reached the port, I already knew what a frantic trip across the park-and-pay lot quickly confirmed. The ship wasn't there. A shuttle driver grimly informed me that the *Liberation* had left in the middle of the night, right after Glorietta hooked north, picked up steam, and headed our way. "She's coming in faster than anybody thought." He gave the water a nervous glance. "Port closes to all traffic at one. Mandatory evacuation order's coming anytime now. If you've got a way out of town, you'd better take it. Now. If not, there'll be buses leaving from the strand as soon as they can set it up."

"I have my van," I muttered, staring numbly toward the harbor, where my ship should have been. How could this be happening?

"If it's not fueled up, you'd better get in line before the stations run out." He pointed across the highway at a Shamrock, its sign a wavy green blur in the heat waves rising off cars. "Not much left on this side of town."

I vacillated in place, weighed down by luggage, jewelry-making supplies, crashing expectations, and a rising sense of panic. Glancing over my shoulder, I checked the harbor again. No ship. Why hadn't anyone called me from the *Liberation*? "When do they expect the storm to make landfall?"

"Eleven tonight, but that could change." Surveying the traffic on the highway, he frowned. "Hard predicting this one since she's turned. They've got everyone from New Orleans to Corpus heading inland. Get in your car and move out. If it comes to Perdida, you don't want to be here."

"Thanks," I muttered, hiking a duffle bag higher onto my shoulder and watching a freighter leave port. What did I do now? Get in line at a gas station? Hit the road? Go back home?

I couldn't just drive off and leave Don. Where was he right now? Did he know an evacuation was being ordered?

Dragging my luggage and the jewelry crate, I hurried across the parking lot and threw everything into the van. The cell phone rang as I was weaving through traffic on the way back to the surf shop. Maggie was on the other end.

"Where are you? Are you on the ship?" The words rushed one on top of the other, hard to make out. "Meredith just checked the website and saw they moved the *Liberation* out of port early."

"I'm not on the ship. I missed it."

"You're not . . ." Maggie drifted into an uncharacteristic silence. When she came back, her voice was two octaves lower. Grim. "Listen, sweetie, you need to get out of there now. The evacuation's already a mess. It's all over the news. As soon as they make it mandatory, it'll be insane."

My stomach slowly sank, the banana suddenly a molten mass of acidic heat in my belly. My mind raced ahead. I passed a gas station, considered pulling in, checked the fuel gauge. *I have a quarter tank. I could wait. . . .* "I am. I will." *What if there's no gas later?* Pulling into the right lane, I slid into line behind at least twenty cars. "I have to get gas and find Don. He went down to Blowfish Billy's last night."

Maggie scoffed. "You just head out of there. Don's a big boy. He knows what to do. We'll keep calling him from here. Wait . . . hang on a sec." She paused to talk to Meredith, covering the phone so that she sounded like the teacher on Charlie Brown. "Listen, Meredith wants me to tell you to gas up at Cap's Store, you know, out by the crossroads at Kaskokee Lake? Don't waste time sitting in the line around Perdida. We made that mistake last time, and they were out of gas before we even got to the pump."

"All right. Thanks." Turning on my blinker, I squeezed into traffic again.

"Don't worry about Don. You just get on the road."

"I have to go back to the apartment." In front of me, cars crawled bumper to bumper. The trip to the surf shop suddenly seemed an impossible distance. "The dogs are there, and I have to pick up some food and water." Even I, who had so far managed to be absent for every evacuation, knew better than to take to the road without supplies. "Listen, the traffic's crazy. I'd better sign off."

When I finally pulled into the surf shop, the place was quiet. No sign of Don's Harley. No lights on, no air-conditioner humming. The dogs ran to me as I checked around the shop and knocked on Don's apartment door. I called Blowfish Billy's, but no one answered. Standing on the deck with Radar and Hawkeye underfoot, I searched across the string of condos, vacation homes, and stores, looked up and down the highway and then up and down the beach. No sign of Don, anywhere. The beach was empty, except for a reporter filming near the surf.

With the traffic, there was no telling how much gas and time a trip to Blowfish Billy's would eat up. There was no point in driving down there anyway. If stragglers from last night's bonfire were still hanging around, someone would be answering the phone. When the fun ran out at Billy's last night, Don and the party must have migrated somewhere else. No telling where that might be.

Gathering food and bottled water, I dialed the number a second time, and a third, then tried Don's cell number. Each time, the response was either no answer or all circuits busy.

Finally, there was no more time to waste.

The dogs followed me to the yard gate, whined and scratched

at the fence as I finished packing supplies into the Microbus. What now? Did I take the dogs along? Leave them where they were? What if Don couldn't make it back to the shop? Even if he could, all he had was his Harley. . . .

Jogging to the curb, I looked up and down the line of cars crawling along the coast toward the highways leading inland. I couldn't leave Radar and Hawkeye behind, trapped in the yard, helpless, unable to escape when the storm came in. There was nothing to do but leave a note for Don and take his dogs with me.

After scratching another message on the chalkboard by the shop door, I hurried back to the yard gate. "Let's go, guys."

The dogs were through the opening and into the Microbus before I could finish closing the latch. Looking up at my apartment one last time, I got in the van, started the engine, crossed the parking lot, and officially became part of the evacuation.

Progress on the coast highway was stop and go, as Maggie had predicted. The back road to Kaskokee Lake was slightly better, but by the time Cap's Station came into view, my gas gauge was down below an eighth. Rolling into line behind three cars at the single set of pumps, I turned off the engine and got out, stretching the stress knots from my back. *Any minute now, I'll wake up. I'll wake up and walk onto the* Liberation, *and everything will be fine.*

*Everything will be fine.*

*This isn't real. It can't be.*

But the situation felt real, and anything but fine. The roads were in chaos, I had three hundred dollars in my pocket, and sometime soon Don would probably come back to the shop and find out I'd hijacked his dogs. He'd think I was out of my mind.

*Maybe I am. Maybe I'm overreacting. Maybe I should have stayed in Perdida.* I let my gaze drift to the road, my mind traveling with it. The way home was completely clear. . . .

Hawkeye climbed into the driver's seat, stuck his head out the window and sniffed the air, then sat panting heavily, his eyes anxious, the dusting of gray on his muzzle making him look like a wise old man, a thinker.

*He knows it's coming. He can feel it.*

"Hey, buddy." I scratched his ears. "Hang on. We'll be out of here soon." But doubt was creeping over me like a tide, slowly rising. At the head of the line, a man in a four-wheel-drive pickup was filling gas can after gas can, then loading them in the back of his truck. Behind him, the driver of a minivan grew aggravated, got out, and started yelling. The confrontation looked as though it was about to turn violent.

Hawkeye tuned in as the gas station owner, Cap, exited the store. Raising a baseball bat like an extension of his arm, Cap pointed at the pickup driver, then motioned the owner of the van back to his own vehicle.

The pickup driver lurched forward and shoved Cap with so much force that Cap landed in a heap against the trash can. I took a step toward them, then stopped, fear tugging me, holding me in place. Wasn't anyone going to do anything? Wasn't I?

A dark blur caught the corner of my vision. I heard the screech of claws on metal, and suddenly Hawkeye launched himself toward the pumps, running with his ears flattened and his teeth bared.

"Hawkeye, no! No!" I cried, bolting after him. "Hawkeye!"

Cap and the customer reacted in unison, Cap staggering to his feet and the pickup driver scrambling into his truck and closing the door. Hawkeye slid to a stop, jumped against the truck, and tried to rip a hole in the glass. The engine roared to life, and the driver ground it into gear, depositing Hawkeye on the pavement as the truck sped away.

Cap chased after the gas thief, moving in a bow-legged run and swinging the baseball bat, but the truck, and the gas, quickly disappeared, driving the wrong way in the empty southbound lane. By the time Cap came back, I'd grabbed Hawkeye's collar and checked him over.

Cap held out his hand to test the dog's mood.

"He doesn't bite."

"Coulda fooled me, he don't bite. Reckon that man'll think twice before he comes here to grab gas again."

The minivan owner, next in line, tore a piece of paper from his pocket calendar and handed it to Cap. "Here's his license number."

Tucking the note into his pocket, Cap motioned wearily to the pump. "You can bring your van on in now. Keep the line movin'."

With a nod of satisfaction and an angry chin jerk toward the road, the minivan driver returned to his vehicle and pulled up. Behind him, a Cadillac SUV moved forward, stopping just a few inches short of causing a collision. The driver stared straight ahead, pretending not to have noticed everything that had just happened.

Patting Hawkeye on the head, Cap gave the gas line a concerned look. Two more cars had pulled in, so that the backup stretched almost to the highway now. "Better move your vehicle on up before someone cuts in front." His grip tightened on the bat. "Some folks lose their minds durin' these things. You'd best get gassed up and hit the road. If we didn't still have fuel and food to sell, we'd be headed that way for sure. National Guard and Highway Patrol are movin' in to help keep things sane."

The minivan driver motioned to a gas can next to the pump. "The guy with the pickup leave that?" Eyeing the container with interest, he reached for his wallet.

Cap hobbled forward and picked up the can. "Guess I better hang on to it as evidence." He lugged the can to the store entrance, and the minivan guy looked disappointed.

After returning Hawkeye to the Microbus, I pulled forward behind the SUV, then tried to call Perdida. All circuits busy. Again.

In front of me, the gas line proceeded slowly. There were cans in the back of the minivan, which seemed ironic. Time ticked by while I waited for both the minivan owner and then the driver of the SUV to fill tanks and cans. By the time I reached the pump, people farther back were honking and yelling, afraid the supply would run out. The guy behind me watched impatiently as I filled my main tank and then the auxiliary. One great thing about my Microbus was that, if you could ever afford to fill it, it held quite a bit of gas at once.

By the time I was finished, the next customer had rolled to my back bumper, the language of road rage indicating that if I didn't move soon, he would push me out of the way. His engine revved, and he rocketed into position at the pump as I moved the Microbus to a parking space near the store entrance, cracked the windows, and went inside. In the store, Cap was pulling six-packs of Coke and packages of doughnuts forward on a nearly empty shelf while his wife, Rhea, stood behind the counter, her attention riveted to a small TV.

"I need to pay for the gas," I said, glancing around the store as Cap moved to the counter. The shelves, usually full when I came to the lake with Maggie and Meredith, looked like they'd been through a looting. "Do you have any dog food?" Mentally, I counted my money, subtracting the chunk I'd spent on gas. When I'd left Don's, I hadn't even thought about bringing supplies for Radar and Hawkeye. They'd need water, too.

Cap shook his head. "All outta dog food. I can give you some deli meat. Power goes down, all this meat'll spoil anyway. You got a cooler?"

I shook my head. "I wasn't planning on evacuating."

"Heard that story before." Cap grabbed a slab of roast beef and put it on the slicer. "I got some foam minnow buckets. That'll work."

I did another mental money count. "How much are they?"

Cap shrugged. "You can bring it back next time you're out to the lake with the M&Ms." He meant Maggie and Meredith. Cap's store was our regular stop on the way to the cabins at Kaskokee. "Don't worry about the meat, either. Better your dog have it than Glorietta. Reckon I owe him a favor anyhow. How's your dog like his beef sliced?"

"I don't think he has a preference."

Cap chuckled under his breath. "We'll just do it medium. There's some bread on the shelf. Little bit of bottled water left. Better grab it if you need it."

I briefly considered the funding issue. If I spent much here, there wouldn't be anything left for a hotel, meals, or supplies down the road. "I think I'm good. I'm not planning to go too far—just up a couple hours inland."

Cap continued with the slicer. "Better go farther than that. You taken a look at this monster lately?" He shrugged toward the television. "She's hookin' it north and they say she'll make category four. Just go ahead and get what you need, all right? You can settle up for it later."

A familiar feeling swept over me, twisting my stomach and causing my cheeks to sting with a hot rush of blood. Growing up, my brother and I were always being sent out to mooch something off someone. Even as a kid, I hated the way it felt. "Really, I'm fine."

"Just take it." Cap packaged the roast beef, tucked it into a Styrofoam minnow bucket with some ice, and moved down the counter. "Take a block of this cheese, too. It'll keep if your cooler don't hold out."

"I'm not . . ." The TV grabbed my attention. The storm had

intensified into a giant swirling mass of clouds covering almost the entire gulf. "Whoa . . ."

"Somethin', ain't she?" Cap and I watched with morbid fascination as I sidestepped to the counter to pay. Rhea slipped from her stool and backed toward the cash register, her eyes welded to the screen.

"I got it." Sliding in front of Rhea, Cap took charge of my bill, the end result being at least thirty dollars less than it should have been. He leaned close as he divulged the final amount. "I ask you a favor?"

"Sure."

His fingers swept my palm as he dropped in my change. "Take Rhea with you. She don't drive, and I can't lock up the store while I got gas people need. Looks like I might be ridin' this thing out. The roads are bumper to bumper already, and it's only gonna get worse. I want Rhea to go before it's too late. In case somethin' happens."

I blinked, surprised, the distance between us suddenly seeming uncomfortably intimate. "You think it'll be that bad?"

Cap winced, sucking air through one side of his mouth, as if he were reluctant to answer the question. "I just want Rhea to get out, you know?"

"Of course I . . . sure . . ." I heard myself say, my evacuation picture shifting. The dogs, me, Rhea . . . "Of course she can come with me."

Rhea turned her attention to us. On television, the scene had changed to one of gridlocked cars on I-10 leaving Houston, frustrated drivers standing atop their vehicles, trying to see the front of the line.

Climbing off her stool, Rhea walked to the cash register. "No."

Cap held up his palms, attempting to placate her. "Rhea, it's—"

"No," she insisted, her accent, European of some sort, cutting the word sharp on the end. She clenched her jaw, her skin gray with determination, her eyes narrowing so that they were nothing but small brown orbs in a nest of fine creases. "We been forty-seven years, Cap, all the way together." She turned to me apologetically. "We been forty-seven years. We never sleep apart."

Rhea's words touched some deep, tender spot in me, settled there and felt warm. How would it be to love someone almost your entire life? To be willing to weather any storm, as long as you were together?

"All right," Cap sighed, frowning apologetically at me. "We'll just hang on here, I guess. Maybe the gas'll run out soon and we'll hit the road." He glanced outside, seeming unconvinced.

His wife patted his arm, then returned her attention to the TV, and Cap followed me to the exit. "Thanks anyhow." Pulling open the door, he handed me my sack, then picked up the gas can left behind by the runaway driver. "You take this. You might need it up the road. Not much fuel on the evacuation routes. Lots of folks stranded already."

"Oh, I don't need—"

Holding up a hand, he walked to the Microbus and loaded the can through the back hatch. "Never know what'll happen up the road." After shutting the door, he headed for the shop without a word.

I stood watching him go, waiting as the door shuddered back into place, the glass reflecting the scenery in layers—a gray sky to the east, swaying pines, the road thick with traffic traveling west.

A minivan melted out of the distance, heading the wrong direction. I turned to look over my shoulder as it drifted off the road and into the parking lot. It paused there, not quite on the shoulder, not quite off it, either. The driver, an older woman with a thin face and red hair mounded into a puffy up-do, scanned the parking lot, seeming confused. In the passenger seat, a silver-haired woman pointed toward the store, and both of them turned my way, checking the place out as if they weren't quite sure where they'd landed or why there was so much commotion.

# Chapter 5

## *Donetta Bradford*

Reckon what's goin' on around here?" Imagene asked, then sniffed and wiped her nose as we rolled into the parking lot. We'd started *Steel Magnolias* after an early lunch, and everyone in the car was a little weepy—even me, and I was just listenin', because it was my turn to drive again. Since we were to the point of needing gas anyhow, we'd decided to pull off when we saw the sign for Cap's Crossroads.

"There's an awful lot of folks headed the other way." Imagene dabbed her eyes and looked out the window at the traffic going west. She had makeup tears clear down to her chin, on account of the movie.

"Maybe is a funeral," Lucy put in.

"That'd be a whopper of a fare-thee-well," I said. During *Steel Magnolias*, the traffic going the other way had got thicker and thicker. I didn't think too much about it because I was caught up in listening to the movie, but now it had me worried. "Lucy, how long's it been since we checked that page about the cruise?" Since we'd gone through all three drivers, Imagene was shotgun and Lucy was in the back again, and they were running the computer together. Lucy's job was to click that little picture in the bottom of the screen and make it big every thirty minutes, and Imagene's job was to have a rigor about how threatenin' that hurricane looked.

"Minute ago, when the movie is finish."

The worry lines around Imagene's mouth got deep enough to grow seed in. "Maybe it don't work."

"It's got wireless intra-net. It works everyplace," I told her, but in my own mind, I was getting worried, and I'd been that way for a while. The hairs'd been creepin' up on the back of my neck, which usually means trouble ain't far behind. Now, pulling into the crossroads station, my fine hairs were standing straight on end. The gas pumps had cars lined up like milk cows at feed time, and I couldn't figure any good reason it'd be that way.

"Maybe is a gas war." You could always count on Lucy to come up with somethin' positive to say.

Letting the minivan roll to a stop in the corner of the parking lot, I caught sight of Lucy's face in the rearview. She didn't think there was any gas war. *We got trouble* is what that face said. *Don't tell Imagene. She'll have a rigor.*

"Let me check the computer." Turning it toward me, I clicked on the screen, and sure enough, everything was fine. The *Liberation* was headed out at four o'clock. The hurricane hadn't gone hardly anywhere all mornin'.

"Maybe we oughta go on and find someplace that's not so busy." Imagene patted her hair and looked out the window, sizin' up the wind.

In the mirror, Lucy caught my eye and shook her head. After working together so many years, there wasn't any words needed between us two. She was thinking, *We better find out what's goin' on. Now.*

"We better stop."

I let my foot off the brake and pulled up near an old van like the hippies used to drive. This one, somebody'd fixed all up. It had a real pretty painted picture of the ocean and some birds flying over, and the words *Gifts From the Sea* on it. Two big black dogs were watching me out the window. It must've been hot in there, because they were panting to beat the band, their noses drippin' on the glass. A cute little girl with blond hair stepped back out of the way when I pulled in. She seemed like the type that'd be friendly, but she didn't smile. She looked nervous and scared, like a little child lost at the state fair, her fingers worryin' a charm on her necklace. The look on her face drilled through me like woodpecker on a dry tree.

Imagene unbuckled her seatbelt and opened the door. "I'm gonna run to the facilities."

"Imagene . . ." I stopped short of mentioning that she just went an hour ago, when we pulled off into an empty campground to stretch our legs and change drivers. "You got your little phone turned on, right?" *If there was anything wrong, Imagene's boys would've called . . . wouldn't they? Kemp would've called, too . . .*

Imagene stopped with one foot on the ground. "I turned it on this mornin'. Why?"

Only right then did it go through my mind that the whole morning'd passed and nobody'd called. "We oughta dial home and check in while we're stopped—let the fellas know we're just a half hour away from the ocean."

"Reckon we should." Imagene closed her door. Lucy got out and followed her inside without sayin' anything, and I set my computer on the seat, then opened the door and unfolded myself like a dried out piece of paper. I'd be glad when we were at the shore and on the boat. Something didn't feel right here. The air smelled wrong. It smelled of the ocean, even though we were still thirty miles away.

The girl with the dogs scooted around the back of her van to make sure the hatch was shut good, and I grabbed my computer out of the seat. "Excuse me, darlin'. Do you know anythin' about how to work one of these?" The girl looked at me like I was a couple sandwiches short of a picnic, but I didn't think anything about it because that happens all the time. "I been tryin' to check the weather, and—"

Before I could get over there to the girl, Imagene come runnin' out of the store, waving her hands in the air and hollerin', "Good gravy, Donetta! Oh, good gravy!" Her eyes'd got big as saucers and her face was picket-fence white.

The girl stepped back and bumped into me, and I just about dropped my new computer.

"Imagene, what in the world?" I closed up that computer right before Imagene grabbed my arm. "Stop pullin' on my arm. What's the matter with you?"

"Good gravy, Donetta, we've drove ourselves right in the middle of a hurricane! That's why all this traffic. Oh, good gravy! We ain't got the sense of a goat!"

I pulled my arm away before she could yank it off. "Imagene, what're you talkin' about? The computer says everything's fine. See?" I opened it up, but the screen was black and the little light on the keyboard was out. I guess I'd mashed the button when Imagene ran at me.

Imagene flipped her hands in the air and hopped up and down like a toad frog. "I *saw* it in the store. That thing's headed smack at us. There's people from here to Port Arthur tryin' to get out. Half of Houston's stuck on the side of the road, and gas is runnin' dry! That man in there said we'll be lucky if we can even get out at all. The station here's about used up their gas. Oh, good gravy! How could we be so dumb?"

"Imagene, the boat's leavin' on time. It *said so* on the *computer*."

Imagene's face was turnin' from white to mad-bull red. "Donetta Bradford, I'm tellin' you . . ."

"The port's closed because of the storm," the girl with the dogs said. She was kind of quiet, like she was afraid to get in the middle of Imagene and me. I would be, too, to tell you the truth. "Most of the ships left as soon as it turned north."

I felt my heart slide down my throat and land somewhere in the pit of my stomach, and all of a sudden, those hairs on the back of my neck made sense. There was a reason the air smelled like the ocean. A great big hurricane was blowing toward shore.

The next thing I knew, I was flappin' up and down, like Imagene. "Why didn't anybody call us on the phone?"

"I don't know, Netta. I did it wrong, I guess. I tried to get that phone out and call Timmy just now, but it's dead as a doornail."

"But the intra-net shoulda said somethin'. It shoulda told us. This computer's got why-five, Imagene. It's the newest thing. It'll pick up the intra-net anywhere, with no wires or anythin'."

The girl took a step closer and squinted sideways at my computer. "There aren't any wireless hot spots around here," she said. We both looked at her like she had corn growing out her ears, but she didn't notice, because she was still talkin'. "A wifi card won't work. There's no cell tower, either. The computer and the cell phone won't receive a signal here. If you update the page on your web browser, it'll tell you there's no connection."

"Up . . . update?" I choked out. I didn't know *browser*, either, but one thing at a time.

Imagene glared at me, and she didn't have to talk for me to know what she was thinking. *This is all your fault, Donetta Bradford. You came up with this trip. You made us drive down here where there was a hurricane on. . . .*

I could've reminded her that she was the one who messed up the cell phone, but I didn't see how that would help.

"Update . . . like, click refresh?" The girl pronounced the

words real slow, like she was talking to the class dunce, which she probably was. I shook my head, and she added, "The little curlycue arrow up in the corner?"

"Oh, that thang! Hon, I didn't mash nothin' extra so I wouldn't lose my window for the cruise ship. I just left it on all night."

Inside the hippie van, the dogs were getting restless, causing a racket, and their owner slapped the window to make them hush up. "Then you're looking at last night's news. Glorietta is about ten hours off the coast now. They expect landfall near Perdida about eleven tonight."

"Oh mercy . . ."

The girl's dogs kept carrying on in there, so finally she excused herself and got in her car. The two of us stepped out of the way to let her back up and get going. She waved out the window as she left, and I hollered, "You be careful, darlin'!"

"She was awful sweet," I told Imagene. "Cute little thing, too."

Imagene didn't want to talk about cute little gals in the parking lot. "What are we gonna do? We've drove ourselves right into the middle of a storm, Netta!" She was working into a rigor, and when she got that way, I couldn't think. It reminded me of my daddy and how, after he'd been hitting the bottle, he'd either go to yellin' or cryin', and I didn't have the first idea what to do to get him to stop.

I closed my eyes and tried to have a moment of meditation, like we gals learned on *Yoga With Yahani*. I pictured a seashore, which maybe wasn't a good idea, what with a hurricane coming, so I switched tracks and prayed instead.

"Donetta, wake up!" Imagene's voice was far off for a minute, like a dog yappin' two blocks away. "The man in there said there's gonna be floodin', and tornadoes, and winds way over a hundred miles an hour, and all the highways are stacked up with traffic. What're we gonna do?"

All of a sudden, my mind was clear. I opened my eyes and looked over our predicament. "We're gonna get gas—Lord willin' and the pumps don't run out—and we're gonna hit the road, just like everybody else."

"Netta, what if—"

Lucy came barreling out of the store before Imagene could list off the things that could happen to three old ladies, stuck in the car alone in strange territory, with a storm coming in and all sorts of people on the road.

"Is a hurry-cane come!" Lucy squealed, then let out a string of Japanese words, and then, "I hear from lady in bat-room!"

"We know," Imagene told her. "We're tryin' to figure out what to do."

A man rushed out of the store, got in his rag-top jeep, and fired it up. The tires burned and spun as he backed that thing out, and I had the feeling he'd mow over anything that got in his way. He looked at us like we'd surely lost our minds. *Why are you standing there?* his face said. *Run!* I wanted to run, but we didn't have much choice other than to get in the gas line, since we wouldn't be goin' far with the tank on empty.

Before the line could get any longer, we wheeled it around and pulled in. While we were waiting, we made good use of the time by praying some more. The prayer worked, because there was still gas in the pump when our turn came, and we filled our tank. Meanwhile, Lucy checked our supplies, then we paid for the gas and hit the road toward Daily. What'd seemed like a little trip that morning all of a sudden looked like a long way home.

We weren't on the go thirty minutes before the cars were bumper to bumper, and the farther we went, the slower it got, until it come to the point where we'd stop awhile, then creep along a few feet, then stop again. You couldn't do anything but keep draggin' on like that, letting time pass by while the mile markers stayed the same. At the rate we were movin', I figured we wouldn't get sixty miles before dark set in, but I couldn't tell Imagene that. I also couldn't tell her we were burnin' gas in a hurry.

"I think we better shut off the air-condition and roll down the windows," I said finally.

Imagene gandered at the gas gauge, which was already down two bars, after just a hour and a half. "Reckon we'd better," she agreed, and we opened up the van, letting in hot, sticky air.

We went on, stop and go, for a long time, until finally we come to a place where the road joined up with another little highway. There was a state trooper's car beside the intersection with the lights flashing, and the poor man was out in the heat, working to mix in traffic from both roads onto one road. A pickup with three fellas in the seat and rifles in the back window tried to cut in front of us, but the officer held him off. The young fella in the pickup wasn't happy about it one little bit, and the patrolman rested his hand near his side iron to show he meant business.

We didn't stay around to find out what would happen next. Traffic moved on, and so did we. Them yay-hoos in the pickup looked like trouble, and I hoped they'd get held up awhile, but pretty soon I spotted them, just two cars behind. Once the policeman was out of sight, they hit the ditch and drove past everybody, carrying on like fools, throwing beer bottles at road signs, hanging out the windows, and cheering like this was all a big, fun game. A real hillbilly Saturday night.

I put in a Hank Williams tape and turned it up loud so Imagene and Lucy wouldn't hear. Imagene was in such a fret she hadn't talked in over an hour, and in the back seat, Lucy had fallen asleep. Neither one of them moved when we rolled through a little settlement that was quiet as a ghost town, the houses shuttered, stores all boarded up, and gas stations dry. On the plywood, people'd painted hasty messages—*No Gas,*

*Looters Beware, No Trespassing, Glorietta Go Home*, and on the shutters of a cute little church, *When thou passest through the waters, I will be with thee; and through the rivers, they shall not overflow thee. Isaiah 43:2.* The chapel was small, a white clapboard building with tiny windows and no steeple. It reminded me of the little Catholic church where Mamee's people went. Back then, it was about the only church I'd ever been to very much, because my daddy didn't favor going to service back home. I hadn't thought about that place in years, but now I remembered it like it was yesterday.

The boys in the pickup turned off to the parking lot, busted a beer bottle against the church shutters, then headed around behind the chapel. I hoped they wouldn't do any damage to the buildin', but even more than that, I hoped they wouldn't come back. Being in a hurricane seemed to bring out the worst in some folks.

I let my head rest against the seat and watched the church inch smaller and smaller in the mirror. In my mind, I could see my grandmother's hands, the veins blue and hard under sun-freckled skin, her fingers knobby and slow as they slid over the ivory rosary, clutching each bead, her mouth just barely movin' in a slow whisper of sound.

*Holy Mary, mother of God, pray for us sinners. . . .*

It was a comfort, thinking of Mamee's voice and her hands on that rosary. I pictured being on the porch with her, listening to her stories, the sounds of the bayou all around.

As much as I hated missing our cruise, it was even worse to think that I might never get back here and find the answer to the question Mamee put in my mind the night she died.

"Netta, look." Imagene's voice seemed far off at first. I was still on the porch with Mamee. Imagene rattled my arm, then leaned close to the window, and I snapped back to the present.

We were inching a few foot at a time toward an overpass

across a four-lane highway. Down below, the cars sat bumper to bumper, still and stagnant as the water in the Dogleg Bayou, where Mamee lived. On the cement barrier, an old woman in a flowered housedress sat fanning herself, her head lolling back. Beside her, a teenager in baggy shorts poured bottled water onto a paper towel, then wiped it over the old woman's arms.

My mind couldn't make out, at first, why they'd be just sitting there on the side of the road, but the reason was clear enough when I looked down a stretch. Alongside the right-a-way, overheated cars'd been abandoned like carcasses, their metal skins giving off a sheen of heat waves far into the distance, like a mirage in the desert.

"Mercy," Imagene whispered. "Look at all them people."

In the back, Lucy sat up, stared out the window, and muttered something in Japanese.

"How're they gonna get out of there?" Imagene whispered.

As we rolled up over the bridge, I thought about that sign on the old church we'd went by, *When thou passest through the waters, I will be with thee; and through the rivers, they shall not overflow thee.* I prayed it over us and over the people stuck below as we drifted into the shade of the pines again.

I didn't stop praying until the bridge was far behind us, and then I let my mind drift to the Dogleg Bayou and Mamee until I was back in her little shotgun house again.

We were sitting on the porch, where the shadow of the cypress trees fell long and heavy, and the air throbbed like the breath of the bayou itself. Around us, the night was thick like one of her old quilts, stitched together from the smells of wet earth and Spanish moss, and saltwater ebbin' and flowin' in the Gulf, far away. Mamee's cane rocker creaked on the wood floor, and mosquitoes gathered thick on the screen. In the dark, gators slid into the water and cicadas thrummed in the trees. The night was so deep, it seemed like there wasn't a thing in the world but us and the bayou, Mamee's little house floatin' out into the black until it was an island, and my uncle's place up the hill seemed a million miles away.

I couldn't remember runnin' up that hill on the last night I ever spent with Mamee, but I remember the story she told right before she passed into quiet and never spoke again. Even before I ran for help, I knew she was gone. I'd heard the angels come for her. I felt their passing in a whiff of sweet, cool breeze that swept over us just after Mamee told me a story I'd never heard before, and never forgot since.

"Macerio," she whispered when the story ended. Her head rested against the rockin' chair, her face tipped toward the screen. She went quiet, and a question turned 'round in my mind. *What happened to Macerio?*

Before I could ask, the cicadas got loud as thunder. "Mamee, you hear that?" I asked, and pushed my hands against my ears. "Mamee, do you hear?" The air closed in, growin' heavier and heavier, sitting on my chest until I couldn't catch a breath. Then there was a waft of something sweet, a flutter of cool, and everything went quiet. When I touched Mamee's arm, her hand fell limp, the cream peas dropping, half-shelled, bouncing off the floor. I stood and looked at her face, and I knew she was gone.

All I could recall, when I thought about that night later on, was the sound of the angels coming, the feel of them in the air, the way it smelled sweet. I remembered my grandmother whisperin' that name, Macerio. I wondered if she saw him that night, if he took her hand and floated her away on the tide.

I never shared her story with anyone, not even my mama, or Imagene, but even all these years later, I still knew it just the way she spoke it. I could hear the roll of Mamee's Cajun words mixing with the bayou's night song as she told me about Macerio.

Mamee was just a girl of sixteen, a child with dark red hair and skin suntanned from hours workin' the rice fields, the summer her family headed east near the end of the harvest season to help an uncle bring in his crop. Even though they didn't travel on the rivers and the bayous by then, she still called it goin' downwater. She told me how the road followed the river, and they bounced along in back of the old farm truck in the heat and the dust, under the gray of a September sky. At night, they camped by the water, cooked on a fire, and shared their food with tramps and fellow travelers.

When they got to her uncle's farm, they rushed around to bring in the harvest ahead of a comin' storm. After more long days than Mamee could count, the work was done and men left for market. Mamee stayed in the barn loft all by herself, and stretched out on a bed of hay, too tired to walk to the house. The sky split open and rain started fallin' hard, but she didn't care. It felt so good to have the work done, she just closed her eyes and let the rain come.

When she woke, it was dark and the bayou'd come up, lappin' at the barn doors. Down in the corn crib, the buckets were clangin' against each other, afloat. The old building swayed like a ship at sea, the rain blastin' in as Mamee clung to the heavy cypress beams and looked out, trying to see through the storm. A flash of lightnin' split the air, and all around, the bayou was like a river. It'd swallowed the foot of the barn and started uphill toward the house. Mamee made the sign of the cross, then fell to her knees and started to pray. She didn't know how long she stayed there, but when she stopped, the storm'd quieted a little. She heard someone callin' from down below, and when she looked over the loft rail, one of the harvest boys, Macerio, was there on his tall brown horse.

"Quickly," he said in his thick Spanish accent, and she scrambled onto the ladder, then slipped and fell into the icy water. He caught her dress, lifted her up with his strong hands, and told her not to let go. He tied her to him with a length of rope, and then he guided the horse out of the barn as the old building cracked, and moaned, and started to crumble. Lightning filled the sky as he whipped the horse into the current, where it swam for its life. Somethin' hard and solid struck the horse, knocking it under, pulling loose the harvest boy and Mamee. She floated away and sank under. Then the rope went tight around her, tugged her forward, and she stretched toward it, trying for air.

A hand caught hers and lifted her up above the surface. She grabbed on, coughing out mud and water, as tangles of brush and wire caught at her dress before ripping free and floating off. She held on to the rope while the horse fought for shore, struggling against the current until finally it found a footing and scrambled uphill, dragging Mamee and Macerio along.

The harvest boy pulled the knife from his belt and cut loose from the horse in one quick motion, then lifted Mamee and carried her to the house. He set her down on the porch, and she watched him go back for the horse, lead it to the porch, and strip off the saddle. Sliding his strong fingers over its muzzle, he stood, his forehead pressed against the horse's white star, both of them spent. Even with the storm ragin', the moment seemed quiet, and still. Then the harvest boy took Mamee's hand, led her inside, and bolted the door behind them. It was the first time in her life she'd ever been alone with a boy who wasn't her brother, but she didn't think of it that way.

"The water comes," he said, and started gathering supplies—the drinking bottle from the icebox, a floating oil lamp the men used for fishing, a pistol and bullets. Mamee grabbed food, blankets, medicine, and piled all of it atop the big double bed in her uncle's room. They propped the bed up high, put the oil lamps on the icebox, where they wouldn't spill into the water, and packed the matches in a jar to keep them dry, and then they waited for the water to come. By mornin', it was up over the furniture.

For four days, Mamee and the harvest boy floated alone on the bed. He told stories of his home in Mexico, where he would someday return. He confessed that the first moment he saw Mamee, he fell in love with her. He'd been movin' on when the storm came, but he turned around because he knew she'd be trapped there alone. He kissed her—the first time anyone ever had—and as the water rose up, she gave her heart to the harvest boy. Macerio.

When the hurricane flood seeped away, the barn was gone, and Mamee knew Macerio'd saved her life. Her family came back, and she told them what'd happened, and all of them worked to salvage what they could of her uncle's farm. In the long evenings, she sneaked away with Macerio, and when it was time to go back home to southeast Texas, she told her daddy she was in love, but her daddy wouldn't hear of it. He said if that boy didn't leave her alone, they'd have him thrown in jail, and since he was just a harvest boy up from Mexico, things would go awful bad for him. Then the man put his daughter in the car and took her back upwater.

True love won't be denied by a man's plans, though—her daddy shoulda known that, if he knew anything. Four nights after they got back to the homeplace, Macerio came for her. Mamee slipped out a window and ran off to marry her beau.

The story ended there, with Mamee in her blue dress, riding away on the back of Macerio's horse in the moonlight, her arms wrapped tight around her love. Whenever I thought of that tale, I knew, just as sure as I knew the sun would rise tomorrow, there are some things in this world that are meant to be. Maybe that's why, all my life, I been so bad about matchmaking. I believe in true love. Even though I know as well as anybody, not everyone finds it. I knew Mamee'd found it that summer she was sixteen.

The boy who rode off into the night with her was her one true love, but there's a reason I never shared that story with anyone.

My grandaddy's name wasn't Macerio. My mama's father was named Burnam. He was Cajun French, not Mexican. He'd lived on the farm next to Mamee all his life. By all accounts, and from the little I could recall, he was a hard worker and a good man.

I'd always wondered, when I thought of that story, the same thing I tried to ask Mamee the night she passed. The question she left this world without answering, as she whispered his name and drifted away through the screen.

*What happened to Macerio?*

The story blazed a path in my heart, the way all good stories do. I always told myself that one day I'd head downwater and find out the truth, but now, with time running out and Glorietta coming in, it looked like maybe I never would.

## Chapter 6

# *Kai Miller*

In the back, the dogs lay listless, panting heavily after hours without a drink or a rest stop. I knew exactly how they felt. With the air-conditioner off and the Microbus barely moving, we were sweltering inside. I'd thought about pulling off a few times, but when vehicles left the line, then tried to reenter, road rage ensued. Desperation combined with survival instinct caused drivers to fight for each new inch of road. Occasionally, traffic bottlenecked completely and people exited their cars, then climbed on top, pounding sunbaked metal with frustrated fists and trying to see what the holdup was. The radio stations kept pumping out dire reports, and the sense of urgency heightened. Glorietta was now a solid category four. She'd hesitated just a few hours off the coast, swinging east, then west, toying with weather forecasters as she picked her time and place to strike.

I tried to call Don, then Maggie and Meredith to see if they'd heard word from him, but in reality I knew that even if he'd started to evacuate, he would have become frustrated and gone back by now. In the nine hours since I'd left Perdida, I'd made it only sixty miles north and west—not nearly far enough to be out of the storm's path.

The cell phone wouldn't connect, and I slapped it down on the passenger seat as Radar barked, whimpered, pressed his nose against the windows, then scratched at the door. I'd have to stop somewhere. Both the dogs and I needed a pit stop. After hours of following evac traffic down tiny county roads, I had no idea where I was, but according to the signs, another town was somewhere ahead. If it was like the smattering of communities before it, everything would be boarded up, no activity except a few desperate travelers pouring water on overheated radiators or checking gas pumps at closed-down stations.

On the roadside, a series of Berma-shave-style signs was passing so slowly, it was hard to remember one until I reached the next. I reviewed them in my mind as I inched along.

*Don't drive no more,*
*Stop at Hornwoods Store.*
*Good gas, good grub,*
*Got pie you'll love,*
*Gumbo, beignets, étouffée,*
*Get some, cher, and be on yer way!*

A National Guard truck passed by in the ditch, the open bed loaded with rescued travelers. Bumping along in the dust with their belongings, they looked like refugees from some third-world disaster area. They were heading south. The wrong direction.

On the outskirts of town, a dirt road led off to the right, toward what looked like a small riverbank picnic area under a bridge. The options wrestled in my mind as I crept closer. It wouldn't be easy to get back into traffic, but I had to stop before dark. The dogs could get a drink and have a few minutes to stretch their legs. I could locate a bathroom au-natural—having been raised on the road, that was nothing new—then head out again and hope someone would let me back in line. A better opportunity probably wasn't coming along anytime soon.

Leaving the highway, I rolled downhill faster than I should have. After eight hours of traffic stagnation, watching the speedometer flirt with twenty-five and feeling a breeze waft in the windows was an incredible dose of freedom.

At the bottom of the hill, fishermen had created a makeshift park with a picnic table, some threadbare lawn chairs, a fire pit, and a propane grill with no tank. Under the bridge, a set of old kitchen cabinets served as a fish cleaning area, the butcherblock countertop crisscrossed with knife marks, the side of the cabinet stained with dried blood. The scent was unmistakably familiar. Studying the gutting table, I had visions of my father outside our camp trailer, cleaning fish—our usual fare when we couldn't afford groceries. Gil and I eventually became pretty good fishermen. Gil was proud of that fact, because he'd read about fishermen in the Bible he stole from the motel.

Now, watching the river drift by in shadow, I thought about that Bible, tucked in my duffle bag behind the seat. I'd used it to baptize my little brother. I felt stupid about it at the time, standing waist-deep in the surf at daybreak, Gil just nine years old, shivering because the water was cold, and he'd lost ten pounds in the past six months. The stolen Bible was propped on a rock, a salt breeze turning the pages. I didn't know squat about baptizing someone. I did it because Gil wanted me to. When he came up out of the water, the look on his face was one of pure joy. He didn't care if I'd done it right, and it really didn't matter in the long run, because a hospital chaplain took care of it a few months later, officially.

My father wouldn't even stay in the room. The chaplain's sermon, he said, took him back to the most painful and humiliating part of his childhood, when he was forced to sit beside his mother in church while the pastor railed endlessly about lust of the eye and sins of the flesh. The sermon was a thinly cloaked warning to the congregation, and to my father, not to follow in the footsteps of his father, a deacon and respected physician who'd created a small-town scandal by divorcing Grandmother Miller and running off with a nineteen-year-old nurse. That sermon, intended to steer my father toward a normal life, was in a way the very thing that prevented him from a white picket fence existence. He wanted desperately to prove to everyone—his father, the pastor, his mother, the people in town—that he was better than any of them. He wanted to make it big with his music and watch them all grovel at his feet.

Being the parent of a terminally ill child wasn't part of his plan. Neither was Gil's desire to be baptized. On a normal day, the memories of my father's resistance to the baptism stayed under the mattress with the family mementos, but today, for some reason, it was all close to the surface. I was glad I hadn't left the Bible, that piece of Gil, behind in the path of the storm. Gil believed in that Bible. He believed the words in it had power. Perhaps, in spite of my father's view that religion was all about guilt, and the only person you could count on was yourself, a part of me believed what my little brother had so innocently placed his confidence in. Having Gil's Bible along made me feel like I wasn't so alone, even here.

As soon as I put the van in Park, the dogs began trying to claw through the doors, so I grabbed the leashes and limped, stiff, sore, and parched, to the passenger side, thinking that I knew exactly how the fish bones drying in the sun by the old kitchen cabinet must have felt. The breeze off the river touched my back and legs, tugging the sweat-plastered shorts from my skin. A shiver tickled my spine, but it had nothing to do with the weather. The camp had an eerie quiet to it, the traffic overhead passing in a soft hum, nearly hidden by the lacy fan of towering pines. The WPA-era bridge groaned under the weight of cars, its arched metal girders sending a dull *ping-ping* through the rebar. In the water below, a trotline bobbed up and down, heavy with the day's catch of catfish—gator bait now that no fishermen would be coming by.

I felt the compulsion to pull up the line and let the fish go, but there wasn't time. Under the thick canopy of foliage, the riverside was getting darker by the minute, less welcoming and more ominous. A shudder ran over my shoulders, and I opened the door just a crack, catching Radar as he tried to bulldoze his way through. Hawkeye followed and sat politely waiting while I connected his leash and closed the van door.

Just past the picnic tables, a trail marked by a hand-painted sign that read *Can* led off into the woods. After pausing at the riverbank for a doggie drink, we followed the path into the trees, Radar pulling ahead and Hawkeye sniffing carefully, checking out the unfamiliar territory. A homemade wooden outhouse marked the end of the trail. It was only slightly better than no outhouse at all, but as my mother had often reminded us, *Beggars can't be choosers.* Since we were beggars at least half the time, the saying fit. It's amazing sometimes, the things a weird childhood prepares you for.

I opened the door, tossed a stick inside, listened. No movement. The outhouse appeared to be unoccupied at the moment, but just to be sure, I poked my head in and looked around. Long streams of late-day sunlight illuminated the facilities, creatively built from a combination of scrap lumber and road markers. A wrong-way sign was posted on the rear wall, with a reflective arrow pointing upward, and a stop sign with the middle cut out served as a toilet seat. The word *Go* had been painted on the rim with a pointer indicating the hole. Someone had a sense of humor.

Hooking the dogs to a crooked nail on the side of the building, I went inside, entertaining myself with a comical picture of Radar taking off with the outhouse in tow. By the time I was finished with the world's fastest pit stop, Radar was tugging his leash, causing the walls to squeak and shudder.

"Radar, stop!" I hissed.

As I was crunching across the layer of raccoon scat on my way out of the privy, Hawkeye growled—not a playful reprimand aimed at Radar, but the real sort of growl. A warning. Radar quieted instantly.

My senses heightened as I unhooked the leases. "Ssshhh," I whispered, laying a hand on Hawkeye's head, listening.

I heard something. An engine and voices.

My mind spun ahead, racing back to the Microbus, as I gripped the dogs' leashes and bolted toward the campground. Everything I needed was in that van—the food, the gas can in the back, my purse . . .

I'd hit the clearing before registering the thought that, having no idea what I was going to find, I should have been more cautious. A pickup truck sat idling, and two men were patrolling around my vehicle, looking curiously in the windows. A third was down by the river with his shirt off, dipping something in the water. The tallest of the three, a guy with long, stringy hair and his shirtsleeves ripped off, snaked a hand through the open window and helped himself to a stale Honey Bun from my dash, then reached in again and came out with my purse.

"Hey!" I hollered, and all three of them turned to look at me.

The purse snatcher paused, his mouth dropping open as I rushed across the clearing with Radar and Hawkeye barking like canine units on an episode of *Cops*.

"Put that back!" My money was in that purse. If I lost it, I'd be stranded somewhere down the road. On the other hand, a few hundred cash wouldn't do any good if I ended up dead under a bridge. This was the kind of place where strolling fishermen discovered decomposing bodies, the clues to the crime long since washed away by the river.

"This yours?" The stringy-haired guy dangled my purse from a long, thin hand with barbed wire and a four-letter word tattooed across the fingers. He smiled, a massive chaw dripping from his bottom lip. He was younger than the redneck outfit and tattoos made him seem, and the one by the creek looked like he might still be in high school—a baby-faced kid who'd obviously had one too many brewskies, celebrating the oncoming hurricane.

Radar wagged his tail and pulled toward the rear of the Microbus, cluing me in to the fact that the third man was slipping around behind me. I turned my back to the vehicle. One thing I'd learned growing up around carnivals, trailer courts, and the parking lots of casinos was never to let some stranger get your back.

"Yes, that is mine, thank you." I reached again, and Hawkeye jumped, growling and snapping.

Radar strained at his leash so hard he started gagging. His tail was circling like a propeller, fanning air against my leg. To him, even sauced-up redneck boys looked like desirable playmates.

A horn blew overhead, and past the tops of the trees, someone yelled, and then a horn sounded again.

The chubby kid walked closer. "Let's go, Dodd."

*Dodd* glanced toward the van, and I seized the opportunity to grab my purse. Lipstick, powder, and a shell barrette fell to the ground and lay there, suddenly unimportant. Throwing open the van door, I tossed my purse inside, reeled in the dogs, and tried to load them through the front door. Radar protested, gagging against his collar and waiting for his usual entry point to open instead.

"Radar!" Picking him up like a seventy-pound Chihuahua, I shoved him into the seat, then climbed in and pulled the door shut.

"Hey, Hawkeye and Radar, like on *MASH*," the pot-bellied kid observed. Someone thumped the van from behind.

*The back hatch isn't locked.*

Hawkeye growled, rushing over the seats to the rear window as I started the engine.

"Eeeewww-eee! She's in a hurry," the third man slapped the back window as I shifted into gear. "She ain't into you, Dodd."

Stepping away, Dodd spit out the plug, then peeled back the Honey Bun wrapper, took a bite, and slowly savored it, smiling at me.

I didn't wait to see if he'd figure out the Honey Bun had been sitting on the dash for two weeks. I just hit the gas, did a doughnut between the picnic tables, and headed for the exit, determined that anyone who got in my way was toast.

"Hey, there's a trotline down there!" the chubby kid hollered. "I think they got somethin'. . . ."

I felt sorry for the fish.

Squeezing past the truck, I mowed over a couple saplings and tossed gravel all the way to the road. The more distance I put between myself and Dodd's group, the better. No telling what he and his friends would be like after a few more beers.

On the highway, a stalled car had brought traffic to a standstill. An elderly couple was marooned on the bridge, the woman clutching her hair in the passenger seat and the man leaning helplessly out the driver's window, trying to solicit help from vehicles squeezing by in the left lane. A custom four-by-four pulling a stock trailer muscled its way into the left lane, then stopped cockeyed at the entrance to the bridge, blocking movement completely. Down the line, horns began sounding in chorus, raucous and insistent.

"Get that thing outta here!" someone shouted, followed by a string of obscenities that, at the moment, seemed fitting.

The pickup driver, a big man in a cowboy hat, was unperturbed. Turning on his flashers, he climbed out, held up his hand to indicate that traffic should halt—as if traffic had any choice at the moment—then solicited the help of three teenaged boys from another vehicle. Both lanes waited as the dead car was pushed across the bridge and onto the opposite shoulder. After shaking his helpers' hands, the cowboy walked back to his truck in no particular hurry.

I inched up the shoulder to the start of the bridge railing and leaned out my window. "What's wrong?"

"Outta gas," he said, motioning to the car, now safely across the bridge. "I'll give 'em a ride into the next town."

*And then what?*

"I've got some gas." The words came out like a knee jerk, not something intentional. Part of me felt good about it, and part admonished, *What are you, nuts? You're going to need that later.* So far, there hadn't been an open gas station since Cap's place. I still had a little gas in my main tank and then the small auxiliary, but even mostly sitting on idle, the Microbus was burning fuel too fast. "I have gas in a can in the back."

The cowboy walked closer, glancing down the road, where stymied motorists were losing patience completely. In the distance, people had climbed onto the tops of their vehicles to see what was causing the standstill. "Wouldn't say that so loud." He motioned to the backup, then pointed toward his trailer, where horses were stomping impatiently. "Pull up behind my trailer and follow on across the bridge. Stay right on my bumper so none of them daggum yuppies can cut you off."

I eased in behind the trailer, successfully fending off a sports car with tinted windows and making my way onto the road. Crossing the bridge, I thought of my father. Wherever he was now, he would be patting me on the back if he could see. My father never passed a broken-down car without stopping to inquire as to whether he could be of assistance. He was experienced in piecing vehicles back together, so he relished the challenge, but there was also the fact that when you helped someone become unstranded, they usually offered you money, and we always needed money. Aside from that, Dad pointed out that it was good karma. You never knew how soon you'd be the one stuck on the side of the road, and generally, soon enough we were.

The cowboy pulled onto the shoulder just past the bridge and motioned for me to move in front of him, so I did. By the Buick, the old man was pacing back and forth, scratching his head helplessly as the cowboy and I exited our vehicles. "My wife's in a wheelchair. I don't think I can get her out of the car here. Her mind's not so good. She don't understand what's goin' on." The pink of the sunset reflected against his glasses, a filmy curtain over moist, red-rimmed eyes.

"This lady wants to offer you some gas so you can get on your way." The cowboy shrugged toward me. "Guess your luck's holdin' out better than you thought."

"I only need a little bit." The man's voice crackled like an old hinge, and he pressed a hand over his mouth, gathering his emotions momentarily. "Soon as we get through town, we're taking the cutoff to my son's place. They got a good sturdy house and a storm shelter."

The cowboy nodded and started toward my van, and I hurried after him. The dogs met us at the back hatch, Radar wiggling and slobbering and Hawkeye surprisingly calm. Pushing them out of the way, I unearthed the gas can, and the cowboy lifted it out. From the road, passing drivers watched, eyeing the container with interest as I shut the hatch and we walked back to the car. When the old man released the Buick's gas cap, it let out a hollow, vacuous sound. Nearby, a driver laid on the horn, and the cowboy looked around warily as he tipped up the can and poured gas into the tank.

Mopping his forehead with his sleeve, the old man dug out his wallet. "I'll pay you. You name what you want for it."

I thought again of my father. He had the routine down pat—act like you didn't want the money, then agree to take it. "The gas was given to me. You don't need to pay for it." I pushed the money away resolutely. My father would have been disappointed, which made refusing the money seem like a victory.

After capping the tank, the cowboy returned to my van with the container. "I'll go ahead and put this in your tank, if you want," he offered. I nodded, and he dumped in the last few gallons, then put the empty can back in my bus.

Below the bridge, shots rang out, reminding me that I needed to get on the road and put some distance between myself and the redneck crew.

"Y'all take care." The cowboy turned partway and tipped his hat. "Y'all hop in your cars and be ready. I'll get you out on the road." As I climbed into my van, he started his truck, the diesel engine roaring. I watched in my side mirror as he turned on his flashers, cut his wheels toward the road, and forced his way in front of a Jeep, despite several obscene hand motions from the driver. The cowboy's message was clear—either let us in or you'll end up like a junk car at a monster truck rally. Traffic parted like the Red Sea, we pulled onto the road, and the line moved out again.

Letting my head fall against the seat, I considered the strange dichotomy between the cowboy and the trio under the bridge. They didn't look so different, but they were. *You can never tell by looking*, my father used to say. But it had always seemed that people could tell, just by looking at us, exactly what we were.

The past and the scene on the bridge grew misty around the

edges, floated slowly away, faded until I'd zoned out completely, leaving behind the inch-by-inch progress of traffic and the constant storm-tracker reports on the radio, as Glorietta taunted forecasters like a Middle Eastern dancer, her long gray veils licking the waters offshore, diaphanous and feather-light. Ahead, far in the distance, the sky was clear, the first stars beginning to twinkle in the narrow slice of sky between the twin walls of pine. Dusky tree shadows fell heavy and thick, swallowing swampy ditches now lined with empty Styrofoam coolers, Coke cans, beer bottles, dirty baby diapers, and abandoned cars.

Sometime after the moon rose in the distance, then disappeared behind thickening clouds, we came to a Y where a highway patrolman was routing the right lane off the highway and onto a rural road. No one protested, as the result was that traffic on both roads had started to move again. The rural road looked dark and ominous, just a snake of taillights winding off into the piney woods, but at the moment I would have driven over the edge of a cliff to get moving again. Glorietta wasn't far from making landfall, and in an entire day of stop-and-go travel we hadn't moved inland nearly far enough.

Crawling along with the flow of traffic as the clouds thickened, I felt vulnerable, alone, lost, like I had as a kid when we pulled into a new town, parked the RV, and my parents headed off to find jobs or hit a casino—whichever seemed more likely to bring in cash at the time. Typically, Gil and I checked out the town, spotted the community centers and the churches. Sometime after the age of eight, I'd figured out that Sunday schools and vacation Bible camps had free food, entertainment, and nice people, usually. Sometimes, they'd even send a van through the RV camps to pick you up. My mother was never thrilled about it, but she let it go because it amounted to free baby-sitting and a savings on the grocery bill.

Being stuck here in the darkness as time ticked by and the

storm drew closer felt like being left alone in those dimly lit trailer parks with parents gone and night closing in outside. There was never any telling when they'd come back. No two days were ever the same. Eventually, my mother tired of that life. After Gil died, she solved the problem by leaving my father and me behind, and getting herself a new family. Unfortunately, there wasn't a place for me in it.

Shaking the thought of her out of my head, I focused on the taillights in the distance, both lanes crawling north and west toward the horizon like a giant beast of wavering electricity, curving and turning, disappearing into the trees, flickering behind swaying pine branches on hilltops.

The flow of cars ahead was slowing, the right lane crowding into the left. Gripping the steering wheel, I pulled forward in my seat, stood partway, trying to discern the cause of the holdup, until finally the source of the logjam came into view.

A minivan sat stalled, mostly on the shoulder, but the driver's side tires were still riding the line, forcing traffic to ease by in a narrow arc.

As I drew closer, then drifted by, I recognized the disabled vehicle. The driver's face was familiar, her tall red hair unmistakable.

# Chapter 7

# Donetta Bradford

One Memorial Sunday, Brother Ervin preached a sermon about prayin' from a foxhole in Korea. He came that mornin' dressed in full battle gear and the whole church smelled like mothballs, so we knew that stuff'd been in the cedar chest since he left the army. He called that sermon "Prayin' From the Foxholes of Life." He said you never really understand what it is to fall on God's grace until there's enemy fire all around and it's so dark you can't see the way out.

I hadn't been in too many foxholes in my life. Mostly, I been the sort to take a problem by the horns, wrestle it to the ground, and tie that bugger's feet so it can't get up and cause more trouble. The foxholes I couldn't handle been few and far between. I prayed from the foxhole when my mama died, and when I miscarried three babies, and when the doctor told Ronald and me we wouldn't ever have children, and as I watched them twin towers come down on September eleventh.

When the engine started to sputter on Imagene's van, and I knew the gas was out, and we were trapped on the side of the road in strange country in the middle of the night with a storm headed our way, I was prayin' from the foxhole. There wasn't a thing I could do to get us out of there, and I didn't even have any *idea* what to do, so I knew whatever happened next was gonna have to be up to the good Lord. Imagene and Lucy'd drifted off to sleep by then, and I didn't even wake them up. I just turned off the key so as not to run the battery down, closed my eyes, and started to pray for somethin' or someone to deliver us from the fix we'd got in. Around us, there was nothing but piney woods, and low country, and cars passing by, one after the other. Glorietta was coming onshore, but I didn't need the weatherman on the radio to tell me that. I could smell the air getting thick, and I knew she was headed our way like a freight train.

Folks around me knew, too, and they were gettin' desperate, and not a one of them wanted to stop for three old ladies stuck in a minivan. We were in God's hands for sure. Somehow, He was gonna have to get us out of this low country and to shelter before the rain and the wind came in.

*Lord*, I told Him, *we're in a fix. We're sure in a fix now. I guess you know that, bein' as you know everything, and we're not the only ones got problems, but I'd sure be grateful if you'd send a little help our way sooner rather than later. Before Imagene and Lucy wake up, for sure. When Imagene finds this out, she'll be like a badger in a barrel. I surely don't want that on my hands, and I know you don't, either. I admit it was pride that made me come on this trip, when I knew there was a storm headin' in. I wanted the chance to rub it in Betty Prine's face. That was wrong. I got no problem admittin' it. You know how I am when I get up on my hind legs about somethin'. I hadn't got the sense, God . . . well, you gave a goat.*

*And I got that curious streak, too. I wanted to find out about Mamee and Macerio. And yes, I know curiosity killed the cat, but a cat's got nine lives, so I guess he can get away with it. I never been one to look before leapin', Lord, but you always caught me. I know you got somethin' in mind here or else I'd be panicked, and I'm not. I'm not panicked. I'll just sit here and wait till you got a minute to . . .*

A red light painted my eyelids, and then it turned white and got brighter and brighter until I felt it all over my skin, like the warmth from a fire. For a second, I was like the shepherds in the Christmas story. I was sore afraid. I figured I'd open my eyes and there'd be an angel of the Lord standin' in front of the van. What in heaven's name was I gonna do then? When I asked Him to get us out of our fix, I had in mind something a little more . . . regular.

I opened my eyes and it wasn't an angel at all. It was just the taillights from a van. It was backing down the shoulder toward us, and when it got closer, I saw that the rear door said *Gifts From the Sea*, and there was a big old dog looking at me through the window. He was wagging his tail to beat the band, and if I'd had a tail, I'da been waggin' right back. I never been so glad to see someone in my life.

I rolled down the window and stuck out my head. "Hey there," I called. "We're outta gas. We need some help!"

The girl probably couldn't hear me for the noise of the cars on the road, so she got out and run around to the passenger side of our car, away from the traffic. She tapped on the window, and Imagene woke up with a snort.

I fumbled around to turn on the car so I could get the window open and talk to the girl. "We're outta gas," I hollered, but the sound just bounced around inside the car.

"Who's outta gas?" Imagene hunted around the dash for her glasses.

"We are, Imagene. We're outta gas and we're stuck on the side of the road."

It figured that right about then, Lucy'd wake up, too. "Who got gas?"

"We are, Lucy. We're outta gas and we're stuck on the side of the road. Y'all hush up now, I'm tryin' to talk to the girl."

Imagene tried to get her glasses unfolded. "What girl?"

"That girl?" I pointed to the window.

"What time is it?" Imagene squinted toward the clock.

"Tirty pass eleven," Lucy answered.

"Eleven thirty!" Imagene sucked in a breath. "The storm was supposed to make landfall at eleven."

"It's hit, Imagene. Glorietta's on land."

The girl knocked on the window again, and Imagene jerked away like the hand was a big old snappin' turtle.

"We're outta gas," I hollered, then finally turned the key and got the window down.

"You need help?" the girl asked. A car honked on the road, and she looked around, nervous.

"Hon, I reckon we do. The car died, and there ain't any way the three of us can walk out of here." Of all things, tears welled up in my eyes.

The little gal checked up and down the road again, once, twice, three times, like she was in as big a quandary as we were. Finally, she pushed loose strings of blond hair out of her face—she had real pretty hair, good highlights, too—and said, "You can come with me. You can't stay here."

Imagene, Lucy, and me looked at each other, and in about two and a half seconds, we were grabbing our purses and abandoning ship. The Gifts From the Sea girl—her name was Kai Miller, I found out pretty quick—opened the side door of her van and pushed some things back to make space, then put leashes on the dogs and moved them out of our way. "Hurry." She darted a nervous look at the cars passing by.

She didn't have to say any more for me to understand. There

was no tellin' who was in those cars, or how desperate they might be. We went to work getting the things we needed, includin' the food, water, and the rest of the pecan pie.

While we loaded up her van, Kai took her dogs down the shoulder to the grass. One of the dogs barked, and I heard something slide into the ditch water. A shiver crawled up my spine. Mamee always kept a dog at her house to chase off gators. Every once in a while, a dog disappeared and we never saw it again.

"Be careful down there, hon," I hollered.

Imagene, Lucy, and me finished getting our things, locked up the minivan, and stood there waiting for Kai to come back. Up above the clouds, a jet flew over, the sound filling up the night for a minute. After the noise died away, I heard an engine revving someplace behind us. When I stepped out where I could see, there was a jacked-up pickup turning into the ditch about a quarter mile up the road. It slid on the grass, fishtailed, then splashed back and forth through the water, spitting clumps of mud into the taillights' glow.

Shading her eyes with her hand, Imagene stepped out and looked down the roadside. "What 'n the world's happenin' there?"

"Nothin' good, I'll bet." I thought of them three fellas that'd been throwing beer bottles at the little church earlier in the day. "Kai, hon, we better go," I hollered off into the dark. "We better go now." The fellas in the truck were close enough that I could hear them whoopin' it up now.

"Hey, Dodd!" one of them yelled, and a spotlight bobbed back and forth across the ditch, while the truck spun 'round again. "Wait, wait, wait! Gator, gator, gator!" The truck roared through the water, aiming at the gator, I guessed.

"Oh, dog, I think you got that sucker!"

The truck revved up again, twirling in the mud so that the headlights strafed the ditch and landed right on Imagene's minivan.

"Hey, we got comp'ny!"

Imagene backed toward the van, and Lucy caught a gasp. I heard Kai running up the hill and the dogs barking, and then headlights swiveled toward her.

"Woo-eee, look'a there!" one of those men hollered, drunk as a skunk. "Hey, sweetheart, where you been?" The truck fishtailed in the mud, then headed straight for Kai and the dogs. Just before they got to her, the driver cut sideways and the rig slid around to a stop, bringing her up short.

"Hey, darlin'," one of them called out.

"Donetta, what're we gonna do?" Imagene whispered.

"Somethin'." But I didn't have any idea what. "Them fellas are drunker than Cooter Brown and twice as ugly."

"Is a knife in the pie," Lucy said, and for a minute I thought she'd flipped her wig, but what she meant was there was a paring knife in the container with the pie.

"They got guns in their back window, Lucy. I saw them whoopin' it up earlier on." My voice shook like a flag on a windy hill. "I don't think a kitchen knife's gonna do us much good."

"We gotta do somethin'," Imagene whispered. "Them boys are trouble."

At the edge of the headlights, Kai's dogs were pitching a fit, barking and pulling at their leashes. One of them yay-hoos got out and slinked around the truck, real careful-like. He peeked over the end toward where Kai was, and the bigger dog went crazy as a market bull, pulled out of Kai's hand, and chased that fella up into the bed of the truck. Good dog.

The man cussed a blue streak, then leaned over toward the window. "Wooh-eee! I think that dog's got rabies. Hey, Jigger, where'z'at pipe wrench? I'll teach that s-s-s-sucker to make a runnn at me."

Jigger tossed a can out the window. "Come on, Dodd. Let 'um be. It ain't funny no more."

The fella in back searched around the bed, stumbling over

empty bottles and pieces of metal, until he finally he came up with something and threw it at the dog. It hit the side of the truck and bounced back, and the boys in the cab hooted.

"Stop it!" Kai tried to go after the loose dog, but the other one was pulling the opposite way.

The next thing I knew, I was headed down that hill with my heart rapping in my chest like the tax man at the door. "All right, that's enough! You boys leave this gal be and move on now. You hear me? Just git on outta here and go sleep off all that liquor before y'all do somethin' stupid."

"Hey, Grandma!" one of them called out.

The fella in the bed of the truck was so surprised he turned real quick and fell over.

I shook a finger at them and kept a'comin'. "I'll tell you what, if I *was* your grandma, I'd grab you up and whoop you from now till next Tuesdey. All three of y'all. Actin' like a bunch of sauced-up yay-hoos. Y'all git on out of here!"

From somewhere behind me, I heard what sounded like a gun cocking, and Lucy hollered, "Hord it righ' there! Stop or I shoot!" She musta got that from a movie somewhere.

I looked over my shoulder, and I could just make out that she was pointing something at us. In the dark, I couldn't tell what it was, so I played along. "For heaven's sake, Lucy! Put that pistol away before you hurt somebody. You don't want to shoot these boys. They look too young to die."

"Go ahea', make my days." Lucy sounded serious. I didn't know she had all that actin' talent.

The fella in the truck bed staggered to his feet, then leaned over with his mouth hanging open, trying to tell if Lucy really had a gun. He probably couldn't see that far, and his friends in the truck were gettin' antsy.

"You gotta excuse Lucy." I moved around toward Kai. "She was in the war. She ain't quite right in the head. She's okay if she takes her medication, but we ain't got any along. I don't think she'd shoot, but I can't be held responsible, either."

The boy in the back squinted at me. He was so drunk, he was probably seeing three or four mad grannies. "She don-don't have a gun."

"She means it, Dodd." The driver ground the gears like the butcher makin' sausage. "Let's go."

I got to Kai and reached for the leash. "Here, darlin'," I whispered while them boys tried to decide what to do. "Give me this dog, and you go get the other one. Real quick, now. Get the leash and take him on to the van." Kai did what I told her, and once the dog was out of the way, that boy started to climb out the back of the truck. I headed toward the van, too, dragging the big silly dog behind me.

I caught up with Kai on the hill. "Hurry up. They're pretty drunk. We'd best go on."

Back behind us, the two fellas in the truck were having fun teasing the third one, hollerin', "Granny's got her gun. Granny's got her gun."

We didn't wait around to hear anything else. We got in that old van quicker than you'd think three old ladies, two dogs, and a girl could, and then hit all the locks.

The engine roared like a freight train, and we took off so fast all our heads snapped. Kai didn't wait for a gap in traffic, just laid on the horn and swerved into the right lane in front of a motor home. The driver honked, but it didn't matter, because we were on our way.

Whatever Lucy had in her hand, she dropped on the floor.

"That ain't a gun, is it?" I twisted so I could see her.

"Is a fire starter." Lucy sounded cool as a cucumber, but the one dog was curled up beside her and she was petting it so hard its eyes were bugging out. In the other seat, Imagene fanned herself, trying to catch her breath.

"Lands," I whispered, all of a sudden feeling like my whole body was full of oatmeal. In the side-view mirror, I watched the pickup turn around in the ditch, then move into line ten or twelve cars back. Kai saw it, too. She glanced over at me, but neither of us said anything about it. "How much gas you got, darlin'?"

"Not enough," she answered.

"It'll be all right." Leaning close to the window, I let my fingers drift in the breeze and started praying from the foxhole again. Ahead of us were cars, and behind us were cars. A gust of wind caught the Microbus when we rolled into a clear space where big metal electric towers stretched up like giants, holding heavy strands of cable that swayed like a rope swing.

"You from down on the coast?" I asked, because I couldn't concentrate to pray or do anything else but talk. When you're a hairdresser and you're nervous, you talk. Actually, when you're hairdresser and you're not nervous, you talk. Hairdressers just talk, period.

"Perdida," she said.

"That's where we were headed, before we run into you at that gas station. Thanks for turning us around when you did, by the way. It's a good thing we didn't go all the way to the coast. We'da been that much worse off." I shifted away from the window so I could hear her better. Outside, the night was getting noisy, the wind shaking the trees around now. "You got family down there in Perdida?"

She didn't answer right off, and I felt the curious cat perk its ears. I got a sense about people sometimes. "Friends," she said. "And an apartment. I live there part time and work cruise ship contracts part time. I was supposed to leave on the *Liberation* today, but I was too late."

"The *Liberation*!" Of all the odd coincidences. "That's where we were headed. The three of us gals were goin' on a cruise. First

time ever. Then the storm come in, of course." All of a sudden, it hit me that it wasn't any accident we'd ended up broke
down when we did, and this little girl picked us up. It wasn't
what we'd planned on, but the Lord was at work here in some
way I hadn't figured out yet. Even through this storm, He was
guiding our path toward somethin'. I didn't know what it was
yet, but somethin'. We gals set off for that cruise to have us an
adventure, and we were sure having one. When we finally got
back to Daily, Texas—however that turned out to be—we'd
have a story even Betty Prine couldn't top.

# Chapter 8

## *Kai Miller*

After a couple hours in the car with Donetta, I felt like I knew everyone in her hometown. I'd taken the virtual tour of her hotel building on Main Street, where she ran a beauty shop in the old hotel lobby and her brother, Frank, did auto repair in his garage around back. She told me about the turn-of-the-century hotel rooms upstairs, which had been closed down for a few years but were now experiencing a rebirth due to the town's recent media status as the home of Amber Anderson, the runner-up singing sensation on last year's TV season of *American Megastar*.

"We got tourism now." Donetta's hands moved along with the words, seeming to stretch the syllables like chewing gum. "With Amber bein' a singin' star, that's brought all sorts of folks, even *famous* folks to town. We got Justin Shay, *the* Justin Shay, plannin' to film a movie ri-ight outside town. Him and Amber bought the old Barlinger ranch—that poor old place'd been sittin' empty fifty years on account of them Barlinger kids were rotten and old Mr. Barlinger changed his will like a flea changes dogs. Nobody could figure out who that ranch belonged to for the longest ti-ime—but anyhow, now Justin and Amber bought the place, and they're fixin' it all up for the movie filmin', and then they're gonna make a home for foster kids out there. Ain't that just wonderful?"

"Yes, it is." It was hard to share Donetta's sense of excitement, considering that it was the middle of the night and there was a hurricane on our tails. In the back seat, the other ladies had already given up and fallen asleep.

"I'm talkin' your ear off, huh?" Donetta surmised finally.

"No, it's fine, really." On ship, I often met people who wanted to tell me where they were from and why they'd taken a cruise, but I'd never met anyone like the hairdresser from Daily, Texas. When Donetta Bradford told a story, it played in your mind in Technicolor, a little brighter than real life, like a movie from the fifties.

After apologizing for talking so much, she started talking again. She gave me the rundown of their trip to the coast that morning, their cruise plans, *Steel Magnolias*, her new laptop computer, and the cell phone that hadn't worked properly. I let her use mine to try to call home. She got to someone's voice mail and left a message that would probably panic whoever picked it up. The phone cut out as she was reading road signs out loud, trying to offer details of our location. When she tried to dial again, there was no reception. She gave up after a couple more tries, put the phone away, and started telling me about her bunko club back in Daily. "We all rode in the Founder's Day parade wearin' tiaras and prom dresses and singin' 'Zip-A-Dee-Doo Dah.'" She paused to poke a fingernail through her lopsided nest of hair, scratching her head. "Don't know what made that come to mind just now. My grandpa used to say I could speak ten words a second, with gusts up to fifty. Your ears are probably ringin', huh?"

"It's all right." The chatter was a good distraction, but even

Donetta ran out of things to talk about after a while. Finally, she apologized again for talking so much, then relaxed in the seat and fell asleep.

Without Donetta and her Daily, Texas, stories, I had no choice but to go back to thinking about the gas gauge slowly sinking toward empty, and noticing that abandoned cars were everywhere. It would only be a matter of time before my bus became one of them, and the storm was moving in fast. The National Guard tanker trucks, which were supposed to be handing out gas along the evacuation routes, hadn't made an appearance here. It was as if someone had guided thousands of people onto this back road and then forgotten we existed.

Donetta woke again as I was trying pick up a radio station to check on the storm. The gale-force winds buffeting the van and the nasty bands of clouds in the rearview told me that Glorietta was traveling much faster than we were.

Jerking upright, Donetta stretched and rubbed her eyes. "Hon, you want me to drive? You gotta be exhausted."

"No. I'm all right."

"How's the gas?"

"Getting low."

"Any idea where we're at?"

"None."

"I see a sign while'go," Lucy offered drowsily. I hadn't even realized she was awake back there. "We near Oddly."

Donetta laughed. "Well, that's the truth, but that don't help much. I hadn't ever heard of Oddly."

"Me either." Leaning close to the window, I combed my hair away from my face and held it in a ponytail, letting the wind cool my neck and travel down the back of my T-shirt, drying the dampness there.

Lightning split the sky behind us, and I turned to look over my shoulder.

"It's comin'," Donetta observed grimly. "I guess the radio won't work?"

"It's not picking up any stations." Something warm slipped under my hand, and I looked down to find that Hawkeye had crawled into the space between the seats.

"Hey, big fella." Donetta scratched his ears, and Radar scooted from the back floorboard, stuffing himself into the space beside Hawkeye. "Poor things. Animals got a sense for when a storm's comin'. My mamee used to say that. She lived on the bayou, down near Perdida. Rice farmers. Went through their share of hurricanes. You ever been in a hurricane?"

"Not so far," I admitted. "The ships circumvent big storms, so I never really had to think about it until I got the apartment in Perdida and quit working so much. I'm still getting used to land life—hurricanes included. I didn't do a very good job of judging this one, that's for sure."

"Oh, hon, there's no judgin' these things," Donetta soothed. "Mamee used to say that. She got trapped in one once and near drowned. And there she was, a gal who'd been raised right on the bayou, and a Cajun to boot. There's no figurin' a hurricane."

I nodded, thinking about Don and the other shop owners in Perdida, and wondering who'd evacuated and who'd stayed. Where were they now and what had happened in Perdida when the storm surge came in?

"You just decide you was tired of sea life, or you got family there in Perdida?" Donetta studied me for a moment, then added, "I asked you that already, didn't I, hon? You gotta excuse me sometimes. My mouth's like a all-weather creek—runnin' all the time. It's the hairdresser in me."

I laughed. "My mother went to hairdressing school for a while." Until that moment, I'd forgotten about Mom's first short-lived venture into cosmetology. Dad had landed a good job managing repairs at an auto dealership in Burnet, Texas, that year, and since we were finally in one place, Mom got a loan for beauty school. Gil and I loved it there. The town was small and friendly, and while Mom was in school every day, the two of us had the run of the place. We played on the baseball field in the city park, spent hours in the library, watched the trains come and go from the station, listened in on a murder case at the courthouse, and scoured the roadsides for aluminum cans we could cash in for change to pay our way into the movie theater. That summer, everything was perfect.

Then life crashed in, like it usually did. Gil got sick, we lost the nice little house Mom and Dad had rented, and we were back in the camp trailer. Eventually, we ended up at Grandmother Miller's. "We had to move before she got through beauty school, though. I think she finally did finish, later on." I'd looked my mother up on the internet once when my ship was in port at Grand Cayman. It was Gil's birthday, and all of a sudden, I wanted to call her. I wondered if she thought about my brother when his birthday rolled around—if she missed him. I found out she owned a salon in Tempe, Arizona, but that was as far as I got.

"Well, isn't that ni-ice? Good for her. A gal oughta git out there and go after her dreams while she's young, that's what I always say. Where's your mama live now, hon?"

"Arizona." *Tempe, I think.* I felt the usual inner pinprick. Even when I was a kid, it was difficult to know how much to tell people about our weird, complicated family. The more I divulged, the stranger it sounded, and in the end people either felt sorry for me or didn't want to have anything to do with me. After Gil died and my mother left, I just started making things up.

"Oh, it's beautiful out there in Arizona!" Donetta's hands fluttered in the air, talking right along with her. "I drove through there one time years ago with my brother and his kids, Kemp and Lauren. We'd been out to California, takin' some horses to a movie studio. Their mama died young—not the horse's mama, Kemp and Lauren's mama—bless her heart, so I took care'a them a lot when they were little. We always been real close. I never could have any of my own—kids, I mean. But my brother's two were just like mine. 'Course, Frank and me got crossways about them kids more than once. You know how brothers and sisters can be."

I nodded, thinking about Gil and all the times it was a miracle that we hadn't torn the trailer to shreds and killed each other.

"You got brothers and sisters, hon?"

I felt a blunt pain, like a clothespin snapping shut on your finger. There was never a good answer to that question. Gil's story threw a damper on any conversation it entered, but acting like he never existed seemed wrong. "My brother passed away when he was eleven."

Donetta laid a hand on my arm again. "Oh, hon, I'm sorry to hear that. I had a little sister who passed young—Sherlyn, but we called her Sherry. It's one of them things you never quite know how to tell people. 'Course, most of the folks I'm around already heard everythin' about my family, but with new people, I never did qui-ite know what to say."

I felt a sense of connection that was immediate and unexpected. "People have a hard time with it. I don't talk about Gil much. I think about him, though. I wonder what he'd be like if he were still here, what kinds of things he'd be doing." It was a strangely honest admission, for me. I'd never even told Meredith and Maggie about Gil. "I always thought he would have gone to college, maybe become an astronaut or a pilot. Every time there was a space shuttle launch, he wanted to go to the library and look all over the internet for information about the mission." Gil was never in any school long before the teachers realized he was smart. When we were on the road, doing homeschool, he was finished with his lessons in half the time it took me. Then he had his face in some book about the Apollo launches or secret spy planes.

"Well, I bet he would've." Donetta's voice was soft, tender. The conversation ran out momentarily, and then she restarted it. "So, you just live down there by yourself, then? Goin' on the ships and all?"

I nodded. *Just living by myself and going on ships . . .*

"Sounds excitin'." Leaning forward, she checked the sky out the front window, studying the clouds. "Must get lonesome sometimes, though, no family nearby to depend on."

"I have friends in Perdida. After a while, it's like a family." The permanent residents of Perdida tended to be a loose-knit bunch, but at least I knew I could depend on them. I couldn't imagine depending on my family for anything at this point.

"It ain't the same thing," Donetta mused. "Your friends are just your friends. Somethin' can happen and they can stop bein' your friends."

*Your family can stop being your family. They can decide to leave you behind and get a whole new life.* I didn't say it, of course.

Donetta laughed softly, shaking her head. "A'course, listen at *me* talkin'. It was me not wanting to depend on anybody that got us gals in this fix. Kemp—that's my nephew. He coaches baseball at Daily High and teaches math. Did I tell you that already, hon?—anyhow, he offered to take a couple days off and drive us down to the cruise boat, and my brother, Frank, offered, too, but I wouldn't let them, and now here we are. In trouble like a one-legged cat in a mouse hunt. Lot of good that phone and that computer did us. If it wasn't for you, we'd still be stuck on the side of the road. Guess that just goes to show there's none of us don't need the kindness of a stranger now and then."

"Guess so."

"Thanks for pickin' us up." Donetta let her head fall against the headrest and sighed. "If I didn't say it in all the commotion before, thanks."

"I don't mind," I answered, and we drifted into silence. Traffic came to a standstill for a while, then started creeping along again as the wind picked up and the sky dipped lower. Behind us, the storm pressed in, lightning splitting the air like a white-hot knife, thunder following behind. Bursts of wind moaned through the pines, rocking the Microbus and shaking the line of taillights ahead. A driver laid on the horn, and someone else honked in return. The frustration was palpable, the unwritten message clear. If we didn't get off this road soon, Glorietta, along with straight-line winds, floodwaters, and whatever tornadoes the storm spawned, would blow right over the top of us.

Another issue stole into my thoughts—something I'd been noticing for a while now. The Microbus was tugging to the right, and it was getting worse. I'd only been vaguely conscious of it while Donetta was talking, but now it was impossible to ignore. The right front tire was slowly going flat.

Donetta leaned close to me. "We got a tire goin' out, hon," she whispered, as if we should keep it between us. "My daddy was a auto mechanic all his life, so I know the symptoms. You got a spare?"

The question tangled in my chest, pushing heat up my neck and into my cheeks. "We're *driving* on the spare." Don had borrowed my vehicle two weeks ago and ended up with a flat. He'd insisted that, since he ruined the tire, he'd get me a new one, but the last time I'd seen the rim, it was leaning against the surf shop with the flat still attached.

The bus listed farther and farther to the side, inching another mile, then two, tilting like a sinking ship, until finally Donetta stuck her head out the window to take a look. A fine spray of mist floated inward, gathering on her hair as the van wobbled down a hill toward a narrow bridge. "I hate to tell ye-ew this, darlin', but we're gonna have to look for a stoppin' place. That's pretty well had it."

"We can't pull off here." The Microbus shimmied clumsily over a joint in the decking as we moved onto the bridge. The steering wheel tugged in my hands, and I slowed to a crawl, the bus leaning and swaying over each joint, top-heavy by nature. Donetta shifted toward the center, eyeing the bridge railing as if she were afraid we might tumble over it. Ahead, traffic inched away, creating a gap, and behind us, the motor home began honking. I hit the emergency flashers and continued limping on.

Donetta balanced on the inner edge of her seat, her face compressing like a Chinese lantern as she squinted into the night. "You just ignore them, hon. We're doin' the best we can here. I'm lookin' for a spot to pull off. If we can get up over that hill yonder, maybe we'll hit it lucky and there'll be a store, or a town, or somethin'. The ditches are too steep here to pull off, that's for sure."

We limped toward the hill, upward, then slowly started down, the van swinging hard to the right and the brakes squealing as the shift in gravity increased the pressure on the front tires, grinding the flat down to the rim.

The motion and the noise stirred Lucy in the back seat. "What go-een on?"

Lucy's voice surprised Hawkeye. He scrambled backward and bumped into Imagene's legs, and she jerked upright, hollering, "The eggs are burnin'!" Catching her breath, she added, "Oh lands, I was dreamin' I was at the café and Bob'd forgot about the fry grill again." She sniffed the air and scooted forward in her seat. "I do smell somethin' burnin', though."

"We got a flat tire. We're lookin' for a place to pull off." Donetta pushed out of her seat and leaned out the window, her legs splayed and her hands braced on the dash. "I think I see somethin'. There's a light down there in the woods, just a little off the road. Must be a driveway, or house there. You see it? I can't tell what it is."

The light flickered through the trees, appearing and disappearing until finally a driveway melted into view. The source of the flickering glow was hidden behind the thick wall of pines, but the driveway looked well maintained, covered in thick gravel with a new culvert over the ditch.

"There's a sign. . . ." Donetta stretched higher, trying to make out the official-looking roadside marker. "Maybe it's a ranger station."

Lucy and Imagene squeezed into the space between the seats, scouting, as well.

"It ain't a gas station," Imagene concluded. "It's . . ."

Donetta finished the sentence. "Somethin' for the power company." Her voice descended as we turned into the driveway, passing a sign that read *TRW Electric Co. No trespassing.*

## Chapter 9

# *Donetta Bradford*

There wasn't nothin' at the end of that gravel drive but a parking pad and chain-link-fenced electric station with *Keep Out* signs everywhere. The place was like a little island floating on a bed of white gravel under a lonesome security light, the woods towerin' all around, dark as ink.

"There's no one here." Imagene's voice shook as our moment of hope collapsed like a cardboard fort in a summer rain.

Kai put the van in Park and turned it off, saying something about a can of Fix-a-Flat in back.

I coulda told her there wasn't any point looking for a can of Fix-a-Flat. My daddy, even sauced up as he was most of the time, was a good mechanic, and he had us working in the shop right along with him. When a tire's off the rim, you're not gonna make it right with a can of Fix-a-Flat. It was a shade more likely we could pray our way out of there. I said that to Kai, but she didn't listen. She just got out to look for the Fix-a-Flat, and I didn't stop her. Sometimes you gotta let other folks butt their heads against the wall on their own. I learned that from my daddy. Not because he taught it to me. I learned it by watching him take that bottle in hand and hit the wall over, and over, and over.

I started getting worried when the lightnin' moved closer and the wind come roaring through the trees like a freight train. Pinecones, needles, and branches pelted the roof, one of the dogs jumped in Lucy's lap, and Imagene hollered, "It's a tornado! Mercy!"

"It ain't a tornado." I knew enough about the piney woods to know them trees could put up a mighty wail when the wind went through. "Not yet, anyhow. But we're gonna have to do somethin'. We can't stay here." I was trying to sound calm so everyone else wouldn't have a rigor, but my heart was pumpin' like the old grinder engine that used to run all day at the mill. You could hear that thing all over Daily, like the town itself had a heartbeat.

The wind quieted a bit, and I stepped outside. The smell of broken pine branches and moss and wet dirt choked the air, and overhead the sky hung low, like it was full of lead and about to fall. My foot sunk in gravel and mud, and I had a bad feeling we shouldn'ta stopped there.

Kai was crouched down with the Fix-a-Flat, and she'd put her shoulder under the wheel fender, like she was gonna lift up the van, even though she wasn't big as a minute. "Hon . . ." I laid a hand on her arm. "That ain't gonna work."

"It has to work."

I squatted down beside her. "Hon, this tire's too far gone." In the soft glow of the security lamp, her hair catching the light and turning a feathery gold around her face, she looked like a little girl, lost and needing her mama.

"It *has* to work." If she hadn't started to cry already, I could tell she was about to.

"Darlin', how old are you?"

She glanced up, her pretty blue eyes wide and desperate in the lamp glow. "Twenty-seven. . . . Why?"

Twenty-seven was about what I'd figured. Just a little younger than Kemp and Lauren. "You got a lot of experience with tires?"

"No."

"They got lots of auto shops on those ships where you work?"

"No." Her shoulders sunk, and she pushed the back of her hand against her forehead, squeezing her eyes shut, like she knew I was right but couldn't stand to hear it just now.

"Well, I'm almost seventy, darlin', and I seen a lot of flat tires in my life, and this one's swan song's done been sung. It ain't comin' back. We gotta do somethin' else before that rain gets here."

Lightning flashed a white ribbon across the sky, and thunder boomed right behind it. I caught a breath and jumped out of my skin, then back in. "Let's get in the van till we figure it out."

Kai stood up and wiped the water out of her eyes, then we got in the car. The wind turned real quiet for a minute. Everythin' was still, so that you could smell the fret in the air. An empty soda bottle toppled off the dash and hit the floor, and all three of us jumped like we'd backed into a prickly pear cactus.

"What we go-een to do now?" Lucy whispered while the bottle was still rockin' to a stop.

"I guess we're gonna start prayin', and start walkin' at the same time," I said.

Imagene gasped. "With a storm comin' and Lucy's bad knee, and in the dark with who knows what kind of people on the road? S'pose them three beer-drinking yay-hoos come along again."

"Right now, I believe I'd ask them can we get in the back of the truck and have a ride."

Imagene snorted. "This ain't a time for jokes."

"I wasn't jokin'," I said. "We got to leave out. Now. Any way we can."

Lucy started gathering her things. "I can go okay on my knee. I been sit all day." She reached around behind and started loadin' her purse with bottled water. I coulda told her in a few minutes we'd have more water than we knew what to do with. That sky was about to bust open.

"We should stay here," Imagene argued, which didn't surprise me. That's Imagene. Measure twice, measure thrice, measure four times, then maybe cut. Or not. "At least down here, we got some protection."

"Down here things are gonna *fall* on us if it gets bad, Imagene. Come a big wind, them pine trees and electric poles'll topple like matchsticks. We gotta get out."

"We can wait a little longer. Maybe someone'll come. Someone from the power company, or . . ."

"Ssshhh!" Lucy cut her off, waving a hand in the air. "Ssshhh! Opening the door a crack, she cocked her ear. "You hear-eeng?"

"Hearing what?" I whispered.

"Ssshhh." She pointed into the dark. "Is a dog ou-side."

The minute she said it, Kai's old dog, Hawkeye, got up and let out a little bark, and all of us jumped.

"Hawkeye, quiet," Kai scolded, and the dog whimpered, then sniffed toward the open door. The young dog got up and wiggled in beside him until the two of them and Lucy looked like three kids at the Barlinger's Hardware display when the new Christmas toys come out.

"Is a man, too," Lucy whispered. "He's sing."

"Oh, Lucy, for heaven's sake," I said, thinking, *Well, that seals it. Lucy's finally gone plumb over the edge. She's hearin' voices. It'll only be a matter of time before the rest of us go, too, and . . .*

Then I heard somethin'. If Lucy was goin' crazy, I was headed right along with her. *They'll just find us here when the storm passes. Three crazy women and one poor girl who got trapped in the storm with them.*

"I hear it, too," Kai whispered.

*Gravy! She's as far gone as the rest of us, and she's young.*

I closed my eyes, thinking maybe that'd get my head clear. A panicky push of wind blew through the clearing, rocking the van, and for a minute there was no noise but pine trees blowing and branches moaning.

The wind ebbed off, and then plain as day coming through the woods was the sound of a man singing. The words to that song were clear as a winter creek.

"'Swing low, sweet char-riot, comin' for to carry me home. Swi-ing lo-oow, sweeeet char-riot . . .'"

"What in the world . . ." Imagene whispered.

Radar and Hawkeye started making a racket again and drowned out everything else until Kai quieted them down. When they hushed up, sure enough there was a dog barking back at them from somewhere in the woods. The long, low bay of an old coonhound was driftin' through the trees, sounding just like the hunting dogs on Mamee's porch.

"It somebody out there," Lucy whispered.

Imagene put her hands on her window, squinting against the dark. "Who'd be walking through the woods singin' at a time like this?"

"I can't imagine." Opening my door, I got out and peered off into the thick black of the woods. "It's comin' from back behind us." I moved around to the rear end of the van to hear better. "I see a light." Lucy and the dogs hung out the side door, their heads all turnin' when I pointed. There was a light bouncing along through the trees, flickerin' in and out of the underbrush, waist high. There one minute, gone the next, then back again.

"I see it," Lucy whispered.

Kai slipped out of the van and tiptoed to where I was. The old dog had a fit about that, and he started trying to push his way through the door. Lucy whispered something in Japanese, and Kai told the dog to stay where he was.

The hound dog bayed out in the woods, then the woods turned quiet as cotton.

Kai moved to the edge of the security lamp's glow, taking steps one at a time, her arms stretched out, like she was feeling the air for danger.

The hound barked in the trees, and it was close this time. Whoever it was had come just to the other side of the underbrush and hid his light. I heard him try to shush his dog. Kai's mutts heard it, too, and that young dog was out the door like a greased pig through a wet gate. Lucy didn't have a prayer of stopping him.

"Radar!" Kai hollered, but it was too late. He was off across the parking lot, and a second later the other dog was out, too. He'd dragged Lucy halfway through the doorway, trying to get past her. Kicking up gravel, he ran across that parking lot and slid to a stop in front of Kai, growling low. The other dog, Radar, was gone in the dark, but I could hear him hopping through the woods and yapping.

"Radar!" Kai hollered, and bolted out of the light and disappeared into the brush. The old dog ran off after her, and I hobbled, stiff-legged, after all of them. Just when I got to the edge of the brush, there was a commotion nearby, and something pushed through into the parking lot, with Kai's dogs right behind.

Lightning flashed overhead, and thunder pounded the sky like a giant parade drum. Things were movin', and blowin', and fallin', and barkin', and squealin', and gravel was flyin' everywhere. Kai stumbled out of the brush, calling her dogs, the hound bayed, and the man hollered, "Ged-down! Ged-down!

Ged-down!" The security lamp was dim overhead, but I could see that man turning 'round and 'round, trying to hold something—his dog, I thought it was—up off the ground while Radar circled around him, yappin' and waggin' his tail and jumpin' up. The man was a black fella, so tall and stout he looked like he could sure enough play linebacker for the Dallas Cowboys. His head was shaved bald as a cue ball, and sort of waxy-like, so that it caught the light and shined, while he tried to hold his dog up and keep the other dog down.

He was a sight relieved when Kai got ahold of Radar and Hawkeye and pulled them off. All three of us just stood there catching our breath for a minute. Time stretched like penny taffy, making everything slow down—the sound of cars going by on the road, my heart poundin', the big shadow man trying to calm down that hound, Hawkeye and Radar barking and struggling to get at that man, Kai holding their collars and hollering at them to be quiet.

I heard a door shut on Kai's van. "What happen?" Lucy hollered.

"I ain't sure."

"What's goin' on out there?" Imagene called.

"There's a fella here."

"I got a gun," Lucy hollered. "Don' try no funny biz-net, understan'?"

"I reckon we're okay, Lucy," I called. I got a sense about people, and that fella looked like we'd scared him worse than he'd scared us. His eyes were big as hen eggs, and he was hugging that hound dog like a fifty-pound teddy bear.

Finally, he set the dog down and bent over to catch his breath. The dog pushed up against his master's feet, scared to death. "Ma'am—" the man's voice was breathless, low, like he was talking in a empty barrel—"just hol' that dog there, all right?" The words rolled together in a smooth strand of sound that reminded me of Mamee's Cajun people. "Jus' hol' that dog, and I'm'ma git my breath, *cher*. Jus' hol' on now."

Kai blew out a long patch of air, and her dogs stopped growling, folded their haunches, and sat down.

I turned back to the stranger. "You all right?" I didn't move closer, just stood my ground. That man's sheer size was intimidatin', even though he didn't seem like he meant any harm. Even bent over, wheezing with his hands on his knees, he come almost to my chest.

"I'm'ma say, I thought that dog, he's gonna eat me up." His voice rumbled in the air like thunder does when it's far away. "I was tryin' to figure out who's over here, and that dog come-a-run out of that brush, and my ol' hound dog, he lookin' for a place to get on up out there, and next minute, *gal-ee*, we all in a tangle."

"You all right?" I asked again.

He nodded but didn't stand up straight. "I jus' gotta catch my breath. I los' my feet, and that dog, he get me down a minute, there in the woods. All I was thinkin' was, Lawd, don't let me get kilt by some dog. One minute, I was goin' though them woods to fetch some water, and the next I'm'ma get ate up." Straightening his back so that he was even taller than before, he looked over his shoulder into the woods. "Dropped my bucket and my lamp and everythin'. Hoo-eee!"

Kai stepped back, like she'd just noticed that he was a big, big man now that he was standing up. Hawkeye heeled at her feet, growlin' again.

The stranger raised his hands like he was a prisoner giving the surrender. "Tell him jus' calm down, all right? Where you gals come from? You live back in here someplace?"

"We were hopin' you did," I told him.

"No, ma'am, I don' live here. We come from down near Perdida—Holy Ghost Church. We all come out together, the whole church." He pointed through the woods. "Our bus, she blow a hose, so we pull off 'round the corner on the county road. I come across the woods to the ditch, to fetch some water in a bucket. I hear your dogs bark, and I wonder, maybe there a house in here someplace."

Disappointment settled over me like a wet wool coat. "Don't sound like you're much better off than we are." The wind kicked up again, and pine straw and dust swirled around us, so that air was rough as cornmeal. "Our van's broke down, and we're stuck. We're in a fix."

Setting his hands on his hips, the stranger whistled through his teeth, shook his head, and muttered, "Ummm, ummm, ummm."

"Truth is, we need help," I told him.

The wind kicked up even more, and he had to holler to talk over it. "We hadn't got much to offer. The bus, she pretty full, but you can come on with me, and we find room. We figure that storm, she comin' soon, and we better cut off down the county road and find someplace fo' shelter. You able to walk out 'cross the woods, like I come? That brush, she heavy, but it's twice as long 'round by the road."

Kai and I looked back and forth at each other. I wished I could see that fella's face, and his eyes, because usually I can figure whether you can trust a person. This time, I couldn't tell anything for sure, except that that storm was coming fast and we were gonna have to do somethin' pretty quick.

# Chapter 10

# *Kai Miller*

Sparse, weighty drops of rain began pelting the van as we grabbed what we could.

Our rescuer, Ernest, took the heavy canvas bag the ladies had packed full of water bottles and leftover food, and slung it onto his shoulder like it was a feather pillow. "We gotta go, cher," he said. "That sky, she gonna come open."

As everyone else started across the parking lot, I grabbed the duffle bag with Gil's Bible inside, then closed up my Microbus and stood looking at it, momentarily torn. Almost everything I owned was in the bus, including the jewelry-making supplies that represented most of my hard-earned savings— semiprecious stones, fine chain, findings, and spools of sterling and gold wire that didn't come cheap. No telling if I'd ever see any of it again. *All of it can be replaced,* I told myself. *It isn't worth risking your life over.* Absently, I slipped my hand into the duffle bag, my fingers closing over something square and solid before I even realized what I was looking for. Gil's Bible.

Something that couldn't be replaced. Something I couldn't allow the storm to take away.

I slid my thumb across the cover, just to be sure, before tucking the keys into my pocket. I ducked my head under the duffle strap, swung the duffle onto my back, and jogged across the parking lot to the underbrush, where the ladies were following Ernest into the woods.

As he cleared a trail, trampling down briars and ripping tangles of vines bare-handed, rain blew in, crashing through the trees like an invisible beast, coming closer and closer until it reached us. The roaring wind and the pounding water eclipsed everything, making even the thunder seem far away. Within moments, the forest carpet of needles and dead leaves became saturated and slick. Our feet slipped and sank as the storm forced its way through, stirring the canopy of trees like a giant mixing bowl, peppering the ground with debris, drenching everything, including us.

Lightning crackled in all directions, illuminating the treetops in flashes as we struggled down a hill and through a low spot that was filling fast. Through the haze of rain, I watched Lucy slide in the mud and land hard against a tree. Ernest's lantern swung as he hooked his arm through hers and picked her up, then continued on, his legs splayed, his body bent against the pounding rain, the dog tugging frantically on its leash, trying to escape the storm.

Overhead, tree limbs whipped in circles like helicopter blades. Donetta grabbed Imagene's arm, then clasped a handful of my shirt, and the three of us staggered over the slick forest floor, stumbling sideways in gusts of wind, calling out to each other, our voices lost in the storm. I reeled in Radar and Hawkeye, held on to their collars, used them to steady myself, felt the soggy leather tugging and stretching in my hands as we climbed a hill, then stumbled blindly down the other side and moved through water ankle-deep. The current tugged at my legs, and behind me, Donetta slid to her knees, then pulled up using my shirt as I braced myself with the dog's collars. Around my feet, the water was getting deeper by the second.

"Come on!" I screamed, but the sound was lost.

Blinking against the curtain of driving water and wet hair, I squinted ahead, tried to see where we were. I couldn't make out anything but the lantern, just six or eight feet ahead but barely visible now. Lucy and Ernest had been swallowed by the storm, but the light was moving, traveling through the underbrush, ricocheting off tangled vines and blowing branches. Radar's collar slipped, wet and slimy, from my fingers, and he surged forward until the leash caught around my wrist. I hung on as Hawkeye's collar slipped away, too.

Suddenly, the shelter of the trees was gone, and the rain was driving so hard I couldn't see anything. I stumbled blindly behind the dogs, down a slope, into water running fast, knee-deep. The ground rose, we climbed out again, scrambling first in mud, then gravel. The dogs barked and tugged, then stopped. I felt someone's hand touching mine, taking the leashes from my fingers. More hands moved me forward, out of the rain.

"Up here," a voice strained over the noise. I staggered up something. Stairs. Three. An arm was half lifting, half guiding me. There were voices all around.

"This way, cher." Someone wrapped a shirt—no, a towel—over me and guided me forward several steps. Grabbing the fabric, I wiped my eyes, tried to see again, to discern where I was. Out of the rain. We were out of the rain, but everything was shifting and rocking, the floor swaying in the wind like the deck of a ship on rough seas. Hands held me up, passed me from one to the next. I felt for something solid, touched a surface that was cool and slick. The back of a seat, and then another, evenly spaced like the rungs on a ladder.

A bus. We were on a bus, rocking in the wind, rain pelting the windows and roof, filling the darkened space with sound. Through the blur of water dripping from my lashes, I made out a narrow slice of light pressing through the front window, illuminating the outlines of heads, shoulders, arms, seats, people moving. Their voices rose over the white noise, the sentences coming in a rolling lilt, some of the words difficult to understand, not in English, I thought. I turned back and saw Imagene and Donetta standing in the aisle, silhouette figures against the light, their hand gestures pantomiming our journey like a shadow-puppet show. A woman with a long ponytail of braids was helping Lucy wipe the mud off her clothes.

Shivering, I pushed my hair out of my face, dried my eyes again, then wrung out my hair.

"Here, cher, you jus' sit down here and rest. You jus' sit down by Mona," a voice said. "What in the worl' you doin' out there in that storm? That lightnin', she strike, and you be knockin' on the pearly gate." A thick, heavy arm encircled me, drawing me into a seat. "Shirlette, go on back there and find this gal somethin' to eat and drink, and a blanket. She gotta be cold in the bone and hon-gree."

"I'm fine. Really." I shifted away, trying to see her, but catching only her silhouette. She was heavyset, the light reflecting off something—braided hair with beads of some kind in it. "Where are my dogs?"

"Don' worry about them dogs," she answered. "My son, Ernest, he got all the animals in his big truck. They safe as the res' of us."

Nearby, Donetta was thanking someone for a towel and at the same time trying to refuse a seat. "No, now y'all don't get up on my account. I'm fine. Don't make that baby get out of her seat. I don't need to sit . . . I'll just stand here. Don't . . .

just . . . oh, all ri-ight." The springs squealed as Donetta gave in and took a load off.

Mona grabbed the towel and started rubbing my arm like she was trying to get the circulation going in a newborn puppy. "You soaked to the middle, *sha*! And mud from the head to the foot. *De'pouille!*"

The bus rocked hard to the left, the wind whistling cold and wet, howling through the spaces around the windows. A tide of gasps circulated, and Mona seized my arm. "Pastor D., we gotta get this bus movin'!"

"She about back together. Hang on!" a man yelled from the darkness near the front door.

"We don' get outta this wind, they not gonna be nothin' to hang on *to*. You kids get down in the seat back there. You hol' on!"

The bus rocked wildly, the rivets groaning. For a moment, I was in Mona's lap. Passengers screamed, a woman started crying, Imagene and Donetta called out for each other, and someone behind me called on Jesus. Grabbing the seat, I braced myself as the bus teetered on two wheels. Lightning flashed, flooding the interior with light, and then the light was gone and there was only the sensation of people all around, bodies holding breath, fear, anticipation, hope. The bus began righting itself, slightly at first, as if a hand were lowering us carefully, then faster, faster, until we were level again. Mona's body collided with mine, and it was quickly clear that she outweighed me by quite a bit. Snatching me up in a hug, she yanked me back into the seat.

"Praise the Lawd!" A moment later, she was shoving me out of the way and heading up the aisle. "Pastor D.! Pastor D.! You men get this bus on the road now! Right now, or I'm'ma come out there and push it . . ."

A shadow figure, rotund with a fuzz of gray hair that caught the light like a halo, rushed up the steps and slid into the driver's seat. A strip of interior lights came on in the aisle. The engine squealed and backfired, then rumbled into action. Outside, the hood slammed shut, and in the glow of the headlights, the men who'd been working on the engine ran toward a large white delivery truck ahead of us.

Around me, hands flew into the air, fluttering like birds. People cheered, and Mona hollered, "Praise ya', Jesus! *Ça c'est bon!*"

I slid to the interior portion of our seat as Mona headed down the aisle. The bus door swung closed, and a moment later we were on the road, behind the delivery truck.

"See can you get the church van on the radio, Pastor D.," Mona called. "Tell them we movin' again!"

"They know already," Pastor D. replied over the noise. Standing above the dash, his legs splayed, he gripped the steering wheel with both hands, fighting the pull of the storm. Ahead, the delivery truck fishtailed in the mud and swayed, the metal wet and slick, reflecting our headlights in long, constantly changing streaks. Leaves and blowing debris clung to the truck like bits of papier mache, slowly sliding downward, then disappearing.

"Hol' on, everybody!" Mona half stood beside me, grabbing the seats and riding the sway of the bus like a surfer catching a wave. "We gonna *drive* on up *outta* of this storm. We gonna be *all right*. I'm'ma say *amen* and hol' on tight."

We moved down a hill, and the storm ebbed under the tree cover. The wind quieted, and the rocking calmed. "I believe we gonna make it," Mona observed, lowering into the seat beside me and whispering under her breath. *A prayer,* I thought.

I laid my head back and let my eyes fall closed. I was too tired to fight anymore, too exhausted to care what happened next. Outside, the bus bounced and slid down a hill, then wobbled across what felt like an old metal bridge. I didn't look, just kept my eyes closed and let my body relax against the seat. The noise of the bus, the sound of Mona's voice, the roar of the storm, the sharp smack of branches and debris hitting the windows faded, and I pulled the towel closer, feeling waves of exhaustion roll under me as the storm raged on, the bus rocking gently now. I listened to its progress, felt it from a distance—another bridge, another curve, the rear end fishtailing up another hill, sliding downward, the brakes grinding, another bridge . . .

Finally, I wasn't aware of anything at all. . . .

Someone was shaking me, speaking close to my ear, but I didn't want to listen. I wanted to sink deeper, keep my eyes closed. "Come on, hon, wake up. We got to get out. We come as far as we can go. We're gonna hole up in this building till the storm blows over. Come on, darlin'. I know you're plumb wore out, but we gotta get out of this bus."

Underneath me, the seat rocked. Metal groaned, and something solid clanged against the roof so hard the bus shuddered. My mind snapped to reality, and even before my eyes cleared, I was aware of the storm raging, people moving around the interior, children crying and mothers calling out, Donetta pulling my arm.

"Let's go, hon, let's go!" There was a sense of panic all around, and in Donetta's voice. "We gotta get out of here, now."

The bus rocked, and passengers staggered in the aisle, colliding with each other and falling into seats. The aisle lights went out, and in the blackness, voices called, "Hurry! Move 'long! Hurry!"

Donetta pulled my hand, dragging me into the aisle, so that I was sandwiched between her and someone else. We staggered forward as the bus rolled and pitched. Near the exit, rain was pouring in the door, driven on the wind like daggers. I stepped into water and mud. The wind struck hard, shooting shotgun pellets of rain into my skin. Hands grabbed me from the side, moved me along. I felt the mud and gravel in my shoes, icy cold, the rain soaking my clothes and peppering my skin. Wind tore at my shirt, pulling it up so that the rain pelted my waist and hips. My feet sank into the mud, slid sideways. Spreading out, I braced myself and kept moving, clinging blindly to the person in front of me, someone else clutching me from behind— Donetta, I thought.

The rain and the wind were suddenly gone. I pushed water from my eyes, tried to see. "Come on, come on, cher, move on in." I recognized Mona's voice. "We got more behind. Be movin'. More comin' behind. Be movin' . . ."

I stumbled into the empty space, feeling my way in the blackness, my hands touching people who were only invisible bodies making sounds, breathing hard, crying, calling out to each other, babies squealing, women screaming. I felt something wooden—a railing—clasped my hands over it, inched along, sightless. I blinked, and blinked again, but there was nothing to see except blackness. Glass shattered somewhere, a woman screamed, high, loud, long. The air roared like a freight train and circled the building. A child cried out.

Crouching against the wet stone floor, I covered my head and clung to the railing. Pressure pounded my ears and crushed my body. Outside, objects thrashed the roof and hammered the walls. The roar grew louder, tunneling into my ears, pressing, pushing, hurting. Overhead, the sections of tin slapped up and down, then vibrated like the tines of a tuning fork. Sharp splinters, bits of glass rained from the darkness, stung my skin, tangled in my hair, burrowed into the folds of my clothing. I curled tightly over myself, debris swirling everywhere, my eardrums pounding inward, my mind exploding.

*Please*, I thought, *please*, but I didn't know what I was asking for, or who I was asking. I'd always had the sense that if something happened to me, it really wouldn't matter. But now, with the sky breaking loose and everything turning over, I felt so far from ready, as if I were being dragged toward a journey I hadn't packed for yet. The thought went out of my head as quickly as it came, and I just hung on to the railing while seconds passed, an eternity of deafening noise and stinging wind.

The roar dissipated as quickly as it had come, like a train rushing past and fading into the distance. An instant of surreal silence followed, and then people were calling for each other all around the room. Something wet touched my arm, and I knew the dogs were there. In the darkness, I grabbed them both, hugged them close and started to cry.

*We're still here. We're all still here.*

A light shone through the room, and I caught the outline of someone—Ernest—passing through with a lantern, checking on everyone. The scene seemed far away, as if I were watching it from an observation tower, as if I weren't really part of it.

"Everybody jus' stay still." Ernest's voice was commanding and deep, calming. "We got glass broke everywhere. Don' move." The lantern glow spread to the far side of the room, where rain was coming through a tall window. What was left of the glass hung from the framework like teeth in a twisted metal skeleton. Lightning flashed, illuminating three more windows, tall and rectangular, arched at the top. A church. We were in a church.

Ernest passed by with the lantern, his feet crunching on broken glass. He touched my shoulder. "You all right?" he asked.

Beside me, Hawkeye stiffened protectively.

"I'm fine." The words rasped in my throat, knotted in a mixture of ebbing fear and rising relief. "What *was* that?"

"Tornado blew over, sha." The lamp lit his face, and I saw him clearly for the first time. He was younger than the shaved head made him look—maybe not much older than me. "The church van, they found us a place to hole up, so we jus' put the pedal to the flo', trying to get here before that storm eat us up."

He rose and moved on, checking others as more lanterns and flashlights lit the interior, and the group carefully began circulating, feet crunching on the mixture of water, grit, and shattered glass. Around the edges of the room, rain pushed through cracks in the decaying stone walls, swelling the puddles on the floor. The room was empty of furniture and the building smelled of must and old plaster, but compared to the bus, it felt like a safe haven.

Mona and several other women herded the kids into the front of the building, where the floor was dry. Imagene's white hair glowed in the dim light as she, Donetta, and Lucy helped to quiet the children. To convince them to stay still, Donetta promised to tell them a story about a cowboy named Pecos Bill, who lassoed a Texas tornado and rode it like a horse.

By the door, men began carrying supplies from the bus, while Ernest and another church member opened a toolbox and struggled to cover the broken window with a tarp. As they worked, the tarp blew inward, flapping like a flag, flicking raindrops throughout the room.

Tying the dogs to the railing, I stood up, gripping the wood unsteadily for a moment before starting toward the broken window. My legs vibrated like Jell-O, my hands shaking as they grabbed a corner of the tarp and held it in place. The scene felt like a dream, something too far away, too strange to be real. When the tarp was secure, shutting out the storm, I moved to the area near the doorway, helped carry in pet crates from the delivery truck, then sort available food, blankets, and dry clothing from luggage taken off the bus. I found my duffle bag among the items carried in. The bag and most of the contents were soaked, but Gil's Bible was all right. I tucked it into the plastic-lined swimsuit pocket on the end of the bag, zipped it up tight, then carried it to the edge of the room and set it by one of the walls before returning to the doorway to help.

My body was boneless and weary when the work was finally done. I couldn't remember the last time I'd felt so completely depleted—perhaps when I was young and we were working in carnivals. Hours of teardown had to be done when the carnival closed at midnight and we prepared to move on.

As everyone settled in to wait out the storm, I moved my bag to a place by the wall near Donetta, Imagene, and Lucy. The room was cold and the supply of blankets and towels limited, so we huddled together under one blanket, trying to keep warm and ward off the dampness. Lucy fell asleep with her head on my shoulder, and I closed my eyes, exhausted. The day spun through my mind, the images as wild and random as if they'd been caught in Donetta's Texas tornado with Pecos Bill.

Listening to the sounds in the room, I tried to push away the noise of the storm, the gusts of wind buffeting the building, the tin flapping overhead, causing the tarp to billow inward like the mainsail on a Spanish galleon. Onboard, we huddled close, unwilling passengers, unable to do anything but wait.

Next to me, Donetta was praying—not loudly enough that I could hear the words, but in little whispers of sound that passed into the air like the wheezing of a napping baby. I listened impassively, thinking that if praying comforted her, then it was harmless enough, but the night my little brother died, I'd learned that prayers are like wishes on stars. No matter how much you want something, how much you need it, the stars don't hear you, and neither does God.

The prayer ended in a weary amen.

"Donetta," Imagene whispered after a while. "You awake?"

"Who could sleep?"

"You think we're gonna make it out of this?"

"'Course we are. Don't say that. The storm'll be gone by mornin'."

I turned my face away, the conversation feeling too intimate to be heard by a third party. I tried to focus on something else, but I couldn't.

"You been the best friend I ever had, Netta. I want you to know that. Nothin' in my life woulda been the same if Miss Laudermilk wouldn'ta put you and me together at that desk in nursery school."

I tried to imagine what it would be like to have ties that long, to have been close to someone since childhood. My childhood was a sea of moving images, people who came and went with the seasons, disconnected pieces that had no relation to one another.

Donetta snorted softly. "Heaven's sake, Imagene, don't talk like that. We ain't dyin'."

Imagene's sigh quivered with emotion. "If it was our time—if another tornado come along—I'd want to've said it, that's all."

"You been the best friend I ever had, too, so I guess we're even." Their bodies shifted, tugging the blanket sideways, and I knew they were hugging. I felt the pull of an old yearning. When Gil and I were growing up, everyone in our lives was transient. We hung out with carnie kids here, and kids on a harvest crew there, and sometimes the kids of some bar owner where my father was playing music, but we knew better than to get too involved. Most of the people who worked with us were just like we were—one step shy of homeless. Either they'd be moving on soon enough or we would, and it was easier to pick up and go when you didn't have entanglements.

Beside me, Donetta and Imagene grew silent, and my mind drifted back to the times when our adventures and our fortunes changed by the week, the month, the season, the only constant being that whatever new place Gil and I landed, we would explore it together.

"I didn't want to be your friend at first," Donetta whispered, her voice bringing me back to the church, casting me into the storm again. "I was jealous of you, Imagene, and that was wrong of me."

"What?" Imagene's voice was drowsy and thick. "Netta, why in the world? You were always the pretty one, and the smart one, and you're still the skinny one—well skinnier, anyhow. You got your own beauty shop and the hotel, and all I done is raise kids and work at the café. Here, you built up a business by yourself, and all I done is listen to Bob Turner flap his gums behind the fry grill all these years. There ain't a soul I ever met didn't think you hung the moon. I always wished I had half the salt you got."

Donetta laughed softly, but it was a sad, resigned sound. "I been jealous of you a lot of times. I was jealous of the way your daddy loved you, the way he used to take you around town with him on Saturdays, and to the café for breakfast, just you and him. I wanted my daddy to do things like that."

*I wanted my daddy to do things like that.* I felt the pull of Donetta's yearning. So many times, I'd wanted to know that my father loved me, that I mattered more than his next big plan, his next trip to the casino, his newest demo tape, the next big gig that was going to get him noticed. I wanted Gil and me to come first, but we never did. Our only choice was to follow after.

Imagene pulled in a soft breath. "Netta, it ain't your fault your daddy took to the bottle. You know that."

Donetta seemed to consider the answer, and something in me understood, before she replied, what the answer would be. "Your head knows that, but your heart don't really understand it. Your heart just keeps lookin' for someone to make you feel . . . special, I guess. I think that's why I ran off and married Ronald so quick after you met Jack. I couldn't hardly stand it the way Jack had stars in his eyes for you, and I wanted someone to feel that way about me. I wanted to know some-body could."

A lump rose in my throat, and I swallowed hard, stuffing down an unwanted swell of emotion. I understood Donetta's words, her feelings. I shared them, even if I didn't want to. Would I end up someday laden with regrets and realizing that the major decisions in my life had been an unconscious reaction to my parents?

"Netta, Ronald loves you. He just . . . don't know how to show it, I guess. He's a man's man—all that huntin' and fishin' he does. There's lots of men know their way around a tackle box and shotgun better than they know their way around a woman's heart. Just because he don't know how to come out and say it don't mean he don't have the feelings."

"Sometimes I wonder." Donetta's voice trembled, the last word ending in a sniffle. "Sometimes I wonder if he'd ever even notice if I just didn't walk in the door one day."

"Netta," Imagene admonished.

"I guess he'd get hungry after a while." Donetta laughed softly, then sniffed again, and Imagene laughed with her.

"Ssshhh," Imagene whispered, and the blanket rustled. I felt them lean away from me and toward each other. "If you start to cry, Netta, I'll cry."

"I just wanted to tell you I always knew you loved me, Ima-gene. And that meant a lot."

"I always knew you loved me, too," Imagene whispered, then they fell silent, and there was nothing but the sounds of the others in the room and the storm pressing in.

## Chapter 11

# *Donetta Bradford*

I didn't close my eyes till it was near mornin'. By then, the wind had died down and a light rain was sprinklin' on the tin roof, just as peaceful as you please. Imagene was sound asleep. Ernest'd cut the light back to one lantern, so the glow was dim, like a candle behind gauze, but I could see Imagene with her head tipped back and her mouth hanging open. She'da died to know she was callin' hogs in a room full of people, but I left her be. We'd been sitting there squeezing each other's hands for hours while that old building rattled and shook. Then her fingers got slack in mine, and I knew she'd finally give it up.

Thinking back on it after she fell asleep, I felt a little silly for all them things I said to her. I hadn't ever admitted that about Ronald to anybody—not even to Ronald. I'd tried to hint around over the years—said things like, "Ronald, guess what Jack and Imagene did? They just hopped in the car and went off to Fort Worth to go dancin'. There's a big ballroom there that plays all the old music. That'd be somethin' to see, wouldn't it?"

Then Ronald, his face still hooked to the TV or a fishin' magazine, would say something like, "Sit in all that traffic up there, like cows in a chute? They coulda just headed over to the VFW Saturday night. Coulda got music and a hamburg. Cheaper."

*That ain't the point,* I'd think, but I wouldn't say it, because then Ronald would think I was holding him up against Jack. Ronald'd always had a chip on his shoulder because Jack'd been all over the world in the service and then he got to be an insurance salesman, and Ronald just worked forty-eight years for the county road service and only left the county for weddin's and funerals.

I could never find a way to make Ronald see I wasn't holding us up against Jack and Imagene; I just wanted to feel like I used to when I was a young gal and I'd load up with my chums and slip off to some Saturday evenin' social, or the street dance after a rodeo. All the boys would come around askin' for a dance, and I'd feel just like Scarlett O'Hara in *Gone With the Wind*.

Back then, I could dance just like Ginger Rogers, except Ginger Rogers didn't do the Texas waltz and western swing.

I was thinking about dancing when the storm finally hushed outside. I closed my eyes and saw myself in my red felt skirt with the horses sewed all along the edge. That skirt was in the window of the Ladies' Store in San Saba, Texas, when I went there with my brother for a rodeo. Frank won the saddle bronc ridin' that afternoon, and he took his prize money and bought me that skirt so I could wear it dancin'. It was the nicest thing any little brother ever did for his big sister. Frank was always good that way, which was probably why Kemp was such a sweet nephew to me. He learned it from his daddy.

My mind turned tired and misty, and I let myself dance to the "Tennessee Waltz," just twirling and twirling and twirling while the horses ran wild on that red skirt.

When I woke up, the air was quiet and calm. The first glint of a cloudy sunrise trickled light over the people curled up around the walls. I don't think I'd ever praised God for the start of a new day quite like I praised Him for that one. There's nothin' like a stormy night to make you grateful for a clear mornin'. I blinked and looked out that window, and thought

*Thank.*

*You.*

*Lord!*

In three separate sentences, just like that.

The rain'd washed the glass clean and bright as a Christmas bulb, and now I could see that, at the top of the windows where they arched up, the panes were colored red, and yellow, and green. The middle window'd shattered, and there were colored pieces of glass all over the floor, catching the foggy light.

Off in the front corner, the door was open and some of the men were trying to read a map and figure out where we were. We'd come a ways from the main road, and the worse the storm got, the more we were turning down one county road, then the next, trying to work our way north, or west, and uphill. We'd probably passed right by houses and such, but there was so much rain, you couldn't see five foot from the bus. The only reason anyone'd noticed the old church was because it sat almost right in the road.

I'd figured out some things while I was on the bus. Mona, who right now was trying to take over the map, was Pastor D.'s big sister, and she had two grown boys, the older one being Ernest, who'd rescued us. Between Pastor D. and Mona, they ran this outfit, which Mamee would've called a Creole church. Being Cajun, Mamee lived alongside lots of folks who called themselves Creoles. They cooked different from the Cajuns, and the ones that talked French spoke it in a different way, and of course they looked different, the Creoles counting their ancestors as some combination of French, black, Spanish, and maybe some Creek, Cherokee, or Seminole even. They farmed rice and knew the bayou just like the Cajuns did.

Mona reminded me of Mamee, some. Her and Ernest and Pastor D. had the sound in their voices that seeps out of the bayou. Their words ran together like a tide, ebbing in and out, soft and pretty.

There was eighteen families in their little flock, give or take. They lived mostly on little rice farms not too far from Mamee's country. The oldest member was Mona's mother, Obeline, and she was ninety-four. The youngest was a baby everyone just called Happy, and then there were all sorts of folks in between, and every kind of pet you could dream up, from turtles to a Chihuahua dog with flowered swim trunks on. They were all members of the Holy Ghost Church, and after sitting through Hurricane Rita and getting flooded out by Ike, they'd made up their minds that come another hurricane, they were all packin' up and gettin' out together. All told, they had a church bus, a van, some cars, and Ernest's furniture delivery truck.

I got up and tiptoed across the room to look at the map with them and see if I could help. When you end up under the manure pile, you might as well start shoveling, I always say.

It didn't take long, standing there by the door, to figure out we were all under the manure pile together. With some reckoning, we decided we were fifteen miles or so off the highway. Ernest'd hiked a mile each way, and he didn't find anyplace to use a phone or get help.

"It's jus' trees down and mess wash up all over the road," Ernest said. "No way we gonna drive out."

Pastor D. muttered something in French that sounded like *Dee-accord,* then studied the map with a big ol' frown. "No way we gonna drive anywhere, anyway. The church van, she outta gas, and the big bus almost there, too. I'm'ma say, we gotta get some help in here, dee-accord?"

Ernest scratched his chin where a little beard was starting to grow. "Could be days before anyone come down this road—trees and branches laid out everywhere, far as the eye can go."

Mona rung her hands, her long gold fingernails—somebody'd done a nice manicure on her with the little glue-on rhinestones on every tip—leavin' little scratches in her skin. "We only got food and water to las' a day. And the *bébés*, they gonna need milk. I'm'ma say, we gotta make a plan now."

We all stood there thinking, and finally the only idea anyone could come up with was that Ernest'd walk one way until he either found help, or a phone, or could get a signal on his cell phone, and his brother, who they called Bluejay (and he did have the prettiest eyes colored blue-gray, just like a jay's wing) would head out the other way.

Bluejay traced a finger on the map, giving his mama and his brother a worried look. The new little baby, Happy, was his, and I reckon he felt a powerful need to get that baby to someplace safer than this. Over in the corner, Bluejay's wife was trying to keep the baby warm. I watched them, standing by the altar rail under the window light, and all of a sudden, I had a vision. That railing and the light made me think of Daily Baptist Church, back home.

I grabbed a pen and started writing the phone number for the Daily Café on the edge of the map. "Listen, you get to where you can use a phone, you call this number and tell them what's happened to us, where we're at, and that Donetta said round up some chain saws and come quick. Tell them Donetta said so, understand?" I wrote the number a second time, then tore off the corners of the map and handed one to each of Mona's sons. "You get that message out, and they'll come for us."

Ernest and Bluejay gave their mama one last hug, Pastor D.

prayed over them, and off they went, opposite ways down the road. They were both jogging at a pretty good clip, Ernest with his hound by his side. They didn't go far before the mist swallowed them up. Standing there with the damp sinking into my bones and scrap elms split like toothpicks all up and down the road, I wondered if we'd ever get out of that place.

The morning went by slow and way too quiet. We got towels and loose boards and swept up the broken glass the best we could, but everyone had to be careful moving around, which was hard on the kids, who were just about happy as puppies in a bucket. They couldn't go outside, because snakes'd come up out of the creek next door, and there were boards with nails sticking out, and twisted pieces of tin everywhere. Through the afternoon, we all just sat around watching the door, waiting and hoping for news, time ticking by slower than you'd ever believe it could.

Finally, Sister Mona stood up by the altar rail and said, "Come on. We gonna get on our feet, here! We gonna praise God. We all right, sha, and the storm, she done pass by, and the river, she don' overflow us. Amen?"

"Amen!" Brother D. called. He was just coming from working on the bus outside. Brother D. swept his hands in the air, like he was picking those people off the floor. "And all the Lord's people say amen."

There was a weak round of amens, and everybody dragged themselves to their feet. Imagene, Lucy, and me got up because we figured we'd better, and after a minute, Kai got up, too. She stood there looking kind of unsure and uncomfortable with her arms crossed over her stomach and her blond hair wrapped close around her face. Sister Mona started to hum "I'll Fly Away," and then in a minute, others joined in. Pretty soon, they got to clappin' and swayin', and all taking different parts of the music, we were having us a old-fashioned singin', raising the rafters. Before I knew it, I got caught in the rhythm, and I was swayin' and clappin' right along. I closed my eyes and I forgot all about where I was, and it felt like a pretty good day. My spirit was light and my heart was smilin', and then I thought, *You know what, Netta, it is a good day. You woke up, and you're still here, and listen to that music!*

When the sound finally died away, I thought I heard somethin' outside. It was far off, and I couldn't make it out for sure. It stopped, then started again, then stopped. Finally, I moved over closer to the door to check that I wasn't imagining it.

I did hear somethin'. Way off in the distance.

Humming, and buzzing, and chugging, loud then soft, then loud again.

A chain saw, clear as day.

# Chapter 12

# *Kai Miller*

The chain saws were drawing closer, but after an hour of standing by the door listening, I could tell that, in spite of Donetta's assurances that we'd be rescued any minute, whoever was coming up the road was making painfully slow progress. One of the scouts who'd left that morning came back at three in the afternoon, after having hiked six miles up the road before being stopped by a flooded creek where a bridge was out. "No way cross that mess," he reported. "That creek, she runnin' like a river. De'pouille! I'm'ma hope Ernest got out. You hear a word from him?"

"*Non.*" Mona shook her head. "But we hearin' chain saws come this way, and Ernest gonna be right along with 'em. You gonna see." Flapping her hands, she shooed two little boys who were listening to the chain saws and trying to work their way out the door. "Out'cha now. You go out there, the Rugaru, he gonna come grab you up, carry you off down the slew." She raised her hands over her head, snarling like a boogeyman, and the boys' eyes widened. I knew the story of the Rugaru. Working outdoor concerts and carnivals, and hanging around carnies, I'd heard about every monster-slash-ghost story ever invented.

"I seen the Rugaru." Bluejay's voice took on an air of drama, and he cast a sideways wink at Donetta and me. "He gone-on down the river in a pirogue, this way." Stretching out his arms and spreading his feet, he pretended to be balancing in a moving canoe. "Rugaru, he big like a tree, covered in the moss, he is."

The story, or his pantomime of a moss-covered boogeyman, triggered a memory. My father collected the carnies' horror stories like exotic treasures. Future song ideas, he called them. He had a habit of acting them out at bedtime for our entertainment. His performances drove my mother crazy, because a scary story or two was all it took to keep Gil awake all night. Even so, for reasons my mother and I could never understand, Gil never stopped begging for one more ghost story or Bigfoot tale.

"I bet Pecos Bill, he bigger than ol' Rugaru," the older boy ventured, nodding at Donetta. "Pecos Bill so big, he ride the tornado."

"That so?" Bluejay crossed his arms over his chest, squinting at the boys and then at Donetta. "He so big as that, cher? You think that Pecos Bill, he can lasso ol' Rugaru?"

Donetta turned her attention from the chain saw sounds, pretending to consider the question with gravity. "Way-ul, I'd have to thank about tha-ut." Compared to the rapid cadence of Bluejay's words, hers dragged like a cassette tape playing too slow. "What do you thank, Kai?" She nudged me, inviting me to get in on terrorizing the children.

"I don't know," I muttered, still remembering Gil. What possessed my father to tell those stories when he knew Gil would end up curled in my bed all night, checking the window every half hour for signs of Bigfoot?

Donetta seemed disappointed that I didn't want to join in. "My mamee used to tell me about the Rugaru. I don't know if him and Pecos Bill ever did meet—Pecos Bill bein' more of a west Texas fella and all. He liked the dry country, pretty much."

"I say Pecos Bill, he gonna whip the Rugaru," one of the boys insisted. "Lasso him right up, skin off all that moss on Rugaru's hide."

Chewing a chipped red fingernail, Donetta considered the contest of tall tales. "Way-ul, I'd have to say I bet he could, too, but what with all the weather we been havin', I imagine ol' Pecos Bill's laid out flat sleepin' somewhere, after havin' to lasso all them tornados last ni-ight and get 'em put up in the barn. It might take him a day or two to get after that Rugaru fella. I wouldn't get too close to the door if I was you kids. No sir, I wouldn't."

The boys' eyes widened, then they giggled and squealed and ran away. I was glad the boogeyman story time was over without my having to contribute. Not to be a party pooper or anything, but it reminded me too much of Gil.

Bluejay wagged a finger and winked at us. "You gals bes' watch out for that Rugaru."

I nodded, and Donetta swished a backhand. "Oh, hon, I'm too old and fat for any old swamp monster to carry me off."

Bluejay's lips parted in a wide smile. "Eiii-eee! What? Forty ain't old. There was a lady over forty won the swimmin' Olympics."

Donetta giggled and blushed. "You know I ain't forty."

Bluejay grinned, elbowing me. "Forty's what I figure, don' you, sha?"

Donetta swatted the air, "Oh, you. Honestly. Kai, hon, you don't even have to answer that. Lyin' is a sin. Bluejay, you better get on over there and take care of that sweet little baby. He's been givin' his mama fits all mornin'. Must be he takes after his daddy."

She slipped an arm around my shoulders as Bluejay left to

check on his baby. "We might as well go sit down, hon. Whoever that is with the chain saws, they're still a long ways off."

"Guess so," I agreed, and we walked to the opposite wall to sit
down. Next to us, Obeline, who at ninety-four seemed too old
and frail for a situation like this, was sitting on a cooler, rocking
a toddler who'd been fussy all day. Watching her hands gently
stroke the baby's arm, it occurred to me to wonder whether
Grandmother Miller had ever comforted us like that. My father
had let it slip a time or two that shortly after I was born, I'd
been left for some months with Grandmother Miller during a
period of time when, in his words, my mother couldn't handle
it. Logic told me that my grandmother must have taken care of
me then, perhaps even rocked me as Obeline was doing now, but
the picture wouldn't form in my mind the way I wanted it to.

"The lil' fella sure looks happy enough now," Donetta remarked, leaning over and lightly stroking a finger along the
baby's cheek.

Obeline smiled. "I midwifed lotta little bébés, and my *mère*,
she a midwife way back when I'z a little bougalee. In the old
day, Mère deliver almost all the bébés on Landee Bayou. The
doctor, he sixty mile away, somebody gotta bring them bébés
into the worl', sha."

Donetta's attention snapped from the toddler to Obeline.
"My mama's people come from down around that way. They
farmed rice near the bayou on a road that went across an old
iron bridge. Did you ever know any Chiassons?"

Obeline laughed. "Oh, honeychil', lotta Chiassons down
in that bayou. Shake a tree 'round there, you find Chiasson, 'n
Guilbeau, n' Thibedeaux, n' Terrebonne come down like rain."

"I guess they would." Donetta's disappointment was palpable, so that I felt it myself and wondered at the cause of it.
Surely she didn't think the odds were very good that in the middle of a hurricane evacuation we'd happen to run into people

who knew her family. "Mamee always called their place the Dogleg Bayou. Did you ever know it?"

Obeline's lips parted contemplatively, and she studied Donetta through bottle-bottom glasses. "Everybody know the Dogleg, sha. The water there crook way, way up in like a hound dog hind leg." She illustrated the shape with her hands. "Oil comp'ny, they drain that out long time ago. No bayou at the Dogleg no mo', and all them farm, they gone."

Donetta's face slowly fell, and I felt her body sink against mine. "Those places are gone?"

Obeline nodded as the baby's mother came and gently lifted him from her lap. Pushing off her seat, the old woman stood with a grunt, her thin bowed legs widening to steady her body. "The rice farmers, they move on downwater. The oil patch, she good to the rich man. Not so good to the rest." She stood a moment longer, squinting toward the altar railing, scratching her head. "I'm'ma think that was the Dogleg they drain. I'm'ma think it was . . ." Sighing, she scrubbed her forehead with her fingertips, then shook her head and wandered away.

Donetta sat looking at the floor, her shoulders rounding forward.

"I guess that wasn't good news," I said finally.

Pressing her lips together, Donetta pushed fallen strands of red hair into what was left of a lopsided rat-up. "Oh, I should've expected it, I guess. A place don't stay the same when you're away from it fifty-odd years. It's just that one of the things I really wanted to do this trip was see if I could find out about my mama's people. Guess I thought they'd all be sittin' there waitin' for me to wander back. Guess I should've known better. Reckon that's why I never said anything to Imagene and Lucy about it."

I suddenly understood Donetta's hope-against-hope that we'd find someone here who knew her family. Occasionally, when I saw a traveler with a guitar case, or when a carnival came to Perdida, or when there was an outdoor music festival, I caught myself eyeballing strangers, imagining that I'd spotted my father. "I don't think it's silly," I offered, and she gave my hand a squeeze, then wiped mascara smears under her eyes.

"You're a sweet girl, Kai. I sure wish we'da got to take that cruise on your boat. I was gonna sign me up for the dancin' class. Guess that was a silly notion at my age."

"I help teach ballroom dancing on ship sometimes. It's never too late to take it up again." I nudged her shoulder, coaxing the way I would have with passengers on a cruise. Sometimes they were hesitant at first, and our job was to bring them out of their shells.

"Pppfff!" she spat, then giggled ruefully. "When I was a young gal, I could sure cut a rug, though. Back before I got married and such." For some reason, *before I got married* had all the enthusiasm of a funeral march. Unhappy marriages were one of the things I saw plenty of on ship. I'd learned to recognize the symptoms. It was none of my business, of course.

"When you finally do go on your cruise, you definitely need to do the dancing class."

Her lips twisted to one side, then sank. "I doubt we'd do all this again. I reckon we'll just get our money back from the travel insurance and stay closer to home. We come into a shade more adventure than we planned for, this time. If I ever get Imagene back to Daily, I don't reckon she'll ever leave the county again. Least not on one of my harebrained plans." Donetta looked like a kid who'd just unwrapped the last box under the Christmas tree and found socks in it. "I was dumb as a post about that computer—all puffed up like a banty rooster because I knew how to use it, and the fact was I didn't know a thing. I wanted this trip to happen, and I wasn't gonna take no for an answer."

"You can still have your trip." Why I felt the need to play Merry Sunshine, I wasn't sure, but Donetta with a frown just seemed wrong. "As soon as we get somewhere, I'll help you re-book your reservation. You could get a better trip, maybe with more ports, even. You didn't miss much in Mexico this time of year. It's still hot in September."

Her answer was a headshake and a sigh and a pause in the conversation.

Something glistening near my feet caught my eye, and I stretched, picking up colorful glass shards and dropping them in my palm. Perhaps when—if—I made it home, I'd work them into one of my creations—a wire-wrap candleholder, maybe, or a picture frame.

Donetta patted my shoulder as I tucked the bits of glass into my duffle bag. "You're a sweet girl, Kai. What kind of name is that, anyway? Kai. It's different. That a family name?"

*Hardly*, I thought, but I didn't say it. The truth was that my handle came on a whim, like everything else. "My father named me after the sound a bird was making when he walked out of the hospital. He heard *kai, kai, kai,* and he thought, why not? I did better than my brother, Gil, though. We were in Lousiana when he was born, and my father named him after a bullfrog."

"I think those are good names. They mean somethin'." She nodded to punctuate. "Like people in a book would have. I always wished I had a name like that. So where's your daddy live now?"

"I have no idea, really."

The answer seemed to surprise, or disappoint her, or both. "It's not good to lose touch with your people. I wish I'da kept better contact with my mama's folk. I guess I figured there'd always be time."

I contemplated the idea that perhaps I'd end up someday regretting the things I hadn't done. "There were issues after my parents split, and eventually we all lost touch." It was an uncomfortably honest admission, something I normally wouldn't have shared. "But it's fine. Life goes on, you know?"

Nodding, she pulled me close, then cradled my head under hers. "Well, you just never know, darlin'. The Lord has it all in mind, though. Everything works for our good."

I didn't answer, because I didn't have an answer. In my mind, God was a blackjack dealer, tossing out cards at random. They landed where they landed and you did the best you could with what you got.

Closing my eyes, I relaxed, letting weariness slip over me. Far back in my mind, I remembered sitting with my mother like this. We were on the beach in Galveston. She'd just told me the truth about Gil. I didn't believe it, so I didn't cry. I pretended to so she would stay there with me longer. It felt good to have her all to myself. Most of the time, she and my father were so wrapped up in each other, that it was like Gil and I were an inconvenience.

I'd always wondered what it would be like to feel that way about someone, or to have someone else feel that way about you—to have your eyes so full of one person you didn't see anything else in the world. But I'd always considered that emotion from a distance—the way you picture living in a mansion or wearing the Hope diamond. A picture so far from reality that you can dream about it without setting yourself up for disappointment, because really, deep down, you know it'll never happen.

Donetta sighed, and her breaths grew long and even.

*It's not good to lose touch with your people. . . .*

Would I end up like Donetta someday, trying to track down a family I hadn't seen in fifty-plus years? I hadn't really considered the question of whether I ever intended to search for my father, or go out to Arizona, knock on my mother's door, and see what she'd say when she opened it. I'd kept myself busy with other things, thought of time as an endless highway with plenty of room for side trips somewhere down the road. How would I feel if I ended up in Donetta's position—with lingering questions and no one left to answer?

The issue circled in my mind while the shadows lengthened in the building, my thoughts stretching with them, drifting as in the distance the chain saws chewed through another piece of wood. . . .

It seemed only a moment later that Donetta was standing over me, shaking me awake. My body was stiff and leaden, so I knew I'd been dozing against the wall for a while. "Listen at that! You hear it? That's an engine! Somebody's comin'!"

I staggered to my feet as Donetta hurried to rouse Imagene and Lucy. Around the room, others had caught the sound and everyone was moving toward the door, listening and whispering, as if too much chatter might make the hum of rescue disappear.

Mona's voice blasted in from the parking lot like a raucous wind. "Praise the Lawd! We're saved!"

"What is it?" someone near me called. For a moment, we were wedged just inside the doorway, trapped behind Obeline as she tried to navigate the uneven threshold.

By the time we made it to the parking lot and around the bus, a vehicle was cresting the hill—I guessed you'd have to call it a vehicle. It looked like something out of a science fiction movie gone wrong. It had the cab of a truck, with a huge winch on the front like the ones carnivals used to raise the rides. In the back, a flatbed was loaded down with toolboxes, chain saws, tanks, and men. They were riding on a tall A-frame that held what looked like a giant corkscrew swinging back and forth like the pendulum of a clock.

"Gal-ee! What 'n the worl'?" Bluejay gasped, pointing at the truck.

"It's the Daily men!" Donetta squealed. "There's my boy, right up top!" She ran toward the road, fanning her hands like a castaway and calling out, "We're here! We're down here!"

Straddling the A-frame of the corkscrew like a circus rider, a man with dark hair lifted a chain saw into the air in a triumphant wave as Donetta splashed through a mud puddle in a stiff-legged run, gesticulating wildly to welcome the truck into the parking lot.

The Holy Ghost crowd backed up uncertainly, murmurs traveling among them as the strange vehicle crossed the muddy lot and rolled to a stop, the brakes squealing out a complaint and the engine backfiring.

Running alongside the truck, Donetta shaded her eyes and peered at the man atop the corkscrew. When the vehicle finally wheezed into silence, she pointed a finger and shook it at him. "Kempner Rollins Eldridge, you get down from that post-hole digger right now. You're gonna slip off there and crack your fool head open like a hen egg, and then where'll we be?"

# Chapter 13

## *Donetta Bradford*

I don't think I ever been so proud in my life as when the Daily boys come over the hill on Pearly Parsons' fencing truck with the post-hole digger swingin' in the back. I feel sure I heard a cavalry bugle call playing in the background. Those boys looked so good to me, riding that truck with their chain saws, and shovels, and ropes, I coulda kissed every one of them. They had Ernest along, too, so I knew he'd got in touch with them somehow and led them right to us.

When that truck hooked into the parkin' lot, I saw Kemp, fifteen foot in the air on top of that post auger, and I coulda wrung his neck. I hollered at him, and he just kicked a leg over and swung off of that thing by one arm—the pitchin' arm that'd had all the surgeries, no less. He landed in the bed of the truck still holding the chain saw and about give me a heart attack, as usual.

I didn't know whether to kiss that boy on the cheek or swat him, but finally I just opened my arms and ran his way. He lifted me plumb off the ground with a one-handed hug. One thing about Kemp, even back in high school, when all the other teen-age boys would act like they didn't even know their own mamas, Kemp was never afraid to give his old auntie a hug.

All around me, I could hear other Daily folk getting off the truck. There was Doyle Banes, stuttering out a story about how they'd cut through oak trees big around as fifty-gallon drums and dragged half a barn off the road with the winch on the post truck. Pearly Parsons was bragging about how that truck'd once pulled the county road service dozer out of a sinkhole. One of Pearly's helpers, Julio, was talking in Spanish, saying *Alamo gordo*, which I think meant *big tree*, and Buddy Ray Baldridge was letting everyone know he was with the Daily Sheriff's Department, and then there was Bob Turner, and Otis Charles Potts, who could probably lift a tree off the road with his bare hands, and my brother, Frank. It felt like the whole town'd dropped whatever was happening and come to rescue us.

I started to cry right there on the spot, and Imagene must've been feeling about the same way, because when Kemp let me go and I looked around through the blur, Imagene was hugging Bob Turner. Bob, of all people! Imagene and Bob been arguing behind the counter at the Daily Café for fifty years. I'd of said them hugging was about as likely as hogs in toe shoes.

After Bob let her go, Frank come over and grabbed Imagene with both arms, and you coulda fried an egg on her cheeks afterward. Her and Frank just stood there looking at each other, all doe-eyed.

Right about then, it come to me to wonder how in the world they'd got there. Surely they didn't ride all that way on the post truck. I turned back to Kemp with a million questions runnin' through my mind and tumblin' out my mouth. "How'd y'all get here? Where'd you find Ernest? Did he tell you where we were—he must've, I guess. Y'all didn't ride all the way from

Daily in the back of the post truck, surely?" I looked around for more vehicles, but there was only Pearly's.

"And who do you think you are, Kempner Rollins, riding up there on that auger—Rambo Balboa? And with a chain saw! That truck could hit a bump and you'd be knocked off quicker than you can say *splat*, or you could get caught in a electric line and hung up like the wash. Ya'll didn't drive over any down power lines, I hope?" All the possible pictures flashed through my mind and my head went light and cloudy. If anything would've happened to the Daily boys because they had to come rescue me, I don't know what I'da done. "How'd y'all get here so fast? Everything all right back home? Y'all didn't have any tornados? We had . . ."

Kemp grabbed me by the shoulders, and I realized I was hoppin' around like a field mouse on a hot tar patch. "Aunt Netta, one question at a time, all right?" He grinned at me, and I remembered how much I loved that smile. It got him away with murder when he was little. He was a stinker, but cute as a bug when he smiled. "We left about nine o'clock this morning, when the first call came through from Ernest. We still weren't sure exactly where y'all were, but he gave us enough information to get started on, so we gathered some equipment and gas cans, and whoever we could find, and we headed this way. In the meantime, Ernest kept walking, looking for road markers or landmarks that'd help us find the place on the map. You'd think it wouldn't take all day to make a trip less than four hours from home, but between the trees and power lines down, and the roads that are flooded . . ."

"You drove through a flood with electric lines in it? What in land's name were you thinkin' about? Y'all coulda got rolled over in a ditch, or carried off in a creek, or—"

"We drove through a little water. That's all," Kemp cut me off, rollin' his eyes. "This county road was slow going, so we left the rest of the trucks a few miles up and worked our way through on the post truck to save gas." He used the chain saw to point back the way they come.

"Put that thing down," I told him, and he looked at the saw like he'd forgot it was there. "Kempner, you are strummin' my nerves, and I'm down to my last one after that storm, let me tell ya."

Laughing deep in his throat, he set that machine on the bed of the truck, then kissed me on the head. He could only get away with that because he was six foot three. "Aunt Netta, you're always on your last nerve." He grinned again. "How are Imagene and Lucy?"

"They're on their last nerve, too. We left Daily wanting us a adventure, and we sure got one. We were stuck on the side of the road, and then a real sweet little gal stopped and picked us up with her two dogs. Kai's her name, after a bird. We went on in a old Microbus—those ones like the hippies had? But the tire got flat. Then we heard someone singin' in the woods and a old hound dog, and we hiked off to the Holy Ghost folks, but the storm blew in, and I'll tell you, I thought we'd get hit by lightnin' or squashed flat by a tree, comin' through the woods. I ain't ever prayed so hard in my life, but then we got on the bus, and . . ." The words kept running like water from a downspout.

It took me a minute to notice Kemp wasn't noddin' along or sayin' anything. He didn't have that glazed-over look he sometimes got when I talked. In fact, he wasn't looking at me at all. "Kemp, are you listenin' to me? Kempner?" I turned and checked over my shoulder, and the only thing back there behind me was Kai. She was giving him the eye, too.

I shut up and just watched for a minute, then I called Kai over and made the introductions. Kemp got tongue-tied, of all things. That boy never had a problem talking to girls in his whole life.

"Kai stopped and picked us up when nobody else would," I offered up, just to see what Kemp would say. "Without her, I don't know what we'da done." I had to nudge the boy a little to get him to come back to the world of the livin'. He snapped to all at once and stuck out his hand to shake Kai's.

"Good to meet you, Kai. Sounds like we owe you a debt of thanks," he said.

My gracious, didn't that sound formal? *Debt of thanks . . .* Someone was tryin' to make a good impression. Hmmm . . .

Kai blushed. Her big blue eyes met Kemp's, and they both stalled again, so I hopped in to keep the conversation going, since no one else was talkin'. "This gal ain't scared of anythin'. She helped us fight off three sauced-up rednecks with guns in their truck."

Kemp's eyes got big and his mouth dropped open.

"Like I said, we had us a real adventure," I told him. "Kai here was a wonder."

"She must be." Kemp looked like he believed it. "Anybody who'd take on you three has to be superhuman." Then he gave Kai one of those grins of his, and it wasn't lost on her, I'll tell you. She laughed, and blushed, and giggled all at once.

The time for talking was over then, and everyone got busy putting gas in the vehicles and gathering the luggage and the kids so we could get on the road. If we headed out soon, we could maybe make it halfway home before dark, Frank said. He talked to Pastor D., and told him, since there wasn't a hurricane shelter that wasn't packed full between here and Daily, the Holy Ghost folks should come with us and we'd put them up in Daily. Frank said it was the least the Daily folk could do, after the Holy Ghost people'd saved me, and Lucy, and Imagene. "It's a slow trip, with the roads flooded, but if we head on out, we'll be back in Daily tonight," Frank said, and Pastor D. didn't waste any time getting his folks moving.

*Back in Daily tonight . . .* The words sure sounded good. Tonight I'd sleep in my own bed, and this crazy, wild adventure of ours would be over.

All of a sudden, something crossed my mind that wasn't there before. In all the excitement when the Daily men'd showed up, I was so excited I never even noticed. Now it hit me like a ton of bricks. Ronald wasn't here. He didn't come.

My heart squeezed. All these folks'd dropped what they were doing and drove down here to rescue us, but Ronald wasn't with them.

My brother passed by, and I asked him, "Frank, where's Ronald?"

Frank had a hose on his shoulder, and he was headed to gas up the bus from the tank on the back of Pearly's truck. "Couldn't find him when we were gettin' together to leave out. Figured he'd headed down the river, fishin'. His truck, boat, and tackle was gone from the house."

*Down the river . . . fishin'.* Frank's words fell over me like cold water. All the while I was traveling, off far from home, Ronald'd never once checked to see if we'd got on the ship all right? He'd just headed off on one of his fishin' trips like it was any normal day. Like there wasn't a thing to worry about . . .

A feeling slid over me that was as sudden and as low as anything I'd ever felt in my life. It sank down my throat and landed in my stomach. I stood there so heavy with the weight of it, I couldn't move.

*Fifty-one years I been with that man, and he didn't even check on me. If you loved somebody, you'd care whether they were safe. Even if you were mad at them for going off on a cruise, you'd care. . . .*

An old pain sneaked from the place I'd buried it, like a dead thing you put in the ground, then it swells up in the summer heat and comes out of the soil. In the blink of an eye, I was a little girl, watching out the back of the community building while all the parents filed in for the 4-H Christmas style show. Our truck pulled up, but it was Uncle Bean in the driver's seat and Frank with him. Uncle Bean looked about as thrilled as a calf in the dehorn chute. I knew Frank'd got Uncle Bean to bring him, and I knew why. My daddy wasn't coming. He was probably back at the ranch with a bottle of whiskey.

All of a sudden, I didn't feel pretty in my Christmas dress. Even though I'd worked months making it, I wanted to run home and take it off and throw it under the bed. All I could think was *A daddy who loved his little girl would want to see her in the pretty party dress she worked on all year. Wouldn't he?*

*Wouldn't he?*

It'd been a long time since I'd let myself go back to that day, but standing there thinking about Ronald down at the river fishing while I was in a hurricane, I felt just the same. It's hard to see, with so many days in a lifetime, how you can circle back on yourself without even knowing it, but I was the girl in the Christmas dress again, waiting out back of the community building for a man who had better things to do. I'd been feeling that way a long time, even though I didn't want to admit to it.

Imagene walked up with our beach bag. "Where's Ronald?" Sometimes I think Imagene and me are like them twins that when one slices a finger with the kitchen knife, the other one gets a pain a thousand miles away.

I realized I'd been standin' there with my head in the past while everyone bustled around like an army in double time, gettin' ready to go. "They couldn't find him when they left out of town." I tried to sound like it was no matter. There wasn't any sense making Imagene feel bad because I was hurting. *Keep the cap on the bluing,* my grandma Eldridge always said. *A little spill stains a whole batch.* I scratched at a spot on my sleeve. "Bob said they figured he was gone down the river fishin'."

Imagene's lips moved like she was chewing a cud and thinking about how it tasted. "I reckon he must be, or else he'd be here, if he knew."

"Reckon" was about all I could get out. If I said anything more about Ronald, I'd give myself away. "I'll go check inside and see if we forgot anythin'. Why don't y'all load on up?" Folks were already getting in the bus, dragging tired kids and suitcases along with them, and Ernest'd finished strapping in the pet carriers and closed the door on his delivery truck.

Ernest and me ended up to be the last ones in the church. He was waiting to drag the door back into place after I got out, but I took a minute to pick up the last couple pieces of trash. Sister Mona and her group'd left that place nearly clean as a whistle. Except for the dirt stirred around on the floor and the tarp hung over the broken window, you couldn't tell anything'd happened there.

"It's a miracle this place held on through the storm, especially that roof." I looked up at the dots of sunlight coming through overhead. "I seen tornadoes peel off sheet tin and roll it up like duct tape."

"This old buildin', she gonna stand here a long time," he said. "I'm'ma say, she been built to las'."

"Reckon so."

"*Mais*, be bad they tear it down to widen up the road someday."

"Surely will." I walked toward the door thinkin' that no matter what happened to this buildin', I'd never forget it. "I almost hate to leave it behind."

Ernest belly-laughed as I stepped out into the light and he pulled the door closed. "My eye, cher! I'm'ma get me some good food, and a shower, and lay up in a soft bed."

"That sounds good, too," I admitted, taking a deep breath and pulling in the smells of moss, and pine straw, and water. "But the low country's where my mamee's people come from. I don't reckon I'll ever get back there again."

"Cher, you get me a hot shower, and some food, and a bed, and when the water go down, I drive you back down there myself and give you the gran' tour." Ernest smiled real big with a twinkle in his eye.

"I think this trip's the good Lord's way of tellin' me to let it go. There were some stories in Mamee's family I always wondered about, that's all." I was talkin' to myself as much as Ernest. I stood there looking around while he worked that stiff old door back into place, just like we found it.

Ernest gave me a real tender look. "I got me a empty spot up there, front a' my truck. You wanna ride wit' me, I listen pretty good," he said, then laughed, his big chest shaking up and down. "I need me somethin' to keep awake."

"Oh, hon"—I batted a hand at him—"I can keep anybody awake."

"You got a deal, then, sha." The words rolled off his tongue in one big string, sounding like *You-god-da-deal-den-sha*.

"It's a bargain, pardner," I said, then hollered up at Imagene to let her know I was gonna ride with Ernest.

The two of us walked around the bus to his truck, and he let me in. Leaning out the window, he wheeled his hand around and hollered at the bus, "Let's ged-on-da-road!"

Just before we pulled out, his stomach rumbled so loud I heard it, and he thumped his middle hard with his palm. "*Gal-ee!* I'm hon-gree. Two hundred ninety pound a' man, he can't go all day wit'out food."

"Hon," I said, "I don't usually go all day without feedin' somebody, so we're a pair. Y'all get us back to Daily and I'll put on a spread that'll fatten you up like a market steer."

Ernest laughed. "Hoo-eee! For true, sha? That a promise or a threat?"

"Little bit a' both," I told him, and then the vehicles rolled out all in a train with the post truck leading the way toward home.

## Chapter 14

# *Kai Miller*

Traveling was slow, and an anxious feeling hung in the bus, pulling the air taut. Along the roadsides, the water was rising, flowing downriver as storm runoff found watersheds. Abandoned cars littered the ditches, where discarded belongings and trash floated like driftwood. Ahead, the road snaked through the water, a pencil-thin island, a lifeline, currents lapping at its edges, running high and fast under bridges that swayed and vibrated with the current. In tiny communities along the highway, residents were out surveying the damage, nervously putting gas in cars that remained above the flood line, or standing on the porches of homes or businesses, watching the water come up and wondering how high it would rise.

"De'pouille!" Sister Mona whispered, shaking her head at the mess outside.

I tried not to think about what might be happening back in Perdida. The storm reports on the radio were spotty, so it was hard to tell for certain. Everything I owned could be washing off to Timbuktu right now.

*They're just things,* I told myself. *They don't matter.* But a part of me knew that without those *things,* I was nobody. I was like my father after one of his potential recording deals collapsed, or his latest cache of lotto tickets didn't pay off, or he bet on the wrong horse at the races, and he had to take whatever work he could get or go begging to Grandmother Miller.

*Come here without two dimes to rub together,* she'd say as she opened the door.

Outside the window, a sign came into view, growing larger in the dusky evening light until finally the letters were clear. *WACO 60.* Waco was just down the road from McGregor. Grandmother Miller's house was closer than I thought. No wonder I was hearing her in my head.

"*Qui c'est que'ca?* Look like they got a problem up ahead there," Sister Mona said, derailing my train of thought, which was probably for the best, since it wasn't headed anywhere good, anyway.

Stretching in my seat, I tried to see what was happening in front of us. Brake lights shined against the pavement and sprinkled pink fog over the water in the ditches.

The radio on the dashboard squawked, and the driver picked up the mouthpiece to answer. Pastor D. stood over him, listening, his face narrow with concern.

"What's goin', Pastor D.?" Mona pushed out of her seat with a grunt and stood teetering above me in a way that convinced me to stuff myself as far as possible into the crack between the seat and the wall. "Pastor D., why we slowin' down? *Sa k'genyen?*"

Pastor D. didn't reply. Clutching the pole behind the driver's seat, he spoke to the driver.

"D., what's goin' on?" Sister Mona demanded.

"The Lawd bless me wit' twenty-twenty ears, Mona," Pastor D. called back, raising a palm as in *Talk to the hand.* "Soon's

I figure out the problem up there, I'm'ma pass that right along yo' way. Don' you worry."

Mona snorted and started up the aisle, grabbing seat backs and swaying with the roll of the bus. "I'm'ma bless you wit' somethin', you tellin' me *Talk to the hand . . .*"

The bus hit a chughole, and Sister Mona landed in the lap of a terrified teenager, three rows from the front. Pastor D. seized the opportunity to make an announcement.

"All right, ever'body." He patted the air like he was silently pushing the congregation back into their seats. "We got trouble wit' Ernest truck. He gonna pull off and let us go on past. We got about a-hour-little-more before we gonna be at this town, Daily. Ernest, he gonna limp along bes' he can and meet us later, and bring all the luggage and the animals. He gonna make it fine, jus' gonna be a little slow. *Pa gen pwoblem.*"

A murmur went through the bus, and from the back, a woman hollered, "*Fiank-o!* We don' leave nobody behind! We go on all together. That's the way we voted it. Them what the Lawd has brung together, let no man take apart, amen?"

A rumble of agreement traveled through the crowd.

"I'm not goin' without my cat," an old woman hollered.

"My eye! I'm not goin' without my boy!" Sister Mona added. "We come all this way. You call up ahead, Pastor D. You tell Ernest to jus' keep on, and we gonna follow behind. We all keep together. Family don' leave family, and this church, it a family. Amen?" Swiveling back and forth, she called up another swell of agreement, then added, "We gonna get there. But we gonna get there together."

The driver and Pastor D. looked at each other, and finally Pastor D. shrugged helplessly. "I'm'ma say amen, then. I can see when I'm outdone. Settle in and we got us a slow trip ahead."

Sister Mona came back down the aisle nodding, muttering under her breath, and looking vindicated. "Tell me he gonna leave *my* boy behind!" she muttered as she sank into the seat beside me. "Nobody, *nobody* gonna leave my boy behind. *Seskonsa!*"

Letting out a long breath, I settled in for what would, apparently, be a long ride. As the miles crawled slowly by, I closed my eyes and let my mind go murky, leaving behind the bus, and the sounds of the people, and the whispers of Mona, uttering a mother's prayer for the well-being of her son.

I woke up to Sister Mona screaming, "Praaaaise da Lawd! I'm'ma say amen!" Outside the window, a sign was passing. Through filmy eyes, I could just make out the letters. *DAILY 10.*

Sister Mona let out a long, loud whoop, and the group responded with a cheer and a fluttering of hands in the air.

I blinked the sleep out of my eyes as we traveled the last few miles of winding road, the headlights illuminating the surrounding terrain in circular bits and pieces. While I was sleeping, the country had become rough and hilly. Rocks, live oaks, and spiny yuccas had replaced thick undergrowth and ditches filled with water. Where tall pines had blocked the horizon, now miles and miles of open country stretched toward the sky. A full moon painted the ground in shades of pearl and iridescent silver, and overhead, a million stars glittered in a velvet blanket of sky.

A sense of peace settled over me as we crested the final hill, passing a *Welcome to Daily* sign. In the valley below, where a lazy river reflected the moon in a curling ribbon, the little town of Daily, Texas, was putting out enough light to rival the Vegas strip—as if every lamp in every window had been lit and left burning to welcome us. As we crossed the river and chugged up Main Street, residents appeared from houses and storefronts, waving and clapping, like we were soldiers returning from war.

The passengers on the bus pressed close to the windows, peering uncertainly at the crowd. "S'pose they been expectin' somebody else?" Bluejay muttered, leaning across the aisle toward his mother. "What time it is?"

Mona looked at her watch. "Pass eleven."

"*Gal-ee*, what're they doin'?" one of the teenagers whispered.

"I don' know . . ."

"What in the he . . ."

"You watch that mouth, T. Ray!" Mona said, pointing at a teenage boy. "I'm'ma say they jus' givin' us a welcome. That's what I'm'ma say. This how they welcome folks here."

"You know that fo' sure, Aunt Mona?" The teenager remained unconvinced.

Sister Mona squinted into the glow, surveying the commotion on Main Street. "My eye . . ." she answered. "I ain't sure of nothin'."

If the members of Holy Ghost Church weren't ready for Daily, Texas, the people of Daily were definitely ready for them. The bus had barely squealed to a stop before we were swept up in a swirl of activity and surrounded by people carrying suitcases, people offering blankets, jackets, and clean clothes, people helping to unload luggage, and telling us that a buffet had been set up in the Daily Café and lodging was ready at the Baptist church and in the Daily Hotel.

"Now, don't you worry, hon," Donetta said to me as we crossed under a sign that read *Daily Hair and Body, Beauty Salon, Auto Paint and Body, Insurance Welcome*. On the windows of the building, fading paint still proclaimed *Daily Hotel*. "I got a place for you at my house." Slipping an arm around my shoulders, Donetta guided me through the door into the old hotel lobby, which had been converted into a beauty shop sometime around 1960, judging by the equipment. "You just wait here a minute, and then I'll take you on over to the house. I got a empty bed in my sewin' room, and you'll be real comfortable there, and we'll put your dogs in the backyard, and it'll be just fine. You must be plumb wore out." Spotting her nephew passing by with a load of suitcases under each arm, she waved him closer. "Kemp, honey, come on over here a little minute."

Kemp veered in our direction, threading his way through the crowd without setting down the luggage. I caught myself watching him move through the lobby, seemingly unburdened by the weight of the bags. He looked vaguely familiar, but I couldn't decide why.

He glanced up and caught me watching, and blood prickled into my cheeks. Something about Kemp Eldridge put me a little off balance.

"You busy, hon?" Donetta asked.

He quirked a brow, looking down at one armful of bags, then the other. "It'll take a few minutes to sort all the luggage and figure out what goes here and what goes to the church and what's too soaked to go anywhere."

I thought about my duffle bag and cast around the room for it. In the rush to load the buses and get on the road, I'd lost track of it. Gil's Bible was in there. . . .

Donetta batted a hand at her nephew, then pulled a pink suitcase from under his arm and set it on the floor. By the old wooden stairway in the back of the lobby, Ernest and Bluejay, also loaded down with luggage and under the field-marshaling of their mother, gave each other confused looks.

"Oh, don't worry about thay-ut, hon." Donetta turned on the sweet-as-molasses southern drawl, like she was trying to sell someone an apple pie. What exactly was going on here? "There's plenty of folks can take care of thay-ut. Ye-ew wouldn't mind escortin' Kai, here, on over to my house and gettin' her settled in the sewin' room, ri-ight? Just move them boxes of junk off the bed and carry them on out to the shed, oh-kaaay? I been gonna make rag rugs for the rummage sale—way-ul, I was, any-how, but I didn't get it done. Just move it out of there for now so Kai can have the room. Ye-ew think ye-ew can do thay-ut, dar-lin'?"

Kemp hesitated, as confused as I was by the obvious sales job. Donetta clearly had some ulterior motive, and even though I couldn't imagine what it was, I immediately felt guilty. There was work to do here. I should have been helping, and aside from that, Donetta's nephew was probably exhausted. His jeans and T-shirt were covered with mud, and his skin was chapped and windblown around a dark growth of razor stubble. His eyelids hung low over his eyes, the lashes touching bottom, then snapping open again. He looked like he was ready to crash somewhere, anywhere, and the sooner the better.

"Oh, listen, he doesn't have to . . ." His gaze caught mine, and the words went right out of my head. *To . . . to . . . to . . .* Up close, he had the most incredible eyes. A warm, rich hazel, not quite brown, not quite green, with thick black lashes. There was a little crinkle at the corners, as if he laughed often. He had tree shavings in his hair and just the littlest bit of sawdust in his eyebrows. His hair, which should have been almost black, was tipped with brown where water or perspiration had formed sawdust-encrusted curls.

It was an oddly appealing look—sort of lumberjack meets Calvin Klein.

"I can sleep . . ." I heard myself mumble. He smiled, and I lost the thought again. He had nice teeth, even. "Anywhere I . . ." The rest of the sentence left my head completely. My body, which only moments ago had been spongy with exhaustion, woke up all at once.

"Don't even bother arguing with her," he whispered, bending closer, so that the distance felt oddly intimate. "You'll never win."

Donetta pushed a puff of air past her lips, giving him the evil eye. "You just hush, Mr. Smartie. Kai's gotta be plumb wore out, and I can't leave here right now. I got folks to feed, and we need to decide who's stayin' in the hotel rooms upstairs and who'll bunk on a pallet downstairs, and who's stayin' down at the church. You can't put a whole busload a' people just any-place." Her gaze circled the interior of the old hotel lobby, tak-ing in the beauty shop, the small square of carpet surrounded by exercise equipment behind the old hotel counter, the empty space at the back by the main stairwell. "We might could put some air mattresses in here, it'd be more comfortable . . ." she muttered, then turned her attention back to Kemp and me.

"Now, there's plenty to eat at the house. Ye-ew just make yourself to home, hon. Kemp'll show ye-ew where everythang's at." Her southern drawl thickened again, like pudding setting up. "I just called over to the house and nobody answered, so you'll have it all to yourself, da-arlin'." A flash of emotion crossed her face, something uncharacteristically dark and sad. "I guess Ronald's gone down the river fishin', still." She pulled more luggage from Kemp's hands, stacking it on the floor. "Somebody else can take these up. Ye-ew just show Kai over to the house and get her settled ri-ight on in, y'hear?"

A familiar sense of uneasiness scratched the back of my neck, like the point of a sandbur, imbedded. Living in the kinds of places I had as a kid, it became a matter of instinct to be careful about people. When someone you barely knew offered you something or was overly nice to you, it was usually a trap. "Really, I'm fine. I can help here. You don't have to make special arrangements for me."

Lips pushing to one side, Kemp shook his head, rolling his gaze over to his aunt, as if he were waiting for the return volley in a Ping-Pong match. His eyes caught the light from the old chandeliers overhead and sparkled in a way that told me he was laughing on the inside. A voice in the back of my head said, *Kai Miller, what you arguing for? Talk about a welcome wagon!*

"No, now, hon, the sooner I can get some bodies out of here, the better. And it's the least I can do, bein' as you saved my li-ife. *Our* li-ives, even. All three of us gals. Now, don't worry about your little duffle bag, either. I know what it looks li-ike. I'll watch out for it and put it aside when it turns up." Donetta continued robbing Kemp of his luggage load. He didn't argue, just helped her make a pile on the floor. No sooner was the stack complete than Donetta's hand found the small of my back, and the next thing I knew, I was being herded through the crowd, out the front door, and onto the sidewalk, where Kemp quickly concluded that his truck had ended up trapped between the bus and Ernest's delivery van.

Donetta suggested we walk, since her house was only a few blocks away, and it was "such a ni-ice ni-ight." Tipping her head to one side, she stood on the sidewalk, watching the two of us like a painter studying a developing piece of work. "All the stars out and a big ol' moon. After so much time cooped up on the bus, a walk'll be just the tha-ang. Stretch yer legs." Her lips, still faintly red, with faded lipstick fanning into the creases, spread into a wide, self-satisfied smile. "Don't worry about a tha-ang, now. We got lots of help here." She grabbed me into a hug, rocked me back and forth, then cupped the sides of my face. "You know, a hurricane in the middle of our vacation ain't what I planned on, but my grandma used to say, 'Sometimes plans gone bad bring somethin' good.'"

Kemp chuckled. "You've got a whole busload of people to feed, Aunt Netta. What could be better than that?" He grinned and winked, and his aunt swatted at him.

"Kempner Rollins! You hush up."

"Yes, ma'am." Kemp's voice was smooth and southern, laced with a playful hint of sarcasm that was . . . well . . . cute.

"And don't be tellin' Kai no tales, either." Donetta gave him a stern look before turning back to me.

"I wouldn't think of it, Aunt Netta." In one quick movement, Kemp maneuvered around the bedraggled, yet still remarkably large, nest of hair and kissed his aunt on the cheek.

The corners of her mouth fluttered upward, and she shook her head with a look of reluctant adoration. "You hush, you rascal."

"Yes, ma'am," he answered again.

"Go on, now. Git." She shooed us off, and we proceeded to Ernest's truck to rescue my dogs, then started down Main Street with Radar and Hawkeye leading the way past the darkened windows of the Chamber of Commerce, Barlinger's Hardware, and an empty building where the window advertised *Television, Radio, and Small Engine Repair* in fading red paint.

"Not too many television repairmen around anymore," I commented, searching for something to say.

Kemp considered the window. "Nah, these days people just throw things away and buy new." The observation seemed to bother him, and he gazed into the store, his eyes sliding over the letters on the glass. "Mr. Mahnken had that store when I was a kid. He could fix just about anything, and what he couldn't fix, he parted out. Watched a little black-and-white TV behind the counter while he worked. Had an incredible memory. He could give you the play-by-play of every World Series for thirty years. He had bins of tubes and transistors from floor to ceiling, and he knew what was in each one. When his kids sold out the store after he died, there were parts for things that hadn't been used since World War II. The transistors ended up in the trash, but the antique dealers went wild over the hardware bins. Turned out they were worth more than all the stuff he'd worked so hard to save."

"That's kind of sad." Absently, I considered the life's work of a person and what it could amount to. Would somebody one day sort through all the rescued treasures in my jewelry bin and decide it was only junk?

Kemp shrugged. "Small town. Things change."

When we reached the end of the block, I glanced over my shoulder. Donetta, Imagene, and Lucy were standing on the sidewalk, watching us. As we turned the corner, I couldn't help feeling that they were still there, observing through the thick limestone walls of downtown Daily, or peering down via the eyes of the stone gargoyles atop the old bank building.

"Don't bother trying to figure them out." Kemp gave a sideways nod in the general direction of the hotel building, and I had the strangest sense of having my thoughts read. "It's like staring into the sun too long. It'll drive you insane."

"Your aunt is very sweet."

"Don't let her fool you." His eyes narrowed at the corners, and I could tell he was kidding. Mostly. "She's a force of nature."

"I had that feeling."

Past the bank building, the side street grew dark. I couldn't see Kemp's face, but I sensed that he was thinking about something. His chin was tipped upward, as if he were contemplating the slice of stars twinkling between the buildings. Beyond the rooftops, they spilled toward the horizon like bits of glass randomly tossed into a dark pool of water. In spite of all the ruin Glorietta had left behind just a few hours away, in Daily, Texas, it was a beautiful night. Even the dogs seemed relaxed and comfortable here. After days of being on edge, they now moved amiably, wagging their tails, sniffing the ground, and nipping playfully at each other.

Kemp and I walked for a while without talking. Around us, the air was soothing, filled with the scents of late summer— grass drying, roses blooming, pecan and pear trees making ready for harvest. Overhead, live oaks twittered in the breeze, the sound stirring memories like grains of pollen hidden in the grass from some summer long ago. Grandmother Miller's house had trees like those. At night, my father, Gil, and I used to lie under them. My father would talk about the stars and name the constellations, relating ancient Greek stories and staggering details about the time required for light to travel from those stars to our eyes. The stars we were looking at, he said, may have burned out long ago.

I thought he must have been the smartest man in the world, my father. In spite of our chaotic life, I did love him then. Over the years, I'd told myself I never felt that way.

"Penny for your thoughts." Kemp's voice was outside the swirl of memories, but even from a distance, the question felt intimate. We'd walked into a patch of moonlight, and he was watching me.

*I was thinking about my father.* For an instant, I was tempted to say it, but then I answered, "It's a beautiful place. Daily, I mean."

He drew back a little, seeming to doubt the answer.

"You're lucky to live here," I added.

He considered the statement, then shrugged. "Well, you know, the hometown always feels a little like an old shoe you haven't worn in a while. You can squeeze back into it, but it rubs in a place or two." He made it sound like a joke, but I had a feeling it wasn't.

*I wouldn't have any idea.* "I think it would be nice to have a place like that—one where you have history."

He laughed softly, the sound a bit rueful. "Be careful what you wish for." His voice lifted at the end of the words, but there was an edge underneath. It stirred my curiosity. Kemp wasn't the devil-may-care post-digger-riding hometown boy he appeared to be. There was more to him. Something deeper. Why I wanted to find it, I couldn't say. *That curiosity will be the death of you one of these days,* Grandmother Miller told me more than once. Usually, she said that right after Gil and I had tipped over the bookshelf by climbing on it, or slid down the stairway banister and discovered there was no way to stop at the end, or tried to jump a skateboard off the porch and landed headfirst in the flower bed. My parents encouraged creativity and experimentation—freedom. In their view, life was to be experienced, an adventure.

Grandmother Miller hated that view. *It's all well and good until you fall on the tile and skin your knee,* she'd point out.

Suddenly, I knew why Daily seemed comforting and familiar to me. The sights and scents here reminded me of McGregor. Despite the fact that our visits with Grandmother Miller were never voluntary, McGregor was the closest thing to a hometown I'd ever had. It was the only place we did the normal things people do—eat supper at a table, say grace over the food, go to bed intentionally instead of falling asleep in a lawn chair while the adults laughed and drank and told stories around a campfire. At Grandmother Miller's house, things were so predictable, the place felt like a box. *It's like being in a straitjacket here,* my father would complain. Then he'd bend close to us and whisper, *Just hang on a little longer, my little krauts. With any luck, we'll be out of here before church on Sunday. . . .*

Now, strolling the streets of Daily, Texas, I realized what I never would have admitted when my father tucked me into the big four-poster bed in the pink room where generations of Millers had lived and passed on. A part of me liked it. A part of me felt safe in the big bed, surrounded by the rose-paper walls. A part of me enjoyed the long table in the dining room and the way it felt to sit down to a meal in a place that couldn't be picked up and moved on a whim.

The realization was strange and startling even now, guilt-coated in a way I wouldn't have anticipated.

"Be careful what you take for granted." As soon as the words came out, I realized that I hadn't really meant to say them out loud.

"Touché." Kemp slapped a hand over his chest as if I'd wounded him. The sound made Hawkeye jump sideways. Kemp leaned over and patted him on the back. "I guess it's a little shallow to be complaining about my hometown when other people are wondering if theirs is still on the map."

I felt like an impolite guest, the kind who comes to your house for dinner and complains that the roast is too rare. He was, after all, walking me to his aunt's house in the middle of the night after having spent hours driving, sawing apart trees, moving debris from the road, and then driving again. "I'm sorry. I didn't mean it that way. I moved around a lot as a kid. We never had a hometown. That's all I was thinking."

"The grass is always greener," he assessed, and both of us laughed nervously.

We walked a little farther, past an old church and several turn-of-the-century clapboard houses. Some had been carefully restored, with lawns manicured, and some were weathered and sinking into the soil. Walking the street felt like a trip through time.

"So, your aunt told me you just moved back to Daily a few months ago," I said, starting the conversation again. "She seems really happy about it." He didn't respond at first, and I looked up at him, but we were walking in the shadow of a tree. I couldn't see his face, just little dapples of light sliding over his hair.

"Aunt Netta's dream was always that we'd all stay in Daily. She had a picture in her mind, and when Aunt Netta's got a vision, you'd better look out. When my sister, Lauren, was in college, the house next to Aunt Netta's came up for sale, and Aunt Netta was all set to take up a contract on it. She figured Lauren would need someplace to live when she got out of school. The thing is that Lauren had just been home a week before that and told us she had a boyfriend in Kansas, and she wanted to go to grad school there. You tell Aunt Netta something she doesn't want to hear, she just doesn't hear it. She likes to control things."

*She likes to control things . . .* My father's complaint about Grandmother Miller. *She has to control everything. . . .*

"She means well," Kemp added, and I felt reality shifting under me in a way my mind, tired and emotional now, couldn't quite grasp.

*What if Grandmother Miller meant well? What if I never understood, because I only knew one side of the story?*

Shaking off the past, I focused on the conversation. It was always easier to talk about other people's lives—something you could look at objectively. "You and your sister and Daily were all she talked about last night when we were in my van." Did Grandmother Miller talk about us when we were away? Did she miss us?

*Stop it. Stop. What's the point in thinking about her now? You're not a child anymore. You have your own life. You don't need any of them.*

I focused on Kemp again, on the present. "Your aunt loves you a lot."

"I know she does." His voice was tender, real. My shoulder brushed his, and I felt the warmth of his skin, the tight cords of muscle underneath. Then Radar smelled something in the ditch and tugged sideways, yanking me away.

Kemp reached for the leash. "Here, I'll take one."

I turned a half circle and gave him Hawkeye's lead, because handing over Radar seemed like a cruel thing to do to someone you'd just met. "So why did you move home? Back to Daily, I mean?"

"Coaching job came open at the school last winter. Baseball.

164

And they needed a math teacher, so here I am," he answered matter-of-factly, as if this were a question he'd been asked more than once. "Couldn't pitch after shoulder surgery, so I told them I'd come take it for the spring semester. Seemed like a way to help everyone out until I could go back to the team."

"Really?" I had a strange sense of déjà vu as we left the tree shadows and stepped into the moonlight again. My parents had always been baseball fans. In our travels, we'd spent countless afternoons in the cheap seats at ballparks. "Where did you play?"

Kemp raised a brow. "You're a baseball fan?"

"I've spent my share of time at dollar-hot-dog nights."

His chin twisted upward and away, as if he were trying to get a better view of me. "You don't seem like a dollar-hot-dog-night kind of girl."

Somehow, that felt like a compliment. "I might surprise you. So where did you play?"

"Frisco, mostly. The RoughRiders. The Rangers off and on when I got called up."

"Wow. Major league." Suddenly it occurred to me that there might be a reason he looked familiar. "Maybe I've seen you play before."

He laughed softly. "I doubt it. I never stayed with the big club a whole season. Would have my last year, if it hadn't been for the shoulder injury, anyway."

A cat ran across the road, and whatever else Kemp was going to say was eclipsed by the dogs barking and Radar tugging at his leash, gagging and yapping. "Radar!" I scolded, but he wouldn't stop. I held on while he lurched forward, propelling me through a ditch and into someone's yard as the cat disappeared under the porch of an old two-story house.

"Ssshhh!" I scolded. "Radar, stop!" But Radar, being Radar, couldn't resist the chase.

A light came on in the house, and I threw my weight against the leash, trying to drag Don's obnoxious dog back to the street. Any minute now, someone would come out with a shotgun, and, having survived the hurricane, I'd end up as a tragic fatality, mistaken for a burglar.

Reeling Radar in, I reached for his collar, but just as my fingers touched it, his quarry bolted from under the porch, ran past us, and scampered up a tree. Radar hung a U-turn, spun me like a jewelry box ballerina, and I ended up on the ground doing the splits with the leash wrapped around my ankle. In the house, more lights came on.

"Who's out there?" a woman screeched from behind one of the darkened screens upstairs. "What's going on?"

"Nothing, Miss Peach." Kemp was laughing when he and Hawkeye caught up with me.

"Kempner Eldridge, is that you?"

"Yes, ma'am."

"Is that *aunt* of yours having a *party* again?" *Party* came out in an obvious hail of spit.

"No, ma'am." I felt Hawkeye licking my face and Kemp's hand on my ankle, unwinding the leash. He was laughing so hard he could barely function.

"Y'all quit that racket. Get off my property or I'll make a citizen's arrest!" the voice screeched. I saw a face in the window, ghostly pale with no sign of a body attached to it, and then the blind slapped shut.

Kemp grabbed my hand and pulled me to my feet. "Come on!" he whispered against my ear. Laughing, he tugged my hand, and we bolted across the lawn, jumped the ditch, and ran down the street with the dogs barking and lights coming on. We didn't stop until we reached an old two-story house at the end of the road. By then, I was breathless, and Kemp was laughing so hard he could only force out one word at a time.

"It's . . . been . . . a . . . while . . ." he coughed out, doubling over as he opened the backyard gate so we could put the dogs inside. I gathered that we'd arrived at Donetta's house.

After closing the gate, Kemp led me into the house through the carport door. When the kitchen light flickered on, he was leaning against the doorframe, red-faced, his eyes glittering wet at the corners. "Sorry . . ." he gasped out. "It's . . . been a . . . while . . . since I've . . . since I've . . . been citizen's arrested . . . by Miss Peach." Wiping his eyes with his thumb and forefinger, he opened the refrigerator and started looking for food, then stopped and leaned on the door handle, doubling over in another fit of hilarity. He had a great laugh—the kind that made you laugh along, even if you weren't in on the joke.

"I gather this is something that's happened before?" I inquired.

Kemp worked to catch his breath. "We gave Aunt Netta some gray hairs," he admitted, then wiped his eyes again and started pulling Corningware from the refrigerator, reading the labels and describing the contents. "Let's see . . . We've got meat loaf, chicken and rice, King Ranch casserole, red beans, and some kind of mystery stuff with noodles and hamburger in it. . . ."

"You pick. I could eat just about anything."

"Lady's choice." He looked over his shoulder with a smile that landed somewhere in the pit of my stomach and fluttered around like a butterfly hopping from flower to flower. "Pop something in the microwave, and I'll go get the dogs some food and water, and clean off your bed. Aunt Netta's probably got some kibble in the storage shed. If there's a stray around, she'll feed it."

He headed toward the laundry room off the kitchen. I stood watching him go, oddly fascinated with . . . well . . . the way he looked walking into the laundry room.

Slipping out the door, he caught me watching.

"Sure you don't care which one I pick?" I asked, holding up a dish of leftovers as camouflage.

"No, ma'am. I'm game for anything." He winked, then went outside. In a few minutes, I heard him come in the front door, then head upstairs, and the ceiling emitted a series of dull thumps as he moved things around overhead. By the time I was finished with the microwave, the noise upstairs had gone silent.

I made two plates of chicken and rice, poured tea from the refrigerator, and set it on the enamel-topped table in the middle of the kitchen, then sat waiting, but there was no sign of Kemp. Finally, I went upstairs looking for him.

I found him in what was obviously the sewing room, cross-ways on the bed that was supposed to be mine, with his head hanging off one side and his cowboy boots hanging off the other.

Sound asleep.

# Chapter 15

## *Donetta Bradford*

When you live in a place, most of the time you take it for granted. You get impatient with the way folks are, and sometimes having them around feels like an old suit of clothes you've worn so much you're tired of it. You think, *I need somethin' different. I need a adventure someplace else.* Maybe that's what my daddy had in his mind when he run off into the world like the Prodigal Son.

Could be it takes something like a storm blowing through to put a shine back on the things you look right past every day. When Glorietta blew me and the gals back to Daily, our little hometown sure had a shine on it. The Daily folk come out for us like we were the stars of a ticker tape parade!

I said a little prayer of thanks, and then, of course, I got to work. When you been given a busload of people to feed and bed down, you can't sit around prayin' for long. One thing you can count on in our little town is that we know how to roll out the Daily hospitality. Usually, everybody'll get involved, and just about everybody sure did on this night. Pastor Harve and his bunch from the little church out on Caney Creek cooked up a mess of barbecue, the Methodist ladies made dessert, and the Presbyterians brought over drinks and ice, while the Baptist men cleaned out space in the fellowship hall there and started laying out air mattresses.

Meantime, Betty Prine and that snooty bunch from the Daily Literary Society didn't do anything except send over a plate of cookies someone'd took out of their freezer. They put a big ol' sign on them that said *Compliments of the Daily Literary Society* so everybody'd know they'd pitched in. Not a one of them showed up to help.

We got all the guests fixed up for the night without the Literary Society pitching in, anyhow. Even though it was gonna be close quarters, it was better than them shelters in Dallas. On the TV, they were talking about how the shelters were packed to overflowing, and every hotel full, too. The reports about the storm didn't look good, either. They showed flooding and power lines down, and buildings knocked flat to rubble some places. Down on I-10, there was a house sittin' smack in the middle of the interstate—a whole house, just like in *The Wizard of Oz*. Sounded like it might be weeks before the roads were all cleared and the power was back on. After one of the stations showed high water levels down around Landee Bayou, Sister Mona fell on her knees and started cryin', and I knew she was afraid they wouldn't have much to go home to.

Somethin' like that'll sure make you look around at your old suit of clothes and be grateful for it, I'll tell you. Before Imagene, Lucy, and me parted ways, the three of us hugged so hard we sounded like the lunch rush at the old folks' home—bones and joints crackling and poppin' all over the place.

"Ronald'd be here if he knew," Imagene whispered close to my ear. I guess she'd seen me call home earlier to check if Ronald was back.

I just nodded and hugged Imagene again and sent her on her way, then I went back in the shop and finished cleaning up the last of the food and sweeping the floor by the door, where everybody'd tracked in mud. Finally, I hunted down Kai's duffle bag so I could take it home to her. Once that was in hand, I couldn't find anything else to do, and Sister Mona was trying to chase me out the door. "I'm'ma say you oughta get on home and get some sleep, cher," she said from the stairs while she was helping old Obeline up to the second floor to bed. "Hooo-ee! You gotta be tired."

"I don't sleep much." I knew when I got home I'd just lay around with my eyes sprung open. So many things were on my mind that it just kept spinning merry-go-round style, questions and worries goin' up and down like iron horses, popping in and out of sight.

My thoughts kept whirlin' while I was telling Sister Mona good-night and headin' home. *Guess Ronald just planned to take off down the river the whole time I was gone on my cruise.* The thought hurt me in a deep, tender place I didn't let myself go very often. *Least he coulda told me, so I wouldn'ta bothered to fix all that food and leave it in the refrigerator. . . .*

I felt low, walking in the door, and I was glad Kai was there and the place wasn't empty. Inside the house, the TV was on the Weather Channel and Kai was on the sofa, fast asleep. She still had her shoes right by her, like she hadn't moved far since she come in. She must've showered, though, because her hair was laying over her shoulder in long, silky blond strands and she was wearing an old T-shirt and sweats that'd been sitting in the rag pile by the washing machine. Poor thing. Kemp should've found her some better clothes to change into than that. What in the world was he thinkin'?

As soon as I got to the sewing room, I answered my own question. There was Kemp, flopped out across the bed with one leg hanging off and his head dangling. I knew right away what'd happened. That boy'd laid down there when he was moving the boxes, and that was all she wrote. Kemp could fall asleep quicker than any normal human. Once he did it, you couldn't wake him up, either. Those fellas he played with on the baseball teams pulled all kinds of tricks on him. They'd pick him up and put him in the hotel lobby, or throw him in the pool, or cart him to the ball field and lay him out on home plate. One time, he woke up in a car headed to the beach in the dead of winter. He pretended to stay asleep until they got there, and then he surprised the boys and pushed the rest of them in the freezing water. Kemp could give as good as he got, usually.

Somebody—Kai, I guessed—had covered him with a blanket, which was real sweet, considerin' he took her bed.

I looked at that boy and shook my head, thinking, *Some Prince Charming you turned out to be. Left the girl to sleep on the sofa and here you are in the bed.* Honestly, if that boy ever found a girl who'd put up with him, it'd be a miracle. Over the years, there'd been a lot of gals gawk at Kemp the way Kai did yesterday. He was a looker. Always had been. Most of the way through high school, and even after that, he was mixed up with the gal next door, Jenny Mayfield, but he was goofy as a bat and his mind always turned back to baseball, and after a while that drove every girl crazy, even Jenny. When it comes right down to it, a gal wants to be more important than a game.

You couldn't explain that to Kemp, though. He was just like his daddy. Stubborn as the day is long. All my brother could see as a young man was rodeo—right up until the minute he walked into a street dance and met Kemp's mama, and he couldn't get a ring on her quick enough. After she died, he just went back to rodeo, dragging Lauren and Kemp along behind him. Maybe that was why Kemp had such a vagabond way about him. He never minded all that traveling around with the baseball teams, and he was willin' to go through surgery after surgery and spend his evenings with his elbow in a bucket of ice water just to keep his arm going.

It's hard to get a girl when you have a bucket of ice water stuck on your arm. I told him that a time or two, but he didn't listen. *Aunt Netta, right now I've got my mind on the game,* he'd say.

So far, Kemp was good at baseball, but that boy was a wash-out in terms of producing chubby-cheeked babies for me to bounce on my knee. At least his sister looked promising since she'd fell head over heels and moved out to California to be near her beau, Nate Heath. I figured any time now I'd be hearing they'd decided to slip off to one of them Elvis wedding chapels in Las Vegas and tie the knot.

Looking at Kemp, asleep there with his boots on and his mouth hanging open, I had a feeling it wasn't gonna be near as easy with him. But then, matchmaking ain't a business for the fainthearted. A real matchmaker's gotta like a challenge.

I pulled Kemp's boots off and pushed his leg up onto the bed, then took off his cap and hung it on the post. He mumbled "Go to second! Go to second!" in his sleep, and I just patted him and kissed his forehead, the way I used to years ago. I went off to bed, wondering what in the world was gonna happen when it was time for spring training and he got the bug again. After the last surgery, the doctors told him if he hurt the arm again, there wouldn't be a thing they could do for it, and it could cause him trouble all his life, and he wouldn't even be able to throw batting practice for the high-school kids. I didn't want to see him get his hopes set on pro ball, then end up crushed one more time. At least right now, he had the coaching job at Daily High. If he went back and tried the minors again, he might end up with nothing at all.

When I put on my nightclothes and slipped into bed, I didn't feel snug and happy to be home, like I thought I would. A case of the blues slipped over me, and I laid there with it sitting on my chest like a overweight house cat. In a minute, I understood why.

I was lonesome in my own house. And I had been for a long time.

The clock downstairs struck four in the morning, and outside the dogs were barking when I finally closed my eyes. The sound took my mind away to the bayou, where Mamee's old hounds stood at the edge of the water and howled at the johnboats passing by. Off in the swamp, other dogs answered as their masters gathered their gator gigs and crawdad seines, and headed out to gather up what the bayou had to give. Mamee was beside me on the porch. She closed her eyes, deep and black as the shadows themselves, and took in air that hung heavy with damp soil and Spanish moss, and saltwater flowin' in the Gulf. Around us, the bayou sang a lullaby of wind and cypress, callin' me home to the dogleg and my mama's people.

I could hear Mamee singing on the hill where the two big magnolia trees framed the lane. I knew the story of those trees— one was planted the day my grandparents married, to celebrate their weddin', and the other was planted when their baby girl, my mama, was born. Mamee's folks'd always figured she'd marry that boy from the next farm and join the places together, so I always imagined that first magnolia tree was planted on a happy day, but after Mamee told me about Macerio, I wondered.

In my dream, she tried to say something, but I couldn't hear her. The wind whipped her voice away. It pulled me back, and back, and back, until Mamee was small, like a little doll under those big ol' trees. Her hands were cupped to her mouth, but the storm had turned to a hurricane, rain and wind washin' away everything.

My body jerked, and I knew I was in my bed. Mamee's voice, the homeplace, the rice field were gone. The dream faded, and I slipped deeper into the dark, into a quiet place where I couldn't see the magnolia trees or the field. I slid into the watery silence. I wanted to stay there, to float in the black still, as Mamee called it. She sang an old song sometimes about a young chambermaid who lost her master in battle. When the girl heard about his death, she laid on his bed, closed her eyes, drifted into the black still, and never rose again.

In the mornin', I woke up feeling like maybe home was a dream, and sooner or later I'd open my eyes and find myself still in the old hurricane church, or on the bus, or in the van, or maybe just getting ready to head off with Imagene and Lucy on the cruise. Maybe we hadn't even left yet and I'd dreamed the whole hurricane and Kai, Ernest and his hound dog, and the bus. It was like something I'd dream, us ending up in such a spot, and then the men from Daily coming in to rescue us. On Pearly Parsons' post-auger truck, of all things.

Kemp riding up top of the post drill with a chain saw in his hand . . .

Heavens to Betsy!

Imagene and Lucy would get a laugh out of this for sure. When we headed off on our cruise today, I'd tell them all about it.

The microwave beeped in the kitchen, the pans rattled, and I realized I was smelling something. Coffee. I smelled coffee. I could hear the pot gurglin'.

No way Ronald would be up getting in the cookware or running the coffee maker. Far as I could ever tell, he didn't even know where the water went in that thing.

What in the world . . .

I got up, zipped on my old housedress, and trundled across the floor. My legs were stiff—more than usual—and my body ached like I'd danced the jitterbug with a market steer. Right by my bedroom door, in a neat little stack near the hamper, was a pile of muddy clothes. The ones I'd laid out to start off on our cruise.

I stood looking at them, thinking, *That wasn't any dream, Donetta. All that really happened.* Right then, I looked back at the clock by the bed. *Good gravy! Here you are sleepin' in past six thirty and you got people to feed!*

When I got to the hall by the kitchen, I heard voices. Kemp's and Kai's. Then the sizzle of bacon hitting the pan. Six slices, and the pan was too hot.

"Ouch!" Kemp must've been standing too close to the stove.

"Turn the burner down some." Kai's voice had a little laugh in it, so that I wondered what they'd been talking about before I got within earshot. I stopped there in the hall, but I wasn't eavesdropping.

Really, I wasn't.

It was research.

"Ouch! Shoot! Dadgumit!" Kemp said again. I smelled bacon smoke. That bacon would be black around the edges when he got done with it.

"Are you sure you're qualified to operate that thing?"

*Well, isn't she a sassy little miss this mornin'? I didn't think she had it in her.*

"I'll have you know I come from a distinguished line of culinary experts."

*Listen at him with all the big words. Culinary experts! That boy couldn't cook his way out of a TV dinner tray.* The only thing Kemp knew about cooking was how to put a hot dog on a fork at deer camp. If it wasn't for me feeding him, he'da starved to death after he moved back to Daily, probably.

"Want to do the biscuits instead?" Kai offered, and there was a big heap of sugar in that voice. "They have instructions on the can."

"Very funny." My boy turned the bacon and said, "Ouch!

Dadgumit!" again. "I've seen this done before." My, but *he* was laying on the charm this mornin'. Good for him, but if he thought he was ever gonna impress a gal with his cooking . . . well . . . that boy was what we used to call *good lookin' but no good at cookin'*.

"It's harder than it seems," he said, making excuses.

"Lots of things are." I heard the silverware drawer rattling, and after a minute she started to giggle.

"What's so funny?" he asked.

She giggled some more. "I can't get the biscuits open, either."

*Good gravy, the girl can't even open a can of whop biscuits. Even Ronald can do that.* The only reason I had those canned biscuits in the fridge was so if Ronald got hungry for food cooked fresh, there'd be something he could make.

Surely even Kemp knew enough to cook them things. The boy had survived on his own through four years at college and six years playing baseball.

"I thought you said the biscuits came with instructions."

*Maybe he don't. Maybe he don't know how to operate a biscuit can. Dear me.*

"It says 'Push at seam with knife,'" she pointed out. "I'm pushing at the seam with a knife, but nothing's happening."

I took a step closer to the kitchen. My fingers started twitching. I wanted to get my hands on the cooking.

"Here, like this," I heard Kemp say, and then *smack*, he whopped that biscuit can on the counter and *boom*, it exploded open.

"Holy mackerel!" Kai sounded impressed. "Is it supposed to do that?"

"You're kidding, right?" His voice was low, like they were standing real close.

"About the biscuits?" It didn't sound like she was talking about biscuits at all. That kind of voice said, *Hey there, handsome.*

"Yeah . . . the . . . uhhh . . . biscuits."

*Forget breakfast, son, you got a live one in the pan. Turn up the heat. . . .*

Nobody said anything for a minute, and if it wasn't for that squeaky board in the kitchen doorway, I'da tiptoed up and peeked around the corner.

"You know, you don't exactly . . . cook for yourself . . . on a cruise ship." Her voice was breathless and heavy.

"Guess not."

"Actually, I don't know anything about cooking."

"Yeah, me either."

"Really? I couldn't tell." Kai's laugh was soft and low, and so was his. I took a step back toward my room, since it sounded so cozy in there. Might be the best thing I could do was go on back to bed so as not to ruin what was cookin' in the kitchen, all on its own.

I heard biscuits slapping into the dish and Kai giggling again. "Whose idea was it to make breakfast, anyway?"

"Yours."

Kai gave a cute little cough. "Mine?"

"You said the least I could do was cook you breakfast."

"Well, you did steal my bed."

Things got quiet again, and I made myself take another step backward. A good matchmaker knows that sometimes the best thing to do is just get out of the way. There was some cookin' going on in the kitchen. It didn't have much to do with food, but there was some cookin' going on. I could feel the heat all the way down the hall.

I could even smell the smoke.

Oh heavens!

I really did smell smoke.

## Chapter 16

# *Kai Miller*

The black cloud billowing down the hall must have awakened Donetta, because by the time the smoke detector went off, she was in the kitchen.

"Good gravy!" she gasped, yanking the flaming pot off the stove. "Y'all don't have to cook. I'da done it." That was probably a nice way of saying, *Get out of my kitchen before you blow something up.* She was actually pretty calm, considering that we'd almost burned the place down. "Watch out, hon," she warned as she took the flaming pot and headed for the carport door.

I looked at Kemp, and he shrugged with his palms raised, then picked up the bacon box and looked at the label, as if this were somehow the bacon's fault. "Guess we could start over." He opened the cabinet, searching for another pan.

Donetta had other ideas, and one thing I'd learned about Donetta in our short time together was that her ideas became your ideas whether you planned for them to or not. She wanted Kemp and me to get dressed and go have breakfast at the Daily

Café, even though it was only a little after six thirty, and as Kemp pointed out, the café didn't open until seven.

"Now, hon," she admonished. "You know that's just for regular folks. We ain't regular."

Kemp's lips curved into a smirk. "They've got medication for that now."

Bracing a hand on her hip, his aunt hiked up one side of her housedress, revealing a skinny white leg with a fuzzy sock balled at the bottom. "Kempner Rollins, you just quit that being smart, y'hear?" She grabbed a wooden spatula and shook it at him, spraying bacon grease across the kitchen. "I'm about ready to medication you."

"Yes, ma'am."

"I mean it. Now, I got to fix some pecan rolls and a big ol' egg casserole for the folks at the hotel, and I don't need anybody messin' around my kitchen. You put down that bacon."

"Aye, aye, Cap'n." His lips twitched at the corners, and there was a playful twinkle in his eye as he slid the box onto the counter and backed away with his hands in the air, surrendering it like contraband.

"It's too early for you to be wartin' me." Donetta's frown cracked around the edges as she turned to the stove to assess the mini-disaster Kemp had left behind. Snorting, she waved the spatula over her shoulder, then swiped it on the towel Kemp had used to try to beat out the flames. "You just got to ignore him, Kai. He's *always* been a pill. Got too much of his father in him, and besides that, he grew up hangin' around the beauty shop with all them ladies wrapped around his little pinkie finger. Wasn't a day went by those women didn't bring him cookies, or penny candy from the grocery, or give him a quarter to run down and ride the little horse out front of the hardware store. He's ruint."

Nodding gravely, I pretended to now have an understanding of Kemp's devil-may-care personality. "So that's how it happened."

Kemp flashed me a wide-eyed look, as in, *Excuse me, but who figured out the biscuit can?* "Aunt Netta, you know those ladies didn't mean anything to me." He produced a wounded tone, which she rewarded with a rotational swipe of the bacon spatula, ringing his stomach like a tightly wrapped drum.

"You hush up now and take this gal for somethin' to eat. I got to get my food down to the hotel the same time as everyone else's casseroles, and to get that done, I need you out from underfoot."

"I could stay and help," I offered, because it didn't seem right to leave her here to do the work by herself.

"Oh, *no*," Donetta's eyes widened, as if she were aware that I was about as much use in the kitchen as a buzz saw. "I do my best cookin' on my own. You just go on and do whatever you need to do. There's some exercise suits in the closet by the bathroom upstairs. They found your bag last night, but everything's soakin' wet in it. I just dropped it there by the washer. We can get that stuff laundered up today. Those exercise suits of mine'll be kind of big, tiny as you are, but at least they're clean and dry. Kemp, them clothes you forgot here when you changed for the church banquet are on the dryer, folded. I washed up your tennis shoes, too. Them things had a gallon of ball field dirt inside, I'll tell you. Run out and check on Kai's dogs while you're back there, all ri-ight, Pickle-poo?"

*Pickle-poo?* I quirked a brow at the nickname, but Kemp just ignored me, gave a good-natured shrug, and headed for the door. I caught myself watching him go, and then I caught Donetta watching me watch him go. I blushed and muttered, "I'll be upstairs."

"There's some hairdryers and brushes and things of Lauren's there in the bathroom drawer, hon," she called after me, her voice honey coated again. "Ye-ew just help yourself to anythin' you need, darlin'."

"Thanks," I said, then circled through the laundry room to check my duffle bag. Just as Donetta had assessed, the clothes were a mess—soggy and smelly from muddy water that had seeped through the walls of the old church. But in the dry pocket, Gil's Bible and my personal papers were safe. Taking the little packet of things that actually mattered, I went upstairs while Donetta hummed happily in the kitchen, pleased to have the place all to herself again.

It occurred to me, while I was tucking my belongings into a bathroom drawer, then selecting an eighties-era green and purple windsuit from Donetta's closet, that Kemp probably had things on his agenda today, other than shuttling me around and baby-sitting Don's dogs. Here in Daily, life was going on as normal. People had jobs to do and business to take care of. The polite thing would be to offer him an out. There wasn't, after all, much chance of my getting lost in Daily, Texas.

When I came back downstairs, Kemp was sitting on a stool with a cup of coffee, watching his aunt roll out dough on the counter. His hair was slicked back in dark, wet curls, and he'd traded the sawdust-covered jeans and boots for a gray T-shirt that brought out the little silver flecks in his hazel eyes, silky black athletic shorts that had a Daily Dawgs logo on one leg, and sparkling white freshly washed Nikes. Today, he looked like a coach instead of a cowboy-lumberjack.

". . . not on Satur-dey, surely?" Donetta was saying, and I stopped in the doorway, counting the days in my head. Was it really only Saturday? It seemed weeks had passed since I left Perdida. Last night when I'd used Donetta's phone to call Maggie and Meredith, it felt like I was checking in with people I hadn't seen in a month. It was hard to know what to say, except that I was safe. None of us could tell much about Perdida from the weather reports. Glorietta had hit a bit west, so there was some hope, but with a ten-foot storm surge and flooding rains, at least some of the historic district and other low-lying areas of Perdida would be under water. Depending on how well the seawalls and the Geotube held out, the stores and homes along the beach might or might not have made it through. So far, there was no news of Don, but as Maggie put it, he'd lived there thirty years. He knew what to do. The M&Ms were trying to call him and other contacts in Perdida every few hours, but right now there was no communication. As soon as they learned anything, they'd let me know.

In the kitchen, Kemp answered his aunt's question. "Need to go by and open the field house. Got kids coming in for a workout."

"Ffff!" Tension puffed into the air like a cloud of flour. "Why can't Coach Groves do that? Why's it always you that's got to do extra?"

I stood in the doorway, feeling like an eavesdropper and thinking, *Maybe I should make a noise or something.* At the same time, the bit of ongoing drama involving Kemp had my attention. Or maybe I was just looking for a reason to deny the obvious evidence that he really did have other things to do today.

He calmly took a sip of his coffee. "It's not a problem."

"He *always* leaves you to do it. It ain't right."

"It's not a problem," Kemp said again, and glanced out the window, as if the needs of the day had floated by and caught his eye. "I'm the new guy, remember?"

"Groves is probably down at the river with a fishin' pole in one hand and a big ol' cup of coffee in the other. Him and Ronald are probably out there together. Nobody worryin' about whether they're needed to home."

Kemp's lips pursed speculatively. "I could drive down the river later and look for Uncle Ronald—let him know what's going on. Most likely, he's camped past Boggy Bend or Rock Island."

Donetta smacked a spoon against the edge of the bowl. "If he was worried about it, I guess he'd check in. Wouldn't be too hard to figure out there's been a hurricane."

"There's no radio in the boat, Aunt Netta, and you know he won't carry a cell phone."

"Ffff!"

Tiny worry lines gathered between Kemp's eyebrows as he studied his aunt.

*So Pickle-poo does have a serious side.* The thought caught my interest. In my line of work, I met too many fun-but-flaky guys who were suffering from Peter Pan syndrome. Those bumming-around-the-beaches-of-Never-Neverland vagabond types always reminded me of my father.

I tiptoed back down the hall, then came in again, making noise this time. Both Donetta and Kemp turned my way. "So, listen," I said, "I think I'll just take the dogs for a walk and grab something at the convenience store. I know you both have things to do today. I've held you up enough already." Suddenly I felt like the dorky cousin from Hackensack—the one your mother forces you to take along to the drive-in, where your real friends hang out.

Donetta turned apologetically to me. "Kai . . . darlin' . . ." Stretching the words and coating them with honey, she gave me a remorseful look. "I'm sorry I don't have anybody better than this rotten rascal to take ye-ew for some breakfast. It's the best I can do on short notice, thay-uts's all. Really, there's plenty of ni-ice people in this town that don't give their poor old aunts gray hairs, but he's all I can come up with ri-ight now. If you get down to the café and you find someone better, just chuck him into the river."

Kemp slid off his stool, crossed the kitchen, and opened the carport door. "Ready?"

All of a sudden, I was. I didn't care if he had other things to do, or if his aunt was trying to get me out of her kitchen, or if I looked like a dork in the oversized purple windsuit with the rolled-up cuffs. My head did a giddy little twirl as I slipped out the door and crossed the carport, passing the cooling bacon pan on the way.

"I feel bad, leaving her with a mess to clean up," I said, really just to make conversation. Obviously, I didn't feel too bad to wander off to breakfast with Kemp. I also wasn't terribly burdened with guilt over the fact that I hadn't even checked on the dogs this morning. *They'll be all right,* the happy voice in my head was saying.

"You try to go back in that kitchen, you'll be in mortal danger." Sliding his hands into his pockets, he slanted a glance down at me. Something tugged and jittered in my stomach. "Don't let that sweet-little-old-lady act fool you. Behind that heart of gold there's an agenda. Always." The words were matter-of-fact—not a complaint, exactly, but a slightly weary observation. I had the unusual urge to probe into it. Normally, I let people keep their stuff in their boxes, and I kept my stuff in mine. Everything calm and cordial. Nothing too personal.

"An agenda?"

He shrugged, as if it were elementary. "Aunt Netta's a natural-born mother hen. My dad is her little brother. She mothered him, right along with the rest of us, after my mom passed. Or at least she tried to. Dad always had a wild streak."

"I hear it runs in the family."

He winced as if I'd injured him. "Ouch. I'm wounded." He actually had a little bit of a pout lip, if you looked closely. How cute.

"You don't *look* wounded, Pickle-poo." I paused to eyeball Miss Peach's house as we came closer. The place was quiet this morning.

"I hide it well." The comment swiveled my attention, and for a moment, I felt the pull of something just beneath the surface. He was gazing up into the trees, so I took advantage of the moment to observe him. I could see his dad in him—Frank's square chin with the cleft in the middle, Frank's straight, dark eyebrows—but I could also see Donetta. He had his aunt's slightly crooked grin, her tall, lean build. I imagined what he must have looked like as a little boy, with the chin dimple and the precocious light in his hazel eyes. No wonder he had all the ladies in the beauty shop wrapped around his little finger.

"So, where does that nickname come from, Pickle-poo?"

Kemp scratched his chin, shaking his head sheepishly. "Depends on who you ask."

That was a vague answer, and of course it intrigued me. "Really? How so?"

Shrugging, he snaked a hand out and plucked a feathery stalk of grass growing from a crack in the edge of the road. "In my family, nicknames are like birthmarks. Everybody gets one shortly after arriving in the maternity ward, and they don't wear off easily. Pickle is a baseball term—you know, getting caught in the pickle—getting stuck between bases?"

He cut a quick downward glance, as if he were wondering whether I was buying.

"So the nickname comes from baseball?"

"Sure," he said, tossing the grass over his shoulder. "Of course."

"And you've been playing baseball since shortly after arriving in the maternity ward?" Having grown up around cheats and con-men, I knew how to sniff out a snow job. "Why do I have the feeling that if I asked your aunt, she'd tell me something different?"

He shrugged, watching a cardinal fly over. "Oh, she'd probably come up with some implausible story about how I arrived in this world with a face like a grouchy old man, and the doctor said, 'Looks like this one's been eatin' sour pickles.' But she'd be wrong, of course. It's a baseball term."

"I'm sure it is," I said, and he just shook his head at me. "So, what was it like, growing up as Pickle-poo?" My own question surprised me. I never ever brought up childhood, because the next logical step, after someone shared theirs, was for them to ask about mine. There was no way to cast an attractive light on my trailer-trash past. It was so much easier just to steer conversations in a different direction.

"It was good." Kemp punctuated the answer with a nod, pressing his lips together as if he were trying to decide whether the word tasted right. "Quiet. Small town, you know, you sort of have to make your own fun. Everybody's into everybody's business, so most of the time our fun got us caught. My dad pioneered every available form of trouble in Daily, anyway. He usually knew what we were up to before *we* did. His philosophy was, You step in a mess, you clean it off your own boots."

"That's cute—'clean it off your own boots.'"

He gave me a lopsided grin. "Thanks. I specialize in cute. My sister's the serious one. That pretty much freed me up to be a goof-off."

*Goof-off* wasn't at all the term I would have picked for him. "You must have been serious about baseball." As soon as the sentence came out, the change in his expression told me I'd opened the wrong door. "I mean, it's a huge accomplishment, making it to the majors. Not many people manage that."

Slipping his hands into his pockets, he pushed both shoulders up like he was trying not to think about it too hard. "My dad always said when you love something, it doesn't feel like work. I love baseball."

"Everybody has something they feel that way about, I think." It occurred to me that the way he felt about baseball was the way I felt about Gifts From the Sea. I couldn't wait to walk the beaches in the mornings, or comb the port markets when I had the chance to debark in Mexico, the island markets of the Caribbean, or points beyond. Every journey was a treasure hunt, a chance to bring home found objects and create something from nothing. It never felt like work. "You're lucky if you get to do it for a living, though."

"True enough," he agreed, flicking a sidelong glance at me. "So, what about you, what's your game?"

His gaze unnerved me. I should have been prepared for my question to ricochet, but I wasn't. "Cooking," I joked.

"No . . . seriously."

"Thanks a lot!" I pretended to be shocked, but I wasn't. Short of boxes, cans, hot dogs, and McDonald's bags, my mother never cooked anything, nor did she have any interest in teaching me. "Your aunt's right. You are a pea-ul," I said, imitating the way Donetta pronounced *pill*, in two long syllables.

He chuckled softly, and I liked the way it sounded. "Okay, actually, I do *have* a kitchen, but I use it for a studio." Every square inch of counter space in my apartment was, typically, covered with tools, supplies, and several small vices I'd mounted on the side of the cabinet, to Don's dismay. "The last few years I've been getting an art jewelry business going. Perdida's a good place for it. Lots of tourists canvassing the shops, looking to take something back from vacation." Home flashed through my mind, and a sick feeling settled in my stomach. "There were, anyway."

Kemp, of course, was oblivious to the jumble of thoughts in my head. "Jewelry . . . so you're an artsy type?"

*Artsy type.* A strange way to think of myself. My parents, being free spirits, abhorred labels. "I guess so. I love creating things. It's interesting, gathering objects from different places— beach glass, stones, beads, fossils, pieces of coral or whatever, and seeing how they fit together. You never know what the tide will turn up. There's something poetic about it."

Kemp chewed the side of his lip. "An artsy type," he confirmed. "I should have guessed that."

I wasn't sure whether to feel insulted or affirmed. "Why?"

"You're different."

I wondered if he was seeing the raggedy trailer-camp girl the town kids made fun of at the carnival—the weirdo they all thought came from another planet. I'd always hated the fact that we were different. I wanted to be like the normal kids—normal house, normal town, normal parents, clothes that actually matched and didn't come from the Goodwill store.

Kemp didn't have any way of knowing that, of course.

"Different, how?" Although maybe I didn't want to know.

"I'm not sure yet."

"That isn't an answer. You can't tell a girl she's weird and then just leave it at that." For some inexplicable reason, my breath caught as I waited for his reply, and I felt my gaze tangle with his. I wanted to know what he saw when he looked at me.

"I didn't say weird. I said different, as in—"

A commotion behind us halted the sentence just as it was about to get interesting. Kemp and I spun around so quickly we collided with each other. The zipper of my borrowed windsuit caught the hem of his T-shirt, and we were attached at the hip as Miss Peach's gray cat streaked up the street. Radar was hot on her tail, bellowing like a foxhound on the hunt.

"Radar!" I gasped.

"How did he get out?" Kemp disengaged my jacket from his shirt by ripping them apart just as the cat made it to Miss Peach's yard and ducked through the narrow crack between the doors of an old garage. Radar, who was too large for the crack, collided with the opening at full force, propelled himself halfway through, hung there a moment with his back legs churning up gravel, then succeeded in bending the entire door inward. Wood cracked, hinges squealed, and the dog disappeared inside the garage.

"Whoa!" Kemp exclaimed, then took off toward Miss Peach's house.

I ran down the road after him and caught up as he was trying to pull the mangled garage door back to the correct side of the frame. Inside, Radar howled like a banshee, gravel pelted the walls, mystery objects clanged against other mystery objects, and something metal fell over and rolled all the way across the room.

Grabbing the door, I added my weight to Kemp's, thinking, *When I get my hands on that dog, I'm going to kill him.* Any minute now, Miss Peach would come out of the house and I'd get shot, or citizen's arrested, or both, and then I'd end up having to pay for a new garage door and whatever else Don's dog was destroying in there.

The blockage gave way suddenly, Kemp and I fell backward and landed in a pile, and the cat ran for daylight. Radar burst through the opening immediately after, running on three feet while trying to kick something white and square off his back paw and dragging a string of Christmas lights. Scrambling onto all fours, Kemp dove for the trailing extension cord but came up empty, and Radar bolted up the street, disappearing around the corner faster than you'd think a three-legged dog could.

Kemp and I scrambled to our feet and took off in hot pursuit. We caught up with Radar in the alley behind Main Street, where the Christmas lights had wedged under the wheels of a Dumpster. The cat was on top, serenely licking her paws.

"Oh, you're dead, buddy," I threatened, but Radar was busy trying to chew the white thing off his foot. "You are so dead."

Kemp and I moved closer, stalking with our arms out, like wildlife biologists on a Discovery Channel feature. Radar succeeded in freeing his foot from the white square of whatever-it-was and came up with the mystery object stuck to the end of his nose. Whimpering, he tried to rub it off on the asphalt, but it was firmly adhered to whiskers, nose, and a section of lolling tongue. When I grabbed his collar, he tilted his head upward with a soulful whine that said, *Look! Here I am minding my own business, and a mysterious rectangle has come and stuck itself to my nose.*

Growling through my teeth, yet managing to maintain admirable self-control, I tried to free the wax-covered square of cardboard. It wouldn't budge. Skin stretched, whiskers popped, and Radar squealed, so I let go.

Leaning in from the opposite side, Kemp studied the problem. I touched the sticky surface and left some skin behind getting my finger loose. "What *is* this thing?"

"Rat trap," Kemp said, and I could tell he was trying not to laugh. "No way that's coming off easily."

"A rat . . . eeewww." I'd seen glue traps for mice, but nothing of this size, or . . . stickiness. There were bugs and pieces of brown hair trapped on the glutinous surface, as if a rat had been there before. "Gross." Swiping my finger on Radar's hair, I tried to rub off the rest of the glue, a shudder traveling down my spine. "Now what do we . . ." I looked up and Kemp was startlingly close. So near, I could see tiny streamers of silver and green set against the earthy color of his eyes. Whatever I'd been about to say left my head. *Dog? What dog?*

My mind hopscotched, and we hovered in a three-way tangle of suspended animation. Suddenly, the dog thrust his head between us, the rat trap boxed me in the nose, and something caught the end of my ponytail.

"Oh, gross!" I jerked back, Radar squealed, and I realized we were now glued together, rat fur and all. "Eeewww! Get it off!" I reached blindly for the trap and Radar yelped in my ear.

Kemp grabbed the dog, or me, or both. "Hold still." His voice was straining against laughter at first, and then he had the nerve to give in to it. I felt his hand on my head and his breath on my ear as he leaned over the dog and me. The proximity might have been romantic, if not for the dog, and the fact that all I could think was, *Rat fur and bugs, rat fur and bugs, rat fur . . .*

Kemp's fingers slid into my hair. "Don't move, all right? Whoa, what a mess."

Painful twinges coursed over my scalp, and follicles came loose at the roots. "Owww!"

Radar whimpered in agreement, or defeat, or both.

Retreating, Kemp stood above us, considering the problem, while I clutched the dog in a bear hug. From that vantage, I could see that Radar also had a trap stuck to his rear end. He was sitting on it. Along the edge of the cardboard, it read *This End Up.* Somewhere overhead, Miss Peach's cat meowed softly, and Radar growled.

"Do *something.*" I had a sudden picture of Radar taking off with my hair attached to his snout.

"The vet's office is right across the road from the school. I'll grab my truck out front," Kemp suggested finally. "Maybe the vet's got something that'll get this off."

"No *way!*" I squealed. "Cut the hair, rip it out, do whatever, but I *am not* going to the vet clinic."

"Darlin'," he said, and he was close again, his voice soft against my ear. "There's a lot of things I'd do for a pretty girl, but I'm not cutting off that hair."

# Chapter 17

## *Donetta Bradford*

By eight o'clock in the mornin', my building downtown was hoppin' like a sale barn on sheep and goat day. Sister Mona's bunch was gathered downstairs, watching the weather news in the back part of the shop where I keep the coffeepot, a TV, some old sofas, and some exercise machines I got at yard sales. The equipment don't get used much, but right now, it was comin' in handy for folks to sit on.

When I walked in with the pecan rolls and casserole, Bluejay was bouncing real gentle-like on the Abs-o-matic with his little baby in his arms.

"He been fussy?" I asked, walkin' by with the food.

Bluejay yawned. He had the nervous look new papas have, and he was holdin' that baby like he expected it to explode any minute.

"Yeah. Jovette been up with him all night, walkin'. She finally come and hand him over, sayin', 'You take him. This yo' bébé.'"

I smelled baby powder and milk, and felt the itch grannies get when there's a little bundle within arm's reach. "Let me set

193

up this food, and I'll take him for a bit. It's hard on a little guy, all this commotion day after day. I'd cry, too."

"Mais yeah," Bluejay yawned again. "*Gal-ee*, he got the lungs."

"Maybe he'll be a singer like his daddy." Somewhere along the way, I'd heard that Bluejay made his livin' singing in restaurants, and he played the guitar and sang in the Holy Ghost Church, too.

I lifted up the blanket and peeked inside. That baby had his nose all scrunched up like he wasn't one little bit happy. "Precious. Oh, he's precious."

Bluejay snorted, but he was smiling a little. "Tha's not what his mama call him las' night. He kept the whole place up. She finally took him out and sit on the curb. The sheriff deputy, he come by and ask what she's doin' out there."

"Buddy Ray Baldridge?" I checked the window just in case Buddy Ray was passing by in his cruiser. I was gonna go thump him on that big knothead of his if he'd been bothering my guests. . . . "Just ignore him. If sense was chickpeas, Buddy Ray wouldn't make a side dish. The only reason the sheriff sends him out in the cruiser at night is to get him out of the way."

"Nah, he's just tryin' to help," Bluejay answered. "He got Jovette a blanket from the trunk and then he sit there on the curb and play the harmonica. Turn out this little bébé, he like country music."

All of a sudden, I got a picture of Buddy Ray Baldridge sitting out in the moonlight, with his long skinny legs folded up and his body bent over that harmonica, playing "Red River Valley" and "So Lonesome I Could Cry" (the only two songs Buddy Ray knew), to quiet that little baby. A tenderness washed over me, and I felt bad for having a mean thought toward Buddy Ray. *A mean thought's just a sin that happens on the inside,* Brother Ervin said in sermon one day.

194

I left Bluejay there bouncing on the Abs-o-matic, and I got the food put out and took the covers off the things Imagene and some of the Methodist ladies'd brought. The guests were glad to have the breakfast, but from listening to the TV and hearing them talk, it was pretty clear the news from down around their homeplaces wasn't getting any better.

I took Bluejay's baby and walked the floor with him while everybody ate. After a minute, the baby quit mewing around and just looked up at me real quiet and still, his big blue eyes thoughtful, like he was trying to figure me out. His little hands grabbed my finger, and I thought how good it felt to hold a baby. Then I got sad, because I knew that the poor little guy might not have anything to go home to.

On TV, a newsman was hip-deep in water, saying could be two weeks, a month, maybe even more before electric got restored and they let people go home to the coast. Lucy come in the back door with a casserole she'd fixed, and I started thinking we better have a meetin' about what in the world we were gonna do with all these people for that long. When I whispered that to Lucy, she said we oughta slip next door to the café and catch Imagene, so all three of us could talk.

Lucy kidnapped the baby from me, and we walked past the dryer chairs and swung open the bookshelf to let ourselves into the café. Nobody knows why that secret doorway's in the wall between the café and the hotel buildin'. There's lots of stories about bank robberies and Confederate escape plans and secret tunnels under the building from way back in the Civil War. Folks used to scare us kids sometimes with tall tales about ghosts. My daddy told us he saw the ghost a time or two—said it walked right by him, droppin' gold coins on the floor. *Clink, clink, clink.*

Pickled as my daddy was, he probably did see it.

Lucy and me caught Imagene behind the cash register. The

morning coffee was brewin', and Bob was scraping off the fry grill. He had the Vent-A-Hood on, so I figured we could talk right there and he wouldn't hear a word.

I turned my back to him so he wouldn't see my face. Havin' spent so much time under the Vent-A-Hood, Bob'd got pretty good at reading lips.

"You seen the news this mornin'?" I asked.

Imagene nodded, then swatted a fly with her ticket book and brushed him off the counter into the trash. Good thing there wasn't any customers at the bar—just old raw-boned Doyle, perched atop his favorite stool, dozing on his hand. His mouth was hangin' open a little, and it looked like he was sound asleep. He was probably tired after the big rescue yesterday, bless his heart.

"Imagene," I said, "the TV's tellin' it that these folks might be waitin' two weeks, a month, maybe longer before they can go home. We can't have folks sleepin' on floors and wearin' the same suit of clothes all that time."

Lucy nodded like she agreed, which is what Lucy usually does. "They got to eat, too," she said. "What we doing about that, all these days? Who go-een to buy all that grocery?"

I scratched my head, nodding along. I ain't one to judge people, but even I could tell from the luggage those folks'd brought, and the fact that a lot of them come on the church bus, that they weren't just rollin' knee-deep in money.

"I don't know," I muttered. "I really don't." Already this morning, I'd used up every bit of the breakfast food I'd bought to keep Ronald going while I was out on my cruise. He'd had a fit when he saw the bill for all that stuff. *I'm retired now, Netta,* he'd said. *We can't be buyin' like we used to.* Ronald didn't talk about much, but he could get stirred up about money. To hear him, you'da thought we were on our very last dime.

Then again, I guess we had plenty of money to buy boat gas,

fish bait, and tackle so he could take off down the river all week while I was trapped in a hurricane. Guess *that* wasn't a problem.

Imagene sighed and leaned over the counter, resting her elbows on it. "I heard Sister Mona and Pastor D. talkin' about how they oughta pack everyone up and try to head for one of the convention center shelters in Dallas or Waco. 'Pastor D., we can't impose on these folks for days and weeks without payin' our way, and we gotta save what money we got left for gas,' that's what Sister Mona said. She told him they'd need to move on pretty quick to someplace where FEMA would take care of them."

I looked over at Bluejay's baby, sound asleep in a wad on Lucy's chest, his little lips hanging open in a tiny cupid's bow, and I tried to picture him cooped up in the Dallas Convention Center with thousands of other folks who'd evacuated. He could catch a cold, and with so much racket, he probably never would sleep. "We can't let them do that, Imagene. They took us in and saved us from the storm. We owe a debt."

I ran a finger along that baby's cheek, and he puckered, smacked his lips, then sighed. "They got babies, and old folks like Obeline, and I been hearin' on the news that them shelters up in Dallas are overflowin' anyhow. They might get up there and not be able to find a place at all. Who's gonna have room for all those people?"

"I uggg-got a room, got a room over to-to my uppp-place." Doyle perked up on his counter stool, and I realized he was listening, not sleeping. "I can b-b-bunk out in the camp-camper. I uddd-don't mind." Doyle might've been a backward old crow, but he had the heart of a prince inside that bony body of his.

"You're a good man, Doyle." I had a feelin' a shelter in Dallas was probably cleaner than Doyle's old house. "But we got a bigger problem than one house is gonna solve, and then there's the foo—"

The door burst open, and in breezed Betty Prine. She looked well rested, which she probably was, since I hadn't seen her downtown last night helping out. "Donetta Bradford, you want to tell me *what* in the *world* is going on over there? It's my wash-and-curl morning, and your *shop* is full of—" she stopped to hunt a word, and finally settled for— "*people*. There are *children* running *everywhere* and the whole place smells of food."

Like usual, Betty's voice crawled up my spine and pulled every short hair along the way. That woman could get my back up quicker than anybody I ever met. "Well, Betty, since they're havin' breakfast, I expect that's understandable."

Betty let the café door fall shut behind her and blinked at me like I was too thick to get her point. "I have an *appointment* this morning. It's my *day*."

Imagene grumbled under her breath, "It's always her day."

The baby started to squirm and whimper in Lucy's arms, like even he felt Betty Prine muckin' up the air in the room.

"I always come on Saturday," Betty chirped, then poked her nose around like a bird sniffing for worms, and spotted the baby. "What's *that*?"

"It's a baby." Heaven forgive me, but any day you can aggravate Betty Prine is a good day.

Betty looked down her nose at Bluejay's little baby, snuggled in Lucy's arms. "What are *you* doing with it?"

"Hor-ding it," Lucy answered.

Now, Betty Prine's been around Lucy for fifty years, but for some reason, even though everybody else in town can pick out Lucy's words just fine, Betty's always got to act like she don't know what Lucy's saying. "*Hording* it? Hording it from what?" She knew Lucy meant *holding*.

"Hording it from me," Imagene said, and reached across the counter. "Here, let me have that baby. I ain't held him yet." Lucy turned over the baby, and Imagene settled him in, then purred like a cat, "I'd give you a turn, Betty, but I don't think I can let him loose."

"Pppffff!" Betty stuck up her nose, her lip curling on one side. "I need a *wash*-and-*curl*. I don't have *time* for that *nonsense*."

Imagene just smiled at her, real pleasant. "Well, we grandmas always got time for a baby. When you're a grandma, that's the way it is. You love 'em all, whether they're yours or not. You'll understand one of these days, Betty."

Betty's face turned three shades of hot. We all knew that her spoiled-rotten daughters lived together in a house up in Dallas, and far as anyone'd ever heard, neither of them'd ever had a date. Betty was about as far away from grandkids as a mouse from moose, and that goaded her right in the flank flesh. Grandkids are one treasure money can't buy, so there wasn't a thing Betty could do about it.

She knew it, too, so she just pretended Imagene wasn't there. "Donetta Bradford, are you going to give me my wash-and-curl or not?"

*I been almost dead in a hurricane and now I got a whole busload of people to take care of. The last thing I got on my mind is washing your hair, Betty Prine.* But I didn't say it. When you own a business in a small town, you got to bite your tongue sometimes, especially with people like Betty Prine. Betty can make a lot of trouble if she wants to. "Betty, you know all appointments been canceled this week on account of our cruise."

Her lips pressed hard together and curved upward just at the corners. Her mouth looked like it ought to have the fur of something cute and fuzzy hangin' out of it. "You aren't *on* a cruise, *Donetta*. I supposed that, since you're *back here* in *Daily*, you'd be getting on with business as *usual*. No sense *throwing* away good *money*."

My collar steamed hot as a kettle spout. It was just like Betty

Prine to backhandedly say I couldn't get by without her twenty dollars for a wash-and-curl.

*Lord, you better put a hand over my mouth, because I'm fixin' to commit a sin of the tongue.*

Imagene must've heard that prayer go through my head, because she jumped in before I could commence to do somethin' stupid. "Heaven's sake, Betty, can't you see we got folks to take care of? There's been a hurricane, remember?"

Betty clicked her big yellow teeth. "Well, I *supposed* that, now that it's *daylight*, they'd be packing up and heading to a proper shelter—someplace prepared for the . . . *displaced*."

"Been a lot of Daily folk helpin' make a place here." Imagene's chin stuck out like she was ready to get in a spittin' match. "Love thy neighbor, and all that, like Brother Ervin was talkin' about in church last Sunday."

Betty licked the lipstick off her teeth, or at least she tried. They were still coated. Coral Surprise #3, to be exact. "Well, of course. Harold and I want to do all we can to help. I hope *those people* enjoyed the cookies last night. Harold is headed by the church this morning to talk to Brother Ervin about getting up a fund to help them *move* . . . I mean, *travel* on to wherever they're going. We'll contribute, of course. It's the Christian thing to do, and we recognize that we're in a position to afford it more than some."

I heard that whistlin' noise a champagne bottle makes right before the cork blows off and flies across the room, and I grabbed the side of the counter, because otherwise I was gonna snatch Betty's hair right off her head. *Next time she comes in for a perm, I'm gonna set the timer ten minutes too long and send her out the door lookin' like Mrs. Mayfield's pet poodle dog. I really am. With them big ears and bug eyes and pointy nose of hers, she's halfway there already.*

"The beauty shop's closed," I said. "And it's gonna have to be closed while these folks're here."

Betty's eyes got wide, then the right one ticked shut. "And just *what* is everyone else supposed to do in the meantime?"

"Wash their own hair at home, I reckon."

Imagene chuckled behind her hand, and Doyle piped in from over on his stool. "Th-they got a b-b-beauty shop right in the Wal-wal-wal, in the Wal-Mart over to Killeen."

Betty acted like he wasn't even there. She got a cold look that turned her eyes hard as glass, and I knew we'd just stuck the twig a little too far into the anthill.

"Those *people*"—Betty stabbed a long, bony finger toward the wall, and her voice crawled up so high I figured they could probably hear her next door—"need to move on to a proper shelter. There are *plenty* of places set up by the *government* to handle this sort of thing, and the Daily Hair and Body is *not* one of them, Donetta Bradford. We have *building codes* and *fire laws* in this county. There's an *occupancy limit* on that building for the protection of the *pubic welfare*." Her chin wagged back and forth on *occupancy limit* and *public welfare*. "Being head of the city council, Harold of course can't just *turn his head* and *ignore* such a matter. What if there were to be a *fire* and the authorities had failed to protect the public safety? What if it were to spread to our buildings next door and burn down all of Main Street? What then, *Donetta Bradford?*"

"Seems to me folks ought to just mind their own business, and everything'll be fine." Oh mercy, sometimes my mouth ran wild when it needed to hunker down. Betty leveled a look like one of them serial killers on TV. I knew we were in for trouble.

"It would be a *shame*, wouldn't it"—she said each word real slow and careful, her nose pointed my way like she was gonna peck me with it—"if the *county fire marshal* found out about this. I mean, my gracious, how long has it been since your building has been thoroughly checked for code violations? If that new young fire marshal were to . . . *happen by*, he might even be forced to put a red tag on your building, and wouldn't *that* be a sad thing for Daily—to have the Daily Hotel closed down for code violations? What with all the tourism showing up nowadays because of Amber Anderson's big win on *American Megastar*, and now the movie project coming to the old Bar-linger Ranch, visitors will need a place to stay. These are exciting times in Daily, and the *last thing* people need to see when they come to visit Amber Anderson's hometown is *run-down vehicles* parked all over Main Street and a bunch of . . . well, not to sound untoward . . . but members of a *certain element* loitering on the curb in front of the only hotel in town."

Blood boiled in my ears, and I gripped the counter so hard I felt a nail tip pop loose. By *certain element*, Betty meant *black folks.* No matter that plenty of our neighbors in Daily were from Pastor Harve's church out on Caney Creek, which'd always been a black church, just like Sister Mona's. "What sorta element, Betty?"

"Well, you know . . . people . . . from other places."

"From other places . . . like all them tourists you were talkin' about?"

Lucy sucked in a breath and started rubbing the locket around her neck, where she kept a lock of hair from the baby she had to leave behind in Japan during the war.

"*Paying* customers are *different*, of course. Daily needs all the tourism it can get." Betty's eyes went half closed, and she smiled at me. "It's important that the town project a certain . . . image. Of course, Harold and I *have* thought about building a *new* hotel outside of town, with a swimming pool and so forth. But we'd hate to be the source of competition for you. No telling what that would do to *your* old place."

Imagene caught my eye, and she started shaking her head like she felt a chill. Her face said, *Hush up, Netta. She'll do it. You know she will.*

Betty tapped her fingernails on her purse, looking satisfied with herself. She knew she'd won. "I guess my wash-and-curl can wait until Monday." Her voice was all sticky-sweet, like a cat purring when it's got a belly full of mouse. "I can see you'll have your hands full *today* helping *those people* find suitable accommodations somewhere *away from Daily*. If you need help, Harold and I have *contacts*, of course." She turned around and breezed out the door just as uninvited as she come in.

None of us said anything for a minute. Imagene looked down at the baby, and Lucy just kept rubbing her locket.

"What we go-een to do now?" Lucy asked finally.

"We got to find someplace else to put that bunch," I said.

Imagene sucked her cheeks in and started chewing. "Just wait till she finds out there's a group bedded down at the church, too."

My insides sank. I hadn't even thought about the church. Betty'd find out about that just as soon as Harold got home from his visit to see Brother Ervin this morning, and then she'd be on a warpath no wash-and-curl was gonna smooth over.

## Chapter 18

# *Kai Miller*

Kemp transported me, along with Don's idiotic dog, to the vet's office. Because there was no way for the two of us and the rat trap to get into the cab of the truck, Radar and I rode through town cheek to cheek on the tailgate. At the vet's office, the receptionist laughed so hard she had a coughing fit and couldn't catch her breath until she'd downed several big swallows of coffee. After checking out the situation for herself, she suggested cutting the trap so that my hair could have its corner and Radar could have the rest. Within moments, we were successfully separated, and I proceeded into the bathroom with a pair of scissors to finish extricating myself, while Kemp headed across the street to open the field house for his ball players.

I came out of the bathroom with a little less hair, but no glue trap.

The receptionist craned to check out my ponytail, then giggled, fanning her face. "Sorry." She handed Radar's leash back to me and opened a swinging gate so we could proceed to the exam rooms. "This way."

Radar, remembering that swinging half doors led to flea dips, vaccinations, and other unpleasant procedures, dug in his claws, and I was forced to drag him down the hall with his toenails plowing furrows in the linoleum. By the time we got to the exam room, I was winded and a laughing veterinary assistant was following behind us, pushing Radar from the back while carefully avoiding the rear glue trap.

After we hoisted Radar onto the exam table, we were joined by a pretty veterinary intern with wide brown eyes and chestnut ringlets pulled up in a hair clip. Everyone stood admiring Radar's accomplishment while I filled out forms, at the bottom of which I was supposed to sign my name promising that I was good for Radar's bill. I considered just writing down Don's address and leaving Radar there.

While the matter of the bill twirled in my mind, Radar sat on the examining table wagging his tail as the intern and the assistant discussed possible removal methods. Reaching around to nip at an itchy spot on his rear end, Radar managed to stick the glue traps together, and after a moment of sheer panic during which it took all three of us to hold him down, he gave up and lay there like a giant chocolate doughnut.

The veterinary intern laughed so hard her eyes watered. "I'm sorry," she apologized, pressing the back of her hand to the bridge of her nose and trying to get control of herself. She had a smile that looked like it belonged on a billboard somewhere. "I'm sorry. It's just . . . this is a new one." She left the room, then came back pushing a cart full of potential glue trap solvents—everything from surgical soap to a tub of margarine from the break room.

"If you'll just stand at his head and help him stay calm, I'm going to give him a sedative to keep him still," she instructed, tucking stray curls behind her ear. "All right, big guy . . ." She pointed the needle upward and squeezed out a bubble.

Woozy at the sight of the syringe heading toward flesh, I looked away, leaning over Radar's head. He had the nerve to roll an eye upward and thump his tail against the table while the needle went in, and I tried not to picture it. Vet trips were one of those errands I'd always refused to do for Don, even though he tried to con me into it. Anyplace that smelled like antiseptic or felt like a hospital brought back memories of Gil and all those times I could barely make myself walk into the room and see his pale, thin body surrounded by IVs and tubes.

*It's okay,* he'd say. *It doesn't hurt.*

Radar went limp in my hands, and for a moment I was back with Gil, standing over his bed, holding him, wondering when my parents were coming back.

The sensation faded as I moved away and stood by the window. Across the street, Kemp was standing in front of the field house with two little boys. Both were too young to be high-school ball players, but the smaller one had an oversized plastic bat in his hand. Memories of Gil and the past floated from my mind and I watched Kemp help the younger boy position his bat as the older boy pitched underhand. The bat smacked the Wiffle ball, and it flew over the grassy lawn beside the field house. Kemp wheeled his arm and cheered like a base coach while the batter ran an imaginary diamond and the pitcher took off after the ball. At home plate, Kemp played both catcher and umpire. When the pitcher threw the ball in, Kemp caught it, got sloppy with the tag, and called the runner safe at home.

A warm feeling slid over me as I watched the game continue. The veterinary office, the cloying scent of antiseptic, and the ongoing discussion of failed glue trap solvents and tender nasal skin faded away, and I focused out the window. A strange sense of déjà vu enveloped my senses, as if I knew exactly how it would feel to be sitting there in the sun, listening to the sounds of the Wiffle ball game. I felt myself leaning closer to the glass, pressing the tips of my fingers against it, trying to decide why the scene was so familiar.

"Ma'am . . . Radar's mom . . . ma'am?" By the time the intern's voice penetrated the fog, I knew she'd been calling me for a while.

I turned from the window unwillingly. I wanted to continue watching the game and searching for the memory attached to it. "Sorry. I was zoned out."

The intern smiled, and in spite of the fact that it's hard to like someone who looks that good in scrubs, especially when you're decked out in an ugly purple windsuit, I liked her. "He's all fixed up. Thank goodness for Parkay." With butter-covered fingers, she held up the plastic tub. "Guess I'll put this back in the break room refrigerator."

I blinked and curled my lip, and she laughed, then tossed the margarine tub into the trash. "Maybe not." She patted Radar, who was lying prostrate and groggy on the table, his eyes rolled back and his tongue hanging out. "It'll take a while for the sedative to wear off. You can wait, or you can come back for him in an hour or so."

"I'll come back," I said, and handed Radar's paper work to her assistant. On the way out, I stroked Radar's damp, greasy ears and had the random thought that Don would get a kick out of this story. So would Maggie and Meredith. I tried to picture all of us back in the coffee shop, life going on as normal, me on my usual stool by the counter, but for some reason, I couldn't.

Exiting the clinic, I took a deep breath of fresh air, shook off the antiseptic smell, and jogged across the street to the field house, where the ball game was still going. Two additional elementary-aged boys had ridden up on bicycles, and things were getting rowdy. Kemp waved as I came closer. "Hey, we need a second baseman," he called.

"I think I'll just watch" was out of my mouth before I even thought about it. *Why?* The voice in my head sounded like Gil's. *Why sit on the fence? You afraid to get dirty?* "I'd hate to make you look bad," I added, and Kemp's brows shot up, disappearing into the brim of his Daily Dawgs baseball cap.

"Oh-ho!" he said. "Look out, boys. Second base is covered."

"She's a girl!" one of the kids protested.

"She's a lady," another corrected, and all four of them studied me from behind home plate. I felt like the newcomer at the neighborhood sandlot. Fortunately, I had plenty of experience. Gil and I were always new somewhere, trying to prove ourselves in games of tag, football, soccer, baseball.

"*She's* got second covered," I told them. "You guys better watch out."

Kemp drew back, surprised, or impressed, or both. "All right, new game. Take the plate there, Sly."

Sly, who couldn't have been more than six or seven—too young to be wandering around the school grounds on his own, actually—stepped up to the patch of dirt that served as a plate, and the game began. By the time the batting order rolled around again, the ranks had swelled to include three kids who'd been riding by on bicycles and several high-school boys who'd just finished their workouts. Someone broke out a bag of old baseball gloves, and the game got serious. Even with a plastic bat, the high-school boys could smack a deadly line drive.

"Hey, hey, hey," Kemp warned when a ball whizzed past Sly at third. "Easy. We've got kids here."

"Sorry, Coach," the batter, a tall, stringy boy named Andy, apologized. Somewhere along the way, I'd figured out that Andy was the brother of the town's blossoming country music sensation, Amber Anderson. To the little kids, Andy was a minor celebrity. "Send me one, Coach. I'll be careful this time."

Kemp dug a toe into the grass, getting ready to pitch. "Hey, Andy, when's your sister coming in, anyway?"

"I don't know, Coach." Andy fanned the bat behind his head. "She called this morning, but I didn't hear what she wanted. She talked to Peepaw. I think she's on tour somewhere in Oklahoma." Looking at Andy now, I recognized the similarity to his sister. I'd watched her make her way to the top on last spring's season of *American Megastar*. No wonder Daily felt so familiar. I'd probably seen it on Amber's hometown feature.

"Next time she's around, tell her to drop by the field house and remind me about those extra pictures of you guys from the playoffs last spring. I think she wants to frame some things for your grandpa to hang in the new house."

"I'll let her know."

Kemp pitched the ball, and Andy swung, lofting it into the outfield. He took off for first, and a runner came in from third. In the outfield, one of Kemp's ball players jumped over a little kid and dove for the ball.

"I got it." Rolling over on the ground, he held up the ball. "He's out, Coach."

"It hit the ground," Andy protested, staying on first. "Digger trapped it."

"I got it in the air, Coach!" Digger defended.

A minor disagreement fired up, and Kemp finally had to step in and play the part of umpire. "You guys are pathetic. You're out, Andy. That's three. Last bat for the other team. Let the little kids hit first."

My team went in to bat, and Kemp stayed on the pitcher's mound. Standing in line, I watched him pour on the drama for the younger kids. "And, stepping up to the plate, it's Slugger Sly Sofar. Back up, outfield, here comes a big hitter. . . ."

Kemp's face was alive with light. The hint of shadow that usually seemed to hang over him was gone, and watching him now, I could tell this was his game, his element. I thought about what he'd said earlier, that playing baseball didn't feel like work, because he loved it.

"But on the mound, it's Robert Leroy Satchel Paige. He likes the corners, folks, and it's batter beware. . . ." Kemp continued to give the play-by-play as he moved into his windup. "Paige's in rare form today. There's steel in his eye and lightning in his arm. Looks like he's thinking about a Midnight Creeper, but he likes the curve, too. No . . . no . . . it's . . . it's a fastball down the middle. That thing's clocking out over ninety-eight. Looks like Sly's lined up on it. He's loaded, he's ready. If he gets ahold of the ball it's gonna fly . . . and . . . it's . . . outta here!"

Sly tossed the bat and took off, then rounded the bases while Kemp did the announcing, and his ballplayers purposely bobbled the ball.

"Oh . . . oh, he's on second, and Anderson guns the ball to third. It's gonna be close, but, but no, Hanson misses the catch and it's all the way to the oak tree. There's Sly rounding third and turning on the speed. He's fast. He's agile. Hanson's recovered the ball. Catcher's checking from the plate. The ball's in the air. Throw's off to the right, but . . . but . . . no, catcher makes the snag! Sly's coming in like a freight train. He runs, he slides. He's . . . he's . . . he's safe! Catcher misses the tag and Sly ties up the score for the Rangers!"

The rest of my team batted through without a score. Now that the game was tied, Kemp's high-school boys were playing for real and slinging so much trash talk that Kemp threatened to make them run laps if they didn't chill out. Even in Wiffle ball, they had an undeniable competitive streak.

Somehow, I ended up at bat with a chance to bring in the winning run. Sly's brother, Jayden, was on third, in position to score. The pressure was on, and to compound things, the play-by-play announcer was in high gear. "And, look out in the stands, it's Highfly Hilda. She's 0 for 5 this afternoon."

I sneered at Kemp. He *would* have to point out that I'd flied out all five times so far. Of course, considering that it had been at least fourteen years since I'd picked up a baseball bat, I thought I was doing pretty well just to hit the ball.

"The batter swings like a girl!" one of the high-school boys joked, and the little kids picked up the chant. "The batter's a girl, the batter's a girl. . . ."

Just for fun, I stretched out the bat and pointed to the outfield.

Kemp's lips parted in the form of an O. He was impressed. "Look out, folks, Highfly Hilda's callin' the upper decks. She's delivered a challenge to the pitcher. . . ." Grinning at me, he palmed the ball, rubbing it between his hands.

"The pitcher's raising the laces. Where's the ump?" I complained.

"It's plastic. It doesn't have laces," Kemp pointed out, but I barely heard him. My mind had snapped back in time. I saw my father's fingers twisting over the ball. I heard Gil say, *Dad, no raising the laces!* For a moment, I was there, on some overgrown ball field in a park someplace. We were all there—Dad, Mom, Gil, and me. Mom was laughing as Dad gave the play-by-play. Her face was turned upward, her long blond hair floating on the breeze, her smile radiant. We were happy. All of us were happy. I saw myself, a stringy ten-year-old girl in an oversized T-shirt, jittering on second base, pigtails bouncing, knobby sun-browned legs protruding from cut-off shorts that might have been converted from jeans on the spur of the moment because the weather had turned warm.

*Burn it by him, Dad. Burn it by him. . . .*

Dad threw a pitch, Gil hit a grounder, and we pretended

we couldn't field it. He ran the bases, his chubby little legs pumping for all he was worth. We were laughing. Everyone was laughing. . . .

I heard something whiz by my ear, and I jerked back out of reflex, realizing Kemp had just thrown an inside pitch.

"Steee-rike one," Kemp announced. "And Hilda's back off the plate. Paige's on the corners today. He's a master. . . ."

I blinked hard, tried to focus, but my mind was still foggy with the memory. Where were we that day? It felt like the best place in the world, a day I'd wished would never end. We'd played until dark because Gil and I wanted to. Gil wasn't sick. His skin was ruddy and tan, his face streaked with red clay dust. Mom had kicked off her shoes. Her feet were red, like the hills in Oklahoma. Maybe we were in Oklahoma then. . . .

Another pitch flew by. "And he burns one right down the middle, but Hilda doesn't like it. She's waiting on her pitch," Kemp narrated.

My team gave a collective groan. "C'mon, Hilda," one of the high-school boys complained. "That was a fastball right down the middle."

Stepping out of the batter's box, I shook my head, shedding the memory like droplets of water in my eyes. "I'm ready now," I said, and stepped up to the plate again. The announcer told the crowd I had steel in my eyes this time. The pitcher leaned forward in the stretch, narrowed his dark lashes, gave a wicked little sneer.

I felt a giggle tickle my throat. "Cut it out and pitch."

"Whoo-hoo, Coach!" Kemp's players cheered. "Cut it out and pitch."

"Unless you're scared," I challenged, and the boys cheered again.

Kemp adjusted the brim of his ball cap. "Sure you're ready?"

"I'm ready. Show me what you've got."

"You're 0 and 2." His eyes focused on mine, and a tingle traveled through my body. "Last pitch."

"Hilda only needs one."

He answered with a wide, white smile, his eyes disappearing behind his cap. He stood up in the stretch, drew the ball back, lifted a foot. I loaded the bat. The ball sailed through the air, hung up like a curve, then started to drop. I waited on it.

*Dad, stop throwing curveballs!* Gil complained in my mind.

I knew how to hit a curveball. My father threw them all the time.

The ball lofted over the plate, I swung the bat, and I heard the crack of plastic on plastic.

"Whoa!" Sly cheered. "Good hit!"

The ball sailed through the empty space at second and dropped before center field could catch it. I ran to first, and the winning run came home.

Kemp announced the end of the game, and my side cheered. Suddenly, I was a hero.

After several minutes of gloating, Kemp wound things up, his players gathered the equipment, and the smaller kids disbursed. On the way back to the field house, Kemp's students were still debating the catch in the outfield.

"I didn't trap the ball, Coach," the outfielder argued, holding up his mitt with the Wiffle ball still in it. "I had it. Andy really was out."

Lashes lowered, Kemp frowned. "It's Wiffle ball, Riley."

Riley flushed behind a peppering of freckles. "I know. I was just saying . . ." His gaze met Kemp's, then he ducked his head. "Never mind, Coach."

"Go hand the kid his ball back." Kemp pointed to the ball, then patted Riley on the shoulder. Giving the ball a surprised look, Riley spun around and trotted off after Sly, who was headed home, dragging his plastic bat behind him.

When we reached the field house, Kemp's players went in, and Kemp and I stopped outside the door. "You'd probably better wait here, unless you're up for skin, jockey shorts, shoe stink, and fart jokes."

"Eeewww, yeah, no thanks." I stopped at the pipe fence by the door. "I'll wait here."

"Good choice, probably," he agreed, then went inside.

I sat down on the fence and waited, listening to the high-school boys talk trash and snap towels inside the field house. The boys' voices slowly faded as I gazed at the empty field, and I heard my family again, felt the warmth of the memory wash over me. How long since I'd thought about all the times we'd camped out at empty city parks, picnicked, and played Frisbee, hide-and-seek, and baseball? How long since I'd thought about those years before Gil got so sick?

So long I'd almost let those memories go, allowed them to fade completely. I'd convinced myself that things had always been bad, always been uncertain, unstable, on edge. I'd stacked up all the unhappy memories, all the resentment and pain like building blocks, mortared them together, and allowed them to dry in the sun—a wall that blocked out everything, even the light, even the laughter, even the times when the freedom to stop at a park in the middle of the week and spend all day playing baseball felt like the greatest thing in the world.

There was a time when I looked at other kids, normal kids, and knew that their parents would never drop everything and just play. For other families, a Tuesday was just a Tuesday—the same routine every week. For us, a Tuesday could be anything.

Tears prickled in my nose and the field went blurry. Something calming and peaceful settled over me. I felt a darkness lifting, floating away, allowing the memories to return.

*Maybe nothing's perfect,* I thought.

Maybe life was always a balancing act between the things

you chose and the things you sacrificed. Maybe my parents were feeling their way through the adult world just like I was now, trying to find a place that seemed right. Maybe they were doing the best they could. Maybe they weren't prepared to raise a terminally ill child, or handle the difficult decisions that had to be made about Gil's cancer treatments. When they found out Gil was dying, Mom was younger than I was now. Maybe she was as confused about her life as I'd always been about mine.

Players started coming out of the field house and walking to their vehicles, and I wiped my eyes. When all the boys were gone, I ventured inside. Kemp was standing in the middle of the locker room next to a massive pile of towels, athletic shorts, sweats, T-shirts, and hoodies. Hands braced on his hips, he sized it up, shaking his head.

"Looks like they left a mess," I commented, thinking that, as tempting as it was to offer to help in the cleanup of sweaty boy clothes, I needed to head over to the vet clinic to retrieve Radar.

Kemp scratched the dark curls near the nape of his neck. "Sometimes they surprise me. Usually, you can't get those kids to clean out their lockers. There's junk in there from two, three years ago. They throw it in a duffle bag at the end of the year and stuff it back in the locker the beginning of the next year." Gesturing toward the pile, he shook his head. "They just sorted out all their stuff, because they thought the evacuees might be able to use it."

Suddenly, I understood the awed expression on his face. "Wow," I whispered.

"Yeah. Guess I've got laundry to do."

"I'll help," I offered, thinking that Radar could wait a little while. Bending over the laundry mountain, I started sorting lights and darks. "Looks like you could use it." I noted that all the white sweats were already various shades of pink—a testament to the fact that someone had been washing lights and darks together in the past.

After some disagreement as to whether the reds and the whites actually needed to be washed separately, Kemp and I loaded two industrial-sized washers in the back room. We ran out of detergent and Kemp had to go get some from the bus barn, so I waited at the field house while he zipped across campus in the official athletic department limo—a rust-streaked golf cart with an office chair welded in to serve as a driver's seat.

I'm not usually the type to snoop, but once I was in the field house alone, some curious, nosy girl I'd never met before possessed my body, and the next thing I knew I was tiptoeing around the building, checking out Kemp's territory like a CSI investigator looking for clues.

A grouping of newspaper articles on a bulletin board caught my interest as I wandered near the coach's offices. There were pictures of Kemp and his team posing after the district championship, an action shot or two from the state playoffs—Kemp with his arm around one of the boys, talking strategy, Kemp giving signals to the catcher, a series of action shots of Kemp trying to outrun a Gatorade bath after a winning game, a shot of him with his players praying at a Fellowship of Christian Athletes meeting.

I settled on that one for a moment, studied his face. His eyes were closed, his lips parted slightly, his arms resting on the shoulders of the boys beside him. Below the photo, the title of the article read "FCA Chapter Finds New Life After Six-Year Gap." Scattered among the text were pictures of student athletes engaged in service projects around town—cleaning up the city baseball fields, mentoring younger children at a challenge camp, leading prayers at See You at the Pole, building a wheelchair ramp for a crumbling house while an elderly man looked on from the doorway. According to the text, the man, whose nickname was Oats, had been the groundskeeper at the school for forty-five years before suffering a heart attack.

In the middle of the article, a quote from Coach Kemp read,

When I played here, Oats and I were the first two at the ball field every morning. Usually, the sun was just coming up, but the mound had already been raked, and a bucket of balls was waiting with a can of Dr. Pepper that had an oatmeal cookie balanced on top. I never forgot that. Oats was quiet about his job. He picked up the trash kids left in the dugout, scraped chewing gum off the cement, scrubbed graffiti, and took care of the crabgrass and the fire ants. If you forgot your glove on the field after practice, it'd be back in your locker the next day, cleaned up with a little oil on it.

As I read the words, Kemp's voice played in my head. I could hear him saying them, his tone slightly tender, filled with fondness.

Oats never offered a word of complaint. He never said the weather was too hot or too cold. He never decided he needed to sleep late, or go on a vacation, or call in sick for a mental health day. He never criticized anyone or said a cross word about anything, or griped when we made extra work for him. He just led by example. He served. It's important for these kids to know how to do that. We all like to win games, but it's not the scoreboard that really matters. Sports are a vehicle to teach the things that count in life—service, dedication, compassion, unselfishness, patience, perseverance. We have to look at the lessons these kids take away from the field. If their involvement in sports doesn't teach them something more than just how to play the game, then we haven't done our jobs.

At the bottom of the article, Kemp was popping a wheelie in grainy black and white as he pushed Oats up the wheelchair ramp. Oats was laughing with his hands in the air like a roller coaster rider's. I raised my fingers, touched the photo, imagined the moment.

Finally, I left the bulletin board behind and wandered into Kemp's office. The place was surprisingly bare—just a desk, a computer, some baseball equipment piled in the corner, a file cabinet and a stack of boxes next to it. Picture frames protruded from the top box. I wandered over and peered in. I felt like a voyeur, but I looked anyway. The thick shadowbox frame in front held a game ball, a picture of Kemp, and an article about a no-hitter he'd pitched at the University of Texas.

Glancing over my shoulder, I silenced a pang of guilt, touched an index finger to the corner of the wood, tipped the frame forward, and leaned over the box to look at the next one. It was upside down. Twisting like a corkscrew, I took in a neatly matted combination of a pitching portrait and a Rangers' ticket stub from last year. There was a shadow over the picture, so I couldn't quite see it. I lifted it a little—just enough to make out the photo of Kemp sending the ball toward home plate, thousands of people only a blur in the stands behind him. His face was intense, determined, his eyes steely and focused.

In my mind, I compared that moment to the one in which he was pushing Oats up the wheelchair ramp. Trying to mesh one with the other was like trying to overlay transparencies that didn't match. There seemed to be pieces of the coach that didn't fit the pitcher, and pieces of the pitcher that didn't fit the coach. What was he thinking of in those two very different moments? How did he feel? Which moment mattered the most to him?

Why were the frames in a box, rather than hanging on the wall?

I found myself wondering about Kemp, trying to figure him out like a cipher for which there was no answer key. Who was the man behind the clever quips, the pile of pink laundry, and the mean curveball?

As I thumbed through the rest of the box, peeking at articles, awards, and another glass-enclosed game ball, a new question scratched the surface of my mind. Who had carefully collected and framed all these treasures? These didn't look like the creations of a man who couldn't even sort the laundry. Some of the photos sported creative mats with cutsie little scrapbook stickers of tiny baseballs, bats, gloves, and printed cheers like *Home run! Curveball! RBI! Strike three . . . he's out!*

Behind that question, there was the original one. Why were these carefully preserved mementos—everything from high-school letter jacket patches to ticket stubs from the first major-league game Kemp had pitched—in a box, chunked haphazardly upside down, right side up, and sideways atop a stack of boxes, in the corner of his office?

The clink-clink of tires rolling across the threshold into the locker room made me jerk upright like a cat burglar caught in the act. I left Kemp's office and met him as he turned off the limo and dismounted the seat.

"Eureka!" he cheered, holding up a bottle of laundry soap like a giant diamond. "We're in business. Let's wash some clothes."

"Gotta like a guy who's enthusiastic about his laundry." The comment was meant to be a joke, but it came out sounding flirty.

Kemp cocked his head, answering with a wry lip-twist.

"Sorry," I said, "little bad laundry humor there."

"Dirty joke."

"Ohhh," I groaned as we headed for the washroom. "Now *that* was bad laundry humor. You've been cooped up with the pink sweat pants too long, Coach."

"Probably," he admitted, and now he was the one sounding flirty. "I think I need a change of scenery." The sentence was open-ended, an invitation to something, but I didn't know what. He waited for me to respond.

Possible answers twirled through my mind, fluttering like brightly colored dragonflies, tickling where they landed. *What did you have in mind? Me, too . . . The scenery looks pretty good right here. . . .*

*This is a hurricane evacuation, not a date.*

The last realization fell like a bucket of cold water. Splash. There was no point even thinking about some guy who lived in a place I'd be leaving in a few days. Once the immediate chaos subsided, I'd have to report in to work, figure out whether I was catching up with the ship for this trip or meeting it for the next one. I was still under contract, after all. Sooner or later, reality would come calling and I'd never see any of these people again. Daily, Texas, would be just a memory—an odd but cozy port of call on the way back to real life.

The idea felt heavy in my chest, uncomfortable and unwieldy. On some level, I'd been settling in here, imagining I'd be staying longer than I really would—that, as time went on, I'd learn more about Daily and about Kemp. Maybe, if I got my courage up, I'd borrow a car and drive over to McGregor. I'd see if Grandmother Miller's big clapboard house was still there beneath the live oaks, the tall white porch pillars stretching imposingly to the second story, the concrete lions still frozen at the gate, their mouths in a perpetual roar.

Maybe I'd walk through the gate, climb the steps—seven, I remembered—and knock on the door.

I hadn't even realized those thoughts were in my head until now. They'd been hiding in the shadows, just vague images, pictures without text. When they took on dialogue all at once, it was overwhelming.

"Whoa, what's that look for? You're as white as a Sunday shirt." Kemp swiveled to check behind himself as we crossed the washroom and stood by the machines. "There a rat back there or something?"

"How far away is McGregor?" As soon as I said it out loud, I wished I hadn't. Now he would want to know why.

He stopped checking for rats and turned back to me, perplexed. "Fifteen miles or so. Why?"

I shrugged. "I was just curious." Fifteen miles. Only fifteen miles. If Grandmother Miller were still there, would she know anything about my father? Did she ever think about us at all? Did she ever go visit my brother's grave? Did she keep it tended? Gil was buried in McGregor. In the family cemetery. Grandmother Miller wouldn't pay for it any other way.

That seemed so long ago now, another life.

I'd never even gone back to visit.

"Curious about McGregor?" Kemp's voice broke into my thoughts.

"Long story. I used to know someone there. No big deal. Are there really rats in here?"

"Just little ones." Raising the washer lid, he dumped in some detergent without bothering to measure, then turned on the water. "Cute little ones with big brown eyes and big furry ears."

"*Cute* little rats?"

"Field mice," he offered. "It's a field house, after all."

"Bad joke."

Leaning over the washer, I decided that with that much soap, either everything would come out really clean or the washer would explode. "You don't catch the field mice with glue traps, do you?"

"No glue traps." His voice was close. "You're safe." I felt him near me. I looked up, and he'd leaned back against the washer, rested his palms on it comfortably, as if he didn't have anything more important to do than stand there and talk. "So, who do you know in McGregor? They're our archenemies, you know. The Bulldogs."

*The Bulldogs.* I remembered that now. I was jealous of the girls in their cheerleader suits on Friday nights at the soda shop. "Oh, nobody special. It's been a long time."

"Mmmm." Nodding, he eyed me speculatively. I felt the power of that gaze, the pull of it.

"I have a confession to make." A tiny sliver of guilt had been needling me since he came back with the soap. "I snooped in your office. Sorry."

He drew back a little, his eyebrows arching upward, as if that pleased him. "Not a problem. I don't have any skeletons in my closet . . . or my office." His voice was soft, low so that it rumbled in his chest. "Find anything interesting?"

*Interesting . . . anything interesting . . .* A pulse fluttered in my throat, thready, aware, expectant. "You should . . . close the washer." What a completely idiotic thing to say. Every fiber of my body had gone wild, thoughts zinging randomly though my brain, as if someone had plugged me into a wall socket and the voltage was too high.

His eyes were the most gorgeous shade of golden brown now, like caramel with a small, silvery pool of mint melting toward the centers. "You're doing it again, you know," he said.

"What?" The word was throaty, inviting.

"Changing the subject. It makes you hard to figure out."

"Sorry." I knew I was leaning closer to him, or he was leaning closer to me.

"Don't be," he whispered, and I felt the room spin.

"What . . ." I swallowed hard, blinked, tried to gather a coherent thought, but I couldn't. "What did you want to know?"

"Everything." His lips met mine and I was lost. Any coherent thought flew from my mind, and there was only the scent, the touch, the feel of him. I felt his fingers slip into my hair, felt his body turn, lean into mine, felt my body mold against his, strangely familiar, as if I'd been imagining this before it happened.

Either the washer changed cycles or the earth moved, but everything shifted at once.

The ending of the kiss was like waking from some alternate state of reality. I leaned against the washer, hot and dizzy, my head floaty and light. I felt his hand trail along my skin, his fingers toying with mine, then letting go.

I stood staring into his eyes, trying to remember why I was there. "I guess we should go . . . ummm . . . pick up . . . the . . . uhhh . . ." Stringing together a complete sentence was suddenly impossible. What was it we were supposed to pick up? *Bulldog . . . bull . . . dog . . . dog . . .*

Kemp seemed as confused as I was. "The . . . uhhh . . ." He blinked hard, shook his head. "Dog."

"Right, the dog. The dog's . . . probably . . . ummm . . . probably ready." I'd never had anyone kiss me like that before. Ever. That kind of kiss was dangerous.

I pushed off the washer and started toward the door, feeling like I was walking in a funhouse with a moving floor and wavy mirrors everywhere. Neither of us said anything as we exited the building and Kemp locked the door. While his back was turned, I caught my breath, patted my cheeks, smoothed stray strands of hair into my ponytail holder, tried to gather my scattered wits and put them back where they belonged.

On the way across the street to the vet clinic, we started a conversation about baseball—a harmless topic that was satisfactorily distant from whatever had just happened in the laundry room. Kemp asked me where I'd learned to play, and I revealed more than I'd intended to about my weird and disjointed upbringing. If it bothered him, he didn't show it.

"Sounds like you've seen a lot of places," he observed.

"We did," I agreed. "You're right. We did."

He held open the door of the clinic, and for an instant we were in interestingly close quarters. Another jolt of . . . whatever . . . zinged through me.

Inside, I inquired about Don's idiotic dog. I could hear him yapping insanely in back, probably annoying the other patients as they tried to recover from surgeries and flea dips. "Guess he's awake," I observed, and the receptionist nodded.

"He has been for a while. He's a talker." She glanced up at Kemp and smiled. "Hey there, Kempner. How's everything today?"

"Everything's good," he answered. "How goes it in the veterinary business, Billie?"

Billie tucked a pencil into her partially gray updo. "Better. We got a new intern." The answer came with a strange private smile, and then she leaned close to the speakerphone and pressed a button. "Ben, can you tell Doc to bring that black lab up here? The noisy one. His mom's back."

I grimaced at the idea of being Radar's mom. Hawkeye, maybe, but Radar was an orphan.

I heard toenails scrambling in the hall long before Radar turned the corner, dragging someone behind him. The veterinary intern skidded through the door frame, narrowly escaped a broken nose, then abruptly dropped Radar's leash and squealed, "Oh my gosh! Kemp! Where in the world did you come from?"

The next thing I knew, I was getting tackled by seventy pounds of slobbering Labrador, and the intern was wrapped around Kemp, who didn't seem to mind at all. He twirled the disgustingly gorgeous veterinarian around the waiting room, then set her down, and a barrage of questions and answers flew back and forth between them.

"When did you get into town?"

"Yesterday. Doc Thomas broke his shoulder—bad cow. He finally admitted he needed some help around here." She smiled and winked. "By the time that shoulder heals, I'll have him to where he can't live without me." She backhanded Kemp playfully in the stomach. "Did you get the box of stuff I sent you? Did you hang everything up?"

Suddenly, Kemp looked embarrassed. "Yeah, not quite. It's in my office, though."

Bracing her hands on her hips, she scowled, and even that was cute. "I worked hard on those! Here I kept them all this time, and now you're finally in one place and you don't even hang them up? Okay, I'm insulted."

Kemp cleared his throat and stretched his neck, as if all of a sudden his collar were too tight. "It's been . . . busy here."

"Yeah, right. You've been in Daily for what . . . eight, nine months?" She rolled her eyes, and if everything wasn't clear about them, the fact that they knew each other well was unmistakable. "I'm not even the scrapbooky type, you know. I wouldn't do that for just anybody. I was going to run by and surprise you this morning, but I couldn't get away. Good thing I didn't. I would've mashed that box right over your head, Kemp Eldridge."

*Good thing she didn't,* I thought, standing there holding Radar and feeling like a big purple third wheel in my eighties windsuit. *Very good thing she didn't.*

*This would be one of the skeletons he doesn't have in his closet. . . .*

"So, what are you doing here?" She nodded toward the reception desk to indicate *here,* as in *the vet clinic.*

"Had to pick up the dog." Kemp motioned in my direction, and suddenly they were both looking at me. Kemp quickly performed introductions. "Kai Miller, Jennifer Mayfield, Jen, Kai." Jennifer looked at me like she'd never seen me before, even though just a short time before we'd been engaged in friendly conversation and rat trap removal.

"Kai's here waiting out the hurricane," Kemp added.

"Ohhhh," Jen breathed, then sailed across the lobby with an outstretched hand and a friendly smile. "Oh, well, great to meet you, officially. Welcome to Daily."

"Thanks," I said, putting on my best friendly-cruise-crew face as we officially shook hands. "Good to meet you, too." Really, it wasn't. Meeting Jen opened up a whole line of questions that hadn't been there before. Who was she? Why was she scrapbooking Kemp's life? Why did I care?

Why had Kemp kissed me? Why did I get the feeling Jen wouldn't have been happy if she knew that? Why were her carefully framed mementos stacked in the corner of Kemp's office, where the cute little field mice could get to them?

I didn't know, and the uneasy look on Kemp's face told me I probably wouldn't be finding out anytime soon—from him, anyway.

I did now know who the box came from.

I wished it were still a mystery.

# Chapter 19

# *Donetta Bradford*

Imagene's daddy told me once, *When you're up against a wolf, you gotta think like a fox.*

Betty Prine and her group were about as much a pack of wolves as I've ever seen. Folks like the Prines only want things one way. Their way.

Sometimes it seems like it'd be easier to let them kind of folks win. You get crossways of Betty Prine, you might end up like Lot's wife. Betty could turn anybody into a pillar of salt, probably. If Betty put in a report on my building, and some inspector said I had to fix a bunch of things, or the insurance company decided not to insure me anymore, I wouldn't have the money for all that, and Betty knew it. My hotel, and my beauty salon, and Frank's auto repair shop in the back would be out of business, lickety-split. My brother and I'd be broke, and the building that'd been in my family over a hundred years would sit empty until it finally got sold off for taxes. The Prines'd bought more than one building on Main Street that way. They knew how to run somebody out of business without ever getting their hands dirty.

After Betty made her threats, my stomach was flippy as fish in a bucket. I had enough worries on my plate without taking on the Prines—there was Imagene's van still stuck on the side of the road, and Kai's bus we'd left in the woods, and my troubles with Ronald, and that little bit of matchmaking with Kemp and Kai. If I thought about it, I coulda come up with a whole list of reasons why it'd be easier to collect up some gas money for Sister Mona's bunch and send them on their way.

But a crowded plate's one of the biggest enemies of good works. Brother Ervin'd talked about it just a few Sundays ago in service. He'd brought some brown hen eggs and just stood there by the pulpit, juggling one and looking out into the congregation and greeting folks—saying whose baby looked cute this morning and who'd come back from being sick. Then he was juggling two eggs and doing the same thing.

"Brother Ervin, what are you doin'?" Amber Anderson's littlest brother, Avery, asked finally. In the Amen pews up front, Betty Prine let out a little snort. She didn't like anything that didn't come straight out of Scripture, and juggling eggs wasn't anyplace in the Bible.

"Well, I don't know," Brother Ervin answered and smiled at the boy. "What do you think I'm doin', Avery?"

"Jugglin' eggs, and lookin' who's here, and talkin' to people," the boy said.

Brother Ervin nodded and picked up another egg. Then he had three. He looked out at the crowd and told Millie Crawford that was a pretty new sweater she had on and did she knit it herself? Then he noticed that Bailey Henderson's little boy'd got his cast off his arm. "What am I doing now, Avery?"

Avery looked at his peepaw, and his peepaw nodded for him to answer the question, so Avery did. "Jugglin' three eggs and lookin' to see who's here, and askin' Sammie Henderson about his arm."

"That's true." Brother Ervin picked up another egg. Those were good, hard-shelled brown eggs, but I was getting worried, with four in the air. I figured Brother Ervin'd better quit gawking around and talking, and concentrate on what he was doin'. The Prines'd put in a big donation for our new carpet, and if those eggs landed on the floor . . . oh mercy!

"Now what?" Brother Ervin didn't look out at Avery that time, which was good. He had to keep focused on the eggs.

"Jugglin' four," Avery said.

"Anything else?" Brother Ervin almost lost an egg again.

"No, sir, just jugglin' four. Well, and you asked me a question, too."

Brother Ervin nodded and shot a quick look at the egg basket. Little beads of sweat were gathering on his forehead, and his mustache was twitching on one side, flashing an eye tooth. "Avery, you keep tellin' everybody what I'm doin', all right?"

"All right." Even Avery sounded worried now, and in the front row, Betty Prine'd pushed Harold halfway out of his seat, like she was gonna have him dive for the altar and catch the eggs before they hit the carpet.

"Okay. Right now, you look like you're gonna get another egg," Avery reported. "Okay, now you got five, but you're just jugglin' and watchin' them hen eggs, and that's all."

A big ol' bead of sweat ran down Brother Ervin's nose and hung off the end. There was one more egg in the basket, and you coulda heard a cat cross a cotton bale in that room. Nobody was sleepin' in church that day, I'll tell you.

"You gonna do six, Brother Ervin?" Avery asked, but Ervin didn't answer.

Now, I got faith in the Lord and Brother Ervin as His instrument, but I was worried, I'll admit.

"Don't you dare!" Betty Prine shrieked. "That carpet cost an arm and a leg."

"It's Stainmaster," Imagene muttered behind me, which woulda made me chuckle, but I was froze in place.

"I hope he does it," Kemp whispered, which was just like Kemp, livin' on the edge. "I'll clean it up."

*Lord,* I started prayin'. *Please don't let Brother Ervin try for that last egg. It'd be a sad end to a good preachin' career. Betty Prine'd get him fired, or worse. . . .*

Half the church council was out of their seats already.

"You're still jugglin' five," Avery reported. "Just jugglin' and nothin' else."

Right then, Brother Ervin caught all the eggs—three in one set of fingers and two in the other, and a sigh went through the whole church.

"My goodness, Lola Fae, I think that is the prettiest pearl necklace I ever did see," Brother Ervin said as he tucked the eggs back into the basket. "But you're just about as white as it is. I didn't scare ya, did I? And Nana Henderson, how're you feelin' today? That sciatic nerve get any better? What am I doin' now, Avery?"

"Talkin' to folks again and lookin' who's here, and asking about Nana Henderson's static nerves."

Brother Ervin nodded, smiling just a little, like he does when he's about to make a point. "You notice anythin' different from the first of this demonstration to the last?"

Avery thought for a minute, his sweet little face getting narrow around the nose. His peepaw leaned over and whispered something in his ear.

"Well," the boy said finally, "at first, you was jugglin' just a couple and talkin' to folks and lookin' out here, but the more eggs you got in the air, the more you had to look at the eggs and not the folks."

Out went Brother Ervin's lightnin' finger. "Exactly! Avery Anderson, you ever think that maybe, when the Levite and the priest passed by that man who'd been robbed and left on the side of the road, maybe they had lots of things goin' on? Maybe they had a couple meetings to get to, and the potluck list to worry about, and some business deal to do, and a fund-raiser goin' on down at the Moose Lodge? Maybe they had so many eggs up in the air, they just didn't hardly look twice at that man layin' all beat-up and bloody. You think?"

"Maybe." Avery shrugged his little shoulders up and down and grinned, enjoying having everyone's attention. He'd be a star like his big sister someday. "But Brother Ervin, I reckon I know one thing for sure about that man on the side of the road."

"What's that, Avery?"

Avery's big brown eyes got wide as a newborn calf's, earnest and sweet. "I reckon it's a lucky thing for him that Samaritan didn't know how to juggle."

The whole church had a big belly laugh, and it was three minutes before things quieted down enough for Brother Ervin to make the point that the biggest enemy of havin' our hands ready for God's work is having them full up with other things.

Brother Ervin and them eggs came to mind when I was thinkin' about all the reasons it'd be easier to give in to Betty Prine and send the Holy Ghost bunch on their way. I figured my rememberin' that sermon was a sign, so I decided to get Brother Ervin and a few others to help come up with some kind of a plan to outthink Betty Prine.

We met at my house so Betty wouldn't know what was goin' on. Lucy and Imagene got there first, and then Frank showed up, hopping mad about Betty's threats, of course. Harlan Hanson drove over in his postal jeep, and then Brother Ervin came in, and Sharon Lee, that sweet little preacher from Daily Methodist,

Pastor Harve from the little church out at Caney Creek, and at the last minute old stutterin' Doyle Banes rolled in, driving his dump truck from the lime plant. He'd stopped off and picked up Bodie Rogers, who ran the Texan Talkies theater until it went out of business. Thinking back on it now, I knew why Bodie was here. It was Betty and Harold Prine that got the theater building condemned and closed down.

Right now, Bodie had a gleam in his eye, and his big square German face was hard set. "That's just what she done to me," he said, striking a big fist in the air so hard the half-dozen hairs combed over his bald spot lifted and fell back down again. "Her and Harold just wanted to get me out of business so people'd come rent from that video store they put in. Just want everybody to sit home and watch movies on TV. It ain't the same as goin' to the theater. It ain't. Any decent town oughta have a place to go watch the picture show."

"All right, now, let's ride one horse at a time, here." Brother Ervin took out his hankie, pulled off his eyeglasses and polished the lenses. "Right now, we got to solve the problem with the hurricane folks—without getting Betty and Harold Prine on the warpath. We got to get the folks out of the church and out of Donetta's buildin', but if they head on to Dallas or Waco, they're gonna end up there with no place to stay. Every shelter from here to the Red River is full up. I did some callin'."

"Them Prines won't stop till they own the whole town." Bodie's eyes squeezed until they almost disappeared behind his big cheekbones.

Frank put in two cents that he probably shouldn'ta said in front of three preachers. You could always count on my brother to tell everybody exactly what he thought.

Sharon Lee mentioned that the Methodist campground might be a possibility, but it'd take a few days, maybe a week, to get all the approvals and the water turned back on and such.

"We hadn't got a week," I told her. "We hadn't got a day, really. Come Monday mornin', Betty'll have the fire marshal on my doorstep first thing, and the fire marshal ain't blind old Burt Battles anymore. It's that new young fella from Dallas. You know and I know my buildin's perfectly safe, but if Betty Prine sticks her nose in, with the way she's got the commissioner's court under her thumb, and that new fire marshal bein' in office, it won't be the kind of deal where they look past the squeaks and creaks of an old buildin', and let business go on as usual. He'll red tag me for havin' too many people sleepin' in my building, and about a dozen other things, too, I'll bet."

"We could use the churches," Sharon suggested. "There's nothing Betty can do about our putting people there."

"Harold Prine's on my church council," Brother Ervin pointed out, and Sharon nodded gravely.

Pastor Harve leaned back in his chair and rubbed the top of his head, where thick white hair stood out against his skin like cotton fluff on polished brown leather. "Well, the churches don't make too good a solution, anyhow." His deep, scratchy voice rumbled around the room in a way that made everyone else stop and listen. "No bathtubs, no showers, not enough restrooms for that many folks. I been talkin' to their Pastor D., and he's afraid it'll be a couple weeks, even a month, before they got power and water back in their area. And that's assumin' they got a place to go home *to*. No way of knowin' that yet. If we put folks in the churches and then the Prines decide to make trouble, they can get every one of our old church buildin's wrote up for code violations, just like Donetta's place, and then the Prines can get the insurance companies all riled up, and we'll all end up in a pickle."

"We could try to put the evacuees in houses around town," Sharon suggested. "I have a guest room." Bless her heart, but she hadn't been in town long enough to know Betty Prine very well.

"Hon," I told her, "even if we could find enough space—which'd be hard, because quite a few local folks already got relatives staying here for the evacuation—once Betty Prine gets around, you won't hardly be able to find anybody who'll give out a guest room. Harold's bank owns half the mortgages in town, for one thing. These days, with the economy bein' what it is, there's a lot of folks a payment or two behind. They can't afford to get Harold mad."

Brother Ervin nodded, and so did Pastor Harve, and we all scratched our thinking caps some more.

Strange as it may be, Doyle Banes was the first one to speak up. "I uggg-got a idea."

All of us turned his way at once. I was scared to ask what he had in mind, because it takes Doyle a long time to spit out a whole idea. The day was rushin' by in a hurry. Any time now, I'd be getting a call from Betty Prine, demanding to know why my building wasn't empty yet.

The phone rang, and I figured it was probably her.

"Which kind idea?" Lucy gave Doyle a patient look.

"W-w-well . . ." Any sentence Doyle started with *well* was gonna take a while. "I was-was thinkin', we uuuh could-could-could, maybe could uhhh s-s-see about, see about uhhh askin' uhhh . . ."

On the other side of the room, Frank smacked the palm of his hand on the chair arm. "I think we oughta just git some pitchforks and a torch or two and head on over to the Prine place. I'll rustle up a wood stake and some garlic."

Imagene giggled and swatted at Frank, and he winked at her where he thought no one'd see it.

"Ssshhh!" Lucy hissed, which was pretty bold for Lucy. Folding her hands in her lap, she turned back to Doyle. "Which kind idea you got? Good idea, I bet."

Doyle's big droopy eyes went wide, and he straightened like

he was Pinocchio and somebody'd just pulled the strings. He cleared his throat real big and said, "I was thinkin' we could put-put 'em out at the Anderson-Shay ranch." That was about the clearest sentence Doyle'd ever spit out. "All-all-all them buildings been fixed up, gettin' ready for the umm-movie filmin' and the foster shelter, y'know."

The thought swirled round the room like a hawk gliding in circles—kind of quiet, and interesting to look at.

"I thought the work out there'd hit a snag," I said. For months, all kinds of construction crews and volunteers had been working to bring the old Barlinger ranch back to life so Amber Anderson and Justin Shay could start filming *The Horseman* and then move on with the plans to turn the place into a new charity home for foster kids. The foster shelter plans'd got put on hold, though, because an *anonymous citizen* brought up questions about whether there was enough water supply out there for the sprinkler systems that a group home had to have. Now the well had to be tested, and probably more wells drilled.

We all knew who *Mrs. Anonymous* was. Betty and Harold were all for our town getting famous with a movie bein' made here, but they didn't want any bunch of foster kids moving in and going to Daily schools.

Doyle had a sneaky little gleam in his eye. I'd never seen sneaky and Doyle in the same seat before. "We-we-we still been workin' out there. Don't tell uuun-nobody. Scooter hooked up the ulll-lectric last week. Marley checked the plummin', uhhh checked it Thursdey."

"He did?" Imagene's mouth dropped open with shock, and mine did, too. The very idea that something so big could have been going on just a few miles outside Daily, and we didn't know anything about it!

"I been haulin' fill dirt from F-F-F-Frank's place."

"You have?" My head snapped toward Frank, who was lookin'

three shades of pale, and rightly so. How dare my brother be in on such a big secret and not share it with us gals!

"Frank never *said* anythin'," I shot Frank a glare that coulda fried an egg. He snatched his cowboy hat off his knee, dropped it on his head, and pulled the brim low.

"B-b-b-b-been on the Q.T.," Doyle added.

I gandered around the room and figured out right then that everyone knew but me. Imagene was looking down at her hands and Lucy'd turned her ear to the dog barking out back, like it was real important.

"Looks to me like everyone thinks Donetta Bradford can't keep a secret," I said.

"Now, Netta," Imagene said, trying to settle me, but I pointed a finger at her before she could finish.

"And you! There you are, my *best* friend, and us about to die in a tornado and a hurricane, and you didn't even fess up then!"

Imagene flapped her lips like a fish trying to spit out a hook. "I didn't think it mattered right then, Donetta, and besides, I . . . promised Frank I wouldn't breathe a word."

"Promised *Frank?*" I coughed out. "Promised *Frank?* Well, since when does—" Every once in a while, the Lord actually gets His hand over my mouth in time, because I was about to say, *Since when does Frank rate above your best friend?* Imagene would never've forgiven me for saying something about her and Frank in front of everybody.

I sat back in my chair, hooked my arms over my chest, and said, "Never mind. If we can't put a bunch of foster kids out there because of the wells, how we gonna put a whole church-load of folks? Betty Prine'll just stick her big nose in and shut us down."

"Unnn-not if she don't know." Doyle gave me a crafty look. "Betty don't-don't-don't have no reason to uggg-go way out there."

"How we gonna feed 'em? It'll be a lot of groceries to buy," I pointed out. "They ain't got that much money left, after buyin' gas to get here."

Brother Ervin cleared his throat, a little smile slowly spreading under his mustache. "I got a big check from Harold Prine just this mornin'. He said it was a donation to help the evacuees get to a shelter."

I sucked in a breath, because it ain't every day the Baptist preacher suggests tellin' a lie and committin' financial fraud. "But that money's for gas."

"And we'll be glad to use it for gas," Brother Ervin said. "Which'll free up the money Pastor D.'s got left in his reserve. That'll buy a bunch of groceries."

"By golly, I'll donate some, too!" Bodie struck a vengeful fist in the air, and I couldn't blame him. "Heck, I'll drive my truck over to the Wal-Mart in Austin and buy the groceries myself."

We went on with the planning from there, until we finally had the details worked out. Doyle, Ervin, and Frank were gonna get busy and gather up all the blankets and pillows they could, then get cots from the Methodist campground. Harlan would finish his mail route, then pick up his wife and they'd head to the grocery store with Bodie. Imagene and I would explain everything to Sister Mona and Pastor D. At four o'clock, the whole Holy Ghost crew would roll on out of town, head down the highway, and loop right around Bee Hollow Road, the back way to the ranch. Meanwhile, Pastor Harve and his bunch from Caney Creek Church would cook up some brisket and beans for a hot supper out there tonight.

"Oh, hang, somebody better get ahold of Justin Shay or Amber Anderson and make sure it's okay to put all them people out there," Imagene pointed out. "It's their ranch, after all."

"Well, that's true." I was mad at Imagene, but she was right. "Amber's on singin' tour someplace. And I saw on *Celebs Inside* where Justin's still in that rehab center way out in the desert somewhere, but he's doin' real good. No tellin' how hard it might be to get ahold of him or Amber. I'll get busy and call Lauren. She's out in California helpin' with the movie script right now. She might could tell us how to get permission to use the ranch."

"If Betty finds out they let us put people out there, she'll make even more trouble about the foster shelter plans, you know." It was just like Imagene to worry about everything that *might* happen. Imagene never took a step in her life without looking three times at where her foot was gonna land.

"One horse at a time," Brother Ervin reminded, and he was right. No sense borrowing trouble when we had enough already.

We went over the plans again real quick, then everyone got up and headed for the door. I ended up in the living room with my brother.

"Where's Kemp at?" he asked as he hauled himself out of the chair and worked on getting upright.

"He's with Kai, I reckon. I hadn't seen them since they left for breakfast."

Frank smacked his lips. One thing about Frank, he never let his kids sit idle for a minute. They always had to be working. "Hope Kemp remembered to go by the house and feed that bottle baby calf in the pen. I reckon I'll try to figure out where he's at, and he can come help with the furniture movin'."

"You don't worry about him." I wagged a finger at Frank. "He's already been over to the school this mornin' to let the boys work out in the field house, which oughta be the football coach's job. And he's been showin' Kai around town, and I got a feelin' about them two."

Frank rolled his eyes, his mustache hiding a new frown. "Leave the boy alone, Netta. You already got my daughter flittin' off to California, in love with a movie writer. Kemp's got enough on his plate, between teachin' and coachin' and havin' them surgeries on his arm. He don't need to be moonin' after some gal that's just here till she can head back home to the coast. He's already facin' a half-dozen doctors tellin' him all different things about his pitchin' arm. He don't need to be settin' himself up for one more heartache."

"Ffff!" Sometimes Frank didn't have even a speck of vision. "Far as I can tell, Kemp's settlin' back in here real good. Seems like he likes livin' out at the ranch again, and he's good with the kids at school. I hear their test scores were up ten percent in math last spring. He's a good teacher and a good coach, and if he could just find him a little gal . . . the right little gal this time . . . he'd quit moonin' over playin' pro baseball and start makin' hisself a normal life."

Frank held up his cowboy hat and sighted down the brim, like that hat bein' straight mattered more than what I was sayin'. "Just let him be, Netta. I want that boy here at home just as much as you do, but maybe his idea of a good life ain't livin' right in Daily and settlin' down and findin' him a wife. Maybe he don't want to give up on baseball until he don't have any other options."

"Ffff! What's one more surgery and one more go-round gonna get him, except back home again in six months, or a year, or two years in the same spot he's in now? There ain't any point in him livin' through it all again. I think deep down he knows that. I think he's ready for somethin' new in his life." Talking to Frank about matters of the heart was like waltzing with a mule. "Maybe he's still tryin' to make peace with it all right now, but you didn't see the way he looked at that girl the first time he laid eyes on her. He was dumbstruck. I ain't ever seen Kemp dumbstruck, have you?"

Frank pulled in air and let out a big sigh. "Cute little gal like that'll turn any boy's head, but that don't mean there's somethin' more on the horizon."

"You ain't got a romantic bone in your body, Frank Eldridge."

"Maybe not." He shrugged like he didn't care one whit. Then he crossed the room and walked out the door. I just let him go and grabbed the phone and called Lauren to track down Justin Shay about using the ranch.

By the time I got done with the call and headed outside, Frank and Imagene were lingerin' in the carport. They were standin' close, like they had a secret between them. Soon as they saw me, they stepped apart like a couple kids caught flirtin'. Frank waved over his shoulder, then walked out to his truck and drove off, and Imagene headed back in. I stopped her at the door, because I'd had just about enough of them carrying on. "You know what?" Even though I could hear Lucy coming up behind me, I went right on. "If you and Frank are gonna be sweet on each other, you oughta just come out with it."

Imagene's mouth dropped open, and I thought she'd faint and fall out right there, but then she just flushed red and looked away. "Gracious, Netta."

"There's nothin' wrong with it. Not one thing—him bein' a widower since the kids were little and you a widow over a year now. Jack wouldn't have a grudge against it, either. He'd want you to be happy. He'd want you both to be happy. He loved you and Frank both. Life's too short to be mealymouthin' around. You got to go after your own happiness."

Imagene poked her hands onto her hips so hard they disappeared in there somewhere. "And what about you, Donetta Bradford? Here you are givin' all this advice, and where's Ronald? Where's he at right now?"

"I don't know." I pulled up my chin, because she'd hit a sore spot.

Imagene whipped out her chubby little finger and pointed it at me. "And you *ain't* tried to find out. You know full well that Kemp or Buddy Ray Baldridge or the sheriff would go down the river and look for Ronald right now if you asked, but you *hadn't* asked, because you got your feelings hurt and you're too proud to say so."

"I hadn't got time to worry about where Ronald's fishin' right now. He'll come back when he comes back, I reckon." I tried to act like it didn't matter, but Imagene knew. She'd got me by the short hairs the way only a best friend can. "There's more important things to think about. We have all these people to tend."

Imagene hooked her eyes on me so hard I felt pulled down by it. "It don't have anything to do with those people, Netta, and you know it. This's been goin' on between you and Ronald a long time. You're just gonna sit here and die on the vine without a word, because you're too stubborn to tell that man how you feel."

Something drew tight in my ribs and stung like a thistle burr in the back of my nose. "Ronald don't listen, Imagene. It's like livin' with a two-hundred-pound sack of beans. You don't understand, because you and Jack never were that way."

"Jack's Jack and Ronald's Ronald." Imagene's voice got quiet. "That man loves you, Netta."

"Not so you could tell it." Even though I didn't want to, even though I was hard in my heart about it, and I had been for a long time, my eyes welled up, and right there in the carport I broke down and started to cry.

Imagene took me in her arms and rocked me back and forth like a baby, and then I felt Lucy join in, too, until we were just a wad of girlfriends, swaying back and forth while the flies buzzed overhead, looking for a warm place to land before the evenin' set in.

## Chapter 20

# Kai Miller

Every once in a while, you experience a day that's perfect, except for the little voice in your head whispering that you'll wake up sooner or later and it will all be a dream, so you shouldn't get too invested. But you can't help it, because everything feels so right.

My day with Kemp was like that. A span of time apart from any reality and unlike any other. After the vet visit and the baseball game, we returned Radar to Donetta's yard and packed firewood into a hole under the fence so the dog wouldn't make another great escape. As we were finishing, Kemp mentioned that he needed to go *feed a bottle baby*, whatever that meant, and asked if I wanted to ride along. With no idea what I might be getting into, I agreed. We grabbed some lunch at Dairy Queen, and Kemp drove us out to his family's ranch, where, I gathered, his dad lived in the main house and Kemp lived in the original farmhouse, as he put it, *on the back side of the place.*

As we drove, I took in the countryside, enjoying the view, as the late-summer breeze wafted in the windows, contributing to the sheen of perfection on the day. Having come to town in the dark, I hadn't fully appreciated how beautiful it was here. Outside the window, the grass grew sparse and feathery among thick, squatty nests of prickly- pear cactus and yuccas with tall stalks that had yielded summer flowers but now were dried brown and hard in the sun. When I asked about them, Kemp laughed and said that as kids, they'd often cracked off the dead stalks and used them for sword fights. "Jen was the champ. She just about poked my eye out once."

All of a sudden, my DQ milkshake tasted sour, and the day felt tainted. There was that name again. Jen, Jenny, Jennifer. He called her all three. She came up repeatedly in little anecdotes about his past. Jennifer was part of all the good times, number three in a trio of musketeers with Kemp and his sister, Lauren. Jen was the only person who lived close enough to their ranch to be a playmate. They rendezvoused in the middle of the pasture to play in the big live-oak grove and wile away the hours, skipping rocks and swimming in Caney Creek.

Kemp pointed to the grove as we bumped along a winding gravel driveway, past his father's place, to an old stone farmhouse on the backside of the ranch, where Kemp was, in his own words, *bunking for now.* Gazing at the rolling, dry-grass sea, I pictured a little-girl version of Jen, crossing the pasture with her yucca sword, trotting high in the knees to clear the tufts of grass, her hair bouncing and catching the sun in waves as she galloped and tossed her head. *Jen never went anywhere without pretending she was riding a horse,* Kemp had commented after he told me about the yucca swords. *I think the only reason she liked us was because we always had ponies around.*

Jen didn't seem to be thinking about ponies when she saw Kemp at the vet clinic. She was thinking about Kemp—slipping comfortably into a pattern of interplay that revealed old affections, turning on a charm even baggy scrubs and a little smear of margarine on her cheek couldn't hide.

In the back of my head, the still, small voice of insecurity whispered that I could never compete with someone like Jen, Jenny, Jennifer, as if I didn't know that already and hadn't been aware of it forever. I understood it in the part of me that had realized it since the day my mother left a note on the table and walked out. *It's for the best,* she wrote. *I don't know where I'm going, or where I'll be. I just know I can't be here.* For a while, I thought it was temporary. My mother had always been flighty, fragile, temperamental. She'd come back eventually, after she worked through Gil's death in her own way.

But she didn't, and time went by, and a couple years later, she sent a note with an address. She had a new last name, a new family. It was then that I knew what I had already suspected. I wasn't all that great. If I were, my mother wouldn't have replaced me with stepkids that weren't even hers. It doesn't take a genius to figure that out, even at thirteen. The truths you establish early stay with you. They're written in the journal of who you are—the one you carry around in your pocket like an operating manual for life.

Of course a guy like Kemp wouldn't seriously be interested in someone like me. He was just being . . . hospitable, a polite host. Whatever was between him and Jen was really none of my business. The man had a life after all, and on a normal day, I wasn't part of it. Jen was. Clearly she slipped into his thoughts quite often, and the two of them were important to each other. That didn't explain why he'd kissed me in the laundry room. Maybe he put the moves on women all the time, just to see if he could—he didn't seem like the type, but you could never tell. Maybe, given the hurricane relocation and my traumatic experience in it, I was communicating particular vulnerability and desperation, and he was just trying to cheer me up. Maybe the purple windsuit and lopsided ponytail made me particularly attractive. . . . Well, okay, not likely, but it made about as much sense as anything else.

*Just enjoy the afternoon,* the voice in my head admonished, and I tried to banish the pointless inner dialogue. No matter where I went or what I did, the negative head talk jumped in the middle of every potential relationship. Not that this was a potential relationship, of course, but why clutter up the day with old insecurities and self-deprecating head talk? Right now, it was just Kemp and me and the mysterious bottle baby.

Shortly after our arrival at Kemp's little stone house, I met the bottle baby, and no amount of negative head talk could compete. Bottle Baby was actually a brown and white calf with soft doe eyes and a squeaky, pitiful little voice that awakened some motherly instinct I didn't know I had. It was living in an enclosure behind Kemp's place. I scratched its head while Kemp went in the barn to "fix lunch," as he put it. He came out with a baby bottle the size of a football and handed it to me.

"Really?" I held the bottle up uncertainly, checking out the giant udder-shaped spout on the end. "I mean, I don't know how . . ."

Kemp laughed and positioned my hands on the bottle, his fingers sliding over mine in a way that sent a current up my arms. "Just hold it out. Yeah, like that. He knows what to do. Oh, hey, don't brace it against your stomach that way. He'll—"

Just before Kemp could finish explaining why I shouldn't use my body to keep the bottle steady, the calf planted all four feet and butted his food source, forcing the air out of my lungs. "Ooof," I coughed. "I think I lost a kidney."

Chuckling, Kemp said, "Guess I should have told you that to begin with," then abandoned me and walked to the fence to refill a water bucket.

"Guess so," I agreed. Gazing down at the calf, now sucking the bottle with his little milk mouth dripping and his brown and white tail spinning like a propeller, I fell in love again. "How old is he?"

"About three weeks." Kemp dumped the bucket, then rinsed and refilled it, and stood leaning on the fence, watching the bottle baby drain the milk so fast the plastic was collapsing in my hands. "Pull it out of his mouth a minute and let the air in."

I pulled, but Baby hung on with impressive strength. "He doesn't want to let . . . go . . . hey . . . there we are." The bottle inflated, the calf blew out a loud, milky complaint, stomping his feet and kicking the air, and then I lowered the bottle, and he latched on again, rapidly draining the rest of the milk. "He's really cute. Can I keep him?"

Kemp chuckled. "Not if you want to trade me a dog for him."

I laughed, picturing the calf down at Blowfish Billy's with Don and Hawkeye. "Sorry, it's the dog or nothing. All my other valuables are stuck in a van somewhere between here and Perdida." The flippancy of the comment surprised me at first. Right now, the Microbus and its contents didn't seem to matter at all. I was more interested in wrestling the bottle from Baby's mouth and watching him stomp and complain like an unhappy toddler. When he tried to use my windsuit as a pacifier, I ran for the fence and climbed to safety, laughing.

"No deal, then." Kemp took the bottle, rinsed it out, and hung it on a loose wire to dry in the sun. "Listen, don't worry about the van." His tone sobered as we walked to the truck. "As soon as the roads are open, Dad's taking his car-hauling trailer and heading down to see about Imagene's van. He'll pick yours up, too." He made it seem simple, as if it were a given that the vehicles would be sitting, undamaged, right where we'd left them. I had a feeling he was making it sound that way for my benefit.

"Thanks. I'm just trying not to think ahead too much."

Actually, at the moment, I didn't want to think at all about getting the van back. Its return meant my vacation in Daily, Texas, was over. As soon as I had transportation and the roads were clear, I had no excuse for not getting back to work.

"Good plan." He gave me a thumbs-up as we climbed into the truck and left Baby behind, headed for our next adventure, whatever it was going to be. When we reached the end of the driveway, he stopped and checked the road in both directions. "So, who do you know in McGregor?"

It took a minute for the question to register. I was looking out the window, watching a huge flock of big white birds dip, dive, and circle against the afternoon sky. As they turned, sunlight caught their wings, then retreated, causing them to shine like silver one moment, then disappear into the sky the next. "What are those white birds? They're really beautiful."

"Cattle egrets. You changed the subject again." Leaning forward, he rested his chin atop his knuckles on the steering wheel and studied me, his eyes a warm gold in the sunlight.

Something tugged inside me, then quickened. My gaze drifted to his mouth, and I thought about kissing him again. "I guess I did." The next thing I knew, I was telling him about my grandmother—about the big clapboard house, the room downstairs, which still held the porcelain sink and glass-fronted cabinets where my great-grandfather had practiced medicine, the banister Gil and I slid down when we could get away with it, the town kids hanging out at the drive-in, the uncomfortable family dinners, and my father sitting stiff in his chair, putting up with *the sermon* until he could leave the table and wander off with his guitar.

By the time I was finished, Kemp had put the vehicle in Park and turned his body so that he was leaning against the door.

Suddenly, I felt stupid for having spilled more of our sordid and slightly pathetic history. By now, he'd probably concluded that I was a total mess. His childhood, by contrast, seemed so normal and . . . well . . . healthy. "Sorry. I didn't mean to dump all that. Our family dynamics tended to be pretty weird."

Kemp smiled slightly. "You haven't seen weird until you've been to a gathering of the Eldridge clan." He rested an arm on the back of the seat, like he had all the time in the world.

"Your family isn't weird."

His brows shot up, then he chuckled. "You've been two days with Aunt Netta and you don't think my family's weird? You *are* a peach."

"A what?"

"Aunt Netta says you're a peach." He winked, and I felt myself melting into a little pool on the seat. *A peach. . . . Me?*

I felt warm all over, flushed in a way that had nothing to do with the afternoon heat. "I'm not sure anyone's ever called me a peach before."

His lips spread into a slow smile that made the nerve endings in my skin go haywire. "I can't imagine why not." Just as my senses were taking a magic carpet ride to Shangri-La, he glanced up and down the road again, then slipped his fingers over the gearshift, like he was ready to proceed with our trip. "So . . . I could drive you over to McGregor. It's only about fifteen miles from here, the back way." He nodded toward the road opposite the direction we'd come.

Uncertainty swept over me, sudden and surprising like the spray off a winter sea. "I don't . . ." For a moment, I couldn't think. What would happen if I said yes? Was the house even still there? If it was, would I have the courage to open the gate, walk past the stone lions, and traverse the pathway in the shadow of the oak trees, knock on the door . . .

What if she wasn't even there anymore? What if, all these years, I'd been mentally role-playing something that would never happen?

What if she *was* there and she didn't want to see me? What if she wasn't any happier to have me standing on her doorstep now than she was to see my father, all those times the wind blew us in?

Did I really want to know? Did I really want to make contact with her while I was homeless in the middle of a hurricane evacuation? She'd only think I was there looking for help, asking for a handout or a place to stay. She'd think things were just like they'd always been.

Wouldn't she?

It was so much easier to leave the questions unanswered, to let time pass by. Just drift . . . from one week to the next, from one year to the next, from one relationship to the next. In spite of all my determination to build a different life, a better life than the one I'd grown up with, the truth was that I was just like my father. I'd drifted around, working in tourist shops, taking contracts on cruise ships, forming surface relationships. Everything I owned, everything I had to show for the first twenty-seven years of my life, could fit in a van and a tiny apartment. I'd grown up to be exactly what I was when Grandmother Miller saw me last. She wouldn't like me any more now than she did then.

The realization was painful.

*Nothing adrift is meant to stay adrift forever.* The words of the street preacher on the pier floated across my thoughts like the shadow of a gull flying over. He'd quoted a Scripture about coming home, then he'd opened his arms to the sky and the sea and the gathering of transients and said, *Come home, brothers. Come home.*

*Home.* My heart didn't even know what that word really meant. Home wasn't a cabin on a cruise ship, or an apartment over a surf shop. It was a place where you looked across a field of grass and saw whispers of your childhood among the live oaks and the yuccas drying in the sun. Kemp had no idea how fortunate he really was.

I would never be home, because for me the past was scattered like dandelion seeds, bits and pieces sprouting here and sprouting there, nothing rooted very deeply.

"How long since you've seen her?" Kemp's voice was quiet, his face empathic. "Your grandmother."

"Since I was a kid. Thirteen, I guess. We visited once after my little brother died—to see his headstone in the family plot. After that, my mom moved to Arizona, and my dad and I spent the year with harvest crews up in the Dakotas. It was someplace different. I guess Dad thought that would be the easiest thing."

Kemp relaxed in his seat again, as if he'd stopped considering whether we would turn toward McGregor or toward Daily. "That must have been hard. I don't remember when my mom passed on. I was too little, but I know it was tough for Lauren. Dad said for months she carried around a lap quilt that was Mom's—just dragged it along everywhere she went. It got smaller and smaller until finally she just gave it up, I guess. I don't remember the end of the story."

"I kept Gil's Bible after he died." I'd never told anyone that before. The Bible was my secret. Something I didn't want to share with anybody, yet telling Kemp felt natural. "It's hard to let go, I guess."

"I don't think you have to let go, really," Kemp's gaze had drifted past me. Not out the window, but into some private thought. "At some point you have to stop dragging around the blanket, but it's okay to tuck a few pieces in your pocket. The bright ones. Good memories. If God intended us to just move on, those things wouldn't stay with us so long."

Watching Kemp's face, I thought of the image he'd created. Gil and me. Little pieces of a quilt, the bright ones, tucked away safely in a pocket, where the sunlight and the weather couldn't fade them. Close by. Beautiful to look at, still.

The Bible was the piece where I stood in the sea and tried to baptize my brother. Gil was never afraid to die. He was only afraid of what would happen to the rest of us after he was gone. When we sat on the rocks that day, he told me everything he read in that Bible. Everything about heaven. He didn't have any doubt.

Now, pulling out that scrap of memory, examining it, I realized that when I'd sat on the shore with Gil, I hadn't doubted, either. I'd believed—right up until God didn't do what I wanted, what I *needed* Him to do. He didn't save my brother. After that, I'd let what Gil believed, what I believed, drift away, let it float so far out to sea that it was only a speck on the horizon, indistinguishable.

The realization was startling, almost painful in its intensity. It wasn't that I'd ever told myself I *didn't* believe, just that I'd never told myself anything. I'd let life go on, like the tide coming in and out, floating faith closer sometimes, and then farther away. It seemed like a workable arrangement, since the boat never moved completely out of sight. There was always a mooring line that tied me to Gil, to the place he was now.

Gil's Bible. Gil's Bible was the thread that stretched from here to eternity.

"Which way?" Kemp's voice broke into my thoughts.

I tried to decide. Wasn't it time to finally confront the very things that kept me separate from everyone? To stop dragging them around like dead weight?

Kemp's phone rang before I could answer. Grabbing it off the console, he looked at the screen. "Huh, wonder what Dad wants," he muttered, then apologized for taking the call.

I waved him off, saying, "No, it's fine." My mind was churning. I felt like a skydiver who'd discovered too late that the chute hadn't been packed correctly. I was spinning and spinning until I'd lost all sense of equilibrium.

The conversation between Kemp and his father was short, and when it was over the question of where to go next had been answered. Kemp's presence had been requested, more like demanded, in a project involving gathering cots and furniture and moving them someplace to better house the evacuees.

"Guess you heard all that," he apologized. "Sorry."

Apparently, he couldn't see relief sliding over my skin like warm oil. "No. It's fine." A quick twinge of disappointment pinched unexpectedly at the thought that this was the end of our day together. "Can I come?" It sounded desperate. Embarrassment prickled where a sense of letdown had been. It was hard to say which was worse. "I mean, I don't mind helping."

"I figured you'd come along." He made it sound completely elementary, as if he'd never considered dropping me off before moving on to Project Furniture.

Something twittered in my chest, like a string of twinkle lights glittering unexpectedly on a warm summer night. I felt the momentary high I had when a piece of jewelry came together as if by magic, and suddenly there was something beautiful where there had been only bits and pieces before, or the sense of triumph I had when a shop owner called me to gloat about a big sale and request new inventory. Those conversations usually took place with me privately jumping up and down while clutching my end of the phone. With Kemp there, I had to make an effort not to seem so giddy.

As we headed off to gather furniture, I was lighter than air, floating like a puffy little cloud in the passenger seat. Driving the back roads, we talked about Daily, the people there, the town's history as a railroad shipping point for wool and mohair, its struggle as downtown businesses dried up in the face of modern commuter mentality. "Everyone just drives to Waco or Temple to shop anymore," Kemp said, the words sounding melancholy. "But I guess you never know what'll happen. Now we're the Home of Amber Anderson, and the future film site for *The Horseman*. All of a sudden, there's tourism. Who'da thought, you know?"

"Kind of amazing what the wind blows in, I guess." Without thinking, I'd quoted my mother. Before our family started falling apart, she used to say that when something good fell our way unexpectedly. *Kind of amazing what the wind blows in.*

Kemp looked at me for so long that I thought he'd forgotten we were in a truck and he was the one driving it. "Kind of amazing," he agreed. The expression in his eyes before he looked away seemed to apply the words to me. *Kind of amazing.*

I floated off the seat again, leaving behind the still, small voice that was saying the wind could blow me out of Daily, Texas, just as quickly as it blew me in.

"What's *that* look for?" Kemp slanted a sideways glance at me, then focused on the road as we navigated a patch of potholes.

"I'm wondering why you're being so nice to me." I made it sound like a joke, but really, I was hoping he'd answer.

His lips twitched into a quirky one-sided smirk. "You're interesting." He shrugged, and the smirk morphed into a playful grin.

"No, seriously." Given Kemp's history, and the obvious fact that he was drop-dead good-looking, there were undoubtedly all kinds of girls—interesting and otherwise—lined up outside the fence at the ballpark, hoping to grab his attention. Jennifer was interesting . . . and cute. Beautiful, actually. And they had history together. A wagonload of fond memories. I, in my purple windsuit, couldn't possibly compete.

"I *was* being serious," he answered, and I felt myself hopelessly tripping off to Never-Neverland, hovering an inch or two over my own life, unable to get a grip on anything solid, with only one thing certain; no matter what else happened, this was one hurri-cation I would never forget.

The rest of the day went by in a strange mix of exhilaration and perspiration. After grabbing a soda at the Buy-n-Bye convenience store and moving the field house laundry to the dryer, we traveled to a church camp out in the country, where we received a quick debriefing on the housing problem with Sister Mona's group, along with marching orders as to how we could help. We ended up scrubbing mildew off cots, with the help of several members of the Holy Ghost Church. It should have seemed like an unpleasant job, but the group laughed and joked and sang gospel songs, making the hours pass quickly. Kemp, Ernest, and Bluejay joked and jostled with each other as they stacked the cots in a horse trailer, and by the time we were finished, I had to admit that I'd never had so much fun scrubbing mildew in my life.

When the trailer was loaded, we swung by the field house to pick up two loads of freshly laundered sweats and towels, then headed out to the Anderson-Shay ranch to watch the Holy Ghost caravan roll up the driveway. There was a sense of triumph in the air as Sister Mona, Pastor D., and the rest of the crew disembarked and looked around. The kids were impressed, and I couldn't blame them. The old limestone ranch house was massive, with two stories plus attic rooms on the third level, and even though the furniture was a mishmash of folding chairs, card tables, army-green cots with assorted bedding, and plastic patioware, the place had the feeling of a grand Western resort—a dude ranch, of sorts. There were even horses and chickens in the barn. When Donetta caught up with us, she urged Kemp and me to take some of the kids out to see the animals.

"Y'all done enough work," she assessed. "Go on and walk the little guys out to the barn. They been cooped up downtown all day, watchin' the storm coverage on TV. They can use a little fun. Get their mind off things." She slipped an arm around my shoulders and squeezed me in a one-sided hug. "Looks like y'all had a good day together." The words left behind a lingering expectation, like a weight pressing down.

I wasn't sure how to answer, so I just nodded and headed off to the barn with Kemp and a gaggle of happy kids, ready for pony rides. Kemp was surprised when he found out that even though I was a novice at calf feeding, I did know how to handle a horse.

"My father played campfire music at a guest ranch in Colorado one summer," I told him as we finished up the pony rides and pulled off the saddles. At the house, the dinner bell had started ringing, and Donetta was calling for the kids.

Kemp sent them on their way, then turned back to me, shaking his head. "Is there anywhere you *haven't* been?" He actually made it sound like a compliment, like he was awestruck by the mishmash of my life.

"Here," I answered, indicating the ranch as I bent over to investigate a tiny crystal at my feet. Next to it lay the limestone fossil of a snail and a small piece of clouded topaz. I tucked them into my pocket as I stood up, thinking that I'd polish them and use them in jewelry, to have something by which to remember this day. "This is a beautiful place. It'll make a fantastic foster shelter someday." I had the fleeting thought that I could have ended up in a place like this. There were so many times when my parents hit rock bottom, financially, emotionally, physically, in dealing with Gil's illness. It would have been easier for them to have just let go and given us over to the state, where Gil's medical care would have been provided. Carnies in campgrounds advised them to do it, explained the process to my father and told him how to work the system. They could get us back in a few years, when Gil's health was better.

My father never even considered it. Instead, he stuffed down his pride and did the thing he hated most—he went begging to Grandmother Miller. I'd never even considered what it must have cost him. I'd only thought about how his failures affected me.

"You haven't seen the half of it," Kemp said, his words seeming prophetic. The next thing I knew, he was swinging, Indian style, onto the back of a gray pony.

"What are you *doing*?" I coughed out, laughing. He looked ridiculous, like a cartoon character ready to stand up and let the pony walk out from under him.

"Hop on." He waved toward the other pony. "I'll give you the tour."

The idea made me giggle. My pony was even smaller than his. "I'm too big for him."

"Are you kidding? These guys were bred to carry big, burly miners up the mountain to the coal mines. You're not too big for him. Hop on."

There was enough of a challenge in the words to convince me to do it. I mounted the pony about as gracefully as a sumo wrestler getting on a balance beam, but I did it. Kemp trotted off, and my pony followed just as I was thinking, *This really isn't such a good idea. . . .*

The next thing I knew, I was crossing the pasture at a trot, gathering the reins in one hand, clutching the pony's thick mane in the other, bouncing side to side, realizing the windsuit was too slippery for horse riding, and giggling out the words "It's . . . ouch . . . been . . . a few . . . shoot . . . years . . . slow . . . down . . . already."

"It's like riding a bicycle—you never forget," Kemp called

over his shoulder, and his pony accelerated into a smooth can-
ter. In spite of the ridiculous size differential, he looked good
up there. He rode as if he and his stubby mount were one.

I, on the other hand, was like a Weeble on a Super Ball.

"Kick him out of a trot. It'll be smoother," Kemp called.

"No!" I hollered back, and my mount and I continued after
him in a fast, yet bone-jarring gait.

Finally, Kemp slowed down as we came to a trail leading up
what had seemed like a hill from a distance, but now looked
like a mountain. Kemp guided his pony onto the trail, making
little smoochy sounds to keep it moving. My mount followed,
and we started to climb, Kemp ducking tree limbs and knocking down spider webs with ease, while I clung to my horse's
mane with both hands and slowly slid tailward, thinking that
this was what it would be like to traverse the rim of the Grand
Canyon on a somewhat overweight burro.

"I'm sliding off!" I clutched the pony's mane tighter, hanging
on for dear life.

"No you're not." Kemp glanced over his shoulder.

"Where are we going, anyway?"

He didn't answer, just continued winding upward on the
trail until finally we emerged in a flat spot atop the hill. He
halted against the setting sun in a pose that would have been
majestic if it hadn't been for the fact that he looked like Gumby
out for a ride.

"Not a bad view, huh?" he said, as I steered into the space
beside his. Happy to be stopping, the ponies nuzzled noses and
chewed each others' bridles.

My breath caught in my throat as I took in the scenery. From
here, the view seemed to stretch endlessly, making the ranch
house and barns look like playthings among the yawning live
oaks. Beyond the buildings, amber grasses extended toward the
horizon, the waving currents of an endless yellow sea. On the

far shores, hills melted into one another, a rocky watercolor wash of violet and smoky blue and deep purple fading into the sky.

The panorama paled suddenly, and I knew Kemp was watching me. I turned to him, and he leaned closer, and just before he kissed me, a last, random thought raced through my mind. *This wasn't a bad idea. This wasn't a bad idea at all. . . .*

# Chapter 21

## *Donetta Bradford*

When I left after the Holy Ghost bunch was fed and bedded down out at the ranch, I headed home on the wings a' victory. We'd pulled the wool right over Betty Prine's eyes. A day don't get much better than that.

I was high as a paper kite in a March wind, I'll tell you. My spirits were so lofty they couldn't be brought down, even by the fact that Ronald's disappearin' act'd come up in conversation while we were fixing dinner for the guests at the ranch. Just out of the blue, Brother Ervin'd said, "Too bad Ronald ain't here. He could've supplied some fish fillets to go with this brisket."

My face went hot and prickly, but I just bent over the choppin' block and kept cuttin' up celery for the salad. "His boat and tackle's gone. Reckon he's off down the river someplace." *Doin' whatever he wants to do. Not one whit worried about whether anybody else got trapped in a hurricane.* "Guess he'll come back when he's ready." There was a sharp edge in those words, and I knew Brother Ervin was lookin' at me, trying to figure out what wasn't bein' said.

"At the lake, maybe," Brother Ervin said. "Harlan was down the river checkin' his trotlines yesterday mornin'. Said he didn't see a soul. The river was up and the fishin' was poor. He'da mentioned it if he saw Ronald's truck parked around the lot at Boggy Bend."

"Well, the lake, then." *There's places all around that lake that got boat docks, with restaurants and phones. From the lake, Ronald coulda called to check on me anytime he wanted, even without a cell phone.* "Could be he drove to Dallas and picked up his brother, and they're camped out at the deer lease." When Ronald and his brother went off in the woods together, they were apt to miss birthday parties, Christmas, and whatever else came up.

Brother Ervin scraped the brisket knife on the edge of the pan. "Reckon. But you might better give him a call and make sure he's all right."

"He won't carry one of them cell phones, Brother Ervin. You know that."

Brother Ervin nodded. He knew how much Ronald hated anything technological—except the fish-findin' radar on his boat. He liked that just fine. "His brother's house, then. Just call up there. Raymond's probably checkin' his phone messages from out in the woods. You know he's always got some horse-sellin' deal goin' on. He don't stay out of touch for long."

"I'll do that," I said, just to end the conversation. Then I realized I'd made a promise to the preacher, which meant, sooner or later, I'd have to break down and call. If Ronald didn't call me first.

I put it out of my mind and just enjoyed the evenin' at the ranch. My promise to Brother Ervin didn't come back to me until I was on my way home. Just as soon as I thought about it, I felt the damper falling over my head, so I turned on the radio and started listening to the *Ophelia Show*, just as she was sending out good wishes to the folks involved in the hurricane. She was doin' a special feature where people called in and told what'd happened to them during Glorietta, and then if they wanted, they could dedicate a song to someone they loved or to their hometown or their family. The show was named "Voices From the Storm," and it was real touchin'. I got choked up and tears come in my eyes, but they were good tears.

Rolling up my driveway, I noticed my house was still empty. Kai hadn't showed back up yet. That was interestin'. . . .

Once I got inside, I called Imagene to let her know. "You sittin' down?" I said.

"Don't have any choice. My legs fell off a hour ago. What's up?"

"Them two still ain't back." I turned on the radio so I could finish listening to the *Ophelia Show*. "Them two been out all day together, Imagene."

"What two?"

"Well, Kemp and Kai, of course. They're still out together. Ain't that somethin'?"

Imagene made a *hmmm* sound. "The way they were lookin' at each other at the ranch, that don't surprise me, but . . ." She trailed off in a way that said there was something more.

"But what? I ain't ever seen Kemp that moony over a girl, especially one he's only just met. It's a good sign."

"Jenny's back in town."

It took a minute for what Imagene said to sink in. "Jenny Mayfield? What? Where?" That wasn't good news. Not good news at all. First Ronald was who-knew-where, and now Jenny Mayfield was back in town. Kemp and Jenny'd been sweethearts since they were kids. They'd wasted years going back and forth with each other, off and on, long distance and otherwise. Those two were like a threadbare brown suit. An old brown suit is comfortable, but it ain't very excitin'.

"She's working for Doc down at the vet clinic." Imagene had a grave sound in her voice, so that it was lower than usual. "I hear Kemp and Kai ran into her today."

"Where'd you hear that?" There's something wrong when your best friend gets the gossip before you do.

"I passed by her folks' place on my way home while ago. They were sittin' out in the carport. I stopped off to say hello, and there was Jenny. She mentioned she saw Kemp today at the vet clinic."

"And you didn't think you better call and tell me that?"

"I didn't want to ruin your day," Imagene said, like she was passing along a funeral notice. "You know what happens every time Kemp and Jenny run back into each other."

A whole series of past hits and misses with Kemp and Jenny scampered through my thoughts—up to and including the first time he hurt his arm in the minors, and had to come home, and ended up actually buying Jenny an engagement ring when she visited for the Fourth of July. They laughed about it later. Kemp went back to the minors and Jenny was off to Galveston to study dolphins, and neither of them seemed too disappointed about calling off the wedding.

"That's about the worst thing that could happen right now, with Kemp having to give up his spot on the Rangers and not knowin' whether those doctors'll ever clear him to go back." If Jenny was between plans enough to be working in Daily, that probably meant she'd be here awhile. "The *last* thing he needs is Jenny back in town."

"I know." Imagene yawned long and loud. "That's why I didn't say anything."

Sometimes, even though we're best friends, I don't understand Imagene's thinkin' at all. "It's better for me to know . . . so I can get prepared—come up with a plan."

"Now, Netta." I could picture her with her hands held out like two chubby little stop signs.

"Don't *now Netta* me."

"Frank says you need to leave things alone. Whatever happens with Jenny'll happen."

My back bristled up like a cat's. "You been talkin' to Frank? You told *Frank* Jenny was back, but you didn't tell me?"

"He called to make sure I was home all right, that's all."

"Imagene Doll . . ."

"I wasn't tryin' to keep secrets," Imagene cooed, like she was dealin' with a toddler about to go into a hissy fit. "I didn't want to get you upset. You been upset enough already."

"I'm not upset. I don't have one other thing to be upset about."

"You're upset about Ronald not bein' home, Netta, and you know it."

Blood washed into my face, and my throat clogged up so that I had to blow it out with a cough before I could talk. "He took his boat and tackle and went off fishin'. What's to be upset about that?"

Imagene gave a long, weary sigh. Even over the phone, she knew that wasn't the truth. "You're my best friend, Netta. I can't be happy if you're miserable."

My eyes stung and I sniffed back tears. "I'm not miserable, Imagene."

"You wouldn't say so if you were." Her voice was tender, but even so, it hurt. "You always do for everybody else, Netta, and that's a wonderful way to be. I hadn't ever known anybody as good as you in my whole life. But you never stand up and say it when you need somethin'. Maybe you should once in a while. If you want Ronald to take you out and dance, you got to just put your foot down and say, 'Ronald, we been married all these years, and I'm tired of waitin' for you to wake up and smell the coffee. I ain't sittin' in this house one more day with an old pooh, so just dust off your suit coat and put on your dancin' shoes.'"

I pictured myself saying those things to Ronald, and I almost got tickled right through the tears. "Imagene, if I walked in here and said 'Ronald, you take me dancin' or else,' he'd have a coronary heart attack."

"Let him." It wasn't like Imagene to sound so hard. She'd been thinking about this for a while. Probably talking about it to Frank, too. "You stick to your guns."

"Ronald don't dance. I knew that when I married the man." Why I felt I had to make excuses for Ronald was a pure mystery, but it just come natural. Every time Ronald stayed home in his chair like a fart, while things were goin' on without him, I tried to keep it from looking bad to other folks. *Oh, Ronald's not a dancer. Oh, Ronald don't like parades. Well, Ronald's arthritis gets him down in the mornin's, that's why he don't make it to Sunday service. Ronald said to tell y'all he's sorry he missed the party. He got tied up at deer camp. . . .*

"I wasn't just talkin' about dancing." Imagene was on this like a coonhound on a tree. She didn't even sound tired anymore. "Just 'cause your daddy never stepped up don't mean you don't deserve better from a man."

I heard a noise in the hall, and I looked up and realized Kai was there. She must've come in the back door after checking on her dogs. "Well hey, hon," I said to her, and then into the phone, "Kai's back. I gotta go, Imagene."

Imagene smacked her lips, letting me know she wasn't happy about leavin' the cows out of the barn. "Think about what I said. When Ronald does come home, you go right on and say your piece."

"No tellin' when Ronald'll come home. Brother Ervin said his truck and trailer ain't at Boggy Bend ramp. He probably drove up to the deer lease to meet his brother. You know how them two are."

"Netta. I mean it. You call him, like Brother Ervin said."

Good gravy, Imagene knew I'd promised Brother Ervin. She'd probably put him up to asking me about Ronald in the first place. I was mortified, of course. Just mortified. "No phones at the deer lease."

"Netta. You give him a call and tell him what's happened, or I will."

"I gotta go, darlin'."

"Don't you *darlin'* me, Donetta Bradford. You listen here—"

"Night-night. Get your beauty sleep. We got folks to feed tomorrow."

"Net—" I hung up, like I didn't hear her still talking.

Kai sailed across the room, and she had the glow a' roses on her cheeks and a dreamy look in her eyes. "Come on in and sit down, hon," I said. "How was your day?"

She blinked like she didn't even know I was there at first, then she said, "Good. I hope the dogs haven't been any trouble this evening." Her eyes flicked toward the radio, and she frowned at Ophelia's voice talking about storm stories. I switched off the sound and turned on the TV instead. Kai probably wanted to see the weather report.

"Oh no, the dogs hadn't been any trouble. There's nothin' they could hurt in that backyard, believe me. One time when we first got married, I thought I was gonna grow flowers, but the flowers've long since gone wild." I laughed, thinking of when we moved into the little yellow house on B Street and how I made all kinds of plans to clean out flower beds and put in plants. I wanted our place to be perfect, so everyone'd see that even though I'd quit college and got married, I could do a sight better at putting together a life than my daddy did. We'd have the place with the mowed yard, and the flowers bloomin' in rows, and the apple pie in the windowsill, and the kids all spit shined—boys in little cowboy boots and girls in bows and Mary Jane shoes fresh from the dry goods store.

When our first-year anniversary rolled around and there wasn't a baby on the way yet, Ronald knew I was down about it. He went to the Women's Auxiliary plant sale and brought me home a pickup load of plants so we could make the yard like I wanted it to be.

I'd forgot all about that until just now. . . .

Kai slipped into the chair across and tucked her hands between her knees, like she didn't know what to say, but she didn't want to be rude and head straight upstairs, either. She watched the Weather Channel while they showed buildings pushed off their foundations and streets hip-deep in water. I wondered if she knew any of them places.

"You and Kemp have fun today?" I asked, to take her mind off things . . . well, and because I can't help bein' nosy.

"We did." There was a little giggle in her voice, like she was remembering something. Oh my, I could recall being a young gal, feeling that way after a date with a beau.

"Heard y'all ran into Jenny Mayfield over to the vet clinic." No sense beating around the bush, I figured.

Kai's eyes snapped back to me, and her cheeks got red. "We did . . . I . . . mean . . . ummm . . ." Cat had got her tongue, all of a sudden.

"It's all right, darlin'. I can pretty much picture what that was like. You must be wonderin' about them two."

Her lashes flew up, all innocent-like, and she shook her head real fast. "Oh no, I didn't, I mean, I don't . . . Kemp was just showing me around town. I don't want to . . ." She took a minute to look for the right words, then finished with ". . . get in the way. It was very nice of him to drive me around today."

A little laugh bubbled up my throat. If that gal was a poker player, she'd lose every time. Her face read like a book in big print and short sentences. "Hon," I told her, "a man don't look at a woman like he's been lookin' at you because he's just tryin' to be nice."

She didn't have an answer for that, but I could tell she was wondering if I was telling the truth.

"Trust me." I stared her straight in the eye. "I can spot that special somethin' from fifty foot away. Sometimes it happens between two people right off. Like when Imagene met her Jack. I knew from the minute I saw them two together it was the real deal. And it was. Everybody thought she was crazy, acceptin' that boy's ring when they'd only just met, and he had years left in the service, but I knew. I knew somethin' like that don't come along even once in every lifetime. You got to grab hold of it when it does, or you spend the rest of your days wonderin' what might've happened."

Kai looked down at her hands, her lips twisting to one side, a little sad, a little thoughtful. "I'm not the grabbing-on type."

"Neither is Kempner, but you never know. I've seen it happen before."

Kai looked up at me, her blue eyes so big and worried and lost, I wanted to take her in my arms like a little child. "I'll have to go back to work soon."

"Ssshhh," I whispered. "Don't spread a trail of worries out ahead of you."

She didn't answer, just sat there looking at her hands.

"Don't fret about Jenny, either," I said finally. Might as well get everything out front, since we were workin' on a short timetable here. A short timetable don't allow the matchmaker to beat around the bush. "The two of them needed to be done with each other a long time ago. Sometimes when you grow up so close together, you're a little too much like a brother and a sister to ever be real romantic."

The dogs barked outside, and Kai turned an ear to it. Whatever was going through her mind seemed to shake off then, and she got up and went to look out the door. When she come back, the melancholy face was gone. "Guess I'd better let you get to bed," she said.

I figured that was her way of saying I'd stuck my nose in enough. "Oh hon, I'm a night owl. I'll be up for hours yet," I told her. "But don't let me keep you awake. I'm sure you're tired. I'm just gonna watch the news and whatnot. See the previews for *Dancin' With the Stars*. It's my favorite show. I don't usually miss, but this last week's been so busy, them stars had to start dancin' without me."

Nodding, she headed toward the hall, then swiveled back just as I was getting the remote to turn off all that horrible storm news. "A lot of the time when the men don't dance," she said, "it's because they don't know how." She blurted out the words so fast it took me a minute to pull them apart. Even then, I was still confused.

"Pardon, hon?"

Her face got pink as a baby's bottom. "On the ship, when I help teach ballroom dancing, a lot of times the men don't dance because they never learned, but they don't want to admit it. They're afraid of looking stupid."

"Hon, I think we jumped the track somewhere here." I couldn't figure why in the world she was on the subject of ballroom dancing. "I don't have a bit of an idea what you're talkin' about."

She fidgeted from one foot to the other, pushing her palms against her shorts, like her hands were sweaty. "Your husband . . . ummm . . . Ronald? Maybe he just never learned. I could give him a few lessons when he comes back . . . if I'm still here, I mean. I know easy ways to teach all the dances. Maybe the two of you could take a cruise together, next time."

I was struck speechless for a minute. Imagine, me and Ronald heading off on some cruise ship together! Right after that thought crossed my mind, I got embarrassed, because I knew Kai'd heard me on the phone with Imagene. I was caught between being full-on mortified and wanting to give her a hug, because it was real sweet of her to try to help Ronald and me. "Oh hon, I think it'd take a joint act of God and Congress to get Ronald to go for that. He just ain't the type."

"Well, like you said, you never know," she pointed out. "I've seen it happen before." Clever girl, chasing my own words right back at me. "Never say never, right?"

*Never say never.* "Hon, I doubt if that's in the cards for Ronald and me, but it's real sweet of you to offer. Don't you worry about us, all right? We been the way we are a long time, and you got enough things on your mind." I stood up and hugged her for being so sweet. "You just go on to bed now and get your rest, all right?"

"All right." She hesitated again a minute. "But, really, I'll help if I can."

"I know you would, darlin'. Sweet dreams."

She padded off to bed, and I stood there thinkin', *If Kemp don't try to grab on to that gal with both hands, he's a fool in a fool's hat.*

I sat there for a while, thinking about a cruise and trying to picture Ronald taking dancing lessons and the two of us cutting a rug. Just the idea of it made me laugh. Wouldn't that be a sight, and boy oh boy, wouldn't Betty Prine spit sour pickles!

Not that any of that would ever happen, of course.

But it was still kind of fun thinking about it. Maybe it was a little easier to imagine without Ronald sitting there in his chair like a lump.

I was still entertainin' the picture and laughing about it to myself when I finally turned off the TV and headed off to bed. I figured it'd be pressing my luck not to keep my promise to

Brother Ervin, so I made myself stop in the kitchen and call Ronald's brother's house. Of course, it went straight to the answerin' machine, which meant he wasn't home and hadn't been for a while. No doubt him and Ronald were havin' a high old time camping at the deer lease and fishin' the ponds there.

I left a message on the answering machine and then went off to bed, figuring that I'd done enough to keep my promise to Brother Ervin. Ronald would show up home when he was ready—probably just about the time I was supposed to get back from my cruise. Which meant he'd be gone a few more days yet. If Ronald wasn't home on Thursday—the day I was supposed to've got back—I wasn't sure how I was gonna feel.

In the morning when I woke up, I sat up and checked out the window for Ronald's truck, first thing. I'd dreamed that he'd got home in the middle of the night with a stringer full of fish. In the dream, he put the fish in the bathtub, and for some reason, I thought that was just fine. I went in and helped him run the water.

Even though that worry was over me like a cloud, everything else that day ticked along just as tight as a eight-day clock. Sister Mona and her people got settled in out at the ranch. The folks from Caney Creek Church took them breakfast, they all shared church service out at the ranch, and Bob even sent fried chicken and iced tea from the Daily Café for lunch.

Frank and Kemp got a flatbed trailer all set up so Frank could head down toward the coast on Monday to look for Imagene's van and Kai's bus, and when they were done with that, they got a TV out of Frank's shop building, took it to the ranch, and hooked it to a big old antenna up on the roof. They had Kai crawling around in the attic to string the wire, because she was the only one small enough to do it. I about pitched a fit at

Kemp when I heard about it, but Kai just laughed and told me her daddy was an electrician one summer and she helped him, so crawling around an attic was nothin' new to her.

"There's not much she can't do," Kemp said, and that boy looked moony as a coyote. Them kids were two peas in a pod if I ever saw. Right after they dropped by the house and told me about the TV wires, they headed off to feed the bottle baby out at Kemp's house, and then they were gonna go down on Caney Creek because Kai wanted to see the place where the Tonkawa Indians had painted pictures on the rocks. Daily Folk called that spot Camp Nikyneck, because it was where the teenagers went to spend a little time romancin', so I figured I knew what Kemp had in mind.

Everything seemed like it was turnin' out right as rain, especially when Betty Prine come by for her wash-and-curl on Monday and let it slip, on purpose of course, that a cousin of hers, Ferla somethin' up in Arkansas, was having tests done and it looked like she was gonna need gall bladder surgery. It'd be Betty's job to go care for her, which meant, of course, that Betty would be a whole state away, and for a good while, if we were lucky.

I never did such a fast job on somebody's hair in my life. I didn't want to delay her packing or anything.

"My, but that was quick." Betty checked side to side in the mirror, patting her loopy gray puff to make sure everything was to her satisfaction.

"Don't want to hold you up, in case you need to leave sooner than you planned." I whipped off the cape and moved straight to the cash register.

"Oh, well, Ferla knows it'll be at least a day before Harold can get away from the bank, so she'll just have to get her neighbor to help out until we can get there. It's difficult for us, you know. When you own so many businesses, you just can't flit off at a moment's notice." Betty wandered up and wrote out her check. "I'm adding an extra dollar in here for tip."

"You might want to save that for your travelin'." It was just like Betty Prine to act like she was doing me a favor, throwing a whole dollar extra my way. "It's a long drive up to Arkansas."

"Yes, yes," she agreed. "Speaking of—I do hope Harold's donation the other day was enough to fuel up *those vehicles* for the trip to Dallas. Being as we have the means, we always feel that it's important to help out the *less fortunate*." She looked right at me when she said that, *less fortunate*.

I wanted to wad up that check and stuff it right in that snooty circle of Passion Peach #2 lipstick, but instead I tucked the check in the drawer. "Oh, surely it was."

"I imagine they're all settled in a shelter by now." Betty stood at the counter, rooted in like crab grass. "Have you heard anything from them?" Why she cared, I couldn't fairly guess.

"They haven't called." *That ain't a lie, Lord. Well, not exactly, anyhow.* Since there wasn't any phone out at the ranch and cell phones didn't usually work out there, Sister Mona and Brother D. didn't have any way to call.

Betty snorted out her nose, her mouth pinched shut. "I'd imagine they might have called, or left a thank-you note at least. I thought it would be nice to publish it in the newspaper—good public relations, what with Daily getting so much attention from the Amber Anderson craze and now the movie deal. Never hurts to let the world know we aren't too high to be charitable."

"Oh, Betty, everyone knows how charitable you are." *Is it a lie, Lord, when you say one thing and think another? It ain't, really. No, it ain't. A body can only put up with so much.*

Betty picked up her purse, purring like a cat. "Well, it *is* our duty, after all. Do you still have that little blond-headed girl stayin' out at your place?"

I got hot around the neck, thinking that now Betty Prine was gonna try to tell me who I couldn't keep at my own house. "Yes, Betty, I do."

She made a little *tsk-tsk* under her breath. "Well, you ought to be careful, you know, having some stranger in your home, what with Ronald gone and all. Wherever *is* Ronald, anyway? Did he make it home in time to drive down toward the coast with Frank to look for Imagne's lost van?"

"Ronald's still on one of his fishin' trips." As if she didn't know. There wasn't a thing went on in town Betty Prine didn't sniff out. That woman was like a rat after trash. "Frank took Buddy Ray along to the coast. Buddy Ray's good with cars."

Betty blinked wide, her eyes droopy and sorrowful. "Well, my heavens, you'd think by now Ronald would have heard about the hurricane, wherever he's at."

"He don't carry a cell phone" was pretty much all I could get out, and that was only because I'd been having a real good day until Betty come in, and with her leavin', it was about to get better again.

She shook her head, frownin' at me, real sorrowful. "What a shame. Well, suppose I'd better run." She give a finger wave like a beauty queen afloat in the homecoming parade. "I've a million loose ends to tie up so we can go look after Ferla."

Watching Betty head out the door, I was feelin' sorry for Ferla. But not too sorry to share the good news with Imagene and Lucy, just as soon as Betty went out the door. We celebrated with a cup of coffee and pecan pie.

"Betty's cousin couldn'ta picked a better time to get a gall bladder attack." Imagene savored a bite of pecan pie, smiling. "Not that I'd be rejoicin' over anybody's misfortune, of course."

Lucy giggled behind her hand. "I don' know what kind is most bad. Get-teeng bad gall bladder or to have Betty come take your care."

All three of us laughed until we were snorting coffee and Imagene about choked on a pecan. Since we were on a roll of the sillies, I popped off and told them what Kai'd said about me and Ronald taking dancing lessons and going on a cruise.

"Can you imagine that?" I asked, and all three of us hooted.

Imagene pushed her plate away and fanned her cheeks. "Maybe you and Ronald ought to take my cruise ticket. Y'all could dance the night away, just like on *Love Boat*."

I threw my head back and laughed until tears come out my eyes. "Ronald'd probably get put in the brig for trying to drop a trollin' line off the back of the ship. He'd be the first fella to ever show up for a cruise with a tackle box and stink bait." We all hooted some more at the idea of Ronald trying to fish off one of them giant ships.

"Imagene, maybe you and Frank ought to take the tickets!" I shot out, since we were all just popping off anyway. "Give him a reward for goin' down to fetch your van and Kai's bus."

Imagene blushed and her eyes went wide. "Donetta Bradford, you are shameful sometimes!" Her face got serious, and her mouth straightened. "But I wasn't kiddin' about you and Ronald. Maybe that's just what y'all two need. A romantic trip together. Somethin' to spice up your love life."

"Ima-*gene*!"

Lucy said something in Japanese, and you didn't have to speak Japanese to get the meaning.

"Lucy!" I gasped out.

We got to laughing again and making jokes about the cruise ship until we were red-faced and out of breath. It felt good to finally cut loose, and better yet now that we knew Betty'd be headin' out of town soon and we'd be home free.

But somehow, even with all the laughing and the cutting up, a little case of the worries was needling the corner of my mind. Try as I might, I couldn't shake the feeling that trouble was hanging over my shoulder, crouched like a mountain lion in the cedar brush, just waitin' for the right time to pounce.

# Chapter 22

## *Kai Miller*

After four full days in Daily I already felt like I'd fallen into a routine. In the mornings, I woke early, then showered and dressed with expectation fluttering in my chest, because I knew Kemp would show up before breakfast. Through the giddy haze, I occasionally looked at myself in the mirror and caught a glimpse of the practical girl, the one who was nothing like her parents and never would be. She frowned at me, wondering why I was still there, why I hadn't called the cruise line to see about catching up with the *Liberation*, why I hadn't been elated yesterday, when Kemp's father and Buddy Ray had driven south with a truck and a flatbed trailer and brought home both Imagene's van and my Microbus. They had even procured a replacement tire for me on the way home, so the van was quickly returned to working condition. Having my vehicle back with everything in it and no damage except a cracked window should have seemed like a miracle, but instead, I felt like a vacationer trying not to count down the days until it was time to go back to work.

276

Even Maggie and Meredith had begun to sense that something about me was off. I hadn't responded like they'd thought I would when they called to tell me they'd finally gotten word from Don, via a network of shortwave radio operators, who were helping to get messages out from the storm zone. Don was back at the surf shop after weathering the storm on the third floor of the Seaside Hotel, two doors down from Blowfish Billy's. Don's shop had been gutted by the storm surge, but the piers were still solid and the apartments on the second story were largely untouched, other than some broken windows. The coffee shop was in similar shape, as were many of the businesses along our section of highway.

Farther down the strand, many of the historic buildings and neighborhoods remained under several feet of floodwater, and debris lay everywhere, clogging streets and hampering attempts to deliver supplies to stranded residents. Despite the lack of basic services, those who'd braved the storm were making plans to dig out, and the National Guard was aiding in the effort to clear debris from the port, which they hoped would reopen within a few weeks. Perdida would rise again.

The news from Maggie and Meredith only reinforced what the girl in the mirror already knew. It was just a matter of time before she'd have to come back to reality and face the months of hard work ahead. Every day, I told myself, *Today you need to call the cruise line and report in. The ball's over, Cinderella.*

But as soon as I would hear Kemp's truck rumble up in the driveway and his voice in the kitchen, the only plans I'd care about were the plans to load the dogs in the back of his truck, grab breakfast at the Dairy Queen or the Buy-n-Bye, then head for the high school to open the field house.

As we drove up the street, Miss Peach would peer suspiciously through her storm door, her chalky legs bare beneath her housecoat. In her arms, the gray cat would hiss as Radar strained against his leash, barking furiously from the bed of the truck. Kemp and I would laugh and wonder whether Miss Peach had noticed that her glue traps were missing.

At the high school, Kemp and I would eat the breakfast we'd brought at a table by the ball fields while his students got in some workout time before school. When they finished, we'd play Wiffle ball. My batting average had steadily improved, as had the reputation of Highfly Hilda. One of Kemp's ballplayers had even borrowed my cell phone during a game, then returned it to me with "Take Me Out to the Ball Game" as my new ringtone and a Daily Dawgs logo on my screen background.

Our daily Wiffle ball contests would end when the first bell rang. As the kids rushed off to class, I'd untie the dogs and Kemp would walk with me to the other side of the football field. We'd linger behind the bleachers like a couple of high-school kids, talking until the second bell rang.

"Looks like you're tardy, Coach," I'd say.

"Don't report me," he'd answer, and grin, and I'd feel like the ground was shifting under my feet.

"I might."

"When?"

"Maybe tomorrow."

"Tomorrow's good for me." As the bells faded, he'd check over his shoulder, grab me and steal a kiss, then melt me with one of those ridiculous one-sided grins and drop his ball cap back on his head before jogging off across the field. I'd stand there and watch him go, trying to catch my breath.

After Kemp disappeared into the field house, I'd walk across town with the dogs tugging happily at their leashes and the crisp morning air slowly clearing my head. The farther I walked, the more I'd remember the days when my mother and father were so caught up in each other they couldn't see straight. *Look what happened to them,* I'd think. Before they met, my father was in college, albeit against his will, and my mother was a contestant in a beauty pageant on campus. If she hadn't been crying on the steps after flubbing her song lyrics in the talent competition, and he hadn't stopped to see what was wrong, she might have continued to compete for the Miss Texas title, and he might have become an engineer, as Grandmother Miller planned. Instead, they met for ice cream after the pageant dinner, spent hours talking about family expectations, the pressure to be something you're not, the life adventures they were being cheated out of. Two days later, they ran off and got married, alienated two sets of family, and proved that love won't pay the bills.

On the walk across town on Wednesday, I tried to force myself to get real, but my parents' story was just a tiny dim spot in the face of something so bright I couldn't see past it. By the time the dogs were safely in the yard and I proceeded to the beauty shop to help with coordinating supplies and meals for the group at the ranch, I was hopelessly floating again. For the first time in my life, I understood the incredible power of infatuation. Try as I might, I couldn't think of anything but Kemp. The feeling was mesmerizing and frightening all at once.

The beauty shop girls saw it, of course. They fed the obsession by sharing Pickle-poo stories—little Pickle-poo making ghostly noises upstairs to scare his sister and her friends on sleepovers, then slipping out the window and shinnying down the drain pipe when they went to see if anyone was there, Pickle-poo knocking out one of the windows goofing around with a ball and a bat on the street, Pickle-poo finding a garden snake hibernating in a bunch of leaves by the curb, taking it inside and putting it in one of the hair sinks to warm up.

"Once that thing got warm, it slithered into one of the hair dryers." Donetta fanned her face, laughing. "That snake hurried out of there when I turned that dryer on, I'll tell you. Shot right into Mrs. Lulu's hair and slid down her dress. She went to bellerin' and screamin' and dancin' around. I thought she'd got the Holy Ghost right here in the beauty shop. . . ."

When Jennifer Mayfield came by for a late-afternoon haircut, I learned more than I wanted to know about the past escapades of Jenny and Kemp. They'd done everything from build a raft and try to sail down the creek like Huckleberry Finn to door-knocking Miss Peach's house on Halloween.

"Kemp and I were just laughin' about that yesterday," she said, and I wondered, *When were they together, strolling down memory lane? He was with me. We were together all afternoon, all evening. . . .*

"It would've worked out all right if Mr. Big Feet hadn't gone and tripped over the garden hose." Jen's voice was a smooth mix of southern belle and cowgirl sweetheart, her laughter jingling across the room. "When I made it around the corner and looked back, Miss Peach had him grabbed up by the collar and she was headin' in to call the sheriff. I just knew he'd get scared and tattle, but he never did. Kemp was always so good that way." When she said that, she gave me a long, interested look. I tried to decide what that meant—whether it was a challenge, or whether she was gauging my reaction to her.

"Y'all two always did get each other into mischief," Donetta said as she finished fluffing Jen's hair, and in spite of Jen's pink scrubs with little kitty paw prints, she looked like she was ready for the cover of a magazine—*Veterinary Vogue*, or *Canine Cosmo*. "His daddy made him go work in her flower beds for a month all by himself," Donetta added, raising an eyebrow and frowning, giving emphasis to *all by himself*. "He's probably still got ni-ightmares to this day." Lowering the seat, she pulled off Jen's hair cape and tossed it into the basket. "There you go, hon. You're done." Donetta was in a hurry to get Jen out the door, and when I glanced at the clock, I had a feeling I knew why. Any minute now, Kemp would show up on his way out to the ranch to entertain the kids of the Holy Ghost Church with a bag of random sports equipment.

Kemp walked in before Donetta could successfully clear the competition from the room, and we shared a few moments of uncomfortable Daily memorabilia during which Jen seemed unusually interested in the evening plans at the ranch and my plans in general, or more specifically my plans to return to the coast, now that I had my vehicle back.

Donetta was quick to cut the conversation short. "Well, no-body can go anyplace right now, with everything bein' such a mess down there. Hadn't you been watchin' the TV? There's a house sittin' in the middle of I-10. A whole house. There's dead gators and cows everywhere, and the water's all polluted. It'll take a while for all that to get cleaned up, sure enough. Frank said he was lucky just to make it down far enough to get Imagene's van."

Jen blinked at the answer, seeming surprised and less than pleased. She was about to pop out another question when Ima-gene appeared from next door to let us know the fried chicken, peach cobbler, and sweet tea were ready to be loaded for the trip to the ranch.

"All ri-ight, here we come." Donetta seized the distraction and proceeded to give Jen the sticky-sweet bum's rush. "Jenny, hon, I know ye-ew got to get back to work now. Thanks for stoppin' by, though. Tell the gals over to the vet clinic hey for me. Kemp, why don't you go out back and clear some space in your truck, all ri-ight?" She hooked arms with Jen and began escorting her toward the front door while Kemp, seemingly oblivious to the female jockeying around him, strolled toward the back door, whistling a happy tune.

Donetta booted Jen out the front, and we proceeded to the café to discuss the best way to box cobblers, pies, and sweet tea for the drive to the ranch. After some packaging and repackaging, the girls were ready for Kemp to do the heavy lifting.

"Where in the world is that boy, anyhow?" Donetta complained. By then, the ladies were in a minor argument about cobbler transportation. "How long does it take to clean out a truck for some boxes?"

"I'll go check on him," I offered, then grabbed a container of deep-fried chicken parts and headed through the storeroom of the café, down a dark, narrow hallway, and stepped out a door into the blinding afternoon light. When my eyes adjusted, there was Kemp, standing with one hand propped on his truck, engaged in what appeared to be an intimate conversation with, of all people, Jen, Jenny, Jennifer. A chill gathered in my chest and worked slowly outward as I took in the body language—Kemp leaning casually against the truck, his elbow crooked over the side of the bed, Jen sitting on the tailgate, as if she'd been there awhile.

The café door slammed shut, and the body language changed instantly. Both of them turned and saw me there, loaded down with fried chicken. I had no choice, really, but to proceed to the truck and dump off my cargo.

"Ready?" Kemp asked, sliding the box into the back of the pickup.

I nodded, but didn't look at him. I was afraid of what I'd see.

Jenny jumped down from the tailgate and dusted off her scrubs. "I thought I'd help y'all load up." She caught my eye and smiled pleasantly, but there was an appraising look behind the niceties, a curiosity thinly masked. I wondered if she was curious about me or if she was trying to gauge my reaction to finding the two of them with their heads together in the alley.

"There's not that much to load," I said as Kemp jogged ahead and disappeared through the café door.

Jen smiled again, and this time the smile seemed genuine,

guileless. "Oh, that's all right. It's been so busy at the clinic, I haven't done much to help those folks out at the ranch. I'm feelin' a little guilty." She rolled her eyes in silent admission, and as much as I didn't want to, I once again found her likable. She seemed like a really decent person.

The café door was locked when we reached it, and Jennifer lifted her hands palm up, then leaned against the side of the building. "This thing always used to do that. It's the ghost of the Daily Hotel."

"I didn't know the place was haunted." Ghosts seemed like a fairly benign conversation, considering that I was trapped in the alley with Jen.

She laughed—a high, musical sound. "Oh sure. Daily's got its secrets, you know. You ask around, you'll get a hundred different stories about the ghost."

"Sounds interesting. I'll have to ask around. Learn a little Daily history while I'm in town."

She quirked a brow at my answer, her demeanor morphing from casual to guarded and serious. "So, how long do you think you'll end up bein' stuck here?"

Suddenly, I knew how Radar felt when Miss Peach's cat hissed at him from behind the storm door. "Hard to know for sure. It depends on the ship's revised itinerary and where I have to go to catch it. They may fly me somewhere to meet up with the rest of the crew." *Of course, I'd have to actually report in first.* As far as the cruise line knew, I was missing in action due to Glorietta.

Jen studied me, her brown eyes narrow at the corners. She turned an ear toward the door, then focused on me again, and I had a feeling we were about to get down to the real reason she'd hung around to load fried chicken. "You know, he never stays involved with anybody. Not for long." Her gaze met mine in a way that, for a moment, seemed earnest, as if we were talking girlfriend-to-girlfriend, and she was only trying to help, but then the look turned sharp, possessive. "He's headed back to *the team* this winter." She spit out *the team* like it was a dirty word.

"It sounds like he's not sure what he's going to do about base-ball." I tried to make the comment sound offhanded, slightly dispassionate, as in *What business is it of mine?* Kemp and I had talked about baseball just yesterday, when we stopped by to give Bottle Baby a late feeding after we finished helping with supper for the evacuees.

"I think your aunt's glad to have you back in Daily," I had remarked as Bottle Baby took in supper with amazing speed, causing the milk receptacle to contort into a crumpled figure eight in my hands. Somewhere in every conversation, Do-netta slipped in the assertion that she was certain her nephew had finally outgrown his wanderlust and was ready to settle down.

Kemp sat on the fence, his elbows braced on his knees. He was wearing a straw cowboy hat, and he looked good in it. "Aunt Netta tries to marshal everyone . . . it's what she does for entertainment." He motioned to the calf. "Looks like he's done."

I yanked the mini udder from Bottle Baby's mouth, then ran for the fence to keep from ending up with milk slobber and calf snot all over me.

Kemp laughed as I scaled the obstacle, then landed on the other side as Baby wailed out a complaint. He let the calf chew on his boot toes for a minute, then swiveled around and slid to his feet.

"So, are you?" I asked, popping the slimy top off the bottle so it could be washed and hung on a wire to dry. Over the past few days, I'd become expert in the calf-feeding routine. A real hand, as Kemp put it.

"Am I what?"

"Happy here." Moving a couple steps to the spigot to rinse the bottle, I tried to appear casual so he wouldn't see that I was probing.

He took a moment to answer. I glanced up, and he was gazing across the pasture, toward the grove of live oaks by Caney Creek. His secret play place with Jenny. "Well, you know what they say about happiness. It's something you decide on."

I finished washing the bottle, then hung it and rinsed my hands before turning off the water. A quote ran through my mind, rumbling like thunder in the distance, *Happiness is a bird that stays on the wing.* A quote from one of my father's songs. A fair representation of his life. Never content, always looking for something new, something better. Always dreaming.

Kemp had that faraway look in his eyes, familiar yet distant. Disconcerting.

As I stowed the milk bottle, he kissed me, and the head talk vaporized instantly. When Kemp touched me, I couldn't think of anything but him.

Now, here was Jen, Jenny, Jennifer trapping me behind the café, smiling like a Cheshire cat up a tree, out of reach. "Don't let him kid you. He'll do anything for a chance to get back with the team, and he knows it. That's why he was up in Dallas having an MRI yesterday. He's getting cleared to go back. He told me last night that the doctor said it looks good."

*He told me last night . . .* The words struck me like a wild pitch, catching me off guard, taking my breath away. Kemp and Jen were together last night? When? Sometime after he and I finished feeding the calf and he took me back to Donetta's?

*He went to see Jen after he dropped me off?* The idea landed in my stomach like a hard right cross, pushing the wind from my lungs.

The effect must have been obvious, because Jen gave me what

seemed like a genuinely sympathetic look, and added, "He didn't tell you that, did he?"

I shrugged, trying to cover. *He was at school all day yesterday, working. Wasn't he?*

Had he gone to Dallas for an MRI and not even mentioned it while we were helping at the ranch, or feeding Bottle Baby, or talking about plans for the future, or kissing as the moon drifted into the deepening sky? Why would he do that, and even more to the point, why would he drop me off and then go discuss his future with Jennifer? *There isn't any reason why he would mention it. We're just friends,* I told myself. *He mentioned it to Jennifer. She knew. He felt the need to discuss it with her.* Why could he tell her the things he wasn't willing to share with me?

"Whatever. He doesn't look at you like a *friend.*" She leaned close, like we were dishing again. "Listen, I'm just giving you the truth. You seem like a nice girl, and I can't even guess what it's like to be in your spot—with the hurricane and all. You can take all this for whatever it's worth, but Kemp and I've been good friends for a really long time. He's had girls dripping off him since he was in high school, and while he was playing for the Rough Riders and the Rangers. It comes and it goes. When he's out of the game, when his arm's hurt and he's off, he gets involved with somebody, but it never lasts. He always goes back to baseball. He always will. Until some doctor finally tells him his shoulder's wrecked for good, he'll always go back, and when he's chasing the dream, he doesn't care about anything else *but* the dream. He doesn't let anything, or anyone, stand in his way. Period."

She didn't wait for an answer. The door was opening, and Kemp was headed out. She turned to him with a bright smile, patted him on the shoulder as she held open the door, and said, "Better watch it, carrying boxes with the arm."

Kemp just chuckled, playfully shrugging off her hand. "Yeah, thanks, Coach. If it gives me any trouble, I'll drop over and let you get after it with a little cortisone and a horse needle."

Lauging, Jen twirled away, her hair orbiting in a shimmering circle. "You let me near you with a horse needle, you're not gonna get it in the arm, Kemp Eldridge."

He laughed along with her, and I felt like the third passenger on a bicycle built for two. I stood numbly watching their interplay, their carefully practiced dance.

"Wouldn't be the first time." Kemp grinned at me as Jen headed toward her car, then he added, "She stuck me in the rear once with a syringe full of tranquilizers when we were working cows. I couldn't feel my leg for two days."

"That was an accident!" Jen's voice floated like a trail of smoke behind her as she slipped into her vehicle and waved good-bye.

Then she was gone, and the doorway felt decidedly uncomfortable—on my end, anyway. Kemp seemed fine. Even after we'd finished loading the rest of the food, he was still laughing about Jen, Jenny, Jennifer. "I can't believe they let her handle sharp objects."

I felt myself go numb, felt the painful yet familiar sting of rejection. Perhaps everything was a game to him—baseball, relationships, keeping his aunt on the string, letting her think he was back in Daily for good, playing this little game of cat and mouse with me.

Why would he do that? Why would he bother? My mind spun like one of the merry-go-rounds Gil and I used to ride in the park. The world was rotating so fast, I couldn't get my feet onto the platform. I was just hanging on, dragging in the dust.

"You ready?" Kemp asked.

"Sure," I muttered. "Guess we'd better get this stuff out to the ranch."

Kemp opened the alley door, then leaned against the frame

instead of walking through. Down the hall, the phone rang. He turned an ear toward it, then looked back at me, his eyes almost black in this light, searching my face. "Something wrong?"

"No." I picked up a broom that was supposed to go out to the ranch. "Why?"

"I'm sensing a cold breeze." I could feel him studying me, trying to figure things out. He wouldn't. After a lifetime of keeping your details to yourself, you learn not to let the truth show. Especially when the truth is a weapon that's sharp on both ends.

"Did Jen say something?"

"No. She was very nice, actually." Jen *was* just looking out for me, after all. She just wanted me to know what the score really was.

His lips straightened into an impassive line. "Jen has a few different ways of being nice. . . ."

"I just have things on my mind, all right?" I cut in, feeling impatient, trapped in a small space with him and the truth. I couldn't think straight. All I could see was Kemp stopping by Jennifer's house for intimate late-night conversations about his medical tests and the future. Intimate late-night conversations and what else? "Guess we'd better head on out to the ranch."

He didn't move. "What things?"

"What things . . . what?"

Pulling off his cap, he scratched his head, then put the cap on again. "What things do you have on your mind?"

"Nothing, I—" *just found out I'm only a little passing entertainment—something to do in the off-season. Not worth confiding in, really—*"just heard from the cruise line. It's time for me to get back to work. My mind's on catching a flight, and . . . I'm trying to decide what to do about my Microbus . . . and the dogs, and . . ." A lump rose in my throat, and I swallowed hard, leaving the sentence unfinished. Why was this so difficult? It wasn't like I'd never broken off a relationship before. What Kemp and I had wasn't even a relationship. It was just a few days . . . a few stolen moments.

Perfect moments. What if I never found anything else that felt so perfect?

*When he's out of the game, when his arm's hurt and he's off, he gets involved with somebody, but it never lasts. He always goes back to baseball. He always will.*

If breaking it off was painful now, how bad would it be if I let things drag on? *When he's chasing the dream, he doesn't care about anything else but the dream.* Wasn't that the thing I most despised about my father? The dream came first. His dream. His needs. His music. The rest of us were a sidenote.

I didn't want to be a sidenote in someone's life again. I wouldn't. Ever.

One way or another, I had to get out of Daily before I fell any deeper, before I did exactly what my mother had done, and history repeated itself.

Kemp tapped a thumb against his bottom lip contemplatively. "When did this come up?"

I fumbled for a lie. My mind was cloudy with emotion, tiny dust devils whirling around the edges of my thoughts. "A few minutes ago. They . . . called my cell."

He looked down, watched a dry leaf skitter in the door. "How long will you be gone?"

"I don't know exactly."

"When do you leave?"

"I'm not quite sure." His face narrowed, and I read the emotions there. Uncertainty, confusion, disbelief. This was probably a new experience for him. No doubt, he was usually the one doing the dumping. "I'm still under contract with the cruise line. I can't just . . . hang around here forever, doing nothing."

His chin jerked upward at the words *doing nothing*, and

his shoulders stiffened, as if he'd just taken a blow, as if I'd wounded him. Where only a moment ago, I'd felt certainty, determination, now doubt moved in like a fog, making clarity impossible. Maybe I was making a mistake. Maybe Jen was just trying to get me out of the way. . . .

But then, why would he have gone for an MRI yesterday and never said a word to me? We'd been together yesterday morning for breakfast, again in the afternoon, all evening. He'd come into the shop that afternoon whistling, with an extra spring in his step. His aunt had asked him how his day was. "Great," he'd said. "You know high-school kids. It's something new every time you turn around." Not, *I went to Dallas. The MRI was clear. . . .*

Why would he lie if Jen's assessment wasn't accurate? He was playing me, maybe even fooling himself, keeping himself entertained until he found out if he would be getting a better offer. The better offer being baseball. That was really what he'd been working toward all along. His life in Daily, this *old shoe*, was just an act, an illusion, a way to pass the time. The coach-slash-teacher-slash-hopeless romantic wasn't real, any more than my pretending I'd be staying there was.

*If something seems too good to be true, it usually is, Kai-bird.* My mother's advice again. Someone in our family had to be remotely practical.

Everything about Kemp's life here made perfect sense now. The office with the personal items still in boxes in the corner, the way he didn't quite seem comfortable when the kids talked about next season, the bottle baby calf he'd told me he needed to get rid of, even the way he dodged my questions about whether he was happy in Daily. *Happiness is something you decide on,* he'd said, but the truth was that he wasn't happy outside of baseball, and he never had been. Jen knew it, and maybe that was why Kemp felt the need to share the good news about his MRI with her. She understood him. She knew him in a way he perhaps didn't even know himself.

An old song played in my head. My mother used to sing along whenever it came on the radio. *Don't fall in love with a dreamer . . .*

*Because he'll break you every time,* the song went on to say. My mother knew all about dreams that didn't come true. Our life was a constant process of my father doing whatever felt good to him at the moment. His art, his music, his quest for fame and easy money always came first, and the rest of us were unwilling passengers on his wandering ship.

Not me. Not any longer. Not when I'd worked so hard to pull my life together. The last thing, the absolute last thing I wanted was to remember what it felt like to be rejected, to be pushed aside by someone you loved, to come in second place. Anything, even making a clean break now, was better than that.

"Are you planning on leaving without ever going over to McGregor to see about your grandmother?" Kemp's words were low and quiet, the tone of them hard to read.

An unsteadiness came over me. Every day when we reached the end of the driveway after feeding Bottle Baby, Kemp asked if I wanted to go to McGregor. *We can drive the back way from here,* he'd say, then he'd lighten the moment with something like, *It's enemy territory, but for you, I'd go,* or *I wouldn't head over to Bulldog land for just anybody. . . .*

*Maybe tomorrow,* I'd tell him. *I promised Donetta I'd help put together the breakfast casseroles tonight, remember?* Or *I'd better check on the dogs. Hope Radar didn't dig his way under the fence again.*

At night when I slept, I made that trip to Grandmother Miller's house over and over again. Each time, the result was different. Sometimes good, sometimes bad, the imaginings as unpredictable as life.

"I don't know," I answered now. "I'm not sure of —" *any-thing*— "my departure time."

Kemp's lips pursed skeptically. I thought of how it felt to kiss those lips, and the familiar headiness slipped over me. It would be so easy. So much nicer to go on pretending.

So much more painful to come back to reality later. It was hard enough now.

"We'll just play it by ear then, huh?" he said finally. "See if—"

"Pickle? Pickle-poo, you still here?" Donetta's voice pre-empted the sentence. Kemp answered as his aunt came up the hall.

Donetta surveyed the distance between the two of us, reading the body language with latent suspicion. "Hon, we got a little problem. Pastor Harve just called from out at Caney Creek Church, and a couple of the older ladies in Sister Mona's bunch ain't getting on too well out at the ranch. Sleepin' on the cots and sittin' around in lawn chairs all day has them stove up. Poor old Obeline can't hardly even walk. A cot's no place to sleep when you're as old as Obeline. You think you and Kai could go out there and bring them back here so they can stay in the hotel? Y'all can drive Imagene's van along with the truck, so there'll be plenty of room to bring the ladies back. Betty Prine was in the café yesterday, and she said her and Harold are packin' up to head for Arkansas so she can take care of her cousin. That means there won't be any Prines nosing around for a while."

"Sure. No problem, " Kemp answered, then hesitated and slanted a glance at me. "You'd better ask Kai if she's got time to drive the van out to the ranch, though."

Donetta drew back, the keys dangling from her fingers, her penciled-on eyebrows knotting in her forehead. "You don't mind helpin' out, do ya', hon? The van's right out front."

All of a sudden I realized that, by telling Kemp I was going back to work, I'd created a situation in which I was going to have to lie to everyone. The only real solution was to call the cruise line, get my marching orders, figure out what to do with the Microbus and Don's dogs, and turn the lie into truth. "Sure. Of course I have time," I answered, and Donetta dropped the keys into my hand.

"I'll bring the truck around, and you can follow me." Kemp headed out the door.

Donetta watched him go before turning to me. "Everythin' all right?" Laying a hand on my shoulder, she leaned close as we started through the café building.

"Everything's fine." *Tell her. Just tell her and be done with it.* But I knew if I told Donetta I was leaving, she'd want details, and I didn't have them yet. I didn't know by what means I was going to break away from Daily, Texas; I only knew I needed to.

She squeezed my shoulder, and I felt the tug of inconveniently tender emotions. Leaving Donetta, Imagene, Lucy, and the rest of the Dailyians behind would be almost as hard as leaving Kemp.

"Well, good. We'll see y'all in a bit, then." We crossed the café, and she held the front door open, then walked with me to the curb, checking the street in both directions. "When y'all get back, come around the alley door to my buildin', all right? Just in case Betty hasn't left out yet. No sense takin' any chances."

# Chapter 23

## *Donetta Bradford*

When Kemp and Kai came in with Obeline, Sister Mona, and two other ladies, we gals'd just sat down for some coffee and pie. We were celebrating like kids on the first day of summer vacation, knowing that Betty Prine was on her way out of town. Buddy Ray'd called from the Sheriff's Department not three minutes before and said he was sitting there behind the desk, watching Betty and Harold load the last of their suitcases and close the trunk, which meant anytime now they'd blow out of Daily like a bad wind.

"Come on in!" I called to Obeline and the ladies. "We got a fresh pot of coffee and there's pecan pie."

The ladies walked up the back hall, looking embarrassed and apologizing for interrupting our day. I guessed they figured they were putting us out by asking for a different place for the older folks to stay.

"Don't even worry a bit," I told them. "Y'all are more than welcome to them hotel rooms. That's what they're for, is for folks to stay in. Sit down and have a bite, and Kemp'll take your suitcases upstairs."

The ladies all wandered in and took a chair, and Kemp took charge of their luggage. After making a stack by the stairs, he went behind the counter to get the room keys.

"Pickle, hon," I said, "while you're up there, would you grab that boot box that's in the white chest of drawers in the Beulah suite? I want to see if I can find a picture of the old farm down on the Dogleg, just in case Obeline would remember anythin' about Mama's people."

"All right." Kemp wasn't cheerful as usual. I wondered what that was all about, and then I noticed that Kai didn't go upstairs or turn around and watch after him with a starry-eyed gaze, like she normally woulda. Somethin' was wrong. That gal had a long, sad look on her face, and instead of sittin' with the rest of us, she stood over in the corner, doing something with her cell phone. Then she got a call and went way up by the front window to take it, where we couldn't hear her.

When Kemp come back with my box, she just kept on with what she was doin'. He gave me my photo books, and I cut him a piece of pie, because he looked like he needed it. "Here, hon. Go fix yourself a cup of coffee before you finish carrying up them suitcases."

I opened up the box and started thumbing through, looking for pictures of the old farm and Mamee's little house down on the Dogleg Bayou. That box was about as organized as my mind, unfortunately, and all I could find was pictures of Kemp and Lauren when they were kids—Kemp with his little baseball suit on, and his sister riding in the barrel racin' and the goat tyin' at rodeos, and the two of them dressed up like Dorothy and the Tin Man for Halloween. Obeline leaned up and looked real close, even though I doubt that was very interestin' to her. I pulled out an old black cardboard frame and found a picture of me in my pretty Christmas dress, all gussied up for the 4-H style show.

Imagene leaned over and giggled. "Oh my word, look at that hair!"

"Is-a not a hair, is-a march-een hat!" Lucy hooted, holding her hands up around her head like she had on one of them tall, furry hats the Daily High School Band wore for marching.

"I worked real hard on that." I tried to act like they'd hurt my feelings, but they knew better. Even I, who understood the value of big hair as much as anybody, had to admit it's possible to go too big. That giant puff with the little bow in front looked like it oughta have hornets livin' in it.

"*Gal-ee!* I'm'ma say that hairdo, that makin' its own patch of shade!" Sister Mona chimed in, and everyone hooted again.

Soon as I caught my breath, I dug back into the box some more. "Hold on a minute, I got to show you *Imagene* at the 4-H style show. Just wait'll you see the hairdo *she* has on." We gals'd fixed each other's hair that evenin', and I remembered clear as day piling Imagene's up so high she looked like the blond bride a' Frankenstein. "Hang on a minute . . . I got . . ."

Right under where the 4-H picture'd been, there was an old photo stickin' out, the corner tore off a little bit, the colors brown and swirled like sugar going to caramel. I knew what it was. Mamee's wedding picture. The one where she was sittin' in a chair with Pap behind her, her dark eyes starin' into the camera, sad and quiet. Until I heard the story about Macerio, I'd always thought she looked that way because she was so young to be gettin' married—just sixteen. After she told me about Macerio, the next time I come across that picture, I wondered if he was the reason for her long face.

I pulled the photo out and set it on the table in front of Obeline, then tapped a finger to it. "That's my mamee and pap when they first got married. Mercy! They're just babies there.

Pap was the kind of man who worked hard and just never said much, but Mamee was sure somethin' special to me. Did you ever know them two? They had a little old house right down on the bayou. Don't recall that it ever had much paint on it. It mighta been blue, or green at one time . . ." I drifted off, trying to recall the place. "Had a big ol' screen porch all the way across the front, and a lane that went on up to the rice fields."

Obeline tipped the picture so she could see it. "That'd be lotta houses on the bayou, sha. Lotta rice field in that country. Everybody farm the rice." Chuckling, she tapped a finger to the picture. "*Gal-ee*, she a Cajun gal, though, is she? You know how to tell a Cajun and a Creole and a regular farmer from each other?"

"No, ma'am, I don't." I was tryin' not to sound too awful disappointed that Mamee's picture didn't jog any memories.

Obeline chuckled again. "Mais, regular farmer, he look at the rice field and he see lotta rice. Cajun, he look out there, he see jambalaya. Creole farmer, he look out there, he see Creole rice 'n' shrimp remoulade. Hoo-eee! That's good!"

The three of us laughed together, then I looked through the box some more, but I couldn't find the picture of Mamee's little house. No telling where it'd ended up over the years.

Someplace down in my heart, I got a sad feelin', thinking that, even though Lauren and Kemp knew all about the Eldridge side of the family, the history of my mama's people would end up lost forever. Maybe before Obeline and Sister Mona left, I'd take down some recipes for that bayou food and pass them along to the kids. It'd be somethin' from Mama's country, anyhow.

"Well, I guess I can't find them pictures of the house," I told them finally. "Probably wouldn't mean much anyway. That's been a lot of years ago. Long time since I even been there. Not since my mamee died, and I was just fifteen then. I was right there on the porch of that little house with her the night she passed on. We were shellin' peas one minute, and the next I heard the angels comin' and she dropped the bowl. It was the strangest thing."

I left off the tale, since there wasn't any more point in it, and I took a bite of my pie. When I finished chewin', I noticed everyone was still looking at me, like they were waiting for the rest. "There was a story she told me that night, right before she passed on, and I always did wonder about it."

"I never knew that." Imagene's eyes got round.

"You never say a word, all the time," Lucy added.

I looked down into my coffee, watching a little pool of Splenda float around like an island. I thought about the tale of Mamee and the flood. "Guess it seemed like a secret, kind of. But really, it ain't. Anybody who'd know anything about it's been gone long ago, anyhow."

"What that story, cher?" Sister Mona asked, and pulled the weddin' picture over so she could look.

I took a big breath then let it out, my mind wandering back. "Well, it was a story about a hurricane, at first," I said, and then I went on and told them the tale about Mamee, and the flood, and Macerio, just like she told me. I ended it up after she run off with him on the back of his horse by the dark of midnight. "That's as far as she got. She never said what happened after that. She just whispered his name real quiet, like a breath almost, and then she passed. I always wondered if she saw him again when she was driftin' off to heaven."

"Mercy," Imagene breathed, her eyes wellin' up. Imagene'll cry over anything.

"How is the angel when you see them?" Lucy asked. "I wonder about that lotta time when I go-een to be a Christian. In Japan, we got hundred, hundred, hundred god and demon, different picture all places, but when I go-een to be a Christian,

I wonder how it is to see some real angel, not just so many picture."

"I didn't see 'em." My mind went back to that day on the porch. "I just heard their comin'—like a roaring in my ears, so loud, and I felt a rush of somethin' cool, like the sweetest breeze ever, like it come across a meadow full of bluebonnets, and then it got quiet and the heat come back in, and I knew Mamee was gone. I just . . ."

Obeline leaned across in front of me to take Mamee's picture, and the look on her face made me stop talking. It was like she was seein' a ghost. "Obeline?" I whispered. The room got quiet and still, like that old buildin' was holding its breath, waiting.

"You remember somethin', sha?" Sister Mona slid a hand around Obeline and rubbed the hump between her shoulder blades.

Obeline slowly shook her head, staring hard into Mamee's face, back into the past. "I don' know this gal, but I know that story. My big sista, Belvette, she tell me long time ago."

My heart got up in my throat, so I could hear it in my ears like a drum poundin', and the air in the room seemed heavy and thick, like the evenings in the bayou. "You know about my mamee? About her and Macerio?"

Obeline nodded. "Belvette, she was there when this gal gonna have the bébé. My mère, she the midwife then. A white man, he come fetch Mère, say his daughter got a bébé comin' soon. Mère, she take Belvette along so Belvette can help out some." Obeline held up the picture, tipping her head back so she could see it through her bifocals.

"Belvette, she come back home near mornin', and I feel her crawl up in the bed, and she jus' shiverin'. I roll over, curl up close, ask, 'What happen, sha?'

"Belvette tell me about the night. She say, when Mère get

there, that little mother-gal, she been hard in labor long time already, and ain't nobody there but her and the man, her papa. Her papa, he tell Mère, that gal's husband gone pickin' up some cows in Houston. So Mère, she tend that poor gal all night. Near mornin' two bébé come, but that gal, she too wore out to know nothin' by then. She got one boy, one girl. That girl bébé she got red hair, like the mama, but she kinda weak and quiet. The boy, he scream loud 'n' long. Mère tell the man, you got two grandbébé. But the man, he don' say nothin'. He pick up the boy bébé, then he tell Mère he gonna carry him to the big house, to the grandma. But when Mère see the man in the eye, he got a bad look on his face. He go out the room and out the door. Mère say, 'Belvette, you creep along after the man, watch out, see what he gonna do. I don' believe he gonna take that bébé to the big house.'"

Right then, Imagene gasped and so did I. Lucy just sat there shakin' her head.

"Mama, you don' ever tell me that story," Sister Mona breathed.

"Been long time ago," Obeline said, and then she went on. "Belvette, she creep along after the man. She quiet, like a shadow. She mighty scared, but she go. She hide and watch, and sure 'nuf, that man, he go on back in the bayou, leave that boy bébé on the water-shore. Jus' set it down and go away, like it ain't nothin'. Belvette, she wait till he gone, then she take up the bébé, sit and rock him. She got *mal pris*! Lotta trouble. She scared outta her mind, sha. She worry that man gonna come back. She worry big gator gonna come. She worry da Rugaru gonna slip up in the bayou, carry her off and eat her up. She mighty glad when Mère come. She cry out, *'Co faire? Co faire?'* She want to know why that man leave the bébé where the gator and the wildcat gonna come get it.

"Mère tell her to shush up till they done walk well away. Then she give Belvette that story you just told, 'bout the gal and the Mexican boy. 'De'pouille!' she say. 'It ain't any secret. Everybody know that gal, she run off wit' a Mexican boy, and the papa catch up wit' them the next day. The papa, he beat her beau half dead, then he tell the gal she either come home or that Mexican boy gonna be all dead. He carry his daughter-gal home, marry her off real quick to the neighbor man, and pretty soon, she big, round, gonna have the bébé."

Obeline stopped talking and reached across the table to get a napkin, then mopped her forehead like even telling that story was hard. Not a one of us took a drink or made a move. We were just froze right there in our seats. I heard Kemp cross the room to where Kai was over by the windows, but I didn't even look to see what they were doing. I just waited for Obeline to give the rest of that tale.

Her hand shook while she took a sip of her coffee. "Then Belvette, she ask why it so bad that the gal have a bébé. Mère open the blanket, she say, 'Belvette, this a Mexican bébé, and he look like a Mexican bébé.'"

"Belvette, she look real hard, and she see it's true. That bébé, he got black hair, brown skin, not red hair, white skin, like that girl bébé have. Belvette ask Mère, 'What we gonna do?'" Obeline stopped for a sip of coffee again, and we hung on her every move until she started back into the story.

"Mère say they gonna take that bébé to the harvest camp, where the Mexican folk stay, and that's what they do. They jus' walk into the harvest camp wit' that wailin' bébé and give it over. The Mexican folk, they promise to take that bébé down to the papa in Mexico, and Belvette, she never know no more about it. On the way home, Mère get right up in her face and say, 'Belvette, you don' tell nobody 'bout this, sha. Never. Fiank! That man crazy. He leave a little bébé in the swamp, he kill us both, sure enough.'"

Obeline made a slash mark across her neck, then shook her

head. "Belvette never tell a soul but me, and I don' say a word. Not all my life." She stopped talking and sank back in her chair, wore out by her own story.

I sat there feeling like maybe I was dreamin' and I'd wake up soon. I remembered Mamee talking about the day my mama was born. Musta been she never even knew she had a baby boy that was carried off to the south. I guessed my pap never even knew it, either. He wasn't the kind of man who woulda gone along with leaving a baby out in the bayou to die. My great-grandaddy musta made that choice all on his own, in the dead of night, and took the secret to his grave. "Mercy," I whispered as it all sunk in. "Mamee had a little boy growin' up down in Mexico, and she never even knew it. Pap wasn't my real granddaddy. Macerio was my granddaddy." Just thinking about that turned my mind inside out like an old shirt that's faded on one side and bright on the other. "Could be I've got people down in Mexico."

"Could be," Imagene agreed, looking as surprised as I was. "Imagine that. Wouldn't it . . ." She stopped and pointed toward the window. Outside, Betty Prine's car was passing by. We all just watched it go, and for a minute I forgot about Mamee's baby and remembered about Betty. In another few seconds, she'd be long gone, and we wouldn't have to worry about her at least. I felt like an outlaw that'd just ducked behind a tree so the cavalry would ride right by.

Imagene chuckled and waved. "Good riddance to rotten rubbish."

"Amen to that," I agreed, and felt a grin tugging hard at me. We'd beat Betty Prine at her own game, and I'd found out the truth about Mamee and Macerio, and I'd learned I might have a secret family down in Mexico. A day can't get much better than that.

But you know what they say about pride before the fall. I guess you could figure it was pride that done it, or me just bein' a little too careless in all the excitement. But really it was a cat, a dog, and a bird that chewed up our plans like meat through a sausage grinder and turned that day from a miracle to a disaster in a hurry.

Just as the Prines' car was passing out of sight, Miss Peach's motley gray cat shot across the street like a bullet. Harold swerved to miss it, and right when he did, that silly dog, Radar, run across the road after the cat. Harold swerved again, skidded on an oil slick, and bumped right up on the curb.

By the time Imagene, Lucy, Kemp, Kai, and me run to the sidewalk to make sure everyone was all right, Harold and Betty were gettin' out to look at the car. By then, the cat'd climbed a light pole, and the dog had him treed. Kemp and Kai headed across the street hollerin' at the dog, which is where the bird come in. All the commotion woke a fat gray pigeon on the highline. While stretchin' his wings, he raised his tail and sent down a blessing that landed smack in the middle of Betty Prine's wash-and-curl. Before we knew what was happenin', Hurricane Betty was headed our way in a dead gallop.

She didn't stop squealing until she come up the sidewalk, run into my shop, and stuck her head in one of the hair sinks. By the time Imagene, Lucy, and me made it in there, she was sputterin' and sprayin' water everywhere, and cursing that pigeon in a way that, well . . . wasn't strictly biblical.

It was just about then, and both at the same time, Imagene and me realized that, not six foot from Betty, right there at the coffee counter, was Sister Mona and her crew, gaping at Betty like a bunch of fish in a bowl. Soon as Betty come up out of that sink, she was gonna know we'd pulled a fast one on her.

"Oh lands!" I ran to the sink, grabbed the spray nozzle from Betty's hand and hollered, "Just stay down there, Betty. It ain't all out yet." I turned up the water and leaned close to Imagene and Lucy. "Get them ladies outta here. Now!"

"What? What?" Betty put her hands on the edge of the basin and tried to raise up, and I squirted her in the face, accidentally, of course.

"Nothin', Betty." I shoved her into the sink again. "Just stay down there."

Lucy grabbed for the drain stopper to plug the sink so it'd fill up while Betty's head was in there, and I batted her hand away.

"We can't drown Betty Prine," Imagene whispered, but then she looked like she was thinkin' about it, too.

"What?" Betty tried to raise up again.

"Hold still, Betty. You don't want that stuff drippin' in your mouth! You'll get worms." I squirted her in the face again, then batted a hand at Lucy and Imagene, and pointed toward the stairs.

"For heaven's sake!" Betty stood up and felt around for a towel, then stumbled forward with wet hair in her face and her arms out like *Night of the Living Dead*. I chased her with the squirter, sayin', "Come back here, Betty. That stuff's gonna stain!"

Imagene and Lucy hurried through the shop and tried to pull them ladies out of their chairs and get them moving.

"For heaven's sake, Donetta Bradford!" Betty roared, with a backward swipe that caught the sprayer and knocked it out of my hand. It flew through the air like a live snake, spittin' water until it'd reeled back into the sink. Betty stumbled over a chair, caught hold of a hair cape, and mashed it to her face, and I knew we were sunk.

When Betty come out from behind that cape, she was lookin' just the right direction to see Lucy and Imagene trying to sneak them ladies up the stairs. "Donetta Bradford!" she roared, pointing a finger and shaking it in the air. "Donetta Bradford, what is the meaning of this?" She swung from Sister Mona's crew to me, and her eyes got smaller, and smaller, just like a pit bull's right before it bites. The room turned quiet, and she growled, "We'll see about this. We'll see about this *right now*. You just *wait* until I get ahold of the *fire marshal*."

About that time, Harold lumbered up to the door, looking confused, like Harold usually does. Betty caught him on the way out and spun him around like a top. "Come, Harold. We'll be delaying our trip. We have a *phone call* to make." She slammed the door on the way out, and we all stood there watching the glass shudder to a stop.

"Uh-oh," Imagene said, the first to speak up.

"Hoos-ten, we have a prob-lamb," Lucy added.

"We got more than a problem." I knew that much was true. "This is a full-scale disaster."

Sister Mona and Obeline started apologizing then, which only made things feel even worse.

"Don't ya'll worry a bit," I told them. "Y'all just go on up there to the rooms and make yourselves to home. This building's been in my family for over a hundred years. No Betty Prine or anybody else is gonna tell me what I can do with it. We'll work things out, don't you worry."

Imagene, Lucy, and me stood there watching and trying to look sure of ourselves as the ladies headed for the back stairs.

"Lucy, call over to the county offices and see if you can find out where that new fire marshal's at," I said. On any given day, catching county officials in the office was about as likely as catching a west Texas raindrop in a shot glass. Normally, if you wanted to complain about potholes in the road, or a dead deer that needed to be drug off, or signs down, you had to leave a message, and you knew better than to hold your breath while you waited for them to call back.

If we were lucky, today would be that kind of day.

I said a little prayer while Lucy hurried off to check.

"Imagene, we got to give this a good think, and quick," I said, listening with one ear while Lucy got out the phone book, then dialed the county offices. "We gotta come up with something to stop Betty Prine before she brings the whole county commissioners court down on us. You know she can do it, too. Her and Harold got connections all over that place."

"Ain't no amount of thinkin's gonna work this out." Imagene's voice was quiet and low, the kind someone uses at a funeral. "Just as soon as Betty Prine puts in a complaint to the fire marshal, it'll be out of her hands, anyway. Lands, Netta, the same thing could happen to you that happened to Bodie Rogers and the theater. You could wind up closed down and out of business. Then Betty and Harold'll go build their fancy new hotel. You and Lucy'll be out of a job, and . . . and Frank'll lose his shop, and . . . ."

"Imagene!" I yipped, and she jerked back like I'd slapped her. Right then, the last thing I needed was to hear all about what *could* happen. "Don't you say a word about this to Frank. He'll be down here with a rifle and, next thing, we'll end up on the evening news."

Imagene's eyes snapped to mine, and all at once, we had what coulda only been called a divine inspiration, "The evening news," we both said at once.

"I wonder how Betty'd feel about kicking four little old ladies, victims of the hurricane no less, out of their hotel rooms, if the news heard about it?" Imagene added.

I felt the plan warming up, like a match head running over sandpaper. "Them all bein' evacuees from the storm, why, that'd look pretty sorry of her, wouldn't it?"

"It would," Imagene agreed.

"No fire marshal," Lucy reported, hanging up the phone. "She sayed he gone to Fort Worth till tomorrow."

Imagene and me let out air like whoopee cushions under a fat man.

306

"We got till tomorrow," I said.

Imagene nodded, but she still looked grim. "What're we gonna do between now and tomorrow?"

Both of us looked at Lucy, and she lifted both hands in the air. "Don' want me to say." What she really meant was, *Don't ask me,* which was pretty much how I felt, too.

"We're gonna start calling the TV and the newspapers." I could feel the idea growing in my head, like God was writing it there. "We're gonna get every reporter we can. Imagene, you give Lucy your mobile phone, and then you go over and use Bob's phone at the café, and I'll use the one here. Call every newspaper and TV station you can think of. Imagene, you call Austin, I'll call Dallas, and Lucy, you call Waco, Killeen, and Temple."

The three of us got busy, but landing yourself on TV ain't as easy as wanting to. After a half hour, Imagene came back with a long face, Lucy'd set the mobile phone down and was just staring at it, and I had my head in my hands. Every news station in Texas was tied up covering the aftermath of Glorietta, or reporting on the troubles of evacuees stuffed in the convention centers, and nobody had any time for one tiny story down in Daily, Texas.

We all sat at the counter, feeling low. "What are we gonna do now?" Imagene asked finally.

"I don't know." There wasn't any point lying about it. We were in a fix. "Pray from the foxhole, I guess. This is gonna take a big dose of divine intervention." I spotted Kemp out on the sidewalk right then, and a idea lit in my brain. "Wait a minute. I just had a thought."

"Uh-oh," Lucy muttered, because sometimes my thoughts ain't for the fainthearted.

"Y'all wait here," I told her, and headed for the door. Kemp was stopped on the sidewalk, and the closer I got to the door, the more I could tell something was wrong. In the first place, he was all by himself, and in the second place, I'd seen that look on his face before. That was the look he got when he'd struck out at the plate.

I opened the door and asked him to come back in. "Everythin' all right, hon? Where's Kai?"

"Yeah." He had the big ol' frown of a kid who'd just lost his trick-or-treat bag. "She took the dog home. She said she'd tie him up so he wouldn't get away again."

"All right." I looked Kemp over again. Whatever was wrong, he wasn't talking about it. When a he was in a mood like that, there was no point pushing. "Hon, there's something I'd like you to help with." A crafty little idea slipped into my head, and I added, "Well, you and Kai, of course. It'll probably take two of you."

Kemp frowned. "That might be a little tough, Aunt Netta. She's getting ready to leave town."

"She's . . . what?" That news flash caught me blindside.

"She's flying somewhere to meet a ship. She says she needs to get back to work."

I was struck silent, which don't happen often. "When did that come about, because just this mornin', she didn't seem in a hurry to get anywhere. She was chatterin' on about y'all helping out at the ranch, and how much the calf was growin', and how y'all two were gonna take some of the evacuee kids down to Caney Creek and she was gonna show you up at bass fishin'. Now all of a sudden, she's headed off to work?"

Kemp rubbed his eyebrows, like he was trying to smooth out a pain. "You know what, Aunt Netta, you're going to have to ask her that question." He bit the words out in a way that made it sound like he didn't care, but I raised that boy from the time he was two, and that wasn't *I don't care* in his eyes. He'd just got his heart broke.

"You know, sometimes a gal just wants a fella to say, 'Don't go,'" I told him. As many gals as Kemp'd always had chasing him around, you'd think he'd know that. "Sometimes she just wants to be sure before she . . . plants a crop, so to speak. Kai's got some tough history with her family. She ain't told me all about it, but she's told me some. I don't think they even talk at all."

"As far as I can tell, she likes it that way." Kemp pulled a breath, then let it out. "I asked her if she planned to leave without even going over to McGregor to see if her grandmother still lived there, and she said yes."

"She's got a *grandma* over in *McGregor*? She never told me that."

"Yeah, well, you don't know her as well as you think." A muscle in his cheek twitched, and his jaw set hard, and I could feel him shuttin' me, and Kai, and everything else outside the door. He'd learned to do that when his mama died. Even though he was too little for us to explain it to him then, he knew his mama was gone. He quit talking for months, and just wandered around the house like he was looking for someone. He never fussed or cried. He just kept to himself.

"I'll talk to her," I told him, and just as soon as the words were out, I knew that was the wrong thing to say. Kemp's eyes got hard as bottle glass.

"Leave it be."

"I just meant that . . ."

"Aunt Netta, I said leave it be."

"Well, hon, sometimes girl to girl, it's easier to tal—"

Pulling his cap back into place with one quick jerk, he pointed a finger at me, which was something I couldn't remember him doing in his whole life, ever. I got the firm feelin' I'd finally gone too far.

Over by the shop counter, Imagene sucked in a breath. She hadn't ever seen Kemp act that way before, either. Normally, he was cool as a cucumber.

"It's finished, all right?" His voice was flat, the words cold as coffin nails. No room for a question there. "Just let it alone. I'm a big boy. I don't need anyone to run my life for me."

I pulled back a little, because that last sentence come out of left field, and it seemed to have to do with more than just a tiff with a girl. "I know that, hon." Looking at him now, standing six foot three and with his dander up, there wasn't any denying he was a full-grown man and he could handle himself. But when you raised that man, there's a part of you that knows the little boy inside and still wants to protect him—even from himself. "I wasn't tryin' to run your life, darlin'. I was only tryin' to help."

He softened, like he'd just remembered who he was pointing a finger at. Back in the day, behaving like that woulda got him sent to his room or a smack on the rear, if his daddy saw it. "I just have a lot on my mind, Aunt Netta. What was it you needed me to help you with?"

"Oh, that . . ." For a minute there, I'd got so wrapped up in Kemp's problem, I plumb forgot about the building and the trouble with Betty. "Kemp, we gotta do something about Betty Prine. She knows Sister Mona's bunch are still here and she's on the warpath now, for sure, and she won't stop till there's a big fat red tag on my door, just like what happened to Bodie Rogers at the theater. We got to come up with a way to stop her."

Kemp cast a hard look toward the street. "It's time somebody went over there and had a talk with the Prines. This is ridiculous." By *somebody*, I could tell he meant himself. He had a glare in his eye that was nothing short of murder.

"No, now you sound like your daddy." Good thing Frank was out at the ranch right now, because if he was there, he'da been banging on the Prines' door already. "Just simmer down."

"They think they can run this town."

I stepped between him and the door, just in case he got any wild ideas. "Kemp, if you go down there and give the Prines a piece of your mind, the next thing you'll have is trouble with the school board. You know Harold Prine has four school board members working for him at the bank and the cement company. He'll lean on the board, and you'll be out of a job."

Kemp snorted under his breath. "I don't need this job."

It bothered me to hear him say that. "Kemp, you're the best thing to happen to those kids at Daily High in a long time, and you know it. You're the only one that cares enough to make them act right and do their work in their classes, and not just win ball games but be good Christian boys, inside and out. If you leave, things'll go back to the way they were, and those boys'll be the losers."

Kemp just kept looking down the road, his chin a hard line. I'd seen that look before. "You *can't* get into it with Betty and Harold Prine," I said, but he didn't answer, so I figured the best thing was to head in another direction. Kemp had something on his mind, but he was locked up tight as widow's wallet. "So, listen, we gals got a plan anyway. What we need is some reporters. Let's see how Betty feels about bein' in the news while she's runnin' people out of town—old ladies and little children who've evacuated from the hurricane, no less. Let's see her do that with everyone watchin'. You still got that little friend who does the news up in Dallas?"

"Ashley?"

"Mm-hmm. Her. You and her still on speaking terms? You think you could get in touch with her? We tried calling the TV stations ourselves, but we hadn't been havin' any luck." Kemp and Ashley'd dated for a while when she was doing publicity for the Rangers. She was a cute little thing, but she had quick, sly eyes like a cat. She and Kemp'd parted ways when he was on the road and she came back to Dallas for the news anchor job. I wasn't sorry to hear about it. "You think you could get her to send a reporter and a camera here in the morning? Even just *one* little reporter and *one* little camera? As a favor to you, so to speak?" I knew Ashley still called Kemp sometimes. Just the other day, I'd heard him answer the cell phone, and it was her.

Kemp sucked air through his teeth, like I'd just slugged him in the belly. "That might be a little tough, Aunt Netta. When Ashley called the other day, she wasn't getting in touch to be social. She wanted a scoop."

Now I really was confused. "A scoop about what?"

Kemp's head bent forward, and he rubbed the back of his neck, letting out a long sigh. "I didn't want to say anything until I knew for sure. I didn't want my ballplayers to hear about it on the sports report." He kept his voice low so no one but me could catch what he was saying.

"Hear what?" From the corner of my eye, I could see Imagene and Lucy inching closer. My stomach twisted up my throat like a constrictor snake. Whatever Kemp was about to say, I wasn't gonna like it.

"Nothing's decided yet."

"Kempner Rollins, you better spit it . . ." *Out.* But he didn't need to. All of a sudden, my mind whip-stitched the strings together, all on its own. Ashley, a scoop, the news, something Kemp didn't want to tell his kids, or me. He was talking to *the team.* He was thinking about going back. "Oh, Kemp. Not again."

"It's a clear MRI, and the big club needs pitching, that's all," he said, but I could tell that wasn't all. He had that gleam in his eye, and I'd known him long enough to know exactly what that look meant.

# Chapter 24

## *Kai Miller*

At Donetta's house, I sat for a long time on a swing in the backyard. Overhead, the oak tree groaned under the burden of the chains, causing the dogs to twitch in their sleep as the day fell into a hush, the sky blushing in shades of crimson and rose.

I thought of Kemp, of the day we rode up the hill behind the ranch and watched the sun go down. The moment replayed in my mind, awakening remembered sensations—the warm summer breeze, the scent of drying grass and cedar, the softness of his touch, the tingle of excitement on my skin as his fingers trailed over my shoulder, slid into my hair, drew me closer until his lips touched mine, until I couldn't think of anything but him. Even now, I yearned for that moment, for his touch, for his laughter, for the heady feeling he awakened in me, for the sense of desiring and being desired until it was hard to say where desire ended and something deeper began. I longed for that feeling the way you long for one more taste of something wonderful after the plate is empty. It was as if all my life, without even realizing it, I'd been waiting to feel that way.

But that was the problem. The need in me was so strong, it eclipsed all sense of logic. I was willing to believe that I'd found the real thing in someone I barely knew, in someone who held a large part of himself in secret. Who was just, as Jen put it, passing time.

My cell phone rang beside me, but I ignored it. It would only be the cruise line calling to leave the final details about the flight that would take me to meet up with the *Liberation*—sooner, rather than later, since the crew members who hadn't made ship the morning of the hurricane were still scattered due to the storm. The ship needed staff before leaving Tampa. In less than a day, I would be a thousand miles from here. It would be that simple.

The arrangements had fallen into place as if it were meant to be. I'd catch a flight from Dallas to Tampa in the morning. The vet clinic would board the dogs. Maggie and Meredith would be flying from Kansas to Dallas as soon as the roads to the coast were open. They'd pick up my Microbus from airport parking, then swing by Daily and retrieve Don's dogs. Meanwhile, Don was holding down the fort in Perdida, trapped with other stragglers, getting occasional messages out on a shortwave radio, while protecting the surf shop building and M&M's coffee bar.

Until Maggie and Meredith could fly in, Jen, Jenny, Jennifer would take good care of Radar and Hawkeye at the vet clinic. She'd probably take good care of Kemp, too. They'd get together, break up, and keep in touch until the next time he was on hiatus from the team. Someday, maybe when the dreams ran out, and he was finished with the game for good, they'd settle down in Daily together.

The idea wounded me in a place I'd thought was closed to everyone. How was that possible? How could he have found the way through a door I thought I'd sealed up long ago? Behind that was the obvious question—Why had I let him? Why had I allowed this to happen when I knew what a painful word goodbye was? When I knew how it felt to know that someone you loved, someone you needed to love you back, was really just marking time with you while making other plans? My mother had other plans, my father's interest was focused elsewhere, and even Gil, as much as he tried to hang on, had to leave me behind.

Relationships ended painfully, every time. Which was why, all these years, I'd kept relationships on the surface—like clothes you could change when they weren't working anymore. Nobody hurt, just an exchange of one outfit for another. This storm had made me vulnerable, sentimental, needy, weak.

It was time to get back to normal.

Even as I tried to convince myself, I wanted to pick up the phone and call Kemp. I wanted to tell him I'd been lying when I stood outside Donetta's shop with him after Radar treed Miss Peach's cat on Main Street. He'd tried to pin me down about why I was leaving, why the sudden change of plans. I'd played it cool, told him I had a job to do, a business to put back together, and of course those things had to come first. There wasn't room in my life for anything more. "There's really no point in keeping in touch," I'd said. "It's just too complicated. We live so far apart, after all. You've got your life, I've got mine."

He'd looked surprised, even a little wounded, maybe. "So you're leaving without ever driving over to McGregor?" He asked again. The look in his eyes seemed to drill right through me, nail me to the wall.

"I don't really see the point." I tried to sound casual, detached. "That's ancient history. With everything that's happening in Perdida, the immediate future's full already." That much was true. The future was full. Full of my own plans.

In spite of my hastily prepared rhetoric, I stood there feeling empty, Kemp and me at a stalemate, a painful haze in the air. I glanced through the beauty shop window to keep from looking at him. A verse written above one of the mirrors caught my eye. *For I know the plans I have for you . . .*

The phrase came back to me now, repeated in my head as I rocked on Donetta's swing. Closing my eyes, I tried to shake it away, force it into a corner and close the door.

*I know the plans I have for myself. My plans.*

Even Kemp, when it came right down to it, had to realize that this was for the best. He was free to keep his focus on the prize, on the big dream that consumed him, that didn't leave room for anything else, just like my father's dream of making it in the music business.

It must have broken my mother's heart when she finally realized that she, and all the rest of us, would always come second to my father's aspirations, to his need to prove himself to the world, to have everyone know his name, to be famous. The problem between my parents wasn't lack of love, or absence of passion. She loved him so much, she wasted half of her life following him from one dive to the next. So often, she wanted him to just stop, stay where he was, build a life that was somewhere close to normal. Every time, he talked her into the dream again, until she believed it, too, and off we went, blowing what little money we had on one more shot at the big time. Eventually, she couldn't live that way anymore, and after Gil was gone, she figured she didn't have to. She broke free while there was still time for a life of her own.

No wonder she never asked me to share it. I just reminded her of my father, of how things were, of how much time she'd wasted with a man who never put her first.

*Sometimes, you have to move on because it's too hard to look back,* she wrote on the sticky note that was still attached to my birth certificate, now safely tucked inside Gil's Bible. *One of these days, you'll understand.*

That day had arrived. Today, it made perfect sense. Today I understood. Those old lyrics *Don't fall in love with a dreamer* were just as true as they had always been.

Tears welled in my eyes, and I let them come. As much as I tried to picture catching the ship in Tampa, satisfying my contract, going back to Perdida, helping Don put the shop together again, listening to Maggie and Meredith talk about the grandchildren in Kansas, the images felt forced, small, sad.

*Home won't be home anymore. It won't be the same.*

Maybe I wouldn't even go back. Maybe I'd just try to go full time on ship, drift from one contract to another, from one port to the next until something seemed right.

Would anything ever be right? How would I know? It felt right with Kemp, here in Daily, with Donetta and the girls at the beauty shop. It felt like I was finally home. I'd allowed myself to sink into the foolish idea that I was just another Dailyian—like all the regular people. Just like the town kids I'd once envied at the Dairy Queen.

Maybe I'd never know how to create a normal life, how to build the house with the painted fence outside and the welcome mat on the porch, inviting people in. Maybe I was more like my father than I'd ever wanted to admit. Where would I ever have learned how to create that picture, how to put down roots, how to be somewhere, or with someone, forever?

*Maybe some people just wander all their lives . . .*

The sunset blurred behind tears.

*I don't want to be lost anymore. I don't . . .*

Headlights strafed the backyard, and I heard a truck rattling into the carport. Wiping my eyes, I stood up and started toward the house, pulling myself together and putting the mask back in place as I reached the back door. Crying over any of this was idiotic and weak. Of course I wanted my life back. I had a good life. I was self-sufficient. I had a business doing something I loved. I had a place of my own where I could open my window at night and hear the tide drifting in and out, the waves rhythmic, even predictable. If Glorietta hadn't come along, I would never have considered the need for anything beyond that.

So why was I standing here now, looking through Donetta's back door, disappointed when it was Donetta, not Kemp, who stepped into the kitchen?

I came in and she slapped a hand to her chest. "Oh gracious, Kai, you scared me!"

"Sorry. I was sitting outside making some calls—getting my flight information and everything." Donetta didn't seem surprised that I was leaving. Obviously, Kemp had told her. "Is everything okay down at the hotel? You look really tired." I knew I should have gone and checked on Donetta before now. As much as she'd done for me, she deserved that, but I didn't want to see Kemp or catch familiar sights around town and replay mental film clips of my Daily memories. It would be better if I just finished packing and left in the morning. Easier.

There was a slight tremble in Donetta's lips as she turned and set her purse on the counter. "Well . . . things don't look so good for tomorrow mornin'. Betty Prine is so mad about the Holy Ghost crew still being here, she plans to turn in a complaint on my building and get the fire marshal here first thing. You know, normally, they just overlook a lot of squeaks and creaks in these old buildings, but if they got a complaint to satisfy, and especially one from Betty Prine, well, that ain't gonna be the case. I keep tellin' myself the good Lord's got this in hand, Donetta, but sometimes it's hard not to wonder." Her voice broke on the final words, and she braced her palms on the counter, slumping forward, seeming defeated. Even when

Glorietta was passing over us in full force, I hadn't seen her surrender like this.

*I keep tellin' myself the good Lord's got this in hand.* Yet here she was, one step from losing her livelihood because she'd tried to do a good deed. If that wasn't wrong, if that wasn't unfair, I didn't know what was. If God wouldn't send down a miracle for Donetta Bradford, who would He send a miracle for? If He didn't listen to someone like her, He didn't listen to anybody.

*He didn't save Gil, either. He doesn't listen. He doesn't hear.* I felt my heart loosening the mooring lines, setting adrift the haphazard vessel of faith that had been clumsily built during anonymous vacation Bible schools and the Sunday school sessions with the free food and nice people. If God was omnipresent, if He knew the falling of every sparrow, why were good people allowed to suffer? If there was a plan, why would this be it?

Stepping into the kitchen, I laid a hand awkwardly on Donetta's shoulder. "I wish there were something I could do."

Slipping her fingers over mine, she held tight. "It's good that you're here. It's good not to be alone." Her voice cracked again. "I thought Ronald'd be here by now, for sure. It's Wednesday, and he knows we were supposed to get home from our cruise on Thursday."

I didn't know how to answer that. Certainly, relationships weren't my strong point. "Maybe he got his days mixed up." It was a lame excuse, but I couldn't think of anything else.

"He knows what day it is. He's just bein' stubborn, since he didn't want me to go on that cruise in the first place. He thought it was a big fat waste of money." Her voice had a cold edge to it, like my mother's when I called to ask about my birth certificate. "You watch. He'll come in here from fishin' and he won't ask a thang about it. He'll act like nothin' ever happened. And whenever he hears about the hurricane, he'll say, 'Well, that's how come I told you not to go. It ain't safe.'"

Unable to find some comforting line to interject, I took a step back and stood by the porcelain-topped table in the center of the kitchen. Maybe the best thing would be for me to go to my bedroom and leave her alone. I was the wrong person to be handing out advice.

She switched on an old mint-green radio on top of the refrigerator. "Ophelia was just comin' on with 'Voices From the Storm' when I got outta the truck. How about we sit and listen awhile? I can make us some cocoa. I don't think I could sleep anyhow."

"All right." I agreed, knowing that getting trapped into a long conversation tonight probably wasn't a good idea. Eventually, she'd want to know what had happened between Kemp and me. I mentally rehearsed the explanation as we made cocoa, then sat down together at the kitchen table. *Oh no, Kemp and I didn't have a fight or anything. It's just time for me to go back to work. I'm still under contract, after all. Can't get away with being AWOL in a hurricane forever. . . .*

Instead of talking, we just sat there, me stirring cocoa I didn't want and Donetta staring into her cup, looking like the world was on her shoulders. Via radio, Ophelia was talking with a woman who'd become separated from her two young children during the evacuation. After days in a shelter, the mother still had no news of them. Ophelia asked their names, and the mother answered, her voice choked with tears. Then Ophelia wrapped up the interview, saying "If anyone has word of Demarius Long, 9, and Raylia Long, 7, you call in to the *Ophelia Show* now. Let us know about it. We're spreading the word and bringing together the 'Voices From the Storm.'"

"I hope she finds her babies," Donetta murmured.

"Me, too," I agreed.

"It's amazin' how many times Ophelia gets a answer from

Lisa Wingate

somebody. Everyone in the whole country must listen to this show." Nodding, Donetta turned her ear to the radio again.

Over the airwaves, an elderly man was describing having held his wife's hand as their car stalled out in floodwater. "We just got out and started walkin'," he said, and Ophelia made a sympathetic sound. "We didn't have no other choice. Ella don't get around too good, but I told her, Elouise, we're either gonna walk outta here together or we're gonna die together. We been married fifty-seven years, and at this point, it's gonna be till death do us part, either now or later."

"He made me get up and try it," Ella added, her voice soft, barely audible over Ophelia's microphone. "I was ready to give up and let the water take me, but I wasn't going to let it take my Johnny, so I climbed out of that car and I did what Johnny said. I guess it's good to be bossy sometimes." She laughed quietly, and Ophelia took the mike again.

"There you go, all you listeners out there in radio land to-night, a little lesson in from Johnny and Ella. There's no storm love can't overcome. Too many times we let go when what we really need to do is cling to each other while the storm rages around us. Let's see who else we can find here tonight. We're at a hurricane shelter tonight, sending out the 'Voices . . .'"

I tuned out as a commercial came on. "Thanks for letting me stay here." It occurred to me that I could have ended up in a hurricane shelter like the one Ophelia was broadcasting from, or worse. Anything might have happened if I hadn't crossed paths with Donetta, Imagene, and Lucy.

Across the table, Donetta looked sad and preoccupied. "Oh, hon, it was nothin'. I wish you could stay longer. Are you sure you've got to go?"

"I'm sure."

"Well, we're gonna miss you a whole lot. You made this the best hurricane evacuation I ever had." She forced a half smile.

I laughed softly. "It's been nice . . . being here." I felt a pang of disappointment that she didn't try to talk me into staying or attempt to ferret out the details of Kemp and me. Maybe she knew this was for the best, too. Jen, Jenny, Jennifer and Kemp had more in common. They had history, a shared childhood, families with the same sorts of backgrounds. Jen was the whole small-town package—everything I wasn't.

The dogs barked outside, and both of us turned to listen. "Guess Miss Peach's cat is around the fence again," Donetta surmised.

"Guess so."

"If I was locked up in a house with that crazy old woman all day, I reckon I'd go on the lam, too." She smiled wanly, staring into her cocoa again. "You know, she was a beautiful gal when she was young, Miss Peach."

"Really?" There was nothing beautiful about Miss Peach now. Her pale, sallow skin hung on a skeletal frame that left her face angular and hard, the cheekbones high and stern beneath sunken eyes that were devoid of joy. Her mouth was narrow and lipless, pleated into a permanent scowl, like the navel of an orange left to rot in the sun. With her thin gray hair rising from her head in stringy flyaway curls, she had the dark presence of a comic strip villainess—the kind of woman who spent her days making fur coats from fuzzy little Dalmatian puppies.

Donetta made a quiet *tsk tsk*, as if she knew what I was thinking. "Miss Peach was a looker back in the day—violet eyes and blond hair that curled up all on its own. She grew up right there in that same house she's in now. Every beau in town wanted to come knockin' on her door, but they were scared to."

"Why?" Suddenly, I was fascinated by the life of Miss Peach.

Donetta's gaze rolled toward the ceiling. "Her daddy was the meanest man I ever knew. Good-lookin' fella, but wicked as a snake, especially if he was drinkin'. He was bad to his wife and bad to them kids. He had three daughters, each one of them beautiful as a movie star, but every boy in town was scared to get anywhere near."

"What happened to the other two sisters?" Obviously, there was only one Miss Peach now. Maybe her dead sisters were dressed for tea and waiting in rocking chairs in the parlor.

Donetta considered the question. "One sister died when she was just a teenager, the other ran off with the preacher's son, and then there was Raeanne—Miss Peach. She worked in the old grocery store across the alley from our hotel. One summer, we had a man helping us in the shop, and he took a shine to Raeanne. For about two months, that gal was all smiles. She was almost thirty years old by then, but you'da thought she was a high-school girl."

I tried to imagine Miss Peach young and in love. On the radio, Ophelia went into a moment of dead air, as if she wanted to stop and listen, too. "Did her father scare him off?"

Donetta shook her head ruefully. "Raeanne did that herself. After a couple months, that fella got some money together and bought a ring, and planned a picnic lunch down by the lake, where he was gonna surprise her. I made up some potato salad and sandwiches for him, and my grandpa loaned him a truck and everythin'. When that fella come back that night, he looked lower than a lizard's knees, I'll tell ye-ew. Raeanne'd told him no, flat-out. Broke the poor man's heart, and he hopped a train out of town the next day. Raeanne lived there with her folks until they died, and after that she got herself a cat, and she's been there ever since. Just her and a cat."

"That's really sad." I imagined Miss Peach and her cat, living year after year, every year the same. No family. Nobody ever coming or going.

Suddenly the existence I'd created for myself, the apartment in Perdida, the job in which people passed in and out of my life in five to seven day increments, seemed pathetic and small. There was only room in it for one.

"It surely is," Donetta agreed, as if she were reading my thoughts. "Right then and there, I promised myself I wasn't gonna cheat myself out of havin' a life, just because my daddy didn't love me like I needed him to. I promised myself I was gonna have a different kind of life. I'll sure enough admit that over the years I hadn't always got it perfect—things aren't like I wanted them to be between Ronald and me, for one thing. I thought we'd have kids, and I didn't think I'd be married to a man who don't see me when there's a TV in the room, but I ain't livin' alone in a house with a cat, either." Reaching across the table, she laid her hand over mine, her gaze pulling me closer. "You can't always see the straight path to where you want to be in your life, but if you don't start walkin', you don't get anywhere. If you want somethin' different, you got to do somethin' different."

The room fell silent as the "Voices From the Storm" music cued. "Hello again, all you listeners out there in radio land," Ophelia's smooth sounds purred through the static. "It's time for Ophelia and more 'Voices From the Storm.' We're here at the evacuation shelter near the coast tonight, spinning out tunes and taking in stories. We've just had buses come in with emergency personnel and volunteers, rotating into the shelter for food and rest, after days of working to rescue residents from storm debris and floodwaters. I have a volunteer here with me who'd like to send out a song to his special lady. This one's for all you listeners out there, warm and safe in your homes with your families tonight. Give the people you love an extra kiss before you go to bed this evening. Remember how lucky you are to be together."

Donetta glanced at the clock. "Guess it's bedtime." She stood up. "It'll be an early mornin', I reckon."

I didn't answer. I barely heard her, in fact. Her voice and Ophelia's faded, and my own life came into focus. *If you don't start walking, you don't get anywhere. . . .*

I'd been walking for ten years, but I wasn't walking *toward* anything. Not toward a future, not toward a relationship, not toward a family. I'd been a runaway at seventeen, and I was still running.

The problem was, I didn't know how to stop, or where. Where was I supposed to be? What was right for me?

Maybe everything would make more sense once I was back on my own turf. I could start thinking through my options, come up with an action plan for the future. Maybe I'd be able to look at the big life decisions more clearly. . . .

The radio started playing "Waltz Across Texas" as Donetta took the cocoa pot and the cups to the sink and began washing them out. Finally, she just stood there, listening to the music and staring out the window.

When the song was over, Ophelia's voice returned and Donetta turned on the rinse water to finish the dishes.

"So, tell me why you requested that song," Ophelia asked of the "Waltz Across Texas" man.

"That's the . . ." Ophelia's interviewee, his voice raw and broken, paused to sniffle and clear his throat. "That's the song that was playin' the night I first saw my wife. She probably don't even know I remember. Guess I hadn't ever told her in so many words, but every time I hear "Waltz Across Texas," I still see her circlin' the floor in her red dancin' skirt. It was like she was on a cloud, and she had a smile that . . . well, I didn't have no idea how to dance, but I told myself I was gonna get to know that gal no matter what. I knew right then she was the one. Over the years, I hadn't told her that near enough. Maybe not at all, I guess. You get busy with life, and you don't think you need to say it to people—to the people you love, I mean, but . . ." The sentence broke up, and Ophelia encouraged her interviewee to continue.

"And, sir, where is your wife tonight? Can we let our listeners know where we're sending 'Waltz Across Texas'?"

"I don't know where she's at tonight." The words were hoarse with emotion. "Her . . ."

Something clattered against the countertop near the sink, bounced off, hit the floor, and shattered. I jerked upright as shards of pastel pink pottery skittered across the black and white tile. By the sink, Donetta stood like a statue, her hand suspended in midair where she had released the cup.

"Donetta?" I whispered, but she didn't respond. "Donetta? Are you all right?"

"Th . . . that's . . ."

"Her and her friends headed off to catch a cruise boat the day the storm come in," the voice on the radio reported.

Donetta swayed on her feet, and I rushed from my chair, reaching toward her, adrenaline zipping through my body. Something was wrong. Maybe she was having a stroke or a heart attack. "Donetta?" I caught her as she staggered sideways and slipped on the broken cup. Her weight knocked me back, and the two of us collided with the table, sending it sliding across the floor.

My emergency medical training raced through my mind. *Reassure the victim. Move the victim to a safe location . . .* "Donetta, everything's all right. Here, let me help you into the chair."

"Ssshh!" she hissed, shrugging my hands away. Bits of pottery crunched under her feet as she stumbled across the kitchen, grabbed the radio, lowered it to the countertop, and increased the volume.

". . . and then a half hour or so after they headed out," the man was saying, "I seen the storm report on TV." His voice blared through the kitchen now. Outside, the dogs stopped barking and came to the back door to peer in. "I couldn't get ahold of my wife on the mobile phone, so I headed out after her and her friends. I thought I'd catch up pretty quick, since they hadn't been gone long and they don't drive too fast. I didn't bother unhookin' my bass boat, even. I just followed the way they were headed, watchin' all the way for their van. I kept goin' farther and farther without seein' them, and finally, I'd made it all the way down to the coast, but there still wasn't any sign. I found out her ship'd left port hours ago to get ahead of the storm, so I knew they couldn'ta been on it."

"That's Ron . . . ald . . . Ronald," Donetta breathed, bracing her hands on the counter, her elbows locked.

I stopped where I was, teetering on bits of debris as the radio played on. ". . . didn't have any way of knowin' what'd happened to them. I started to head back toward home, but by then the roads were clogged up for miles. I couldn't get out, so I just drove back into Perdida, run my truck and boat up in a hotel parkin' garage, and hunkered down there. When that storm was over, the whole area was flooded and there was water way up on the parkin' garage. Turned out it was a good thing I had my bass rig hooked up behind my truck, because it come in handy. I just backed right down the parkin' garage, like a boat ramp, put her in the water, and headed out to see if I could help anybody.

"After a while, I got with some other fellas, and we went around town, carrying out folks who'd got stranded by the floodwater. It was nothin' but chaos around here all that time, no way to get any communication out. We did that for quite a few days, checkin' neighborhoods and movin' folks, till finally the emergency people come to the area where we were.

"All this time, I didn't have any means of contactin' my wife, to let her know where I was, or make sure she was all right.

When you're in a spot like that, you recall all the times you been together—all the good times, and the moments you got crosswise with each other, and all the times you shoulda said somethin' nice but you didn't bother. When it could be you'll never see somebody again, you sure wish you'da done better, so this is for Donetta Bradford of Daily, Texas. Wherever you are tonight, I hope you're hearin' my voice. Marryin' you was the best thing I ever done. I shoulda said *I love you* more often. If I get home, and you get home, I won't be cheap with them words anymore, you can bet on that. I want to send that message to every fella who's out there right now fallin' asleep in his easy chair in front of the TV. Get up. Hug your kids and kiss your wife. Say the things you hadn't bothered to say, while you still got the chance. It don't make you less of a man. It makes you more."

When Ophelia took the mike, she sounded teary, as well.

"Well, there you have it, all you husbands and fathers out there. Some good advice. And Donetta Bradford of Daily, Texas, if you're listening right now, you have a very special man—a hero who's been helping storm victims in the flood zone, waiting to come home to the woman he loves. That's it for tonight, all you listeners in radio land. Good night and Godspeed from Ophelia, near Perdida, Texas, with 'Voices From the Storm.'"

When I turned to Donetta, tears wouldn't let me speak. It didn't matter, because she was already weeping.

"That's my Ronald," she sobbed, and we staggered across broken bits of pottery into each other's arms, then rocked back and forth in a hug.

We'd barely let go when the phone started ringing. The first call was from Imagene, but before they'd finished recapping Ronald's radio show appearance, Donetta answered the Call Waiting, and I listened to her end of the conversation as I dried my eyes with a napkin, then started picking up the shattered mug.

"This is *who*?"

"Well, I'll be . . ."

"All the way from Fort Worth? Well, great hearin' from ya!"

"Oh yes, I did just catch Ophelia's show."

"Yes, ma'am, that was my Ronald. I'm Donetta Bradford of Daily, Texas. *The* Donetta Bradford." Donetta's southern drawl turned thick and sweet as she opened a kitchen drawer and rummaged through scissors, glue bottles, rubber bands, twist ties, screwdrivers, and other assorted flotsam until she came up with a notepad and paper. "Oh yes, ma'am, I surely would lo-ove that. I truly would. Matter of fact, if ye-ew'll show up in Daily, say about . . . oh . . . eight thirty tomorrow mornin', I'll give you a hurricane story like you ain't ever heard. All righty, then, it's a date. Ye-ew just come ri-ight to the Daily Hotel buildin' on Main Street. Ye-ew can't miss it."

She hung up the phone with a triumphant squeal. "That was the Fort Worth newspaper! They heard Ronald on Ophelia's program and they're gonna do a story about Ronald and me. Praise the Lord! There's gonna be a surprise waitin' for Betty Prine in the mornin'. Oh, praise the Lord!"

For the next half hour, Donetta took calls from friends and neighbors who'd heard the show. Finally, she turned off the phone, and we stood in the center of the kitchen, the house oddly quiet after all the excitement. She looked tired but triumphant as we hugged good-night.

"I guess this is good-bye," I said quietly. "I'll be leaving pretty early. I'll drop the dogs at the vet clinic."

"Oh, hon, I'll see you in the mornin'. I'll be up." Smiling, she cupped a hand over my cheek. "I sure do hate to see ye-ew go. I'll miss ye-ew bein' here."

"I'll miss being here," I admitted, and a corkscrew twisted in my chest.

"You could just change your plans and stay awhile longer. The dogs can stay, too."

I shook my head, because I didn't trust myself to speak. Everything in me wanted to say yes.

Donetta smiled sadly, as if she knew I wouldn't. "Well, it ain't good-bye," she said finally. "I'm gonna be in touch. The gals and I got to book another cruise yet. When I get on that ship, I want ye-ew to show me all that stuff regular folks don't get the chance to see—like the engine room and the crow's nest. It'll be just like on *Ti-itanic*."

Nodding, I hugged her again, then headed off to bed for my last night in Daily, Texas.

There was no point, really, in telling Donetta that Festivale Cruises owned numerous vessels operating out of countless ports. Donetta Bradford and I would probably never end up on the same ship again.

# Chapter 25

## *Donetta Bradford*

After all that excitement about Ronald bein' on the radio and the Fort Worth newspaper calling, I went to bed and slept like a baby. Of all things, I dreamed about Mexico, about travelin' way down south of the border to a big hacienda. My mama's twin brother, Macerio's baby boy, was there. He was an old man now, but I knew his smile. That was my mama's smile. Around him by the gate, there were kids and grandkids, and great-grandkids—my family, greetin' me with open arms, like they knew all this time I'd be coming someday.

I stayed in bed, enjoyin' the dream until nearly seven o'clock, when Imagene come bangin' on the door, about to have a rigor out there. She'd probably been trying to call all mornin', but with the phone turned off from last night, there was nothing to take me away from that sweet dream about Mexico. I didn't get woke up early by the dogs barking at the mail truck, and soon as I started down the hall to let Imagene in, I knew Kai was gone and so were her dogs. The house was quiet as an undertaker's parlor.

Imagene asked about Kai after she got done chewin' me out for sleeping late and keeping the phone turned off. "She left early this mornin'," I said. "I didn't even wake up, I guess." I went to the back door and looked out. The yard was cleaned up and the dogs' dishes had been emptied and set on the steps, so it was like they were never there at all.

Imagene gave me a mouth-down look. "I was hoping she wouldn't go."

"Me, too. I tried to talk her out of it, but she wouldn't budge. Sure is gonna be lonely around here until Ronald can get home from the hurricane. It's somethin', isn't it—my Ronald a big hero, rescuing people? And here I been all this time, mad at him for goin' off fishing. Wait till I tell him about that. We'll have a laugh over it, I bet." Imagene nodded with a light in her eye, like she was happy about the idea of me and Ronald having a laugh. She still had a fret on her mouth, though, so I said, "You look like you need some coffee and a sweet roll."

"Donetta, we ain't got time for coffee. We got to get down to the hotel buildin' before Betty shows up." Her mouth worked like she was chewing a worry to pieces. She wouldn't be happy when she found out the Fort Worth newspaper called last night and I didn't even tell her about it.

"We got time for coffee. We're showing up at the buildin' at eight thirty sharp, and not a minute before. If Betty gets there with the fire marshal before that, she can just sit on the curb and wait." I put water in the coffee maker, thinking about Kai and wishing she woulda woke me up before she left.

Imagene followed me around the kitchen, giving me a bug-eyed look, like she thought I might be runnin' a fever. "Why're we waitin' till eight thirty to go down to the buildin'?"

"That's a full-cup story. Wait'll I get the coffee made." My

332

mind jumped tracks, which was never a problem, because Imagene and me always could carry on more than one conversation at a time. "She's a sweet little thing, ain't she? Kai, I mean."

"Real sweet. I drove by the field house just now and there was Kemp, just standin' on the pitcher's mound, starin' off into the haze. Looked like the saddest human I ever did see."

"That boy's so stubborn. They're both stubborn. Anybody with half a brain can see them two're meant to be."

Imagene set the cream and sugar on the little table and nodded. "Well, you know how young folks are. They don't always see what's right in front of their eyes."

"True enough." I watched the coffee brew a minute, waitin' until I could sneak a couple cups. "That's sad, though, ain't it?"

"Guess that's what keeps meddlesome old ladies like us in business."

"Guess so."

I took a couple sweet rolls out of the freezer and microwaved them, then fixed the coffee and brought it to the kitchen table.

Imagene didn't even doctor up her coffee. She was more interested in why we weren't breakin' out the artillery to fight Betty Prine. "Now you gonna tell me why we're waitin' to go to the buildin'?"

I started in on the tale while I was doctorin' up my coffee. "A reporter called last night, Imagene—from the Fort Worth newspaper. I told her to show up at the buildin' at eight thirty this mornin'. Betty's gonna get a welcomin' committee like she won't believe."

"A reporter?" Imagene's bottom lip dangled. "What'd she want? Why didn't you call me?" She ended the sentence in a huff.

"It was late, Imagene. I didn't want to wake you up. She called about Ronald on the radio, on 'Voices From the Storm.'"

"As if I could sleep when I'm worryin' about my best friend getting kicked out of her building and her livelihood, and Kemp havin' his heart broke. As if I'd be noddin' off with all that goin' on." Imagene's mouth and eye squeezed together on one side of her face, and I knew she was on her way to blowin' a gasket. "And here *you* are, sleepin' like a baby at seven o'clock in the mornin', thank you very much. Not worried about your best friend pacing the floor all night."

I should've known she wasn't gonna take it well that I didn't call her right away about the newspaper. "I had to turn the phone off because it wouldn't stop ringin'. Every cousin I ever had called the house."

"I was *up* at midnight. And after."

Sometimes, Imagene was like a record with a scratch—stuck on one thing. "All right, well anyhow, everybody wants to know the rest of the story about Ronald and me—was I okay? What happened to me when I was in the hurricane evacuation? How'd I make it back to Daily and did I know where Ronald was all this time? What'd I think when I heard him on the radio? Are we gonna do somethin' special together when he does get back? People got all sorts of questions—some of 'em kind of, well, *private* . . . truth be told."

"Private?" Imagene's eyebrows shot up, and all of a sudden she wasn't mad at me anymore. She leaned close, like the walls had ears. "Do tell."

"Someone asked me how were we gonna rekindle the romance when Ronald got back, and wanted details, too. I guess it's not every day a man who ain't said I love you in over forty years spits it out on a national radio show."

Imagene's cheeks and the end of her nose got red, and her eyes filled up. "I'll be," she whispered, shaking her head. She checked over her shoulder, then leaned close again. "How *are* you gonna rekindle the romance?"

"Ima-*gene!*" I gasped out, and we had us a good giggle before starting in on our sweet rolls.

Imagene sighed, chewin' on a bite. "Guess even after hearin' Ronald on the radio, Kai didn't decide to stay, or Kemp didn't come rushin' over here to ask her not to go?"

"Young folks can be single-minded sometimes." I pulled my sweet roll apart to let the inside cool. "Them two both got things in their past that makes them afraid—Kemp losin' his mama when he was young, and then all his trouble with Jen and baseball, and Kai with her family bein' such a mess, and her little brother dyin' young. Them two got to overcome the feelin's of loss before they can move on and form healthy new relationships."

"You been watching Oprah again."

"It helps to know psychology when you're dealin' with folks," I said, and Imagene nodded like she agreed with me, and so I went on. "But don't you worry. I got a plan."

Blinking real slow, she leaned away from the table, her head twisting to one side like she was afraid to ask. "A plan? For which—Kai and Kemp or Betty and the building inspector?"

"Both, actually. First one, then the other, but with the order reversed."

"Oh lands." Imagene deflated like a blow-up Santa after someone'd pulled the plug. "I don't think I even care to know."

I grabbed my coffee and stood up. "You don't need to for right now. Just sit here and have your coffee while I go get dressed. It's almost time. Betty Prine ain't gonna know what hit her."

I hurried off down the hall with my mind cranking like the old mill engine. While I was getting myself ready for the big day ahead, I went through the plans in my mind. Then God and me went over the plans together. I was sure hoping we were both on the same page this time. I was nearly finished fixing my hair, and (aside from wishin' I was twenty years younger) I was feelin' ready to talk to that reporter and Betty Prine, when all of a sudden Imagene gave a scream that rattled my makeup mirror from all the way down the hall.

"Donetta! Don-*etta*, come quick!"

I ran toward the kitchen with a trail of hairspray puffin' behind me. Imagene was in the living room doorway, waving like she was bringin' a race-car driver in for a pit stop. "Look! It's 'Voices From the Storm' on the *Good Mornin' America* show! There's Ophelia in person. . . . I thought she'd be younger than that. . . ."

By the time I rounded the corner, Ophelia was on the screen with Diane Sawyer. Imagene'd stopped waving, and she had a hand over her mouth. "She's talkin' . . . about Ronald," she whispered between her fingers. "Look." She pointed at the screen, and, sure enough, down there at the bottom was a blue bar that read *Deep in the heart of Texas*, and then in smaller letters, *radio message touches tender spot nationwide.*

On the show, Ophelia was retelling the story of Ronald, *my Ronald*, and how at the shelter in Perdida, he come right up to her and said, "Ma'am, I need you to put me on the radio. I've got to get a message out to my wife."

Right there on *Good Morning America*, Ophelia told about how Ronald's face looked when he said those words over the radio, and how he spoke through tears, and how it made her think about all the people in her life that she'd never told how she felt. She told how she offered to get Ronald out of there in their radio helicopter, but Ronald said no. His truck and bass boat were still in Perdida, and as soon as he got some food, he was headed back with the volunteers to keep helpin' folks.

Diane Sawyer said Ronald was a true hero. Ophelia agreed that he was, then she told how, after Ronald's message aired, phone lines lit up all across the nation. "I knew that what he'd said was special," Ophelia told Diane. "And that it went deeper than just the storm, or the families who have been separated, or the people who've lost homes or loved ones. Mr. Bradford's message goes to the heart of who we are, and what we are as human beings, and what we could be. So often, our work and our activities, and the ordinary business of life get the best part of us, and the people we love get the least. On the show, I frequently receive calls from listeners who have lost loved ones unexpectedly—either through death, divorce, arguments, family estrangements—and those callers all carry one characteristic in common. There are things they wish they'd said when they had the chance. Ronald's message speaks to all those people for whom there's still time to step up to the plate."

Diane Sawyer nodded along, then turned to look at the TV screen. "Let's give a listen to the words of Ronald Bradford."

At the bottom of the screen, the blue bar changed, so that it read *voice of Ronald Bradford*, and as Ronald talked, the GMA cameras filmed the New York City street, showing folks in a hurry to go about a normal day. Watching them, I wondered how many went home at night and did just what Ronald and me'd done—spent time with their computers, and their TVs, and their quilts for the church bazaar, instead of spending time with each other. Whenever Ronald finally made it back to Daily, it wasn't gonna be like that between us anymore. Not ever again.

Diane Sawyer came on again and reported that flower shops on the East Coast had already had a spike in sales that morning. "So I guess we owe a debt of thanks to one man, Ronald Bradford, a hero of Hurricane Glorietta in more ways than one, and a voice from the storm reminding us that even when so much is lost, some things are found. Oftentimes, those things we discover in the storm are the most valuable of all." She went on to report that GMA had tried to contact Donetta Bradford (me) of Daily, Texas, but been unsuccessful, although, according to sources in the town, Mrs. Bradford and her friends had all made it safely home. GMA was in the process of getting word to Ronald that I was all right, and they'd have an update later in the week.

When the report was over, Imagene ran to the kitchen and grabbed a napkin to blow her nose into. She brought me one, too, because by then I needed it.

"Land sakes, Donetta, if you'da had your phone on, you coulda been on *Good Mornin' America*!"

The idea made my head whirl like a tail-chasin' dog, and I had to reach out and catch hold of the sofa. "If *Good Mornin' America*'d called my house, I think I woulda fainted dead away, Imagene. It was hard enough to believe when the Fort Worth newspaper wanted to talk to me, but this . . . this is . . . well, I hadn't even got words for what this is!"

"This is a miracle." Imagene's eyes met mine, and I knew she was right. While I'd been worryin' and plottin' and plannin', my foxhole prayers'd been answered in more ways than one. The Lord had His hand on the situation all along.

I shoulda known that, of course. He always does.

"Yes, it is," I agreed. "It is a miracle." The clock caught my eye, and I grabbed my purse off the table. If I'd been a gunfighter in the old West, I would've been strapping on my six-shooters. "We better get on down to the hotel."

"Right behind you like a cart on a horse," Imagene answered, and I could tell them were fightin' words. "We'll see how Betty Prine feels about comin' up against a star on *Good Morning America*."

The two of us headed off for town like Wyatt Earp and Doc Holliday goin' to the O.K. Corral. When we turned onto Main Street, there was Betty Prine waiting on the sidewalk with the young fella who'd got the fire marshal's job when Lloyd Graves retired. Word was, the new fella was a stickler for the rules and all that sort of thing. Word also was that Harold Prine'd sold him a foreclosed chunk of land from the bank, on the cheap.

"Well, there she is," Imagene groused as we parked down the street past the café, which must've been busy this morning, because cars were lined up all the way to the hotel building. "Got her big nose up in the air, like usual. Maybe she'll fall off the curb and twist an ankle."

"Imagene!" I felt a chuckle bubblin' up. Imagene and me could always count on each other for a laugh in the bad times. Your best gal friend'll do that, if she's a really good one.

Imagene shrugged. "You know, like in that old Irish proverb about your enemies—If God can't turn their hearts, may He turn their ankles, so we'll know them because they're limpin'."

I leaned over and looked her in the eye. "That wasn't what you were thinkin', Imagene Doll."

She let out a wicked giggle. "Well, all right, I really was hopin' Betty'd fall off the curb and land in the gutter. I'll repent later. Right now, that's how I feel."

"You see anybody that looks like a reporter from the Fort Worth paper?" I checked the rearview mirror.

"Nope."

An itchy, worried feelin' crawled up my back like a nerve about to pinch. "I hope she shows up. . . ."

"Well, even if not, we got *Good Mornin' America*."

"Betty don't look like she watched *Good Mornin' America*." I grabbed the door handle. "Might as well get out, she's headed this way."

Imagene reached across and caught my sleeve. "Wait. Maybe she'll fall off the curb yet."

"Imagene Doll, you got some of the devil this mornin'." I started laughing again, and we clambered out of the car, giggling and carrying on.

Betty stopped on the sidewalk in front of the café, her hands working at her sides, like her trigger finger was itchin'. She had on a black skirt and a black short-sleeved sweater, which seemed to fit the occasion.

"All she needs is a pointed hat and a broomstick," Imagene muttered close to my ear, and we broke up in giggles again.

Betty drew her chin into her neck like an old toad about to croak. "Well, I don't see what *you two* have to cackle a—" all of a sudden, there was a commotion inside the café. I saw Betty's lips finish—"bout," but I couldn't hear her at all.

All I could hear was chairs scraping and people hollering, "There she is! There she is!" There was a rush at the door, and then Imagene and me were surrounded by folks, all talking at once.

"We saw you on the show!"

"How about that Ronald?"

"That man knows how to tell it!"

"Did you ever think he had it in him?"

"*Gal-ee!* You better give that man a hug and a kiss when he come home, cher!" That one was Sister Mona, I could tell by the voice. I caught of glimpse of her two sons, Ernest and Bluejay, towerin' over the crowd. Guess they didn't have any reason to hide out at the ranch, now that word was out.

"I think we oughta print that speech on a T-shirt and sell it in the souvenir shop!" Bailey Henderson called out. For Bailey, everythin' was a moneymakin' opportunity.

"Daily, Texas, on *Good Mornin' America*! How's that for a fine bunch a' taters?"

"And-and-and y-you thought he was f-f-fishin', he was fishin'." That last one was Doyle. Beside him, Lucy was jumping up and down like Zacchaeus, tryin' to see over the crowd, her hands flapping in the air.

"Is a *Good Morn-eeng Amer-ca* call the café! They wanna you come give the story in New York City on TV!"

Outside all the commotion, I caught sight of Betty Prine,

just standing on the sidewalk, looking plumb dumbfounded. She unbuttoned the neck of her sweater, like all of a sudden it was too tight, and her lip began curling on one side, flashing an eyetooth. The inspector started past her, but she stuck out an arm and caught him in the chest.

A car pulled up and stopped in the street. It had the name of the Fort Worth newspaper right on the side. The driver's door opened, and a young lady hopped out and jogged up onto the curb. "I'm looking for Donetta Bradford of Daily, Texas. The wife of Ronald Bradford."

Everyone pointed at me, but they probably didn't need to. I was the one red as a ripe plum and floatin' about a foot off the ground.

The crowd parted then, and I heard Doyle offer to park the reporter's car, and I saw Betty hustlin' that young fire marshal back to his vehicle, and Bob asking if we wanted to do the interview in the Daily Café, but all of it seemed far away, like it was happening to someone else.

For just a minute, I slipped out of my own shoes and I could see the bigger picture, like a scene in a shadow box. I saw it the way it would look from high above, up there with God and His angels. There was the main street of our little town, the buildings just catching the morning sun, yawning and stretching, and waking up to a new day. A day when anything might happen. There were friends and neighbors, and new friends gathered 'round, laughing and cheering, sharing in the certainty that, even with all that can be wrong with the world, or the weather, or a marriage, or a person, or in one little town, there's always more that's right.

We can see it, if we look from a distance. All things work together for our good.

"That's me," I heard the woman with the tall (and might I add, nicely done) red hair say. "Ronald's my husband." The woman smiled then, underneath that big hair. She had on Rumba Red #5, but you probably wouldn't know it if you didn't know your lipstick. It didn't matter anyway. That smile would've been somethin' special in any color, because it was soul-deep.

"I'm Donetta Bradford of Daily, Texas," she said.

And for the first time in her whole life, she couldn't think of anyone else she'd rather be.

## Chapter 26

# Kai Miller

From turquoise waters off the Yucatan, I watched Donetta and Ronald on *Good Morning America*. I caught the show completely by happenstance. I was walking past the casino lounge, getting ready to follow the last passengers onto shore in Cancun, and a familiar voice brought me up short. I stood there with my mouth hanging open.

Suddenly, I was back in Daily, Texas. Seeing Donetta on the screen was like going home again. The camera, and the GMA crew, loved her, and she seemed surprisingly comfortable in the spotlight. Beside her, Ronald, the tall, heavyset man I'd seen in fishing photos around Donetta's house, looked like he'd rather be staked to an anthill than making a guest appearance on national TV. He wasn't embarrassed about what he'd said on the radio, he told the anchor while stroking his salt-and-pepper goatee; he just couldn't believe all the fuss it had started.

"Guess when admittin' your feelings is a national event, that ain't a good sign," he commented dryly, and the anchor laughed. "I can only figure it was somethin' a lot of regular folks needed to hear." Turning a cowboy hat nervously in his fingers, he looked up at the camera, his eyes piercingly direct. "I needed that reminder myself, and I'm about as regular a fella as you can get. I come from a normal family, and I grew up in a nice little town. My daddy was a wheat farmer and a fine, honest man, and he was married to my mama for sixty-one years. In all that time, I never once heard them talk about how they met or why they got together or how they felt about each other. I guess sometime while I was comin' up, I got the idea that a real man don't talk about that kind of thing. But I'll tell you, when you see something big as Hurricane Glorietta breathin' down your neck, being a man's man don't matter half as much as you thought it did. All you care about's that the people you love are safe."

Donetta cast an adoring gaze and reached across the sofa to slip her hand into his, as she and Ronald related their hurricane stories. The Gifts From the Sea van and I got a mention, as did the members of the Holy Ghost Church. Donetta cleverly slipped in a plug for a benefit fund accepting donations to help the members of the Holy Ghost repair damage to their homes, businesses, and church building. "They got a lot of work ahead of them, but they're strong folks, and we're gonna stay friends for a long time. That's the good thing in all this, I think. God uses storms to bring folks together. You learn that we all got to depend on each other. Not a one of us is strong enough to go it alone, when there's a hurricane overhead. It's a good lesson, and you're never too old or too young to learn it." Donetta looked right at the camera and winked, like she knew I'd be watching.

The wink reminded me of Kemp. He had Donetta's smile.

At the end of the segment, Diane Sawyer asked if Donetta planned to take a cruise to make up for the one she'd missed.

She regarded Ronald hopefully, but then said, "Well, we'll see. Right now, we're just enjoyin' the time together, and we're makin' plans to go down and help the Holy Ghost Church with rebuildin', when they're ready. My nephew's even gonna take the Daily High School baseball team to get in on the work, eventually. Meantime, Ronald and me are keeping ourselves busy puttin' in some fall flowers in the yard. Been a long time since we did that." She gave Ronald a tender smile, and he returned it likewise, then cleared his throat and turned back to Diane Sawyer as if he'd forgotten for a moment that they were on national TV.

"It's amazin' how much trouble a truckload of mums and pansies'll get a fella out of," he joked. "You fellas out there remember that."

Everyone laughed, and then Diane Sawyer closed the interview with, "A few words of wisdom from deep in the heart of Texas." Then she thanked everyone and went to commercial.

I stood holding my tote bag and sun hat, oddly captivated by the TV. A shampoo commercial came on, but in my mind I saw Donetta and Ronald planting pansies outside their little yellow house on a sunny fall afternoon in Daily. I knew how the air would smell, the way the grass would sound rustling in the no-man's-land outside the fence, how the light would filter through the canopy of overgrown trees above.

Tears crowded my eyes when Good Morning America came on again, and Donetta and Ronald were gone. The bartender looked at me like I was nuts.

I moved on with all the enthusiasm of a commuter driving the usual route to and from work. In Playa del Carmen, when I normally would have relished the challenge of perusing the markets looking for beads, antiquities, tiny Mayan totems, and other potential treasures, my mind was miles away. I finally gave up and stood in the ferry line to go back to Cozumel and the ship. I listened as a Mexican tour guide returning from the ruins at Tulum entertained his group with tales of the Mayan prophecy that the end of the world was approaching with an upcoming winter solstice.

He laughed when one of his charges said that, since there were only a few more years left, she was cashing out her 401K to spend her time traveling.

"I would save the *dineros*." The tour guide's thick accent rolled over the noise of crowds and street vendors selling sun hats and sombreros. "People only use this prophecy to sell books and movies in Hollywood. On the Mayan calendar, this day is the end of an age. In the end of the age, the prophecy says that the people will have ceased to live as human beings, and something big will happen, and the people will see each other again. I think it is like this here, when the hurricane comes. Before the hurricane, I am a busy man, and my neighbor, he hurries each day, as well. I do not know him, and we pass on the street, and our eyes are filled with many concerns, and so I do not see him and he does not see me. But the hurricane comes, and there is no electricity, and no light, and we cannot go anywhere for days. I notice my neighbor standing at the fence, and I go out to him and ask if his family is well. I give him cheese and a tin of crackers, and he gives me candles and matches. We stand and talk for many hours, and after this, when we pass on the street, we no longer walk by without seeing."

The tour guide paused, his eyes dark and soulful as he took in the crowd. "This is how the change comes. The storm opens the eyes and then the heart, as well. A crisis is only an opportunity riding a dangerous wind, *si*?"

The ferry came in, and the tour guide waved good-bye, leaving his charges with something to think about.

I boarded with the ferry line, rode the choppy waters back to Cozumel, and went to my crew cabin to stow my purchases. When I opened the jewelry boxes, nestled in the top tray lay a tiny handful of quartz crystals, amethyst, limestone fossils from

Daily, and shards of thick colored glass from the old church that had sheltered us during the hurricane.

Letting my tote bag fall to the floor, I touched the treasures one by one, dropping them into my palm. I sat down on the bed and carefully turned each object, studying from every angle. Finally, I clutched them in my palm, lay back against the pillow, and stared at the ceiling until my eyes fell closed.

My mind traveled back to Daily, settling first at Donetta's yellow house on B Street, then drifting toward downtown, through the shadows of the oak trees, past the fading house where Miss Peach stood behind the storm door with her cat, past the live oaks that shook hands over B Street, to the intersection of Main, where I turned the corner, rocking like a ship at sea, sailing past the Daily Café, the hotel building, the *Daily Hair and Body* sign, across town to the high school, where the baseball stadium lay empty in the evening light, the chalk lines drawn and the scoreboard lit up, but the stands vacant.

I searched for Kemp, but he wasn't there.

Laughter drifted from somewhere beyond the field house. I followed the sound to the practice area out front, where an impromptu Wiffle ball game was underway. Sly stood at home plate, his plastic bat waving in the air, ready for the pitch. The ball flew toward home, a curve. The batter swung, missed. The catcher caught the ball, stood up in one graceful movement, pulled off the face mask. Long tresses of chestnut hair tumbled over her shoulders, toying with the sunlight, shimmering like liquid.

She smiled at Kemp, tossed the ball up and caught it, then dropped her catcher's mitt on home plate. "He's out," she purred, as long, lithe movements carried her toward the pitcher's mound. "Game over."

Kemp grinned as Jen, Jenny, Jennifer floated to the mound and hooked her arm in his. "Let's go," she whispered in his ear, and then the two of them turned and left the field.

At home plate, Sly stood bewildered, the tip of his plastic bat slowly descending toward the ground.

"Wait!" I called after Kemp. "Wait! The game's not over! Wait!" Then suddenly, Kemp was Gil. My little brother was walking across a long field with no buildings in sight. He was healthy, his body lean and boyish, his skin tan and ruddy, his blond hair streaked by the sun, falling in curls over his ears. He stopped, turned toward me, smiled, his blue eyes alive with light. "A crisis is only an opportunity riding a dangerous wind," he said, and then he continued across the field, moving farther and farther away.

"Wait!" I called. "Wait! Stop!"

The notes of "Take Me Out to the Ball Game" drifted to my ear, pulled me away from the field and Gil. I tried to stay where I was, to follow Gil, to call him back to me, but the music grew louder, more insistent.

In a gush of air, I was back in bed, jerking upright, aware that I was crying out my brother's name. For an instant, I wasn't sure where I was. Then I realized I was in my cabin on the ship. With the dawning awareness came a familiar disappointment. For the past five days, every time I'd fallen asleep, my dreams began in Daily and ended in a strange mishmash of the past. The experience was joyful, then painful.

The music began playing in the room again—the cell phone ringing. "Take Me Out to the Ball Game." Since leaving Daily, I'd told myself a dozen times I should change the ringtone, but I hadn't.

I picked up the phone, surprised. We were miles out to sea right now, somewhere off the Yucatan. Even though some ships were equipped with antenna-to-satellite cell signal converters, the *Liberation* was not. The cell shouldn't have been ringing.

I picked it up and answered.

"Hello?" The male voice on the other end was far away, almost lost in static. "Hello? Is this Kee Miller?"

"Kai Miller," I replied, wondering if this was yet another insurance adjuster. Between the damage to the Surf Shop and the fact that I had merchandise in stores all over Perdida, I'd been contacted by several adjusters already. "This is Kai. The connection's not very good. Can you call back and leave a voice mail?"

"This is Ronald Bradford." The voice was suddenly clear, almost brusque. "Ronald Bradford from over in Daily, Texas."

My mind spun like a car hitting an oil slick at ninety miles an hour, and I blinked hard, struggling to focus, trying to get the steering wheel under control. *Maybe I'm still dreaming. . . .* "Donetta's husband?"

"Yes, ma'am. I need yer help with somethin'. I only got a minute. Donetta's in the shower right now. We're in a hotel room in New York, so I can't get away from her for long."

"Ohhh-kay," I murmured, wishing I were up higher on the ship so I could look out a window and see if we were really in the middle of the Gulf or if I was losing my mind. Ronald Bradford shouldn't have been able to get through to my phone. "What did you need?"

"This mornin' I was talkin' with that producer on *Good Mornin' America*, and I just called home to talk to Imagene Doll, and we got a plan. Now, you might not know this, but the first time Donetta and me got married, we didn't get a honeymoon . . . well, or a weddin' really, either. I want to do somethin' about that. That producer and I come up with an idea, but I'm gonna need some help to keep Netta from sniffin' it out that somethin's up. Keeping a secret from her is about like trying to hide a bobcat under a bedsheet. I'll call ya with more details later on, but can I count on yer help?"

What was I supposed to say except "Yes. Of course. I'm on contract for a couple of weeks yet, and then I'll be back in Perdida on September twenty-ninth."

"Good deal. I'll call ya on October first. That'll be enough time before our annivers—" Ronald's voice vanished as quickly as it had appeared, and I had no choice but to live with the mystery of his call for the remainder of my time at sea.

⌒

As soon as I returned to Perdida, I was caught in a tangled web of communications with Ronald, Imagene, *Good Morning America*, various businesses struggling through hurricane recovery on the strand, and the Perdida Board of Tourism, which was hoping Ronald's plan would help show the world, and the tourists planning for next year's vacations, that Glorietta may have given Perdida a hard right cross, but the little town by the shore was coming back swinging.

The hoopla and planning went on for a month. Even as dozers worked to fill Dumpsters with debris, construction workers replaced saturated Sheetrock, and the Port Authority reopened the port, the buzz about Ronald's plan was all over Perdida. In the midst of the cleanup and recovery, and the reality of discovering things that would never be the same, there was something to look forward to. Even Maggie, Meredith, Don, and the members of the Holy Ghost Church got in on the act, helping to keep Ronald's secret plan moving along.

The day before Donetta and Ronald's anniversary, Maggie, Meredith, and I sat in the coffee shop with the Perdida Board of Tourism director and Sister Mona, who'd driven over to Perdida to rehash the plans, minute by minute. The coffee shop had the air of a Secret Service war room as we ticked through the final schedule, one item at a time: camera crew in place at 2:00, members of the Holy Ghost Church arriving by bus before 2:45, flowers in place at 3:00 (on the beach if the weather was good, inside the ballroom at Le Grande Hotel if it was raining). At 2:30, Donetta and Ronald would arrive in town, ostensibly for a romantic seaside night at Le Grande, in celebration of their anniversary, courtesy of *Good Morning America*. When they arrived in town, Ronald would make an excuse to drop Donetta off for some last-minute shopping at the high end of the strand, where stores were beginning to reopen, and then he'd leave to go check in to the hotel. But he wouldn't *be* checking in to the hotel. On the strand, Donetta would discover that she'd been chosen as Tourist of the Month. The store owners planned to take over from there, and hidden cameras would film Donetta's prepaid shopping excursion, courtesy of the Perdida Board of Tourism.

Meanwhile, Ronald would be meeting me at the coffee shop.

If everything went perfectly, Perdida, *Good Morning America*, and Donetta Bradford would have a day to remember.

*If* everything went perfectly. Ronald reminded us repeatedly that, with Donetta involved, it was never a straight trip from A to B.

When Ronald's truck rolled by the coffee shop on the afternoon of November second, Maggie, Meredith, and I breathed a collective sigh of relief. My phone rang shortly afterward, but I didn't answer, because the number was Donetta's. She was undoubtedly calling to see whether I'd be able to meet them for supper while they were in town. I'd already told her I'd probably be gone working.

Just as Donetta gave up repeatedly trying to ring my number, Ronald rolled into the coffee shop parking lot. After having talked to him long-distance so many times, it was strange to finally meet him in person. We shook hands, and once the introductions were made, Maggie and Meredith headed off to meet the GMA camera crews and supervise the final preparations, while Ronald and I continued with our part of the plan.

"I want to thank you for all the help with this," Ronald offered, looking sheepish and out of place in M&M's eclectic coffee shop, with the strings of seashells in the doorway and the trails of incense in the air.

"It's been my pleasure." A giddy sense of anticipation fluttered in my stomach as I thought ahead to the moment when our plans would come to fruition. "Did you get the video I sent?"

"I did." Ronald stood in the light of the coffee shop's only remaining plate glass window. "It was real good. I watched it every time I could get Netta out of the house, where she wouldn't see. She come in for lunch one day and caught me in the livin' room with the mop. I had to pretend I'd got the urge to clean the tile."

The image of Ronald gliding across the living room with the mop made me chuckle. "You ready to get started?"

He shifted from one foot to the other, burying his hands in his pockets as I walked to the counter, where I'd stashed everything we would need.

"Kemp says hey." Ronald's voice drifted across the darkened interior of the shop and brought me up short as I set Maggie's boom box on the bar. All these weeks, as I talked to Ronald and heard little snippets of what was happening in Daily, I'd wondered if my name ever came up with Kemp or if he had forgotten all about me. I'd come close to asking a couple of times, but if the answer was no . . . well . . . it was easier just to live with the question.

"He said to tell ya hey for him," Ronald repeated.

*If Kemp really wanted to say hello, he could have called. It's not like he doesn't know where to find me. . . .*

Emotion choked my throat, and I didn't trust myself to speak at first, so I just nodded. Every time my cell phone rang, I grabbed it and looked at the caller ID with a rush of excitement. I couldn't admit that to anybody. Not even to myself.

I swallowed hard, taking a breath. "Tell him I said hi back."

It sounded so juvenile, like a couple of high-school kids playing a silly game of hearts. "How is he doing, anyway? I know he was getting ready to go back to playing ball."

Ronald laughed softly. "Well, he hadn't really made any decisions, I don't think. He's had his mind on other things, I reckon."

I nodded again. *Jennifer.* He probably had his mind on Jennifer.

I pushed the idea away, because there wasn't anything else to do. *Time. It'll just take time to move on.* Once this business with Donetta was over, there wouldn't be so many reminders. Even the few Daily details Ronald sprinkled into our phone conversations made it harder to forget.

"I got a feelin' he'll figure out what's best," Ronald said, and chuckled. "Young fellas hadn't always got the clearest vision at first. If they did, I wouldn't be here with you, seventy-one years old and only now doin' somethin' I shoulda done years ago. Sometimes a fella's just gotta get out of his own way, ya know?"

Shaking off the cloud of emotion, I straightened my shoulders and turned around. "Guess we'd better get busy then, huh?"

Ronald smiled, his eyes sparkling with anticipation. "Guess we better."

I turned on the boom box, and Ronald and I completed the first part of our mission for the day. It went much more smoothly than I'd anticipated, and an hour later, we were heading toward the beach right on schedule. Beside me, Ronald was as nervous as a teenager driving to the prom. He even looked the part, having changed into a tuxedo in the bathroom of the coffee shop.

"I don't think I was this tied up in knots when we *got* married," he said, dragging the palm of his hand along his pants. "The first time."

I laughed. In the past hour, I'd become better acquainted with Ronald. I was learning to enjoy his dry sense of humor and his habit of referring to almost everything in hunting and fishing terms. We had fishing in common, so he was easy to talk to. I was sorry we hadn't been able to spend time together in Daily.

"You'll be all right," I assured him. "You look very handsome."

"Are we almost there?"

"We're almost there."

"Is Donetta where she's supposed to be?"

"Maggie and Meredith will walk her out the back of the Le Grande Hotel as soon as we give them the signal."

"I hope she don't string me up when she finds out what I done. She ain't much for surprises, unless she's the one givin' them out."

"She won't. My gosh, what woman wouldn't be thrilled?" *What woman wouldn't be thrilled?* My heart tugged. I wanted to find my own happy ending. I wanted it so badly there was a dull, constant ache inside me each day. I couldn't distract myself from it, no matter how far from home I traveled or how busy I stayed. Even the commotion of helping orchestrate Ronald's big surprise couldn't take away the heaviness, the yearning for something different. My life had become exactly what Kemp had described—an old shoe that didn't quite fit anymore.

I felt it rubbing and pinching as Ronald and I drove down the highway, parked in the shadow of the imposing Le Grande Hotel and hurried to our places—Ronald at the bottom of the hotel terrace steps, and me among the crowd of spectators seated in chairs on the beach, wedding guests doubling as an audience for the GMA taping. As I made my way to a chair, Sister Mona stood up and hugged me, Obeline patted my hand, and Ernest looked over the blue dress I'd put on in the coffee shop storeroom and said, "*Gal-ee*, I'm'ma say you clean up pretty good there, cher."

As I slipped into my seat, Pastor D. waited up front under an arch of gossamer loops and palm leaves, his hands clasped expectantly behind his back. Nearby, where a portable cabana had been draped with filmy white cloth, Bluejay and his Kings of Creole band waited to play. Behind them, the small section of beach, specially cleaned and prepared by the Bureau of Tourism, lay pristine in the afternoon light, sand catching sun and creating a glistening backdrop that surrounded the spectators and outlined the long red carpet stretching from Brother D. to the hotel steps—an aisle awaiting a bride.

A florist slipped a bouquet of roses into Ronald's hand as he took his place at the base of the hotel steps, the segment producer cued the cameras, Bluejay's band began to play, and a sentry standing atop the old stone steps waved toward the hotel. Ronald gazed expectantly toward the stairs, and a moment later, Donetta appeared on the upper landing, looking—as Ronald would have phrased it—like a deer in the headlights.

The bridegroom beamed, clutching the bouquet of roses against his chest as Donetta made her descent one hesitant step at a time. The breeze caught the long white cotton lace beach dress that had been given to her as part of her Tourist of the Month package.

"Good gravy. What's all this?" Her voice echoed over the crowd, shattering the hush of silent expectation. "I reckon I'm in the wrong place. I was just supposed to have my picture made on the beach, bein' as I'm Tourist of the Month."

Ronald took a knee, and the movement drew Donetta's attention to the base of the steps. Her mouth dropped open, and her eyes grew wide. "Ronald? What'n the world're you doin' here? I thought you were at the hotel room."

"Donetta Bradford"—Ronald's voice was so loud, he didn't

need the microphone the television crew had hidden in a potted palm beside him—"the first time we got married, we didn't have a big weddin', or a honeymoon. I know you always wanted them things, so now we're gonna have both. Miss Donetta Eldridge, you are the most beautiful thing I ever did see. Will you do me the honor of bein' my bride and then joinin' me on a cruise on the good ship *Jubilation*?"

Donetta's eyes widened and her lips trembled, hanging open in a half moon. "Ronald?" She tiptoed to the edge of the center landing and teetered there.

"I'm gonna be awful embarrassed if you don't say yes here pretty quick, darlin'."

The crowd bubbled with muted laughter.

Her lips spreading into a wide smile, Donetta gathered her skirt and ran down the remainder of the steps. "Oh, of course yes. Good gracious, of course yes!" She slipped her hand into Ronald's, and he slowly kissed her fingers, then rose to his feet.

Tender emotions sent a warm flush over my skin as Blue-jay's band played the Creole wedding march, and the bride and groom walked down the aisle to become husband and wife. Again.

Donetta saw me in the crowd and shook a finger at me as she passed by. I only smiled back at her. She'd forgive me once they were on the ship enjoying a seven-day adventure, all expenses paid.

The service was short, but sentimental, as Ronald had requested. When it was over, the spectators stood and tossed flower petals into the air. I tipped my head back, watching them float slowly to the ground as the band played *"La Valse de la Vie,"* "The Waltz of Life," and the newly remarried couple proceeded up the aisle. On the way, Donetta stopped to give me a hug, and Ronald shook my hand, thanking me for my help, and then he smiled in a way that acknowledged there was still one secret left between us.

When they started toward the steps again, the bridal bouquet was in my seat. I picked it up and held it in the air as Ronald and Donetta dashed toward the veranda overhead.

"That's a wrap," the GMA producer reported a few moments later. I barely heard the words. Ronald and Donetta had paused again on the upper landing. Donetta was hugging someone. I knew who it was as soon as I saw the baseball cap in Daily Dawgs colors and the pink-tinged polo shirt. Everything— the crowd disbursing, the TV crew wrapping up their cables and packing away their cameras, the band finishing the last of the song—seemed to disappear. Air caught in my chest, and I couldn't breathe.

Donetta kissed Kemp on the cheek, and Ronald took something out of Kemp's hand, then he pointed toward the beach, toward me. I realized I'd stepped to the middle of the red carpet, and I was just standing there all by myself, holding the bridal bouquet. Ronald slipped an arm around Kemp's shoulders, leaned close to say something, then propelled Kemp forward, so that he half stepped and half tripped off the top stair. After he caught his balance, his eyes met mine across the distance, and I felt myself smile as he descended, the ball cap now dangling from his fingers, which were partially tucked into his pockets.

The next thing I knew, I was tossing the bridal bouquet into a chair, walking, then running up the carpet. All I could think was *He's here. He's really here.*

I skidded to a halt just short of tackling him at the bottom step. So much for playing coy.

"Your uncle didn't say you were coming." *Tell him how you feel,* a voice urged inside me. *Just be honest. What have you got to lose?*

"I didn't know I was." He looked down at the carpet. On

the beach, a crew from the florist shop was starting to dismantle the archway. Soon they'd want the carpet. Kemp and I would have to move . . . somewhere. "Uncle Ronald forgot the passports." His lips twisted to one side like he was fighting a smile. "He accidentally left them on a table at the Daily Café this morning. Good thing Imagene found them and sent me after him."

"Yes, it is." I smiled and blushed at the same time. It looked as though, while I was helping Ronald plot a surprise for Donetta, Ronald and Imagene were plotting one for me, as well.

"Funny how Imagene knew right where to send me to catch up with them." Tipping his head back, Kemp eyed me ruefully.

"That *is* funny." A pulse fluttered so hard in my throat, I was sure he could see it. "Did you get here in time for the ceremony?" In a way, it had seemed a shame that none of Donetta's friends or family had been present at the renewal of vows, but that was the way Ronald wanted it. *If there's a secret around Daily, Texas, Donetta Bradford'll sniff it out*, he'd said. *The less people we tell, the better. They can all watch it on TV later.*

"I didn't know Uncle Ronald had it in him." Kemp surveyed the beach. "This is pretty impressive for a guy whose idea of luxury is a deer blind with carpet *and* cup holders in it."

"He learned to dance, too," I told Kemp. "We just had a lesson down at the coffee shop. Waltz, western swing, and two-step. He's not bad."

Kemp laughed, looking down at his boots. "Tell me about it. He's been spending at least three hours a day watching that instructional video you made for him. When he advanced past the mop and the broom, he started stopping by the field house during lunch so he could practice in the film room. He made me be his dance partner. My feet may never recover."

I giggled at the picture of Kemp and Uncle Ronald dancing in the field house while I demonstrated on-screen, counting out the steps. "You did a good job. He was pretty light-footed by the time I got to him."

"He didn't start out that way, I can promise you." Kemp grimaced, as if it hurt to remember.

"Donetta will be so surprised." I imagined the moment when, after the Captain's Circle Reception on the *Jubilation*, Donetta descended the stairs and Ronald offered his hand and asked, *May I have this dance?*

Donetta would have her *Titanic* moment on ship after all, even if I wouldn't be there to see it.

"Yes, she will," Kemp agreed. "It was worth being Uncle Ronald's dance partner for weeks."

"I guess by now your skills are pretty good."

He grinned mischievously. "If you're lucky, I might show you." The invitation brushed anticipation over my skin, and my heart quickened in response. I felt the walls between us melting in the heat, drifting out to sea, disappearing far into the distance, where the sun was trailing into the water.

"I *feel* lucky."

"Me, too," he said quietly.

Studying me, he slipped his hand into his shirt pocket and pulled out a square of yellow paper. "I brought something for you. Uncle Ronald was supposed to give it to you, but he left it behind with the passports. Guess he knew I'd get the chance to give it to you myself." He held out the colored paper, an envelope. It had my name on the outside. The penmanship was meticulous, but the hand that wrote it had been shaking. Something about it was familiar, but I couldn't place it.

"What is this?" I felt him watching me as I turned the envelope over.

"I went to your grandmother's house."

The muscles in my neck tightened, and I felt as if I were choking. The moment seemed to stand still. "You went to McGregor?"

My mind spun through the times Kemp and I had paused at the end of his driveway, talking as he waited patiently for me to decide which way to go.

"She sent you a letter." He nodded at the envelope.

"You saw my grandmother?" Tears crowded my eyes, and a rush of tenderness pierced me, the sensation sudden and surprising. Even when Kemp and I were far apart—physically, emotionally, even when it seemed like we'd never see each other again, he had completed the journey I didn't have the courage to make on my own.

On the heels of that thought came another. One so powerful it took me back a step. If he didn't care about me, if what was between us wasn't something special, why would he have bothered?

Tears welled in my eyes and spilled over. I felt them hot and wet on my cheeks, tasted them on my lips.

He reached across the space between us, trailed a thumb along my cheek, wiping away the tears. Sliding his fingers into my hair, he pulled me closer until our bodies touched. The contact brought a jolt of electricity at first, then a deep, spreading warmth. "I missed you," I said as I stared into the eyes that had haunted me so many nights. I'd dreamed about him. I'd dreamed about this.

"I didn't think about you at all." His breath touched my lips, and then he kissed me, and every question in my mind was swept away. There was only room for this moment, for the kind of emotion that can't be planned for, or controlled, but only experienced.

When our lips parted, Kemp folded me into his arms, and I laid my head against his chest, watching the sun seep slowly into the ocean. For the first time I could remember, I felt completely at peace.

"I can't believe you did this for me," I whispered, holding up the letter and looking at it again.

His chin rested gently on my hair, so that I heard his voice and felt it. "I thought it might give you a reason to come home."

*Home.* After a lifetime of wandering, of seeking and failing, I finally understood the meaning of the word. Home isn't a place, a structure you create from wood or bricks or mortar, building the walls high and strong, to keep out the storms of life. Home is in the things you carry with you, the treasures of the heart, like Gil's Bible, or the memories of a family baseball game on a sunny summer day, or the feeling of singing "I'll Fly Away" in an abandoned church as the storm passes over. It is a dwelling place you share with the people who matter most, a refuge in which you're never alone. The Builder is always nearby, tearing down old walls and adding new rooms, repairing the damage of wind and weather, filling empty spaces with new gifts.

Gifts beautiful and mysterious and unexpected.

Like all beautiful gifts, a surprise to everyone but the Giver, who seeks us in our hidden places and beckons us home from our wanderings. Who knows that nothing adrift is meant to stay adrift forever.

# Discussion Questions

1. Donetta, Imagene, and Lucy's vacation takes a completely unexpected turn, but in the end something good comes of it. Have you ever had an experience in which a vacation gone wrong brought something new and unexpected into your life?

2. When the women are trapped on the side of the road, Donetta finds herself "praying from the foxhole." Have you ever found yourself praying from the foxhole? When?

3. Even when her own resources are limited, Kai chooses to stop to help others. Why do you think she chooses to do this?

4. Donetta feels that her marriage as a young woman may have been, in part, an attempt to find the love she never received from her father. How do our childhood relationships influence our adult decisions?

5. Donetta's marriage began in hope, but over the years slowly grew distant and stale. What causes couples to drift apart? Do you think this is what God intends for us? What can we do to prevent it?

6. In dealing with her difficult childhood, Kai has cut herself off from her family. Do you think this is healthy? How should we react to those who have caused us pain in the past?

7. Donetta confesses that she was always jealous of certain aspects of Imagene's life. Have you ever harbored secret jealousy toward a friend? How did it affect the friendship?

8. Brother Ervin's sermon about juggling contends that an overly busy life is the greatest enemy of good works. Do you agree or disagree? Do our modern schedules keep us from seeing and attending to the needs of those around us? Examples?

9. When the members of the Holy Ghost Church arrive in Daily, Betty Prine quickly becomes determined to run them out of town. Is her reaction typical? Understandable? Why or why not?

10. The community of Daily rallies together to help the storm victims. Has your community or your church ever done something similar?

11. One of Donetta's goals for the trip to the coast is to finally learn the truth about Mamee. Have you ever searched for the truth about a family secret?

12. Because of her past, Kai rejects the idea that Kemp could really love her, and she returns to her old life. Have you ever found yourself stuck in one place, unable to take a leap of faith?

13. The storm changes the paths of everyone involved. How do tragedies change us? Has a storm or unexpected event ever moved your life onto a new path?

**Lisa Wingate** is a former journalist, inspirational speaker, and *New York Times* bestselling author of thirty novels. Her work has won or been nominated for many awards, including the Pat Conroy Southern Book Prize, the Oklahoma Book Award, the Utah Library Award, the Carol Award, the Christy Award, and the RT Booklovers Reviewer's Choice Award. Her latest book, *Before We Were Yours*, was the winner of the 2017 Goodreads Choice Award for Historical Fiction. Lisa writes her stories at home in Texas, where she is part of the Wingate clan of storytellers.

# Sign Up for
# Lisa's Newsletter!

Keep up to date with Lisa's news on book releases
and events by signing up for her email list at
lisawingate.com.